The passions, scandals and hopes
of two fabulously rich families...

Welcome to the glamorous and cutthroat world
of Australian opal dealing, in this first of
two collections featuring Miranda Lee's bestselling
six-book series, HEARTS OF FIRE.
The Whitmore saga begins with...

Seduction & Sacrifice
Desire & Deception
Passion & the Past

FAMILY TREE

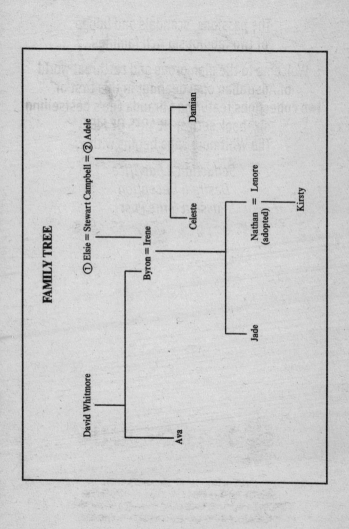

Miranda LEE

SECRETS & SINS

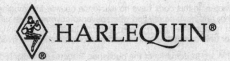

HARLEQUIN®

TORONTO • NEW YORK • LONDON
AMSTERDAM • PARIS • SYDNEY • HAMBURG
STOCKHOLM • ATHENS • TOKYO • MILAN • MADRID
PRAGUE • WARSAW • BUDAPEST • AUCKLAND

HARLEQUIN BOOKS

by Request—SECRETS & SINS

Copyright © 2002 by Harlequin Books S.A.

ISBN 0-373-18504-9

The publisher acknowledges the copyright holder of the individual works as follows:
SEDUCTION & SACRIFICE
Copyright © 1994 by Miranda Lee
DESIRE & DECEPTION
Copyright © 1994 by Miranda Lee
PASSION & THE PAST
Copyright © 1994 by Miranda Lee

This edition published by arrangement with Harlequin Books S.A.

Visit us at www.eHarlequin.com

Printed in U.S.A.

CONTENTS

CONTENTS

SEDUCTION & SACRIFICE

CHAPTER ONE

SHE didn't cry. Neither did anyone else attending her father's funeral.

Not that there were many mourners standing round the grave-side that hot February morning at the Lightning Ridge Cemetery. Only the minister, Mr Gunther, Ma, and Gemma herself. The undertaker had left as soon as he'd dropped off the deceased. If you stretched a point, the grave-digger made five.

Admittedly, it was forty degrees in the shade, not the sort of day one would want to stand out in the sun for more than a few minutes unless compelled to do so out of duty. Gemma watched the coffin being lowered into the ground, but still she couldn't cry.

The minister didn't take long to scuttle off, she noticed bleakly, nor did Mr Gunther, leaving her to listen to that awful sound as the clods of dirt struck the lid of the coffin.

Why can't I cry? she asked herself once more.

She jumped when Ma touched her on the shoulder. 'Come on, love. Time to go home.'

Home...

Gemma dragged in then expelled a shuddering sigh. Had she ever thought of that ghastly dugout with its primitive dunny and dirt floors as home? Yet it had been, for as long as she could remember.

'Do you want me to drive?' Ma asked as they approached the rusted-out utility truck that had belonged to Jon Smith and which was now the property of his one and only child.

Gemma smiled at Ma, who was about the worst driver she had ever encountered. Her real name was Mrs Madge Walton, but she was known as Ma to the locals. She and her husband had come to try their luck in the opal fields at Lightning Ridge more than thirty years ago. When Bill Walton died, Ma had stayed on, living in a caravan and supplementing her widow's pension by fossicking for opals and selling her finds to tourists.

She was Gemma's neighbour and had often given Gemma sanctuary when her father had been in one of his foul moods. She was the closest thing to a mother Gemma had had, her own mother having died at her birth.

'No, Ma,' she said. 'I'll drive.'

They climbed into the cabin, which was stifling despite the windows being down. Bushflies crawled all over the windscreen.

'What are you going to do now, love?' Ma asked once they were under way. 'I dare say you won't stay in Lightning Ridge. You always fancied livin' in the city, didn't you?'

There was no use lying to Ma. She knew Gemma better than anybody. 'I might go to Sydney,' she said.

'I came from Sydney, originally. Nasty place.'

'In what way?'

'Too big and too noisy.'

'I could take a bit of noise after living out here,' Gemma muttered.

'What will you do with Blue?'

Blue was Gemma's pet cattle-dog. Her father had bought him a few years back, fully grown, because he was a fierce guard-dog. He'd chained him up outside the entrance to the dugout and God help anybody who went near him. Gemma had rather enjoyed the challenge of making friends with the dog and had astounded both her father and Ma by eventually winning the animal's total loyalty and devotion. The dog adored Gemma and she adored him. She didn't have to think long over her answer to Ma's question.

'Take him with me, of course.'

'He won't like the city, love.'

'He'll like wherever I am,' Gemma said stubbornly.

'Aye, that he probably will. Never seen a dog so attached to a person. He still frightens the dickens out of me, though.'

'He's as gentle as a lamb.'

'Only with you, love. Only with you.'

Gemma laughed.

'That's better,' Ma said. 'It's good to hear you laugh again.'

Gemma fell silent. But I still haven't cried, she thought. It bothered her, very much. A daughter should cry when her father died.

She frowned and fell silent. They swept back into town and out along Three Mile Road.

Both Ma and Gemma lived a few miles out of Lightning Ridge, on the opposite side to the cemetery, near a spot called Frog Hollow. It wasn't much different from most places around the Ridge. The dry, rocky lunar landscape was pretty much the same wherever the ground had been decimated by mine shaft after mine shaft. Picturesque it was not. Nor green. The predominant colour was greyish-white.

Ma's caravan was parked under a fairly large old iron-bark tree, but the lack of rainfall meant a meagre leafage which didn't provide much shade from the searing summer sun. Gemma's dugout, by comparison, was cool.

'Come and sit in my place for a while,' Gemma offered as they approached Ma's caravan. 'We'll have a cool drink together.'

'That's kind of you, love. Yes, I'd like that.'

Gemma drove on past the caravan, quickly covering the short distance between it and her father's claim. She began to frown when Blue didn't come charging down the dirt road towards her as he always did. Scrunching up her eyes against the glare of the sun, she peered ahead and thought she made out a dark shape lying in the dust in front of the dugout. It looked ominously still.

'Oh, no,' she cried, and, slamming on the brakes, she dived out of the utility practically before it was stopped. 'Blue!' she shouted, and ran, falling to her knees in the dirt before him and scooping his motionless form into her lap. His head lolled to one side, a dried froth around his lips.

'He's *dead*!' she gasped, and lifted horrified eyes to Ma, who was looking down at the sorry sight with pity in her big red face.

'Yes, love. It seems so.'

'But how?' she moaned. 'Why?'

'Poisoned, by the look of it.'

'Poisoned! But who would poison my Blue?'

'He wasn't a well-loved dog around here,' Ma reminded gently. 'There, there…' She laid a kind hand on Gemma's shaking shoulder. 'Perhaps it's all for the best. You couldn't have taken him to Sydney with you, you know. With everyone but you he used to bite first and ask questions afterwards.'

'But he was my friend,' Gemma wailed, her eyes flooding with tears. 'I *loved* him!'

'Yes…yes, I know you did. I'm so sorry, love.'

The dam began to break, the one she'd been holding on to since the police came and told her that her father had fallen down an abandoned mine shaft and broken his stupid damned drunken neck.

'Oh, Blue,' she sobbed, and buried her head in the dog's dusty coat. 'Don't leave me. Please don't leave me. I'll be all alone…'

'We're *all* alone, Gemma,' was Ma's weary advice.

Gemma's head shot up, brown eyes bright with tears, her tear-stained face showing a depth of emotion she hadn't inherited from her father. 'Don't say that, Ma. That's terrible. Not everyone is like my father was. Most people need other people. I know I do. And you do too. One day, I'm going to find some really nice man and marry him and have a whole lot of children. Not one or two, but half a dozen, and I'm going to teach them that the most joyous wonderful thing in this world is loving one another and caring for one another, openly, with hugs and kisses and lots of laughter. Because I'm tired of loneliness and misery and meanness. I've had a gutful of hateful people who would poison my dog and...and...'

She couldn't go on, everything inside her chest shaking and shaking. Once again, she buried her face in her pet's already dulling coat and cried and cried.

Ma plonked down in the dirt beside her and kept patting her on the shoulder. 'You're right, love. You're right. Have a good cry, there's a good girl. You deserve it.'

When Gemma was done crying, she stood up, found a shovel and dug Blue a grave. Wrapping him in an old sheet, she placed him in the bottom of the dusty trench and filled it in, patting the dirt down with an odd feeling of finality. A chapter had closed in her life. Another was about to begin. She would not look back. She would go forward. These two deaths had set her free of the past, a past that had not always been happy. The future was hers to create. And by God, she hoped to make a better job of it than her father had of the last eighteen years.

'Well, Ma,' she said when she returned to the cool of the dugout, 'that's done.'

'Yes, love.'

'Time to make plans,' she said, and pulled up a chair opposite Ma at the wooden slab that served as a table.

'Plans?'

'Yes, plans. How would you like to buy my ute and live here while I'm away?'

'Well, I—er— How long are you going for?'

'I'm not sure. A while. Maybe forever. I'll keep you posted.'

'I'll miss you,' Ma sighed. 'But I understand. What must be must be. Besides...' She grinned her old toothless grin.

'I always had a hankerin' to live here, especially in the summer.'

'You could have your caravan moved here as well. Give you the best of both worlds. I won't sell you Dad's claim but you're welcome to anything you can find while I'm gone.'

'Sounds good to me.'

'Let's have a beer to celebrate our deal.'

'Sounds *very* good to me.'

Gemma spoke and acted with positive confidence in Ma's presence, but once she was gone, Gemma slumped across the table, her face buried in her hands. But she'd cried all the tears she was going to cry, it seemed, and soon her mind was ticking away on what money she could scrape together for her big adventure of going to Sydney.

Though a country girl of limited experience, Gemma was far from dumb or ignorant. Television at school and her classmates' more regular homes in town had given her a pretty good idea of the world outside of Lightning Ridge. She might be a slightly rough product of the outback of Australia, living all her life with a bunch of misfits and dreamers, but she had a sharp mind and a lot of common sense. Money meant safety. She would need as much as she could get her hands on if she wanted to go to Sydney.

There were nearly three hundred dollars in her bank account, saved from her casual waitressing job, the only employment she'd been able to get since leaving school three months ago. She'd been lucky to get even that. Times were very bad around the Ridge, despite several miners reportedly having struck it rich at some new rushes out around Coocoran Lake.

Then there was Ma's agreed five hundred dollars for the ute. That made just on eight hundred. But Gemma needed more to embark on such a journey. There would be her bus and train fare to pay for, then accommodation and food till she could find work. And she'd need some clothes. Eight hundred wasn't enough.

Gemma's head inevitably turned towards her father's bed against the far wall. She'd long known about the battered old biscuit tin, hidden in a hole in the dirty wall behind the headboard, but had never dared take it out to see what was in it. She'd always suspected it contained a small hoard of opals, the ones her father cashed in whenever he wanted to go on a drinking binge. It took Gemma a few moments to accept that nothing and no one could stop her now from seeing what the failed miner had coveted so secretly.

Her heart began to pound as she drew the tin from its hiding place and brought it back to the table. Pulling up her rickety chair once more, she sat down and simply stared at it for a few moments. Logic told Gemma there couldn't be anything of great value lying within, yet her hands were trembling slightly as they forced the metal lid upwards.

What she saw in the bottom of the tin stopped her heart for a few seconds. Could it really be what it looked like? Or was it just a worthless piece of potch?

But surely her father would not hide away something worthless!

Her hand reached into the tin to curve around the grey, oval-shaped stone. It filled her palm, its size and weight making her heart thud more heavily. My God, if this was what she thought it was…

Feeling a smooth surface underneath, she drew a nobby out and turned it over, her eyes flinging wide. A section of the rough outer layer had been sliced away to reveal the opal beneath. As Gemma gently rolled the stone back and forth to see the play of colour, she realised she was looking at a small fortune. There had to be a thousand carats here at least! And the pattern was a pinfire, if she wasn't mistaken. Quite rare.

She blinked as the burst of red lights flashed out at her a second time, dazzling in their fiery beauty before changing to blue, then violet, then green, then back to that vivid glowing red.

My God, I'm rich, she thought.

But any shock or excitement quickly changed to confusion.

Her father had never made any decent strikes or finds in her various claims he'd worked over the years here at Lightning Ridge. Or at least…that was what he'd always told her. Clearly, however, he must have at some time uncovered this treasure, this pot of gold.

A fierce resentment welled up inside Gemma. There had been no need for them to live in this primitive dugout all these years, no need to be reduced to charity, as had often happened, no need to be pitied and talked about.

Shaking her head in dismay and bewilderment, she put the stone down on the table and stared blankly back into the tin. There remained maybe twenty or thirty small chunks of opals scattered in the corners, nothing worth more than ten, or maybe twenty dollars each at most. Her father's drinking money, as she'd suspected.

It was when she began idly scooping the stones over into one corner to pick them up that she noticed the photograph lying underneath. It was faded and yellowed, its edges and corners very worn as though it had been handled a lot. Momentarily distracted from her ragged emotions, she picked up the small photo to frown at the man and woman in it. Both were strangers.

But as Gemma's big brown eyes narrowed to stare at the man some more, her stomach contracted fiercely. The handsome blond giant staring back at her bore little resemblance to the bald, bedraggled, beer-bellied man she'd buried today. But his eyes were the eyes of Jon Smith—her father. They were unforgettable eyes, a very light blue, as cold and hard as arctic ice. Gemma shivered as they seemed to lock on to hers.

Her father had been a cold, hard man. She'd tried to be a good daughter to him, doing all the cooking and cleaning, putting him to bed when he came home rolling drunk, listening to his tales of misery and woe. Drink had always made him maudlin.

There were times, however, when Gemma had suspected it wasn't love that kept her tied to her father. It was probably fear. He'd slapped her more times than she could count, as well as having a way of looking at her sometimes that chilled her right through. She recalled being on the end of one of those looks a few weeks back when she'd mentioned going to Walgett to try to find work. He'd forbidden her from going anywhere, and the steely glint in his eyes had made her comply in obedient silence.

A long, shuddering sigh puffed from Gemma's lungs, making her aware how tightly she had been holding her breath. Her gaze focused back on the photograph, moving across to the woman her father was holding firmly to his side.

Gemma caught her breath once more. For the young woman appearing to resent her father's hold looked pregnant. About six months.

My God, she realised, it had to be her mother!

Gemma's heart started to race as she stared at the delicate dark-haired young woman whose body language bespoke an unwillingness to be held so closely, whose tanned slender arms were wrapped protectively around her bulging stomach, whose fingers were entwined across the mound of her unborn baby with a white-knuckled intensity.

So this was the 'slut' her father refused to speak of, who had died giving birth but who still lived within her daughter's genes. Gemma's father had told her once that she took after her mother, but other than that one snarled comment she knew nothing about the woman who'd borne her. Any curiosity about her had long been forcibly suppressed, only to burst to life now with a vengeance.

Gemma avidly studied the photograph, anxious to spot the similarities between mother and daughter. But she was disappointed to find no great resemblance, other than the dark wavy hair. Of course it was impossible to tell with the woman in the photograph wearing sunglasses. She supposed their faces were a similar shape, both being oval, and yes, they had the same pointy chin. But Gemma was taller, and much more shapely. Other than her being pregnant, this young woman had the body of a child. Or was it the shapelessness of the cheap floral dress that made her look as if she had no bust or hips?

'Mary,' Gemma whispered aloud, then frowned. Odd. She didn't look like a Mary. But that had been her name on Gemma's birth certificate. Her maiden name had been Bell and she'd been born in Sydney.

A sudden thought struck and Gemma flipped the photograph over. Written in the top left hand corner were some words. 'Stefan and Mary. Christmas, 1973'.

The date sent Gemma's head into a spin. If that was her mother in the photograph, pregnant with *her*, then she'd been born early in 1974, not September 1975! She was nearly twenty in that case, not eighteen...

Gemma was stunned, yet not for a moment did her mind refute her new age. It explained so much, really. Her shooting up in height before any other girl in her class. Her getting her periods so early, and her breasts. Then later, in high school, the way she'd always felt different from her classmates. She hadn't been different at all. She'd simply been older!

Distress enveloped Gemma as she stared, not only at the date on the photograph, but at the Stefan part. Stefan had to be her father's real name, not Jon. Lies, she realised. He'd told her nothing but lies. Why? What lay behind it all?

Gemma conceded she'd always suspected her father's name of Jon Smith might be an alias. He'd been a Swede through and through, with Nordic colouring and a thick accent. But the opal fields of outback Australia was a well-known haven for runaways, mostly criminals or married men who'd deserted their wives and families, all seeking the anonymity and relative safety of isolated places. People did not ask too many questions around Lightning Ridge, not even daughters.

But the questions were very definitely tumbling through Gemma's mind now. What other lies had her father told her? Maybe her mother *hadn't* died. Maybe she was out there somewhere, alive and well. Maybe her father had stolen her as a baby, changed his name and lied about her age to hide them both from anyone searching for them. Maybe he—

Gemma pulled herself up short. She was grasping at straws, trying to make her life fit some romantic scenario like you saw on television, where a long-lost daughter found her mother after twenty years. Life was rarely like that. There was probably a host of reasons why her father had changed his name, as well as her age. He'd been a secretive man, as well as a controlling one. Maybe he'd thought he could keep his daughter under his thumb longer if she believed she was younger. Or maybe he'd simply lied to authorities about her age that time when they'd tackled him about why he hadn't sent her to school yet.

Gemma could still remember the welfare lady coming out here to see her father. Despite her being a little girl at the time, and dreadfully shy, the visit had stuck in her mind because the lady had been so pretty and smelled so good. It was shortly after the social worker's visit that Gemma had been sent to school. Her 'birth certificate' had surfaced a few years later when she had wanted to join a local netball team.

Gemma was totally absorbed in her thoughts when suddenly the sunlight that was streaming in and on to the table vanished, a large silhouette, filling the open doorway of the dugout. She froze for a second, then quickly shoved the photo and opal back and snapped the lid of the tin shut.

'Anyone home?' a familiar voice asked.

'Oh, it's only you, Ma,' Gemma said, sighing as she stood up and walked forward across the dirt floor.

Her relief was unnervingly intense. For a split second, she'd been afraid her unexpected visitor might have been someone else. Which was silly, really. It had been six years and he hadn't come near her, hadn't even spoken to her when they'd passed on the street. There again, her father was no longer around to act as a deterrent.

And neither was Blue, she realised with a sickening lurch in her stomach. Oh, my God, was that who had poisoned her dog?

'Come in and sit down, Ma,' Gemma offered, trying to keep her steady voice while her insides were churning. 'You're just the person I need to see.'

'Really? What about?' Ma bulldozed her bulk over to the table and plonked down in a chair, which protested noisily.

'I was wondering if you'd mind if I slept in your caravan tonight. I feel a bit nervous staying here on my own.' Which was a huge understatement at this moment.

'Do you know, that's exactly what I came over here to see you about? I was thinking to myself that Gemma's too good-looking a girl to be stayin' way out here on her own. There are some none too scrupulous men living around these parts.'

Gemma shuddered, her mind whisking to one particular man, a big brute of a miner who had large gnarled hands and had always smelled of body odour and cheap whisky.

'Well, I wouldn't say I'm God's gift to men, Ma, and I could certainly lose a pound or two, but, as you say, some men aren't fussy.'

'Lose a pound or two?' Ma spluttered. 'Why, girl, have you looked at yourself in the mirror lately? Maybe a few months ago you might have had a layer of puppy fat on you, but you've trimmed down this summer to a fine figure of a woman, believe me. And you've always had the prettiest face, though you should start usin' some sunscreen on it. Mediterranean brown is all right for legs and arms but not for faces. You don't want to wrinkle up that lovely clear skin of yours, do you?'

Gemma didn't know how to take this welter of compliments. It wasn't like Ma to rave on so.

'You make it sound like I'm beautiful or something,' she protested with an embarrassed laugh.

'Or *something* just about describes it,' Ma muttered. 'You'll have to watch yourself when you get to Sydney, my girl. City men are vultures.'

'I'm not much interested in men at the moment,' Gemma replied stiffly. God, she'd thought she'd got over that other business. But she hadn't at all. It had been there lurking in the depths of her mind, waiting to be dragged up to the surface again, just as *he* had been lurking, waiting for the opportunity to assault her again.

Ma reached out to pat her on the wrist. 'Stop thinkin' about him, dear. He isn't worth thinkin' about, you know. Men like him never are.'

Gemma gaped a moment before the penny dropped. Ma wasn't talking about him. She was talking about her father. 'What do you mean by men like him?'

'Cruel. Selfish. Mean.'

The word 'mean' struck a chord with Gemma. Was that why her father hadn't sold the opal? Because he was a miser, like Scrooge? Had he gained pleasure by bringing the stone out late at night to drool over its beauty all by himself in secret?

She would never know now. That she was certain of. Jon Smith had not shared the existence of the opal with anyone, even his daughter. He'd dressed her in second-hand clothes and accepted food hand-outs rather than part with his precious prize.

Oh, yes, he'd been a mean man.

Suddenly, she was sorely tempted to show Ma the opal and ask her advice, but people had long stopped showing valuable finds around Lightning Ridge. Greed and envy did strange things to even the closest of friends. So she kept her own counsel and said, 'Yes, he was mean. But he was my father and he could have been worse.'

'You'd find excuses for Hitler,' Ma scoffed. 'How are you set for money?'

Once again, Gemma resisted the temptation to confess all to Ma. 'There's a small parcel of opals Dad saved that can sell,' she admitted. 'Other than that I've got about twenty dollars left out of the housekeeping, three hundred dollars savings in the bank, and the money you're going to give me for the truck.'

'Which I brought over with me,' Ma said, and pulled a roll of money from the pocket of her dress. 'Don't tell the taxman but I did rather well with my fossicking this year.'

Gemma laughed. 'I won't breathe a word.'

'So when are you off to Sydney?'

A nervous lump immediately formed in Gemma's throat. My God, the furthest she'd been from Lightning Ridge was Walgett, a whole forty or so miles away. Sydney was another world, a big frightening exciting world! But wild horses wouldn't keep her away. Not now. Sydney held even more attractions than ever. Her mother had been born in Sydney. Maybe she had relatives there. Maybe she could find them.

'As soon as I can get myself organised, I suppose,' she said, her resolve deepening.

'Mr Whitmore's due in town day after tomorrow if you want to sell those opals. He'll give you a fairer price than most. Don't take his first offer, though, haggle a little.'

Gemma frowned. Her father hadn't liked Mr Whitmore for some reason, had refused to have anything to do with him, saying slick city buyers couldn't be trusted.

'Dad used to sell his opals to Mr Gunther,' she said hesitantly.

'That old skinflint? Look, I know he came to the funeral today and Jon might have been able to bully a fair price out of him, but he'll try to fleece *you* blind. You listen to me, love, and try Byron Whitmore. A fairer man never drew breath. Just go along to the Ridge Motel any time next Friday and ask for his room.'

'All right, Ma. I'll do that.'

'Good. Now you can get me a beer, love. It's bloody hot today.'

Gemma rose to get her visitor a beer. There were still several cans in the small gas fridge and a full carton leaning up against the far wall. If there was one thing her father never stinted himself on, it was beer.

'So tell me,' Gemma said on returning to the table and handing the beer over, 'what's this Mr Whitmore like?'

Ma snapped back the ring top on the can and gulped deeply before answering. 'Byron?' She wiped her mouth with the back of her hand. 'A big man. Around fifty, I'd say, but he looks younger. Thick wavy black hair sprinkled with grey and the most wonderful blue eyes. Very handsome. Too old for you, though, love. He's married as well, not that that seems to bother some men once their wives are out of sight.'

Gemma's eyes rounded and Ma gave a dry laugh. 'You are an innocent, aren't you? Better wise up before you go to Sydney. City men live fast and play fast, and they have an insatiable appetite for lovely young things with big brown eyes and bodies like yours. Still, I don't think you need worry about Byron Whitmore. He's a man of honour. A rare commodity indeed!'

Ma made Sydney sound like a huge dark forest full of big bad wolves. Surely it couldn't be as bad as that! Besides, no man would get to first base with her unless he was good and decent and kind. Maybe no man would *ever* get to first base with her, she worried anew.

That experience years ago had scarred her more than she realised. She'd thought she'd shunned boys up till now because they bored her. Now she interpreted her lack of interest in the opposite sex as a very real wariness. But was it a wariness of the boys themselves, or her own inner self, incapable perhaps of responding to a man in a normal, natural way? Dear God, she hoped that wasn't so. For if it was, how was she ever going to be happily married and have children of her own?

'Don't you believe me, love?' Ma said. 'About Mr Whitmore?'

'What? Oh, yes, Ma, I believe you. I'm sorry. I was wool-gathering.'

'You've had a long, trying day. Look, come over around six and I'll have a nice dinner ready for you. And bring your nightie.'

Gemma's eyes blurred. 'You're so good to me.'

'What rubbish! What are neighbours for?'

But Ma's faded blue eyes were a little teary too as she stood up. Gemma vowed to write to the dear old thing as often as she could from Sydney. And she would come back to visit. Often. It was the least she could do. If that black opal was worth what she thought it was worth, she'd be able to fly back in style!

CHAPTER TWO

MR WHITMORE, Gemma was told, was in room twenty-three, and no, he had no one with him at that time.

The Ridge Motel was the newest in Lightning Ridge, an ochre-coloured assortment of buildings, with reception and a restaurant separate from the forty units which stood at rectangular attention behind a kidney-shaped pool. Room twenty-three was on the second of the two storeys.

Gemma's stomach was churning as she climbed the stairs, something that would have surprised many people, including Ma, who had often commented on how confident she was for a girl of her upbringing and background. Gemma knew better, recognising her supposed assurance as little more than a desperate weapon to combat her father's volatile and often violent nature. She'd found over the years that if she were *too* docile and subservient he treated her even worse. So she'd learnt to stand up for herself to a degree, sometimes to her sorrow.

But none of that meant she had the sort of *savoir-faire* to deal confidently with a city opal trader like Byron Whitmore. Lord, she was shaking in her boots, or she would have been if she'd been wearing boots! Gemma's only consolation was that she'd decided not to try to sell the big opal today, only the smaller ones.

A couple of nights' sensible thinking since her astonishing find had formulated a plan to take the prize to Sydney and have it valued by a couple of experts before she sold it. It had come to her as late as half an hour ago that it might bring more money if she put it up for auction as a collector's piece. Six-figure amounts kept dancing around in her mind. She'd be able to buy herself a house, pretty clothes, a dog…

Her heart contracted fiercely. No, she wouldn't buy another dog. Not yet. Maybe some day, but not yet. The pain of Blue's death was still too raw, too fresh.

Gemma dragged her mind back to the problems at hand. Selling these infernal opals. By this time she was standing in front of room twenty-three but she couldn't bring herself to knock, gnawing away at her bottom lip instead and trying to find a good reason to abandon this idea entirely.

But that wouldn't get her any money, would it? She'd already booked tickets for the bus leaving tomorrow night for Dubbo, and the train from there to Sydney.

If only her father had let her go with him when he'd sold opals, she groaned silently. If only she'd met this Mr Whitmore before. Ma said he was OK but it was hard totally to dismiss her father's warnings about him.

Oh, get on with it, you stupid girl! Gemma berated herself. God knows how you're going to cope in the big bad city if you can't even do this small thing. Stop being such a wimp!

Taking a deep steadying breath, Gemma curled her fingers into a tight fist and knocked on the door.

'Oh!' she exclaimed when it was wrenched open, practically from under her knuckles. 'Oh!' she cried again, once she'd fully taken in the man who'd opened it.

He was nowhere near fifty, neither did he have black hair or blue eyes. At most he was thirty-five. His hair was a golden wheat colour and his eyes were grey. He was, however, very handsome in an unnervingly sleek, citified sort of way.

'I…I'm sorry, I must have the wrong room,' she babbled. 'I was wanting Mr Whitmore.'

Lazy grey eyes swept down her body and down her long bare tanned legs, one eyebrow arching by the time his gaze lifted back to her face. Gemma stiffened, not sure if his scrutiny was flattering or insulting.

Surely he couldn't be surprised by how she was dressed. No one wore anything other than shorts in Lightning Ridge in the summer, no one except visitors like this chap. *He* was all togged up in tailored grey trousers and a long-sleeved white shirt. There was even a dark red tie at his throat. A travelling salesman, Gemma decided. On his first trip outback, probably. It wouldn't be long before that tie was disposed of and those shirt-sleeves rolled up.

A small smile tugged at his mouth, as though he were amused at something. 'Now I know why Byron always looked forward to his trips out here,' he said drily.

Gemma frowned. Byron? That was Mr Whitmore's first name, wasn't it?

'I'm *Nathan* Whitmore,' the man elaborated before she could put her confusion into words. 'I'm standing in for Byron this trip, a fact that seems to have gotten around. You're my first client this afternoon, and only my third for the day. You *are* a client, aren't you?' he asked, amusement still in his voice.

Gemma was unsure now what to do. Ma had recommended *Byron* Whitmore, not his brother.

'You look concerned, Miss—er…'

'Smith,' she informed him. 'Gemma Smith.'

'Aah…and have you had dealings with my father before, Miss Smith?'

'No, I…your *father*?' Rounded eyes stared into Nathan Whitmore's face, seeing the age lines around his eyes and mouth. Either Byron Whitmore was older than Ma thought or his son had been living the life of a rake. Handsome he might be, but *that* young he wasn't. 'I…I thought you were his brother.'

'I understand your confusion. Byron adopted me when I was seventeen and he was thirty-two. We *are* more like brothers than like father and son.'

'Oh…oh, I see.' She didn't actually. Seventeen was

rather old to be adopted. Still, it wasn't any of her business. Her business was getting a good price for the opals in her pocket.

'Let me assure you, Miss Smith,' Nathan Whitmore said, 'that I know opals, and I won't cheat you. Byron would have my hide if I did anything to ruin his reputation for honesty and fairness.'

'He certainly comes highly recommended.'

'Whitmore Opals has a reputation second to none. Shall we go inside, then, and get down to business?'

Gemma hesitated, her eyes darting over Nathan Whitmore's shoulder and into the motel room. It was an oddly personal place to do business in. Intimate, even. Now her eyes darted back to that cool grey gaze.

'Dear Miss Smith,' he said in a rather droll tone, 'I have not come this far to compromise young women, however beautiful they might be.'

Beautiful? He found her *beautiful*?

My God, I'm blushing, she realised, feeling the heat in her face.

Hoping it wouldn't show underneath her tan, she kept her chin up and her eyes steady. He was probably only flattering her, she decided. Hoping, perhaps, to compliment his way into giving her less money than her opals were worth. Ma had warned her about city businessmen. Cunning, ruthless devils, she'd called them only this morning.

But this one didn't look like a devil. More like an angel with that golden hair and that lovely full-lipped mouth.

'Shall we sit down at the table?' he suggested, stepping back to wave her inside.

One swift, all-encompassing glance took in a typical motel room with a king-sized bed in one corner, a built-in television opposite, an extra divan and a round table and two chairs, over the back of which was draped a grey suit jacket.

Gemma chose the other chair and sat down, feeling conscious of her bare legs now, especially since the room was air-conditioned and much cooler than outside. She could appreciate now why its occupant was over-dressed. She clasped her hands together between her knees and gave a little shiver. Even her neck felt cool. If she could have taken her hair down out of its pony-tail she would have.

'The air-conditioning too cold for you? Shall I turn it down?'

'If you would, please, Mr Whitmore.'

How attentive he was, she thought. And how observant. Ma was right. City men were clever. Gemma determined to be on her guard.

The air-conditioning unit hissed when he turned it right off.

'Please call me Nathan,' he said suavely as he sat down, a lock of blond hair falling across his forehead. He swept it aside and smiled at her. 'And may I call you Gemma?'

Despite her earlier resolve not to be distracted by flattery or false charm, Gemma found herself smiling fatuously back at the man opposite her. She nodded, her tongue seemingly thick in her mouth. A light tangy pine smell was wafting across the table from him which she found both pleasant and perturbing. Did all city men smell like that?

'Well, Gemma?' he interrupted her agitated day-dreaming. 'I presume you have some opals with you?'

'Oh...oh, yes.' Squirming both physically and mentally, she pulled the small canvas pouch out of her shorts pocket. Fumbling because her fingers were shaking, she finally undid the drawstring and poured the stones out on to the table, then watched with heart pounding while Mr Whitmore put a jeweller's glass to his eye and started examining them.

'Mmm,' he said once. 'Yes, very nice,' another time.

Finally, he put the glass down and looked over at her with a slight frown. 'Did you mine these yourself?'

'No, my father did.'

'And you have his permission to sell them?'

'He died a few days ago,' she said, so bluntly that the man opposite her blinked with astonishment.

'I'm sorry,' he murmured politely.

Then you'd be the only one, Gemma thought.

'You couldn't have known,' she returned, her voice flat.

It brought another sharp glance. 'Do you want individual prices, or are you selling these as a parcel?'

'Which will get me more money?'

He smiled. Gemma noticed that when he smiled he showed lovely white teeth, and a dimple in his right cheek. That was because his smile was slightly lopsided. There was no doubt that he was by far the most attractive man she had ever met, despite his age.

'There are twenty-seven stones here,' he resumed, 'most worth no more than ten dollars. But this one I particularly like.' He pointed to the largest. 'It has a vivid green colour that appeals to me personally. So I'll offer you two hundred and sixty dollars for the rest and one hundred dollars for this one. That's three hundred and sixty in all.'

Gemma remembered what Ma had said about not accepting the first price. 'Four hundred,' she countered with surprising firmness.

He leant back in his chair, breathing in and out quite deeply. Gemma was fascinated by the play of muscles beneath his shirt and his surprisingly broad shoulders. He would look something with that jacket on. 'I was already being over-generous with the three hundred and sixty,' he said.

'Why?'

Gemma's forthright question seemed to startle him for a moment. Then he smiled. 'Well you might ask. Very well. Four hundred. Do you want cash or cheque?'

'Cash.'

'Somehow I knew you were going to say that.'

Extracting a well-stuffed wallet from the breast pocket of the jacket beside him, he counted out four one-hundred-dollar notes before returning the wallet.

They rose simultaneously, Gemma folding the notes and placing them carefully into her back pocket.

'Thank you, Mr Whitmore,' she said, and extended her hand.

He shook it, saying, 'I thought we agreed on Nathan.'

'Sorry,' she grinned. 'I find it hard to call my elders by their first name.' Now that the business end of proceedings was over and Gemma had her money safely tucked away, she was feeling more relaxed.

'Elders,' he repeated, a grimace twisting his mouth. 'Now that's putting me in my place. Might I ask how old you are?'

'Eigh—' Gemma broke off. She'd been going to say eighteen, but of course she wasn't. 'I'll be twenty next month,' she guessed.

He looked surprised, and, for a moment, stared at her hard. She gained the impression he was about to say something but changed his mind, shaking his head instead and walking over to open the door for her.

She walked past him out on to the balcony, but as she went to turn to say thank you one last time, she saw something out of the corner of her eye that made her heart leap and her stomach flip over. For there *he* was, standing down by the pool, looking huge and menacing, watching and waiting for her.

Panic-stricken, she bolted back into the room, almost sending Nathan Whitmore flying. 'Close the door,' she said in a husky, frightened whisper.

'*What*?'

'Close the door!' she hissed, backing up till her knees were against the bed.

He did as she asked, then turned slowly to view her fear-filled face with concern in his. 'What is it? What's out there that's frightened you so much? Is it a man?' he asked sharply. 'Is that it?'

'Yes,' she squeaked, appalled with herself that she'd started to shake uncontrollably. Dear God, she'd always thought herself a brave person. But she wasn't brave at all. Not even a little bit.

'Your boyfriend?'

She shook her head vigorously.

'Who, then? Dear God, what did he do to you to make you react like this?'

He was standing in front of her now, holding her trembling shoulders with firm but gentle hands.

Memories of other male hands surfaced from the backwater of her mind, large calloused hands that pinched and poked and probed...

A strangled sob broke from her lips, haunted eyes flying to warm grey ones.

'It's all right,' the owner of those eyes soothed. 'You're safe here with me.'

Another sob welled up within her and all of a sudden, she was wrapping her arms around him and hugging him for dear life, a whole torrent of emotions cascading through her, leaving her awash with a fiercely instinctive need to hold and be held.

After a momentary hesitation, Nathan Whitmore answered that need, holding her tightly against him, stroking her neck and back with fatherly tenderness, whispering soothing words as one would to a frightened child. But there was nothing fatherly in the effect such an intensely intimate embrace eventually had on his male body, nothing fatherly at all.

Nathan abruptly held her away from him, pressing her down into a sitting position on the bed. 'I'll get you a drink,' he said curtly, and turned away before the situation became embarrassing. 'And then you're going to tell me what the problem is,' he called back over his shoulder.

Gemma stared after him as he crossed the room, her head whirling with an alien confusion. Who would have thought she would ever find a safe haven in the solid warmth of a man's chest, or enjoy the feel of male arms encircling her?

She was still looking up at Nathan with startled surprise when he returned with a glass of brandy. For a moment their eyes locked and she could have sworn his were as puzzled as her own.

'Here.' He pressed the glass into her hands. 'Drink this up. Then start talking.'

In a way it was a relief to tell someone after keeping it to herself all these years. But she'd been so ashamed at the time. She'd felt so dirty. Yet the words did not come easily. She stumbled over them, faltering occasionally, and finding it hard to explain exactly what had happened.

'So he didn't actually rape you,' Nathan said with relief in his voice after listening to her tortured tale.

'He...he tried,' she explained huskily, 'but he...he... couldn't d-do it. He was very drunk.'

'And where were your parents while this was happening?'

'My mother's dead,' she explained. 'My father had passed out. He'd been drinking. *He* came home with him. When Dad fell asleep he climbed into my bed. When I screamed, he put one hand over my mouth while he...he...you know what he did,' she finished in a raw whisper.

'And does this bastard have a name?'

Gemma shuddered and shook her head. 'I never found out and I never asked. I...I see him in town sometimes, watching me.'

'But he hasn't come near you since.'

'No, but now that my father's dead, I...I'm scared.'

'How did your father die?'

'He fell down a mine shaft.'

'Are you sure he fell?'

Gemma blinked her astonishment.

'I think we should go to the police and tell them about this creep,' Nathan decided.

Gemma gasped and jumped to her feet. 'No! I don't want to do that. I can't tell them what I've just told you. I simply can't! Besides, I...I'm leaving Lightning Ridge tomorrow, on the bus.'

'To go where?'

'To Sydney.'

He stared at her for a long moment. 'Sydney's a tough town for someone alone,' he said. 'Do you have any relatives there?'

'I'm not sure.'

'Don't you *know*?'

She shrugged. 'My mother was born in Sydney but I never knew her folks. I…I was hoping I might be able to track them down some time.'

'How much money do you have?'

'Enough.'

His smile was sardonic. 'Independent, aren't you? Look, I'll give you my card. If you find yourself in a hole when you get to Sydney, or you're desperate for a job, look me up, OK?' Striding back over to his suit jacket, he drew a small white card from another of the pockets and brought it back to her.

'Tell me what I can do to help right now,' he added after she'd slipped the card into the breast pocket of her blue checked shirt. 'Did you drive yourself here? Can I walk you to your car?'

'Yes, I'd appreciate that.'

'And what about when you get home?'

'That'll be all right. Ma will be there.'

Nathan frowned at her. 'But I thought you said your mother was dead.'

'She is. Ma's not my mother. She's a friend.'

He sighed. 'Something tells me you're a very complicated girl.'

Gemma laughed. 'Ma says I have hidden qualities. Is that the same thing as complicated?'

'Could very well be. But I don't think I should try to find out.' Having uttered this rather cryptic remark, he picked up his room key, took Gemma's elbow and ushered her outside. 'Can you still see him?' he asked.

Gemma's heart pounded as she looked around. 'No,' she sighed.

'Right, well, let's get you safely home.'

CHAPTER THREE

'SHE'S become impossible, Nathan. Simply impossible!' Lenore glared at her ex-husband as he sat behind that damned desk of his, looking not the slightest bit perturbed.

'Kirsty is a typical teenager. You shouldn't let her upset you so.'

'That's easy for you to say. You don't have to live with her.' Lenore slumped down into a chair and sighed heavily. 'I'm at my wits' end. They're threatening to expel her from school. She's smoking on the sly, swears like a trooper and dresses like a trollop. I...I've been thinking of sending her to boarding-school,' she finished, flicking a nervous glance at Nathan through her long lashes.

Lenore knew what he thought of boarding-school, having been dumped into different ones by his drug-crazed mother whenever a new man came on to the scene, only to be dragged out once she was alone again and wanting company. By the time he was sixteen a totally screwed-up Nathan had run away from the latest five-star school, just in time to find his mother, dead from a heroin overdose.

With such a history, it was no wonder Lenore felt a little edgy about suggesting boarding-school for their daughter.

Nathan reacted just as she'd feared.

'She won't be going to bloody boarding-school,' he bit out, snapping forward on his chair. 'She can come live with me for a while.'

Lenore's lovely green eyes widened with genuine surprise, then narrowed into a frown. 'Where? Not at that beach-house of yours. Who would mind her till you got home from work?'

'I'm living at Belleview till Byron gets out of hospital and on his feet again.'

'Oh, yes, I forgot. Poor Byron. How's his leg?'

'On the mend. He might have to use a cane for a while, though.'

'He'll hate that.'

'Better than being dead, like Irene. Though maybe Irene's death isn't such a tragedy. She was a miserable bitch, and she made Byron miserable too.'

'For heaven's sake, Nathan, don't you ever have any pity for anyone?' Lenore snapped, irritated with this hard man whom she'd tried to love, but failed. He just wouldn't meet her halfway. Or even a quarter way.

'I have pity for a daughter whose mother doesn't want her around,' he said coldly.

'That's not true and you know it! Oh, Nathan, you can be so cruel sometimes. Cruel and heartless.' Tears flooded her eyes and she rummaged in her handbag for a tissue.

Nathan watched her mop up her tears without turning a hair.

'Let's get back to the point, shall we?' he said when she was sufficiently composed. 'I suggest you go home, get Kirsty to pack her things and bring her round tonight after dinner. But if she comes to live with me, she comes for a whole term at least. No chopping and changing mid-stream.'

Lenore felt as though a huge weight had been lifted from her shoulders. Maybe Nathan would straighten the girl out a bit. Kirsty loved her father. And Nathan loved her too. His daughter was the only female who'd ever been able to get past the steely cover Nathan kept around his heart.

Kirsty was the main reason Nathan had married Lenore. That, and his mistaken belief that she would be the sort of wife to suit him: an independent woman who wouldn't lean or demand, who would be there at his side when he needed a social partner, and there, in his bed, when he needed sex.

Well, Lenore had needed more than that. Much more. So after twelve years of the loneliest marriage she could ever imagine she'd called it quits. People had condemned her for their divorce, saying she'd put her acting career in front of her husband. And maybe there was a bit of truth in that. But she had to have *something*.

A depressing sigh wafted from Lenore's lips. If only things had been different with Zachary all those years ago. If only he hadn't been married. If only he'd loved her as intensely as she'd loved him, as she still loved him.

'If you've finished daydreaming...' Nathan drawled caustically.

Lenore blinked and looked up.

'Maybe you'd like to tell me what or who is bringing that wistful look into your eyes. Surely not Kirsty. It wouldn't be Zachary Marsden, would it?'

'And if it is?' she retorted, piqued by his sarcasm. 'Don't tell me you're jealous, Nathan. Jealousy is an emotion reserved for people in love. You never loved me any more than I loved you so don't pretend now, thank you very much.'

'I never pretended a thing with you, Lenore. It was you who seduced me in the first place, you who used *my* body, not the other way around, you who pretended I meant more to you than I ever could mean.'

'Are you saying you *wanted* me to be in love with you?' she asked, disbelieving.

'I'm saying no man likes to be had on the rebound. We could have had a good marriage, if it hadn't been for Zachary Marsden lurking around in your heart. We could still have had a good marriage if you hadn't indulged in sentimental rubbish and deliberately kept your supposed love for him alive. Do you think I didn't notice how often you contrived to put yourself in Zachary's company? The poor bastard. You've done nothing but tease him for years.

You know he's a decent sort of man, that he wants to stay faithful to his wife and family. Give him a break and find someone else to try out your *femme fatale* talents on.'

'Oh!' Lenore jumped to her feet. 'Oh, you're just impossible! You don't understand true love. But one day, Nathan, one day you're going to really fall in love and then you'll know what it's like. Who knows? Maybe it'll make you human, like the rest of us. Maybe I might even learn to like you, as I once mistakenly thought I did.'

Gemma was sitting in a deep leather two-seater in the plush reception area of Whitmore Opals when the most stunning-looking woman she'd ever seen stormed out of Nathan's office, masses of gorgeous red hair flying out behind a face so arrestingly beautiful that one could only stare. She banged the door shut behind her before covering her luminescent green eyes with sunglasses and striding across the grey-blue carpet on the way towards the exit.

''Bye, Moira,' she threw at the receptionist on her way past. 'My commiserations that you have to work for that man. He's impossible!'

'Goodbye, Mrs Whitmore,' the middle-aged receptionist called after her.

Gemma's head snapped round to stare after the redhead. So! Nathan Whitmore was married.

She shook her head, smiling ruefully at her own stupidity. Of course a man like him would be married.

Gemma almost laughed at the silly thoughts that had been tumbling through her head since she'd parted company with Nathan in Lightning Ridge three days before. It had been crazy of her to imagine he'd been genuinely attracted to her, that he'd been loath to let her go. He'd simply been kind to her, that was all. Nothing more.

I'm as naïve as Ma said, Gemma realised with some dismay.

When she'd told Ma about what happened at the motel, the old woman had been aghast.

'Good God, girl, and there I was thinkin' you'd got your head screwed on where men were concerned. But you're just as silly as the rest. Fancy huggin' a stranger like that in his motel room. And acceptin' a drink as well. The danger wasn't from that ugly old bugger outside, love, but the handsome one inside!'

Gemma didn't agree with Ma about that. She was sure Nathan Whitmore was a good man. But she had to agree about herself. Clearly, she was as vulnerable to a handsome face as the next girl, and twice as silly as most. Her actions in that motel room had been incredibly naïve and foolish. If Nathan hadn't been an honourable man, God knew what might have happened, for there was no doubting she'd been blown away by how she'd felt when in his arms. Her only consolation was that the incident had eliminated her worry that a man's touch would repel her.

The receptionist stood up from behind her desk and went over to knock on the door that Mrs Whitmore had slammed shut. After a brusque command to enter, she went inside, exiting a few seconds later with a polite smile on her face. 'Mr Whitmore will see you straight away, Miss Smith. Please go right in.'

Gemma stood up, feeling suddenly fat and frumpish in her new pink cotton sundress with its tight bodice constraining her full breasts. Yet that morning, she had thought she looked…inviting. But seeing Nathan's wife, so sophisticated and slim in a green silk suit, had put a dent in Gemma's confidence over her appearance. She should have left her hair out, she thought unhappily, not tied it up into a childish pony-tail with an even more childish pink ribbon.

A dampening dismay was beginning to invade when Gemma checked her self-pity with a stern hand. What did it matter what she looked like? The man was married. Decent girls did not try to attract married men. And she was a decent girl. Or so she hoped.

Clutching the straw handbag in which she'd placed her precious legacy that morning, Gemma lifted her chin and strode purposefully into the office. But the moment her gaze rested once more on that handsome blond head and those fascinating grey eyes, she was lost.

Was she imagining things or was he looking at her the way some of the male customers at the café back at the Ridge had started looking at her? As though they'd like to have *her* on their plate and not a hamburger and chips. Gemma was quietly appalled that for the first time in her life she liked being looked at like that.

His hunger was fleeting, however, if that was what she'd glimpsed, Nathan Whitmore getting to his feet and coming round to shake her hand with a cool and impersonal politeness. 'Miss Smith,' he said matter-of-factly. 'How nice to see you again. Would you like to sit down while I get the door?' And he indicated an upright wooden-backed chair that sat in front of the desk.

Gemma sat down, trying not to look as depressed as she suddenly felt. Couldn't he at least have called her Gemma?

She watched him walk back round behind his impressive desk, equally impressive in a dark blue suit which fitted his body to perfection and highlighted his golden hair. He'd had it cut since she last saw him, she realised, for when he bent forward slightly on sitting down no wayward lock fell in boyish disarray across his forehead. The sleek, ultra-groomed look gave him a crisp, no-nonsense, almost forbidding air which she still found disturbingly attractive.

Her mind flew to his wife and her dramatic exit. What had he said or done to upset her so much? Why had she called him impossible?

The man who'd been so kind to her out at the Ridge was far from impossible. He'd been sweet. Sweet and warm and caring. Still, it appeared that man had been left behind in the outback of Australia. The pragmatic individual sitting behind his city desk in his plush city office seemed like a different person.

'So, how can I help you?' he opened up.

Gemma stared at him. No questions about how she was,

or how was her trip to Sydney, or where was she staying, just straight down to brass tacks. Her disappointment was sharp, but she gathered herself to answer coolly.

'I have an opal I would like valued.' If he was going to be all business, then so was she. 'You do valuations here, don't you?'

'We do.'

'I realise they aren't free. I'm quite prepared to pay whatever the going price is.'

He waived her offer with a dismissive gesture of his hand. 'That won't be necessary. Do you have this opal with you?'

'Yes.'

'I could give you a reasonable estimate immediately, if you like.' He smiled, and she felt a lurch in her stomach.

'Thank you. I'd appreciate that.' Gemma was only too glad to drag her eyes away from that handsome smiling face to dig the opal out from the depths of her handbag. She'd wrapped it in an old checked teatowel. As she stood up to place her treasure on the desk before him, butterflies crowded her stomach. What if it wasn't worth as much as she hoped? What if she'd been mistaken about its rarity? Maybe it would prove to be flawed in some way. She didn't have any experience with opals of this size and quality. Nathan leant over and picked the stone up, turning it over in his hands as she had done.

'My God,' was the first thing he said, his voice a shocked whisper.

He peered down at the black opal for a long time, turning it this way and that to catch the brilliant and glowing flashes of light. Finally, his gaze snapped up to hers. 'Where did you get this?' he demanded to know.

Gemma was startled by the accusation in his question. It flustered her. 'I…I…my father left it to me.'

'And where did *he* get it?'

She blinked. 'I suppose he found it. In one of his claims.'

'I doubt that very much,' he said slowly.

Gemma's mind was racing. What was he thinking? That Dad *stole* it?

This solution to her father's possessing such a treasure had not occurred to Gemma before. The ramifications of it being true struck a severe blow. Ashen-faced, she stared across at the man peering at her with steely eyes.

'You think he stole it, don't you?' she cried.

When Nathan didn't deny it, she groaned, and slumped back into her chair.

'Oh, my God...' Her head dropped into her hands, all her dreams crumbling on the spot. She should have known, should have guessed. Her father would have sold that opal if he'd had a legal right to it. But he hadn't... And neither did she...

'Gemma...'

She glanced up through soggy lashes to see Nathan squatting beside her chair. His face had softened to a semblance of the face she remembered from the motel and her heart turned over.

'I have no proof at this moment that your opal was stolen,' he said gently, 'but it resembles a stone that disappeared over twenty years ago. If you like, I can have it looked at by the man who owned it before it vanished. Believe me when I say you will not get into trouble, no matter what happens.'

'Who...who is the rightful owner?'

'If it is the opal I think it is, then it's Byron...my father.'

Gemma gasped. 'But how incredible!'

'Not so incredible. There was a time when Whitmore Opals was one of the only two opal-trading companies in New South Wales. They owned many precious opals, this one included.'

A thought struck Gemma and she frowned. 'How do I know you're telling me the truth?'

Nathan stood up, his eyes cooling. 'The theft was registered with the police at the time, as was a detailed description of the opal. You can check it out if you like.'

Gemma felt small for having doubted him. 'No,' she mumbled. 'I believe you.'

'If you like I will have a photograph taken of the opal and give you a receipt for it, then if it turns out not to be the opal in question it will be returned to you. Of course, if this happens, we would like the opportunity to buy it from you. An opal of this beauty and rarity does not come up for sale very often.'

Gemma decided it would be foolish to be too trusting, so she accepted this offer, at the same time agreeing to give Whitmore Opals first right of purchase. But intuition told her this would never come about. The opal had not legally been her father's, and it would never legally be hers. All her dreams had been dashed. Suddenly, she was here in Sydney, staying in a cheap hotel, with just under a thousand dollars in her purse, no job, no friends and no opal.

A deep depression settled on her, making her shoulders sag.

'I'll have Moira get you a cup of coffee while you wait,' Nathan said. 'Or would you prefer tea?'

'No, coffee,' she said limply.

'Black or white?'

'White with one sugar.'

Moira brought her a couple of biscuits with the coffee, which Gemma ate gratefully, knowing she would have to conserve her money now. She was thinking about what her next move would be when Nathan returned with the photo and receipt, and a black leather briefcase.

'I'll take the opal to the hospital for Byron to look at this afternoon,' he said, patting the briefcase.

'The hospital?'

'Byron was in a boating accident a few weeks back. He was lucky to survive. His wife and a couple of friends were killed.'

'Oh, how awful! The poor man.'

'Yes.'

Gemma interpreted Nathan's curt tone as grief, since

Byron's wife would have been his adopted mother. But his closed face didn't allow gushes of sympathy and she fell silent.

'I can understand this opal business has come as a great shock to you,' Nathan resumed. 'You were probably relying on the money. But I'm sure Byron will give you a substantial monetary reward for its return.'

Gemma brightened. 'Do you think so?'

'I guarantee it. Call back in the morning and I'll have either the reward for you, or your opal back again. Where are you staying, by the way?'

'The Central Hotel for the present.'

A dark frown scrunched up his high forehead.

'That's no place for a young girl like you to be staying. Look, you'd better come home with me. We've plenty of rooms, then tomorrow we'll see if we can't find you a decent flat.' He glanced at his watch. 'Come on, I'll take you to your hotel right now and get your things, then I'll drive you home to Belleview.'

Gemma scrambled to her feet. 'Oh, but I...I can't let you do that. What will your wife say?'

'My wife?'

'Yes. Mrs Whitmore.'

His smile was ironic. 'I dare say Mrs Whitmore might have plenty to say. But it won't make a blind bit of difference. Lenore Langtry ceased to be my legal spouse two years ago. Does that put your sweet mind at rest?'

No, Gemma thought as he swept her out of his office. Not at all, she reaffirmed once she found herself being settled into the most luxurious car she'd ever seen. Most definitely not, when Nathan stayed leaning over her for a second longer than necessary, peering down her cleavage then up into her eyes with an expression no female could mistake a second time.

Ma's warnings came back to haunt her. What was she getting herself into here? This was no schoolboy she was going home with. They were *easy* to ward off. Neither was he a safely married man with a chaperoning wife in tow. He was a mature man, a divorced man, a...a *city* man. And she was letting him take her home for the night. Ma would be having apoplexy by now if she knew!

But no sooner were they under way than Nathan started chatting away with her quite naturally, putting her at ease, making her feel very relaxed in his company. Soon she began wondering if Ma's warnings had made her paranoid about city men. So he'd glanced at her a couple of times. What did she expect after wearing this type of bare-necked dress? She'd bought it specifically with Nathan Whitmore in mind after all. Oh, she'd denied it to Ma at the time, but there was no point in denying it to herself. She'd wanted him to look at her and he had. But looking was only looking. Nothing to work up a head of steam about.

Finally, the questions came about her trip down and her impressions of Sydney, Nathan listening with gentlemanly politeness as she babbled on about how large and intimidating she found everything, how she hadn't been able to sleep the night before because of the traffic noise, how she thought everything was awfully expensive, even a rather dingy hotel room.

'I don't think I'll ever get used to a sandwich costing over three dollars,' she said, with awe in her voice.

'Yes, you will,' he returned drily, then smiled across at her. 'But not too soon, I hope. I like you just the way you are.'

Gemma flushed with pleasure at what she saw as his seal of approval. He liked her. He really liked her. How exciting. Not even thinking about Ma or her warnings could still her dancing heart.

It must have taken them over an hour to get from the city office block which housed Whitmore Opals down to the hotel then back over the Harbour Bridge. But Gemma didn't really mind. Her eyes were everywhere. There was no doubt that, despite the claustrophobic feeling the city gave her, it had the most beautiful setting in the world.

Her mouth remained open as they drove across the Bridge. There was so much to see with Darling Harbour and the Opera House and the Quay and all that lovely blue water. How different from the dry, dusty, grey crater-filled landscape that had been her world for eighteen years.

No, twenty, she corrected herself again, a frown forming as she remembered her other mission in coming to Sydney. Would she be able to find out more about her mother? A trip to the registry of Births, Deaths and Marriages would be a start. Hopefully, she'd be able to get a copy of her parents' marriage certificate, which she hadn't located among her father's things. Then there were electoral rolls to check. Motor registry lists, maybe. Driving licences, perhaps.

But would the authorities give her such information freely? If not, maybe the missing-persons division of the police could help, because she certainly couldn't afford a private detective. Not now. She had to be very careful with her money. And she simply had to get a job.

'Mr Whitmore. Nathan…'

'Mmm?'

'Do…do you think there might be a job for me at Whitmore Opals? I've learnt a lot about opals over the years, you know.'

'I'm sure you have. What would you like to do?'

'I don't know. I could serve behind the counter, I guess. Do you have shops like that, ones that sell opals to the public? Or do you just make jewellery?'

'We have two retail outlets. One down at the Rocks, and one in the foyer of Regency Hotel. Yes, I'm sure we could use someone with your knowledge behind the counter, though you'd be required to do a course in Japanese first. A lot of our customers are Japanese businessmen and tourists.'

'How long would it take me to learn Japanese?' she asked, concerned about her money situation, not to mention

her ability to learn another language. She'd only been average at school.

'With intensive lessons, most people are able to com-
municate on a basic level after a couple of months.'

'A couple of months! But I'll have run out of money by
then.'

'I doubt that. I'm sure Byron will be very generous with
his reward. That opal is conservatively worth over a million
dollars.'

'You're joking!' Gemma gasped.

'Not at all. Prices are on the rise again.'

'A million dollars...'

'Are you upset that you're probably not going to be an
instant millionaire?'

'Yes,' she admitted. 'I am.'

'Money doesn't always make you happy, Gemma.'

She laughed. 'Neither does being poor.'

Now *he* laughed. 'You could be right there. Well, at least
you have a better chance than most poor people of ending
up rich.'

'How do you figure that out?'

His head turned to rake over her once more. And once
again, Gemma was shocked. Not so much by what she saw
behind those grey eyes, but by the way they could make
her feel. All hot and heady and helpless.

'A beautiful young girl like yourself should have no trouble ensnaring a rich husband. Who knows? I might even
marry you myself.'

Gemma sat there, stunned. Till he bestowed a wry little
smile on her and she realised he was only teasing.

'You shouldn't make fun of me,' she said with reproach
in her voice, but turmoil in her heart. For she would marry
him in a flash if he asked her, this man she'd only met
twice, but who already had her in the palm of his hand. It
was a shocking realisation and one which underlined her
own foolishness where Nathan Whitmore was concerned.

Gemma had often wondered why women made fools of

themselves over men, not having ever understood the strange power of that alien emotion, love. She'd also scorned girls who claimed to have fallen in love at first sight. What rubbish! she had used to think.

Now, as she wallowed beneath the onslaught of a tidal force of longing, she had to accept she'd been wrong. This had to be love, this dreadful drowning feeling, this mad desire to go along with anything and everything this man suggested, even something as insane as marrying him.

But of course he hadn't meant it. She had to keep reminding herself of that. No doubt city men couldn't resist teasing silly, naïve country girls. She simply had to pull herself together.

He was smiling at her again, amusement in his eyes. 'Who says I was making fun of you?'

A very real resentment began to simmer inside Gemma, who was not a person to simmer in silence. 'I can just see you marrying someone like me,' she countered indignantly. 'People would think you'd gone mad after having someone like Mrs Whitmore as your wife. Now *she's* what I call beautiful!'

'Is she now?' he drawled. 'Yes, well, Lenore is lovely to look at, no one would deny. But there are all kinds of beauty, my dear Gemma, and all kinds of wives. Speaking of which, you'll be meeting Lenore tonight. She's bringing my daughter over to stay for a while. Apparently, the little minx has been creating merry hell at home and is in need of a firm hand.'

'How old is she?' Gemma asked, picturing a recalcitrant six-year-old.

'Fourteen.'

Her head snapped round before she could stop it.

'Yes, I know,' he said drily. 'I was a child groom. Twenty-one years young the day before my wedding. And yes, it was a shotgun affair.'

Gemma caught his bitter tone and wondered if his marriage had been under duress right from the start. Marriage simply because the woman was pregnant seemed fraught with danger. The couple had to be in love as well. Still, it was hard to imagine a man not being in love with Lenore Whitmore. Maybe Nathan's bitterness came from her not being in love with him.

'Kirsty's basically a good kid,' Nathan went on. 'But the divorce hit her hard. She just can't seem to come to terms with it. Not that I blame her.'

'You…you shouldn't be bothering with me, then, if you've got your daughter coming.'

'Why not? As I said, there's plenty of room. Besides, you're not that much older than Kirsty. She might relate to you better than Melanie or Ava.'

'Melanie and Ava?' Gemma must have sounded as perplexed as she felt, for Nathan chuckled.

'Don't worry. I haven't got a harem installed. Melanie's Byron's housekeeper. She's not that old—thirtyish, I guess—but unfortunately projects a personality that would make Mrs Danvers seem warm.'

'Who's Mrs Danvers? The previous housekeeper?'

Nathan smiled. 'A housekeeper certainly, but one of the fictional kind. I'll tell you about her one day.'

'Perhaps you should tell me who Ava is first.'

'Ah, Ava. She's Byron's kid sister. A change-of-life baby. As scatty as anything and young at heart, but as old as Melanie. No, I think Kirsty'll get along best with you. In fact, I might hire you as her minder while you learn Japanese. What do you say? Bed and board for nix in exchange for keeping an eye on the little devil before and after school?'

Gemma's head was whirling. Everything seemed to be going so fast. In the beginning, she'd only been going to stay the night. 'I…I'll have to think about it.'

'Will you? Pity. I was hoping you'd just say yes. It would have been the perfect solution.' His sideways glance carried an odd little smile which Gemma found quite unnerving. It was as though it hid some secret plan only he was privy to.

'P-perfect solution?' she found herself stammering.

'Yes. *You* would be safely accommodated till you find your feet and *I* wouldn't have to worry about my wayward daughter. Still, I have to warn you, Gemma, I don't take no for an answer lightly. I can be a very stubborn man when I want something.'

Gemma gulped. She didn't doubt him for a moment. But what, exactly, was he wanting?

Oh, Ma...I'm trying to keep my head. I really am. But it's hard. It's really hard. If only he weren't so...so...

'How long before we get to your place?' she blurted out, her stomach in knots.

'Not far now. But it's not my home. It's Byron's. It's called Belleview Manor. But mostly we just call it Belleview.'

CHAPTER FOUR

FOR a girl who had spent her entire life living in a dirt-walled dugout, Gemma's introduction to Belleview was an overwhelming experience.

'My God!' she gasped when Nathan swung his dark blue sedan into a driveway, stopping in front of high iron gates which had the name 'Belleview' carved into one of the sandstone gate-posts. They'd been travelling along a quiet, tree-lined avenue for some time, in a suburb called St Ives, where Gemma had already glimpsed some splendid homes behind high security walls, but this…this was something else.

'I agree. It *is* rather ostentatious,' Nathan said, pressing some sort of remote-control unit so that the gates began opening all by themselves.

'Oh, no,' Gemma denied, embarrassed that he might think she was criticising his home. 'It's the most beautiful house I've ever seen. Why, it's even more beautiful than Tara in *Gone With The Wind*. In fact, it looks a bit like Tara.'

'I suppose it does, superficially. All those white columns. But it's a lot more modern inside. More modern than Tara, that is. Certainly not all that modern by today's standard. It was built by Byron's father in 1947, just after the war. Byron has made some renovations over the years, however. Put in air-conditioning and a pool.'

The gates now properly open, the car purred forwards, following the curve of the red gravel driveway to stop in front of the huge two-storey white mansion. Gemma couldn't stop admiring the house and gardens. There was so much colour. And the lawns were so green. But it was the pond complete with lilies in the centre of the circular driveway that entranced her the most, perhaps because water had been such a sparse commodity out at Lightning Ridge.

'This is like something out of a fairy-tale,' she said, and beamed across at Nathan.

The corner of his mouth lifted in one of those small sardonic smiles which Gemma wasn't sure she liked any more. Did he always view the world with that air of wryly amused cynicism?

'And who are you in this fairy-tale?' he asked. 'Cinderella?'

Gemma's face fell with his mocking tone. She turned away so that he wouldn't see how hurt she was. When she went to get out of the car, he stopped her with a hand on her arm.

'I'm sorry, Gemma.'

His gentle apology moved her so much that she almost burst into tears. With great difficulty Gemma controlled herself and turned back to face him. A foolish move. He was very close, having leant over to grab her arm; so close that she could smell that pine-scented aftershave he always wore.

She stared into his eyes and a trembling started deep within. His hand lifted to lay against her cheek. Amazingly, it too was far from steady.

'God, but you're lovely,' he muttered thickly, and, curling his hand around the back of her neck, he slowly began to pull her mouth to his.

She gasped back from him, brown eyes wide like those of a startled fawn. 'No!'

Her rejection clearly shocked him. Or was it himself he was shocked at? 'I was only going to kiss you, Gemma,' he said sharply, 'not ravish you. Do you think I would try to force myself on you like that brute you told me about?'

'No,' she admitted shakily. 'You're nothing like him. You're nothing like any man I've ever met! But I hardly know you, after all. And I...I...' Her words trailed into a dazed silence, her thoughts a mess.

'What you're saying is that you're not that type of girl. Do you think I don't already know that, Gemma? You're the sweetest, nicest girl I've ever met. Do you honestly think I invited you home tonight with the sole intention of having my wicked way with you?'

Her blush was fierce, her embarrassment total. When he actually put it into words she felt a fool.

'If you're having second thoughts,' he said coldly, 'then we can turn round right now and find you a hotel near by.'

'No!' Gemma burst out. The thought that she might have offended Nathan, who'd been so good to her, was unthinkable. 'I'm sorry, Nathan. Truly. I...I know you're a gentleman.'

'I like to think I am, though you do have a way of making me do things on the spur of the moment, like that kiss. You must know how lovely you are, Gemma. Lovely and desirable and very very tempting.'

'T-tempting?'

'Yes, tempting. Damn it all, perhaps I *should* take you to a hotel!'

He might have driven off too, if a white sports car hadn't careered into the driveway at that moment, screaming round to screech to a gravel-scrunching halt right in front of them. The driver's door was flung open and a young woman unfolded herself from behind the wheel, a wild-looking creature with very short, impossibly white hair and kohl-rimmed eyes, which flashed curiosity at Nathan once she spied Gemma in the car beside him.

Gemma stared as the girl strode over, her tall athletic body looking extremely sexy in tight white jeans slung low on her hips and a man's white shirt tied around her tanned midriff. Outlandish gold loops dangled from her ears, and she had to be wearing a dozen gold bracelets, which jingled and jangled as she walked. They weren't the only things that moved as she walked, her generous breasts clearly bra-less beneath the shirt.

'Hi, there, darls. I'm back,' she said, pouting full pink lips at Nathan through the driver's window.

'So I see,' he returned drily. 'I thought you were mending your grief-stricken heart with Roberto in Fiji.'

'Nah. He turned out to be a drag. No fun at all.'

'You mean he wouldn't jump when you said jump.'

The girl pulled a face at him then cocked her head to one side as she surveyed Gemma, who must have been still staring with her mouth open.

'Who's this, brother, dear? Some stray you picked up off the streets?'

'Watch your mouth, Jade,' Nathan snapped.

'Oooh, you've gone all masterly and protective.' She gave Gemma a more thorough once-over. 'Mmm. Not your usual style, Nathan, dear. And it's bordering on cradle-snatching.'

'Jade,' he warned darkly.

'All right, all right, I'll behave. You do have that effect on me, don't you? So, are you going to introduce us? No, I suppose you aren't. I'm Jade Whitmore, darls....' And, leaning into the car through the window so that one of her breasts was practically stuffed into Nathan's face, she shook Gemma's hand. 'My, you *are* pretty. I'm Nathan's adopted sister, by the way, only daughter of Byron and his dear recently departed wife, Irene.'

'Jade, for God's sake!' Nathan finally lost his temper and shoved her back out through the window. 'Don't take any damned notice of her, Gemma. She has this tasteless sense of humour and no tact at all.'

'Which makes me just the opposite to you, Nathan, dear,' Jade countered airily. 'You have no sense of humour and all the tact in the world. So it's Gemma, is it?'

She bent over, showing ample cleavage as she peered into the car from a safe distance. 'Well, Gemma, watch yourself with this so-called brother of mine. He has the habit of making silly women like us fall madly in love with him, but he doesn't ever love them back. Oh, he'll make love to you. And very well too, for a machine. But when it comes to matters of the heart, you'll find out he just hasn't got one.'

By this time Nathan was getting out of the car, his expression coldly threatening.

'Now don't get mad, Nathan,' Jade laughed, wagging a finger at him. 'I'm going. I've decided even Roberto is better than nothing. And that's all I've ever got from this place. Nothing!'

Gemma glimpsed a flash of the most crushing pain in the girl's face before she whirled away and dashed back into her car. Gravel flying, she accelerated away, leaving a furious-looking Nathan glaring after her.

Heaving a frustrated sigh, he turned to face Gemma, who was sitting in stunned silence in the passenger seat. Nathan walked round and wrenched the door open.

'You might as well get out and come inside. Don't worry. You'll be safe enough now. Jade has a sobering effect on most people, especially me.'

Gemma climbed out, her mind still on the vivid Jade and that shattered look.

'I think she's very unhappy,' she murmured.

'If she is, it's her own damned stupid fault,' Nathan stated. 'She would have to be the most selfish, spoilt, wilful woman I've ever known. No, she's not a woman. She's a child, with a typical child's way of only wanting what she can't have.'

Namely you, Gemma guessed, her thoughts flying back to Jade's astonishing hint that Nathan had once taken her to bed. Had he? she wondered. She didn't dare ask but she rather suspected he might have. Nathan pretended to be a cool, controlled man, but Gemma knew better. Hiding behind that urbane manner lay a man whose hand could tremble when it touched a woman's cheek, and whose voice could grow thick with desire in a split-second. What had Jade said about him?

'He'll make love to you…and very well too, for a machine. But when it comes to matters of the heart, you'll find he just hasn't got one…'

Gemma's mind whirled over those words as she stood on the flagstone patio, waiting while Nathan lifted her old black suitcase from the boot of the car. Jade was wrong about that last part, she decided. Nathan did have a heart. He just didn't like to wear it on his sleeve. But the other part about his making love to *her*… Such a thought sent a shiver rippling down Gemma's spine.

'Don't let anything Jade said worry you,' Nathan advised on joining her. 'She's an incorrigible liar and a troublemaker of the first order. As if *I* would ever make love to someone like her.' He shuddered in revulsion. 'I'm just thankful she decided to leave again. The longer she stays away, the better!'

Lenore bundled a sulky Kirsty into the car straight after dinner, and set out for the relatively short drive from her villa home in Turramurra to Belleview.

'I keep telling you, I don't *want* to go live in that ghastly old mausoleum!' Kirsty complained. 'It's not as though Dad'll ever be there. Not in spirit, anyway. He works at Whitmore Opals all day, writes those boring old plays of his all night, then goes down to the beach-house to write all weekend!'

Lenore resisted arguing with her daughter. Setting her lips firmly, she simply kept on driving.

'Why can't you and Dad get back together again?' Kirsty resumed in a whiny voice. 'He didn't want a divorce. He told me so. It's your fault. You and your stupid bloody career!'

'If you keep using that disgusting language,' Lenore threatened her daughter, 'I'll wash your mouth out with soap.'

'You and whose army?'

'Wait till I tell your father the way you're speaking to me!'

'I'm shaking in my boots.'

Lenore shot a truly pained look across at her daughter, who looked sorry for a second, before she lifted her nose in a disdainful sniff and turned her face away. But not before Lenore saw tears pricking at Kirsty's eyes.

Lenore felt like crying herself. Maybe Kirsty was right. Maybe it *was* all her fault. Did she expect too much from life? Should she have settled for a lonely, loveless marriage? Struggled on regardless?

She hadn't really been happy since the divorce, despite having a lot more success on the stage. Already, she'd secured a marvellous meaty part in a play this year, rehearsals to start next week. As for being lonely...well, she was still lonely. She hadn't been with a man in two years for one thing, yet she enjoyed sex. Nathan had been an expert lover, knowing exactly what buttons to push to turn her on even when she wasn't in the mood. But their lovemaking had never been anything but a meeting of bodies in bed, often in the dark. She could have been any woman and it wouldn't have mattered to Nathan.

But men were like that, weren't they? That was why prostitution was the oldest profession. They could separate love and sex. No trouble.

Maybe some women could too, but in the end Lenore had not been one of them. Slowly but surely, she hadn't been able to stand the way she felt after Nathan rolled from her and invariably fell into a sound sleep. She had always lain there, wide awake, thinking about what it would be like if it had been Zachary in bed with her.

Nathan's taunts that morning about her teasing Zachary all these years still stung, maybe because they were partially true. Yes, she *had* lived for the times she ran into Zachary at social functions, a reasonably frequent occurrence since he was the Whitmores' solicitor and a good friend of Byron's. She and Nathan had lived at Belleview during part of their marriage, and Zachary and his wife had come there often for dinner parties and other celebrations.

Lenore might have taken extra trouble with her appearance on those occasions. But she had never deliberately teased Zachary. Her only deliberate action was the one time she'd gone to his office, ostensibly to employ him in his professional capacity as a solicitor with one of her acting contracts. All she had wanted was to see him, not seduce him. Zachary, however, had treated her with such cool propriety that she hadn't gone through with that idea. He'd made her feel vaguely ashamed, as though it had been beneath her.

Yet she did so love him. He was more of a man than any man she'd ever known. Strong and gallant and good, and so handsome he made her go weak at the knees. He might be over forty now, but age had lent a broad-shouldered maturity to his super-tall frame and a dignity to his lean, angular face. He stood head and shoulders above most men in stature *and* character, in Lenore's opinion. Felicity didn't know how lucky she was to have such a man as her husband.

Felicity...

Lenore suppressed a sigh. If only Felicity weren't so damned pretty. And so damned delicate. Lenore sensed Zachary wasn't in love with his wife, but she could imagine a man's ego being constantly stroked by all that blonde, blue-eyed fragility. A lot of men liked the clingy, vulnerable variety of woman. Clearly, Zachary did.

'You've just driven straight past Belleview,' Kirsty said scornfully.

Lenore swore under her breath.

'Such language!' her daughter mocked.

Lenore's head snapped round to find her daughter grinning at her. When she grinned back, Kirsty's face began to crumple.

'I...I'm sorry, Mum,' she said in a strangled tone, 'I

know I've been acting like a bitch. I don't know what's wrong with me.'

Lenore patted her daughter's bejeaned knee. 'It's all right, sweetie. I understand. I haven't been the best mother lately, either. Perhaps we both need some breathing space.'

'I'll try to be good for Dad.'

'I think that would be a wise idea. It was good of him to have you, you know. He's very busy at the moment with Byron still in hospital. If it hadn't been for the accident, he would have given up his position at Whitmore Opals to write full-time. For your information, Hollywood has just bought the rights to one of his boring old plays, so I wouldn't knock them if I were you. Your Dad happens to be a creative genius, my girl, and it's time you realised it.'

'Wow, Mum, do you realise you just stuck up for Dad? You still love him, don't you?'

Lenore sighed. 'Let's not get back to that, please. I couldn't stand it.'

By this time Lenore had negotiated a U-turn and they were approaching Belleview from the other direction. The clock on the dashboard showed eight, and the sun had just set.

'Do try to be pleasant to Melanie,' Lenore said pleadingly as they swung into the driveway. 'And don't make fun of Ava.'

'Melanie's a wet blanket and Ava's a dill. She *asks* to be made fun of.'

Lenore heaved another sigh and pointed the remote control at the gates.

'But I'll do my best,' Kirsty promised.

'Good. Oh, and one last thing. *No more smoking.*'

Kirsty turned an innocent-looking face towards her mother. 'Of course not. Smoking's bad for your health.'

'So's trying to con your father!'

Melanie came to greet them at the door, looking her usual prim and proper self with her black hair scraped back into a tight roll, no make-up on, and her figure disguised in a black shirtwaister uniform dress one size too large for her. Ghastly beige-coloured stockings and chunky black flatties completed the quite erroneous picture of a stodgy, boring, sexless woman the wrong side of thirty.

But there was no pretence in the dullness of her black eyes as she smiled her dead smile at both of them before taking Kirsty's bags. 'Hello, Kirsty…Lenore… I'll take these upstairs to your usual room, Kirsty. Nathan's waiting for you both in the billiard room, Lenore.'

Kirsty started walking ahead across the marble entry, under the huge semi-circular staircase and down the hallway that led down to the entertainment rooms.

'He—er—has someone with him,' Melanie told Lenore quietly as she went to follow her daughter.

The odd note in Melanie's voice stopped Lenore in her tracks. 'Wait a sec, Kirsty,' she called to her daughter. 'Who?' she asked, running her mind over Nathan's very few male friends and not coming up with anyone who would be playing billiards with him at eight o'clock on a Monday night.

'Her name's Gemma Smith,' the housekeeper said, throwing Lenore a look that was overly bland even for Melanie. It suggested something was up which was highly unusual.

Nathan had been seen around town with several women since his divorce. But he hadn't brought one home. Not to Belleview, anyway. This Gemma person had to be someone quite special.

But if Nathan was getting tangled up with some woman why hadn't he mentioned her this morning? And why had he invited Kirsty to live here with him if he had some female in tow? No way would Lenore condone Kirsty living here while her father was having it off with some blonde bimbo down the hall.

Lenore was shocked at her crude thoughts, and the undeniable stab of jealousy that had inspired them.

'Is there anything I should know about this Gemma?' she asked.

'Seeing is worth a thousand words,' Melanie said drily.

Lenore hurried on after Kirsty lest the girl get a nasty shock. Not that Lenore really thought Nathan would be making love to this Gemma on the billiard table when he was expecting his ex-wife and daughter to arrive at any moment. But it was better to be safe than sorry.

The billiard-room was the very last room on the left. Lenore caught up with Kirsty just as she reached the heavy wooden door which wasn't properly shut. The sounds of laughter came floating through the gap: light and musical and very, very young.

Lenore's eyes widened. Kirsty frowned over at her mother.

Unaccountably infuriated, Lenore pushed the door open without knocking, only to reveal the most astonishing sight.

Nathan was trying to teach a young woman in a pink sundress to play billiards. He was standing behind her— *close* behind her—and they were both bending over the table. Nathan's broad shoulders were wrapped around the girl's slender ones, his long arms extending to where he was showing her how to aim the cue stick.

'No, not like that,' he was saying. 'Slowly... Smoothly... You don't jab!'

'I'll never get the hang of it, Nathan. I'm a duffer. Oh!' she gasped, straightening abruptly when she saw Lenore standing in the open doorway. Nathan grunted from behind her.

Lenore's gaze swept over the girl, her already green eyes even greener with envy. What a beauty this gorgeous young creature was! Those eyes! And that figure! Why, her breasts were having trouble staying within the confines of that dress, yet her waist was so tiny a man like Nathan could put his hands right round it.

Her own eyes darted to her ex-husband, reproach replacing shock on her face. What, in God's name, was he doing with such a child? Why, the girl could be no more than seventeen or eighteen, only marginally older than his daughter. It was disgusting!

'And good evening to you too, Lenore,' Nathan drawled, coming out from behind the girl at long last. 'Come in, Kirsty,' he directed over Lenore's shoulder. 'I want you both to meet Gemma. She hails from Lightning Ridge and has just been employed as Whitmore Opals' newest sales-girl. Unfortunately, Byron won't let her start till she's done the mandatory Japanese course, but while she's doing that she'll be staying here at Belleview.'

'*What*?' Lenore exclaimed. But before she could launch into an argument with Nathan he cut her off.

'I've offered her a live-in position, keeping an eye on madam here before and after school, *and* at the weekend.'

'I don't need a babysitter!' Kirsty protested.

'Not a babysitter,' her father refuted. 'More of a minder. Which you *do* need, according to your mother. From what I hear, you're not doing your homework, you're being cheeky and you're smoking.'

Kirsty glared at her mother. 'Traitor,' she whispered fiercely.

'If this is an example of your manners, young lady,' Nathan said sternly, 'then I can see your mother was not ex-aggerating. Now say hello and goodbye to Gemma in one breath, then skedaddle off to your room. I'm sure you have some unpacking to do and your mother and I have some things to discuss with Gemma.'

Kirsty flounced off, muttering something about how *she* looked older than her minder. Which she almost did. At fourteen Kirsty was fully grown and developed, though her figure had a layer of puppy fat over it. By contrast, Gemma's face and body had fined down to those of a woman. It was only the way she was dressed and the way she did her hair that was trapping her age as an adolescent in other people's minds.

Nathan walked over and closed the door after Kirsty's

grumbling departure. 'I see exactly what you mean,' he remarked to his ex-wife. 'But I still think it's a stage she's going through, nothing serious. What do you think, Gemma? You're closer to her in age than we are.'

'Which would have to be the understatement of the year,' Lenore muttered.

Nathan's look was scathing. 'Gemma happens to be twenty.'

'No, Nathan,' Gemma corrected, blushing prettily. '*Nearly* twenty.'

'How nearly?' Lenore snapped. 'The year 2000?'

'Oh, for pity's sake,' Nathan muttered.

Lenore rounded on him. 'Don't you "for pity's sake" me, Nathan Whitmore,' she spat at him. 'You come home with some strange girl I don't know from Eve and expect me to let her mind *my* daughter!'

'*Our* daughter, and I'll have you know that—'

'Please don't argue about me,' the girl interrupted in a quiet but surprisingly forceful dignity that Lenore had to admire. 'I… Mrs Whitmore is probably right, Nathan. This wasn't a good idea. Thank you so much for all your help but I think I should go to that motel you spoke of.'

'You will *not*!' Nathan pronounced with a passion that stunned Lenore.

Good God, if she didn't know better she might think he'd finally done the unthinkable—fallen in love.

'Lenore, I'm disappointed in you,' he swept on. 'You're usually a sensible clear-thinking woman. Do you honestly think I would bring someone into this home who wasn't above board? Besides, where's your Christian charity? The girl's mother is dead, her father died recently and she's all alone in the world. I met Gemma when I went to Lightning Ridge a few days back and promised to help her get on her feet if and when she came to Sydney. And I aim to do just that. If she can help us with Kirsty in return then so much the better.'

Lenore bit her tongue to stop herself from snapping back

that since she wasn't a mind-reader she couldn't have been expected to know all that. She bestowed a less emotional, more assessing gaze on their visitor from Lightning Ridge and had to admit she liked the way the girl stood up straight and was studying her in return with unwavering eyes. There was integrity in her stance and honesty in her face. It was too bad that face was so lovely and that Nathan was obviously so susceptible to it.

'I'm sorry, Gemma,' she apologised drily. 'But you did come as rather a shock.'

'I understand, Mrs Whitmore. I have been rather shoved on to you without warning.' The girl smiled a softly sweet, but incredibly sensual smile that worried the hell out of Lenore. What man could resist *that*? She resolved to speak to Nathan privately, tell him that she would not tolerate Kirsty being exposed to any kind of shenanigans. If he had to have this girl, then he could do so somewhere else!

The thought of her ex-husband actually sleeping with this innocent began to bother the life out of Lenore, yet it didn't feel like jealousy any more. More like concern for the girl. What was it about this creature that made one warm to her on sight, made one want to protect her?

Perhaps she was misjudging Nathan. Maybe that was what he felt too, an urge to protect.

And I'm Mahatma Gandhi, she told herself with rueful cynicism.

Lenore addressed both her ex-husband and his newly found friend with a politeness she wasn't feeling.

'Maybe Gemma could go upstairs and get to know Kirsty while I have a few words with you, Nathan.'

His sardonically arched eyebrow suggested he wasn't fooled for a moment by Lenore's saccharine tone.

'Would that be all right with you, Gemma?' he asked softly. 'Kirsty will be in the room right next to the one I put you in.'

The girl smiled nervously up at him. 'Are...are you sure

about this, Nathan? I would hate to think I've caused you any trouble. You're been so kind…'

Nathan actually took the girl's hands in his. 'Don't trouble your pretty little head about a thing. It's time you went upstairs anyway. You must be tired. You've had quite a day.'

'Yes… Yes, I have.'

'I'm sorry about the opal, Gemma, but I was fairly sure as soon as I saw it.'

Her sigh carried a weary resignation. 'I should have known it was too good to be true.'

'I'll ask Byron again tomorrow about the reward. If it hadn't been for that physiotherapist arriving, I would have settled the matter this afternoon.'

'Tomorrow will do just as well,' the girl assured him, their conversation totally confusing Lenore.

But she watched the interchange with growing interest. Nathan was different with this girl than any person she had ever seen him with, even his own daughter. Anyone not knowing Nathan might think he was acting in a fatherly fashion, but Lenore suspected it was nothing of the kind.

He coveted this girl, as one would a rare jewel. An opal, maybe, in its raw state. There was a glittering of suppressed passion in his eyes when he looked at her, as though he couldn't wait to get his hands on her, to strip away the superficial rough edges, to fashion and polish her till she was a priceless piece of art that all the world could see but only he could touch.

Lenore gave herself a mental shake. She was getting too fanciful for words. First thinking Nathan was in love, then this. She had to be going crazy. The Nathan she knew did not fall in love, or blindly covet, but he did have strong male needs. Which brought her right back to the problem at hand.

'It was nice meeting you, Mrs Whitmore,' the girl was saying and holding out her hand.

'And you, dear.' She briefly shook the proffered hand.

'But I think you should call me Lenore. Nathan gets peeved when people call me Mrs Whitmore these days.'

'I do not,' he growled.

'You do too.'

'Goodnight, Gemma,' he said curtly. 'Tell Kirsty I'll be up to see her after her mother has left.'

'All right. Goodnight again.'

'No wonder I'm having trouble with Kirsty's manners,' Nathan remarked testily once the sound of Gemma's departing footsteps receded.

Lenore was determined not to be side-tracked. 'Are you sleeping with that girl?'

She had never seen Nathan's eyes grow so cold. 'You would think that, wouldn't you?' He came forward to place a fingertip under her chin, tipping her face till her wide green eyes were staring into the wintry depths of his. 'Just because you can be had quite easily, Lenore, don't think every other woman is like that.'

Lenore gasped her hurt and would have spun away had not Nathan grasped her whole chin with his hand.

'What's the matter, darling?' he taunted in a low dangerous voice. 'Are you worried I'm getting something you're not? What's the matter, haven't you been able to seduce Zachary yet? Isn't your latest leading man coming across?'

'You're disgusting!' she exclaimed, and slapped his hand away.

Her action sent a wild fury into his face. Grabbing her by the shoulders, he yanked her hard against him, his mouth plummeting to take hers in a kiss of sheer spite and anger. Lenore struggled beneath its brutal onslaught but he seemed beside himself with an uncontrollable need to punish her for she knew not what. One of his hands slid round to grip her hair and he began pulling her head back so hard she thought her neck would break. Using her brains, she abruptly surrendered to his kiss, trying to defuse the situation by sighing and melting into him, opening her mouth to accept the violent thrusts of his tongue.

Neither of them saw the wide-eyed Gemma, standing just outside the open door, staring. She'd returned to get her cardigan from where she'd left it on a chair, only to be confronted with an oblivious Nathan kissing his ex-wife.

With a tortured groan, Gemma fled, her second departure going totally unnoticed.

CHAPTER FIVE

GEMMA ran blindly along the dimly lit hallway, tears stinging her eyes. God, what a fool she was. What a stupid, stupid fool!

Up the sweeping marble staircase she raced, intent on getting to her room where she could hide or cry or whatever. But as she turned right at the top of the stairs for the short dash down the hall to the guest bedroom Nathan had put her in, she crashed headlong into Ava.

Gemma had met Byron's 'kid' sister earlier that day, and she was the loveliest lady. They'd had afternoon tea together and a long chat, after which Gemma had happily accepted Nathan's offer of a live-in position at Belleview.

But the dear woman was carrying far too many pounds for her small-boned frame. So it was Ava who fell when Gemma collided with her, landing on her plump bottom and sliding across the marble-floored hallway to crash into the wall with a loud thud. A picture hanging on the wall above the point of impact was dislodged from its mounting and fell, just missing Ava's head. The corner of the gilt frame shattered as it hit the hard floor.

'Oh, dear,' Ava groaned, seemingly more concerned by the broken frame than her own physical condition. Gemma rushed over. 'I'm so sorry, Ava. Are you all right? I shouldn't have been running. I'm not usually so silly and clumsy. Here, let me help you up.'

It was a struggle to get Ava up on to her slippered feet which kept shooting out from under her. 'It's not you who's the clumsy one around here,' Ava said with an unhappy sigh. 'I fall over on average once a week. I'm just too fat!'

'You're not fat,' Gemma said kindly. 'You're pleasantly plump. And much as I think these marble floors are magnificent, they're also very slippery.'

Ava laughed, her bright blue eyes lighting up. It came to Gemma as she looked into Ava's round but pretty face that she would be extremely attractive if she lost a little weight and let her hair go back to the brown colour of her dark roots. That ginger frizz wouldn't have flattered any woman.

'How sweet of you to make excuses for me, but I *am* clumsy, and I also recently crossed the line from plump to fat. Why do you think I wear black pants and tent tops all the time? To hide the bulges!'

'What's happened?' came a sharp voice from behind them.

Gemma and Ava turned to see the housekeeper descending with a frown on her face. When they'd been introduced earlier that day, the woman had told Gemma to call her Melanie, but she preferred Mrs Lloyd. Melanie was far too warm a name for this frosty-faced martinet. She was a childless widow, Nathan had informed Gemma, who wondered again what man would ever marry such a coldly forbidding woman. No doubt the fictional Mrs Danvers Nathan had compared her with wasn't exactly a bundle of laughs, either.

'I…I'm afraid I've broken the frame of this picture, Melanie,' Ava said haltingly.

'Yes, so I see,' the woman answered in that monotone voice of hers, and picked the painting up from the floor. It was a landscape, reminiscent of the beautiful brush valley visible from the back windows of Belleview. St Ives was apparently on the fringes of Sydney—so Ava had enlightened Gemma—with a lot of national parks and reserves enhancing the much sought after locale.

'Please...don't tell Byron,' Ava said worriedly. 'I'll have it fixed before he comes home.'

'But it was all *my* fault,' Gemma protested. 'I was running up the stairs and I knocked into Ava. *I* should be the one to have the picture fixed.'

Melanie turned her deeply set black eyes Gemma's way, and Gemma could have sworn she saw surprise and respect in their usually expressionless depths.

'No, no,' Ava denied. 'It was clumsy me, as usual.'

'If Gemma says it was her fault then I believe her,' Melanie Lloyd pronounced firmly, then floored Gemma by smiling at her. It wasn't much of a smile, admittedly, a slight lifting of the corners of that thin-lipped mouth. But oh, the transformation to her face. Why, the woman was quite beautiful! And she didn't have thin lips at all!

'Byron makes adequate provision in the housekeeping money for simple breakages,' she advised. 'I'll see it's fixed and hanging back up well before he comes home from the hospital.'

'You're so efficient,' Ava praised with an envious-sounding sigh. 'I never seem to get anything done. I started a watercolour a few weeks ago and it's only halfway finished.'

'Speaking of getting things done, Ava,' the housekeeper said, 'do you think you could come downstairs and help me plan the dinner menus for the next week?'

'You want *my* help?' Ava looked shocked, but delighted.

'I certainly do. You have creative talent and I think the meals around here have become a little bland lately. I would value your suggestions.'

Ava fairly beamed, and Gemma smiled approval at the housekeeper. For a second their eyes locked, and a silent message passed between the two women. It bespoke an understanding that Ava was not as strong as they were, that she was a gentle creature who needed to be stroked and cosseted. All of a sudden, Gemma knew she would not think of the housekeeper as Mrs Lloyd any more. She would be Melanie from that moment on.

'I'll go and see how Kirsty is doing,' Gemma said.

'Yes,' Melanie agreed. 'I think that might be a good idea. Come along, Ava... We have work to do.'

Ava went off with Melanie quite happily, and Gemma turned to continue up the hall, the incident having provided a welcome interruption to the emotional breakdown she might have indulged in a few minutes before. Now, it seemed silly to burst into tears. Her misery was no less acute but her common sense had come to the rescue, making her see that it was a misery of her own making.

She'd been getting carried away all evening with Nathan's feeling towards her, misinterpreting his gallantry, mistaking his attentions in the billiard-room as the attentions of a man as smitten with her as she was with him. As if he would be!

The man was way out of her league, for heaven's sake. Years older in both age and experience. A man of the world. She'd been crazy to start thinking she could mean anything to him other than an amusing distraction. He would never fall in love with her. How could he? He was still in love with his ex-wife!

Gemma's stomach curled just thinking about that kiss she'd witnessed. She'd never seen anything like it. Such passion. Such intensity. Much as the memory pained her, she couldn't stop thinking about it, couldn't stop wondering why they had divorced if there was still such passion between them.

Gemma recalled Lenore's fury that morning as she'd stormed out of Nathan's office, how she'd called him impossible. Maybe they just hadn't been able to live together in harmony, maybe their personalities had not proved compatible. But it seemed there was one matter in which they were still highly compatible.

Tears hovered again, but Gemma steadfastly pushed them aside.

I wasn't really in love with him, she reasoned bravely. I was only infatuated. I'm not used to men like him with their city polish and their smooth charm. I lost my head for a minute, Ma, but it's back on again now, and I'm not about to lose it again in a hurry.

Gemma squared her shoulders and was continuing along the hallway when another thought had her grinding to a startled halt. Was a kiss—however passionate—proof of love?

Maybe not on Nathan's part, if Jade was to be believed about her adopted brother's cavalier treatment of women. Nathan had said not to believe a word Jade said, but what if she'd been telling the truth? What if…?

The possibility that her knight in shining armour was far from a saint in sexual matters crashed through Gemma, bringing dismay, but also a disturbing quickening of breath. She flushed to think of his supposed 'spur-of-the-moment' impulse to kiss her in the car. She had believed his excuse at the time.

But what if he'd been lying? What if he *had* brought her to Belleview to have his wicked way with her. Maybe not straight away, but eventually…

Gemma's head began to whirl, her pulse-rate picking up even further. She kept remembering how it had felt when Nathan had wrapped his body around hers at the billiard-table. At the same time she'd laughed in a vain attempt to relieve her blistering awareness of his hard flesh pressing into her soft buttocks, but in truth, she wouldn't—or couldn't—have stopped him from going further if he'd wanted to. Lenore and Kirsty had arrived in the nick of time.

But she couldn't always rely on someone arriving in the nick of time, could she?

Maybe she should clear right out. Leave Belleview.

Gemma frowned. But that would mean falling back on her own meagre resources in this enormous and extremely daunting city. She'd have to be insane to do that, to turn her back on this beautiful home, on a good job, and on the reward Nathan said Byron would give her. And she wasn't insane. Silly, maybe. And susceptible to a handsome face, as Ma had said. But she was learning, wasn't she? And now that her eyes were more open, she would be on the alert against being taken advantage of in any way. Given time, this infatuation or sexual attraction or whatever it was she felt for Nathan was sure to wane. Soon, she probably wouldn't even turn a hair when he came into the room!

Feeling slightly better, Gemma took the remaining steps that brought her to Kirsty's bedroom door, deciding she'd better get on with what she was being employed to do and break the ice with the girl. When there was no answer to her knock, she slowly turned the handle and peeped around the door. Kirsty was sitting, cross-legged, on her bed, puffing away on a cigarette.

The bold little hussy!

But neither Kirsty's defiant behaviour nor her smoking fazed Gemma. She'd been there, done that. Adopting an indifferent face, she walked right in, shutting the door behind her, then strode across the room where she flung open the window. 'Better get some air in here,' she said. 'Your dad will be up shortly and I don't think he'll want to smell smoke.'

Turning, she leant against the window-sill and looked around the room. It was a delight of femininity. All pink and white, with pink walls, off-white shag carpet, a white four-poster bed with a pink lace quilt and matching pink and white curtains at the windows. It was the sort of bedroom Gemma would have given her eye-teeth for while growing up—*any* bedroom would have done. But she suspected Kirsty hated its little-girl prettiness.

'God, this is frightful, isn't it?' Gemma remarked.

Kirsty blinked. 'Huh?'

'The room. It's frightful. We'll have to see what we can do to make it liveable-in.' Gemma levered herself away from the window and came over to take the cigarette out of Kirsty's suddenly slack mouth, taking a couple of puffs herself—to check for grass—before walking back and tossing it out of the window. 'Heck, Kirsty,' she said to the gaping girl, 'the least you could do is smoke a decent brand. That sucked.'

Kirsty was still staring at her when there was a tap tap on the door and Nathan strode in. Gemma was pleased to find she didn't go to mush, though her eyes did fly to his mouth. The bottom lip looked even fuller than usual—sort of soft and swollen and appallingly sexy. Gemma stiffened, her hands curling over the window-sill.

Nathan immediately sniffed the air. 'Do I smell smoke in here?' he growled.

Kirsty looked at Gemma, who shrugged. 'I can't smell anything.'

Nathan gave her a dry look. Gemma was now finding it hard to look him straight in the face without thinking about the last time she'd seen him, with a moaning Lenore in his arms.

Yanking her mind back from that path, she lifted her chin and launched into another minefield—winning Kirsty over. 'One thing I wanted to ask you, Nathan,' she said in an amazingly steady voice. *See*, she told herself. Progress already.

'Yes?' Nathan said curtly.

'Would Kirsty and I be able to redecorate this room? Pink and white lace is rather babyish for a fourteen-year-old. I do realise this is Byron's home, but...'

'Oh, *please*, Dad,' Kirsty joined in. 'I won't change it too much. Just a few posters and stuff.'

He sighed. 'All right, provided you clear it with Melanie. She's in charge of the house.'

Kirsty's face fell. 'That miserable bitch.'

'*Kirsty*!' both Nathan and Gemma chorused at once.

'Well, she *is*,' Kirsty insisted sulkily.

'You wouldn't feel like laughing all the time if you saw your husband and only child incinerated in a car accident,'

Nathan berated his daughter. 'It's a wonder the woman's still sane, let alone a functioning human being.'

Both Kirsty and Gemma gaped at him in shock.

'Gee,' Kirsty said at last. 'That sucks.'

Nathan gave his daughter another reproachful look. 'Maybe you'll look for the reason behind a person's behaviour before you make a judgement next time, madam. And please don't use that expression. I find it offensive.'

'What? Sucks? Gemma said it earlier, so why can't I?'

Nathan swung surprised eyes her way.

Gemma cringed inside but kept her chin up.

'Has Mum gone home?' Kirsty said. 'Why didn't she come and say goodbye?'

'She said she'd call you as soon as she got home.'

The telephone beside the bed started ringing at exactly that moment.

'That'll be your mother now.'

Kirsty snatched up the receiver. 'Mum? Hi there. No, it's OK. I didn't mind. Gemma and I have been getting to know each other. Yeah, I think so. She's real cool...' And she flashed Gemma a wide smile.

Gemma smiled back, feeling pleased with herself. But when Nathan gestured brusquely for her to come out into the hall with him, everything inside her tensed. No doubt he was only going to haul her over the coals for encouraging his daughter to use such language, but she still didn't want to be alone with him. Her susceptibility hadn't waned yet, not even a little bit.

'I don't know how you've managed it so quickly,' Nathan started once the bedroom door was safely closed, 'but Melanie speaks highly of you, Ava thinks you're a darling and my difficult daughter actually seems to *like* you. Care to tell me your secret?'

'I don't think I have any secret,' she returned tautly. 'Mostly, I just try to be myself.'

His smile was wry. 'How come I don't think the Gemma

Smith I've come to know and respect would use an expression such as something "sucks"?'

Gemma felt a smile tugging at her lips. 'When in Rome, do as the Romans do.'

'Aah...and are you going to take up smoking as well?'

Now she laughed, her tension easing. 'Maybe,' she admitted. 'For a while.'

'And the room? Will I have to gird myself the next time I dare to enter?'

'Definitely.'

'Should I accept anything and everything with po-faced indifference?'

'Good heavens, no. Kirsty would be disappointed if you did that. You have to cringe and say how simply ghastly it all is. What would be the fun if your parents accepted the way you did up your room?'

'Oh? And did *your* father cringe at the way you did up your room when you were a teenager?'

Gemma flinched at the mention of her father. 'I didn't have a room of my own, for starters,' came her bleak reply. 'And I'm still a teenager,' she reminded him pointedly.

Nathan frowned. 'So you are, Gemma. So you are. One day, perhaps, you might like to tell me all about your life at Lightning Ridge, and your father. I realise that with his death being so recent you might not want to talk about him right now, but I would like to know what events made you into the woman you are today. And before you say differently, you *are* a woman, not a teenager. You're as far removed from Kirsty as night is from day.'

Gemma felt uncomfortable with his saying such flattering things about her. She was also uncomfortable with the way his eyes started travelling down her face and neck to where her breasts were rising and falling in an uneven rhythm.

Fear curled her stomach. Not so much of him, but of herself. All of a sudden, she wanted to be in his arms as Lenore had been, wanted him to do what she had stopped him doing in the car. She couldn't stop looking at his

mouth, his lovely full-lipped mouth. The yearning to have
that mouth on hers was so sharp she almost moaned.

'I…I must be going to bed,' she blurted out instead. 'I'm
very tired.'

His eyes lifted, and while they looked cool enough, she
suspected their owner wasn't. There was a stillness about
him that made her hold her breath, that sent her eyes flaring
with wide apprehension. The air around them seemed to
crackle with a dark electricity which felt both ominous and
threatening.

Don't, she screamed silently at him with an internal
panic close to hysteria. *Please* don't…

'Did Melanie tell you the arrangements we have here for
breakfast?' he said, his voice clipped.

Gemma nodded, unable to find her voice.

'Fine. Would seven-thirty be too early for you to meet
me in the morning-room?'

'No,' she croaked.

'Good. I'd like to discuss a few things with you before
I go to work. I'll see you at seven-thirty, then. Goodnight,
Gemma. Sweet dreams.'

She watched him walk away, aware that she had started
to shake. Sweet dreams? The man was mad, or bad, or
both!

When Gemma presented herself in the morning-room at
seven-thirty the following morning, Nathan was sitting at
the oval-shaped breakfast table, an empty coffee-cup in
front of him, his face buried in the morning paper. Any
other time, Gemma would have turned to admire the room
with its cool green walls, attractive cane furniture and wide
picture windows through which the morning sun was
streaming. But her attention was riveted on the top of that
gleaming golden head as she waited, breathless, for the moment those grey eyes would lift and notice her standing
there.

But it was Melanie, gliding in to top up Nathan's coffee,
who spied her first and said good morning. Only then did

Nathan glance up, his gaze unreadable as it rapidly surveyed her from top to toe then back again. Her simple floral dress with its dropped waist and tiny white buttons down the front was cheap, price-wise, as were all her clothes, but it was fairly new, the cotton material still crisp, the cream and apricot colours suiting her dark hair and olive complexion. The brown leather sandals on her bare feet were real leather, a gift from Ma at Christmas.

It was her hair, however, that seemed to hold Nathan's eyes for an extra moment or two, her thick dark wavy hair which she'd left down this time to curl gently around her face and shoulders.

'Good morning, Gemma,' he said, folding the newspaper crisply and placing it on the table beside his now full coffee-cup. 'You're looking refreshed this morning. I trust you slept well?'

She had, surprisingly, maybe from sheer exhaustion, or because her bed was so comfortable.

'I did,' she said stiffly, and came forward, determined to conquer this spell he seemed to have cast over her. It wasn't love, she'd reasoned again on waking. But it *was* powerfully disturbing.

When she hesitated over which chair to sit in, Nathan made up her mind for her by pulling out the one nearest his right. She sat down, noting ruefully that not all the common sense resolutions in the world could control her wildly beating heart in his presence, nor stop herself from staring at him all the time.

But he was just so handsome. And sleek. And polished. And *clean*!

She was used to men stinking of stale sweat and body odour, their hands and nails thick with grime, their clothes looking as if they hadn't been washed in a month. Which they probably hadn't.

Nathan sat there, his freshly shampooed hair gleaming in the sunlight, no stubble on his just-shaven jaw, his broad-shouldered body elegantly encased in a pale grey three-piece suit that didn't know the word 'crease'.

Gemma could have sat there forever, drinking in his beauty, her nostrils being pleasantly teased by his pine-scented aftershave, had Melanie not asked, 'What would you like for breakfast, Gemma?'

Now, Gemma had never in her life had anyone ask her that question before. Last night at dinner she'd been in awe of Melanie's home-made celery soup, mouth-watering steak and salad, and custard cake afterwards. But that meal had simply been placed in front of her. She hadn't been required to make a choice.

'Oh…I—er…'

'Bring her the same as I had,' Nathan intervened, much to Gemma's relief.

'Coming right up,' Melanie said briskly, and departed through a sliding door which Gemma presumed led into the kitchen. Ava had given her a tour of the house yesterday but they'd missed some sections when Ava had suddenly decided to take Gemma back upstairs and show their new visitor her watercolours.

'You must be a little nonplussed over all that's happened to you this past week,' Nathan remarked thoughtfully as he lifted the coffee-cup to his mouth.

Gemma didn't know what to say to that. What did nonplussed mean? 'Er—yes, I am,' she agreed. When in doubt, always agree with one's elders or betters. Another one of Ma's pearls of wisdom.

'I just realised this morning I hadn't even enquired about what you've been doing with yourself since you left school.'

'Not a lot,' she admitted. 'The only work I could find around Lightning Ridge was some part-time waitressing in a café. I wanted to go to Walgett to find work but my father wouldn't let me.'

'I see… And what were you like at school?'

'Average, I suppose. I didn't set the world on fire with

my HSC marks but I was sick with glandular fever at the time of the exams.'

'Ah…the kissing disease…'

'The what?'

'Glandular fever is sometimes called the kissing disease. It races through high school and colleges because it's easily passed on by kissing.'

'Well, it wasn't passed on to *me* that way.'

Gemma found herself on the end of an intense look from Nathan which might have truly flustered her if Kirsty hadn't dashed into the room at that moment. She was still in her dressing-gown and looked as if she'd just jumped out of bed.

'Gosh, Dad, I'm running late. Nobody got me up and I haven't even had a shower yet. Can you drive me to school when I'm ready?'

'Firstly, madam,' her father returned sternly, 'nobody around here is going to get you up of a morning. You're old enough to take some responsibility for your own life. You have a radio beside your bed with a built-in alarm. Set it before you go to sleep in future and when it goes off, get up! Secondly, I am not driving you to school. I have to leave for the office in a couple of minutes or I'll be late. Gemma will drive you to school, *and* pick you up this afternoon. And one last thing before you go. I don't want to hear you weren't wearing your proper uniform, which also means no jewellery and no make-up. Is that clear?'

'You're worse than Mum!' Kirsty wailed as she flounced out.

'I'm bigger too,' he called after her, then turned to grin at Gemma before seeing how pale and panicky she looked.

'What have I said?' he asked, frowning. 'You do drive, don't you? You did out at Lightning Ridge. Ava has said you can borrow her car. It's small and automatic. Very easy to handle.'

'It's not the driving part that worries me,' Gemma croaked. 'It's the traffic!'

'Oh, you don't have to take her into the city,' Nathan said dismissively. 'Kirsty's school is only a few miles up the road. Not far at all. The traffic's light around here. Look, I have to away.'

'But…but…what will I do for the rest of the day?'

He frowned. 'Never had the problem of telling a woman how to spend her day. I have no idea. Read a book. Watch television. Go shopping. Keep Ava company. I don't know. Ask Melanie. She'll know what you can do. Perhaps you could start planning what horrors you're going to perpetrate on that bedroom. You've probably only got this week to do that. Come next Monday you'll be fully occupied learning Japanese.'

He stood up, reminding Gemma how tall he was. Her neck crinked as she looked up at him.

'Will Ava be up before it's time for me to take Kirsty?' she asked worriedly.

'Should be. If not, Melanie keeps a spare set of keys to all the cars. Ask her. Oh, and there's a Gregory's Guide in the glove-box of the car in case you get lost.'

Gemma couldn't help a small groan.

Nathan's hand curved over her shoulder in what she supposed was a comforting gesture, but Gemma's immediate reaction to his touch was not comfort. Everything tightened inside her and she dropped her eyes away from his, lest he see her instant tension.

'You'll be all right,' he said. 'I have every confidence in your abilities to cope with anything life can throw at you.'

Something in his voice drew her to glance up.

It was a mistake. For his eyes fastened on to hers and in no time she was drowning…drowning…

Through a swirling haze she heard him mutter something, saw his eyes darken and narrow, saw his head begin to descend. Her lips gasped softly apart in anticipation of feeling his mouth on hers, but at the last moment he didn't kiss her. He straightened, lancing her with a savage look while adjusting his tie and doing up his suit jacket.

'Let me give you a little bit of advice, Gemma,' he warned darkly. 'If it's your intention to keep me at a distance, then do not look at me like you did just then. Take a leaf out of Melanie's book! She's mastered the art of freezing any man's desire at a single glance.'

He exited the room with long, angry strides, leaving Gemma to stare after him with a flushed face and madly thudding heart. She didn't hear Melanie come in with her breakfast, so she almost jumped out of her skin when the woman spoke.

'Nathan's a very handsome man, isn't he?' she commented coolly as she placed the plate of scrambled eggs before Gemma. 'Has women throwing themselves at him all the time.'

Gemma looked up into Melanie's intelligent dark eyes. 'Watch yourself with him,' the housekeeper said in a hard voice. 'He's trouble.'

CHAPTER SIX

LENORE couldn't believe any of it. First, that Kirsty had invited her to come over and see what she had been allowed to do to her bedroom, then that Melanie had actually *allowed* her and Gemma to turn the previously pretty room into such an eye-popping horror.

Kirsty stood there, giggling, while Lenore's wide gaze took in the never-ending posters, all of them seemingly of the one male pop singer who had sleepy dark eyes and a perpetually sulky mouth. Since the name 'Johnny' appeared with regularly monotony, she assumed that was his name.

The black and white poster wallpaper was only part of it, however, the lovely lace bedspread having been replaced by a black and white geometric print throwover that made one's eyes water just looking at it. The only consolation was that they hadn't hung matching curtains at the window. There were *no* curtains at the window, she suddenly realised.

'Get real, Mum,' Kirsty said when Lenore mentioned this. 'Curtains suck.'

Lenore groaned and threw an anguished look at Gemma who mouthed for her to 'stay cool'.

'Melanie and I put the curtains and quilt carefully away,' she whispered when Kirsty was preoccupied raving over her favourite poster. 'The posters are attached with a special glue-tack that comes off easily. Nothing's been done that can't be undone in a day.'

Lenore was beginning to feel a grudging respect for this girl. She'd been surprised when she arrived at Belleview today to find that Nathan had taken himself off for the weekend to his beach-house at Avoca—*alone*. Apparently, he'd extended an invitation for the two girls to go with him, but Gemma, it seemed, had been the one to talk Kirsty into staying behind to finish redecorating the room. This was hardly the action of a girl with her eye on snaring the highly eligible Nathan Whitmore for herself.

Still, Lenore was in no doubt that Gemma found Nathan very very attractive. It had been in her eyes the other night whenever she looked at him. Nathan hadn't been much better. He'd been drooling with desire, though he tried not to show it.

Not that he would have any intention of *marrying* the girl. He'd vowed after their divorce that he would never marry or have children again. No, Nathan would have a less permanent position in mind for this breathtakingly lovely creature. God, just look at her! How many girls could look a million dollars in that cheap little dress she was wearing? *And* without a scrap of make-up. What she could look like in the right clothes and with the right make-up was anyone's guess.

But perhaps it was her very ingenuousness that was bewitching Nathan. Maybe, like a lot of men, he harboured the fantasy of taking a beautiful but innocent virgin and moulding her into the perfect sexual partner for himself. He would teach her how to please him in every way. Yes, she could imagine that fantasy appealing to Nathan very much. He didn't hold a high opinion of women in general, especially ones of the more experienced kind. A virgin would suit him very well. And Gemma, unless she was severely mistaken, was just that!

A wry smile hovered round Lenore's lips as she pretended to look at the various posters. She could well imagine Nathan's irritation that his plans for Gemma were being side-lined by the girl herself. Lenore didn't believe his angry assertions the other night that his helping her had been a gesture of Christian charity. If it was, it was the first time Nathan had played Good Samaritan.

No, there had to be another reason for his sudden interest in the girl, and Lenore knew exactly what that reason was. His totally unexpected but explosive kiss the other night was very telling. Nathan, it seemed, was in a state of high sexual frustration. Thank God he'd quickly got a hold of himself on that occasion or she might eventually have been forced to kick him.

Hopefully, for Gemma's sake, he would pick up some willing little floozy this weekend up at Avoca and rid himself of all that tension. There were always plenty of beach bunnies hanging around on the weekends, and Nathan, in swimming-trunks, was an enticing sight. Golden Greek gods never had any trouble finding women to satisfy their sexual needs, especially when they didn't have a conscience to get in the way.

Lenore's mind drifted inevitably to Zachary Marsden and she sighed.

'I know this isn't your style, Mum,' Kirsty said quite happily, 'but I think it's awesome.'

Lenore turned to her daughter and smiled. 'I'm happy if you're happy, sweetie.'

'Are you? Great. Then can I have twenty dollars to go to a blue-light disco tonight? It's at the school hall and I'll be *real* happy if I can go.'

Lenore frowned. She'd grounded Kirsty for a month less than two weeks ago. Would her daughter think her weak if she gave in? Damn it all, this was the kind of problem she'd hoped Nathan could solve for a while. That man hadn't changed. He was still as selfish as ever. He had no business going off for the weekend and leaving Kirsty behind. He should have *insisted* she go with him.

'I think not, Kirsty,' she said.

'Oh, *Mum*!'

'You know you're grounded for another two weeks.'

'Yes, but that was *before*...'

'Before what?'

'Before I came to live here. Before Gemma. She'll take me and pick me up, right outside the door. She knows her way around now,' Kirsty laughed. 'She got lost last Tuesday, though, didn't you Gemma?'

Suppressing a jab of very real jealousy, Lenore turned to face Gemma, who gave her an understanding smile.

'I think, Kirsty,' Gemma said in her melodic but surprisingly mature voice, 'that if you've been grounded, you shouldn't be asking your mother to go back on her word. We can just as easily get some videos and enjoy ourselves here at home.'

'Yeah, I suppose that would be just as good, provided we can get some funny ones. None of that serious stuff.'

'Do you think I could stay and watch them with you?' Lenore asked, not happy with feeling left out of her daughter's life, which was crazy since a couple of days ago she'd been happy to get rid of her for a while.

'Sure thing, Mum.' Kirsty beamed and gave her a hug. 'We'll have a ladies' night. We'll even invite Ava.'

'What about Melanie?' Gemma suggested.

Lenore frowned. 'I don't think Kirsty likes Melanie much.'

'No, Mum, I was wrong about Melanie. She's not too bad.'

Lenore blinked over at her daughter.

'Did you know about what happened to her family, Mum? I suppose you must have since Dad knew. He told Gemma and me about it and boy, were we shocked!'

'It *was* a shocking thing,' Lenore agreed, 'but for heaven's sake don't mention it in front of Melanie. She's trying to forget it.'

'She must be a very brave lady,' Gemma murmured.

'Yes, I think so,' Lenore agreed. 'But even the bravest of us have breaking points...' Once again, her mind drifted to Zachary and she felt the most awful pain in her heart. How long, she thought, before *my* breaking point comes, how long before I go to him and make an utter fool of myself again?

Tears pricked at her eyes and she just managed to stop them gathering force.

'I'll tell you what,' she said with false brightness. 'How about we go and visit Byron in hospital this afternoon, then we can pick up the videos on the way home? I haven't been to visit him since just after his accident and I've been feeling guilty. Have you met Byron yet, Gemma?'

The girl looked startled and a fraction worried by the suggestion. 'N...no. But surely he won't want to see me from his hospital bed. I'm not family.'

'Neither am I, strictly. What do you call an ex-daughter-in-law of an adopted father?'

'A right pain in the bum,' Kirsty giggled. 'Now Mum, don't deny it. That's what Pops said you were when you wanted to go back to acting and Dad didn't want you to.'

Lenore sighed. 'Byron's a dear man,' she explained to Gemma, 'but he thinks a woman's place is firmly in the home. But I won't hold that against him today. He's got his own problems now and I'm sure meeting you would give him a lift. You must know a lot about opals, coming from Lightning Ridge, and opals are his greatest passion!'

Gemma stayed just inside the door, feeling awkward and embarrassed. The man propped up in the big white bed in the private hospital room was a formidable figure, and exactly as Ma had described. Very handsome for a man of his age, with thick black hair going grey at the temples, piercing blue eyes which missed nothing and a mouth that stood for no nonsense.

'What are you doing skulking over there, girl?' he said in his deep rumbly voice. 'Come over here where I can get a good look at you; have to see what's impressed my family so much. All I heard from Ava this past week was "Gemma this" and "Gemma that".'

Gemma didn't miss the slight raising of his eyebrows as

she walked forward, nor the way those incisive blue eyes encompassed her thoroughly with one sweeping glance. 'You're certainly a good-looking girl, I'll say that for you. And you're twenty, Nathan tells me?'

'*Nearly* twenty,' Lenore corrected in a tone that brought a sharp look from Byron.

'I wasn't talking to you, Lenore.'

'Pardon me for breathing,' she said without turning a hair. Gemma received the impression that these two rather enjoyed sparring with each other. There'd already been several caustic interchanges since they'd arrived.

'It's been sweet of you to come and visit me, Lenore, but why don't you take yourself and Kirsty down to the cafeteria for a coffee?' he suggested. 'It's down the end of the corridor. I have some business I wish to discuss with Gemma here. In private.'

Gemma felt awful at Lenore and Kirsty being summarily dismissed like that, though they didn't seem to mind. Kirsty especially had been clearly bored by the visit. But seeing them disappear down the corridor increased the butterflies in her stomach. Byron Whitmore was an intimidating man who, despite Ma's glowing reference, radiated an aura of ruthless power. She admired Lenore for the way she stood up to him.

'Right,' he began sternly straight away. 'Now tell me how you think the Heart of Fire came to be in your father's possession?'

'The...the Heart of Fire?'

'The black opal, girl. It was named that by my father over fifty years ago. What do you think I'm talking about, a romance novel? Now there's no need to look like that. My bark's worse than my bite. I'm not accusing your father of anything criminal. He might have been an innocent dupe in all this. Just tell me what you know.'

Gemma stared at Byron, her mind ticking over with his words. An innocent dupe... Maybe her father hadn't been a thief at all. Maybe someone gave him the opal. Or maybe he simply found it somewhere.

'Well, girl? Speak up. If you're to work behind the counter of one of my stores you'd better get rid of that shyness of yours.'

Gemma's eyes flashed and her chin shot up. 'I'm not shy,' she denied. 'I was thinking.'

'By gum, she has spirit as well. Nathan can certainly pick them. Tell me what you were thinking.'

His reference to Nathan distracted her for a second, but with those blue eyes boring into her Gemma quickly re-grouped her thoughts and told him the little she knew.

'So, in fact, you know nothing!' Byron announced, clearly disappointed.

'I'm afraid so.'

'Ah, well, maybe it's all for the best,' he grumbled. 'That opal's brought nothing but bad luck. I think I'll have it cut up into several smaller stones and be done with the damned thing.'

'*What*?' Gemma saw red, and when she saw red, she said things that perhaps were better left unsaid. But she never thought of that till afterwards. 'I would have expected more from an opal man than to hold with that old wives' tale about opals bringing bad luck,' she burst out. 'You must know that garbage was put around by diamond traders because they were scared people would start buying opals instead of diamonds. And why wouldn't they? They're far more beautiful. As for cutting up that magnificent stone...'

She drew herself up straight with righteous indignation. 'I can't think of a worse travesty against mother nature. An opal like that doesn't come along very often and its beauty should be protected for posterity, not desecrated. Now I see that my father had the right idea, keeping such a precious prize hidden away like that. Maybe he knew once he surrendered it to someone like you it would be gone forever!'

Her tirade finished, Gemma found that, as was usually

the case, her anger dissipated quickly, to be replaced with horror that she had spoken in such a way to her employer.

'Oh,' she said, her face crumpling with remorse. 'Oh, dear…'

Byron's laughter was a surprise and a relief. 'Don't stop now,' he chuckled. 'I haven't had such a good dressing-down in years. You'd make even the matron around here sit up and take notice when your blood is up, girl. You'll make a damned good seller of opals, I'll warrant. You have a passion for them that's truly rare. Yes, rare…' He seemed to be mulling something over in his mind before saying unexpectedly, 'You're an orphan, is that right?'

'Y…yes.'

'Mmm. The reward… You thought it fair?'

Gemma recalled her shock when Nathan told her Byron was giving her a hundred thousand dollars, invested for her in a secure bank account till she decided what she wanted to do with it. She still couldn't comprehend the amount.

'You've been more than generous,' she said.

'It'll provide a deposit for a roof over your head if you ever need it.'

She frowned. 'Only a deposit?' That amount would have bought her a whole house and land out at the Ridge.

'This is Sydney, my dear, the dearest place in Australia to live. But you don't have to worry about where to live for now. You're staying at Belleview for the time being, aren't you?'

'Yes.'

'It'll be good for Kirsty to have someone nearer her own age around.'

'She's a nice kid.'

'Yes, I think so too. Still upset, though, over her parents' divorce. A bad thing, divorce…'

'Maybe Nathan and Lenore will get back together again,' Gemma said.

Byron gave her an odd look. 'No, I don't think so. Not now…'

'That's a shame.'

'Oh, I don't know about that. Lenore never was the right woman for Nathan. Too ambitious. He needs a girl who will devote herself to him and his needs, not crave for her own moon and stars all the time. Call me old-fashioned, but I think most men want that. If more women stayed home and looked after their families there would be fewer divorces.'

Gemma refrained from making comment. She'd already said enough, she thought. But she didn't agree with Byron. Women were better educated now and there was no way they could live the lives their grandmothers had led and not feel bored and unfulfilled. Sure, they had obligations to their families, if they had them, but they had obligations to themselves as well. They were people too, weren't they, with needs and desires of their own? They had a right to careers if that was what they wanted and, if husbands understood and supported them in that, *then* there would be fewer divorces.

But Gemma resisted saying so. Instead she studied the man in the bed and wondered if his poor dead wife had stayed home and if she'd been happy. Privately, Gemma didn't think being married to Byron Whitmore would be a recipe for happiness, despite all his money. He was far too bossy, not to mention chauvinistic. As for his opinion on Lenore and Nathan getting back together again…well, maybe she knew something Byron didn't know…

'We've finished our coffee,' Lenore announced from the doorway. 'Have you finished talking business yet, Byron? Because if you have, we must away.'

'Yes, we're finished.' Byron bestowed a softer, more charming goodbye smile on Gemma which showed another side to his personality. She suspected he'd been quite a one with the ladies over the years. 'Nice meeting you at last, Gemma. And good luck with your Japanese lessons. I want to see you behind that counter selling opals for Whitmore's as soon as possible. Er—could I have a quick word with you, Lenore, before you go? *Alone.*'

Lenore frowned, then handed Kirsty her car keys with a resigned sigh. 'You and Gemma wait for me at the car. I'll try not to be long.

'Well, what is it?' she asked as soon as the others were out of earshot. 'If you're going to go on about Nathan and me again you're wasting your time.'

'I realise that. I have a favour to ask of you.'

'Oh, yes?' Lenore's tone was wary. She didn't trust Byron, whom she considered a tyrant of the first order. He meant well but he liked trying to run other people's lives because he thought he knew best. But his standards were impossibly high and no one could live up to them. It was no wonder that his own daughter, Jade, had gone wild after she came of age and inherited her own money. She'd had twenty-one years of strict discipline and stupidly old-fashioned ideas shoved down her throat. Only Ava had completely given in to Byron's tyranny, and just look at her, the poor thing. Stripped of every ounce of confidence and self-esteem, waiting for some mythical Prince Charming to sweep into her life and make her happy. As if any man could make Ava happy. Didn't she know she had to be happy with herself first?

'I want you to help that Gemma girl with her wardrobe,' Byron said. 'Get her to buy some decent suits and blouses that would be suitable for work. And some other clothes as well. Casual, as well as dressy. And do something with her hair. Have it cut. Not short, but shaped properly around her face. And teach her to apply make-up without it seeming overdone. You know what I mean. Give her some class.'

'I think Nathan likes Gemma the way she is,' Lenore said drily.

Byron's eyes snapped to hers. 'So! You've seen the attraction for yourself, have you? What is this, Lenore? You don't want Nathan but you don't want anyone else to have him?'

'She's only a child,' Lenore muttered, still struggling with how she felt when she thought of Nathan really wanting another woman. Maybe he hadn't loved *her*, but he had desired her. Often.

'Only in superficial ways,' Byron argued, 'and you're going to fix one of those.'

'What makes you think I'll do what you ask? And if I do, what makes you sure I won't deliberately make her look awful?'

Byron's smile was smug. 'Because I'm going to bribe you not to.'

'How?' she scoffed. 'I have enough money of my own from the divorce settlement.'

'Have you read Nathan's new play?'

Lenore frowned. What was the conniving devil getting at now? 'Nathan doesn't show me his work any more,' she said coldly.

'It's very good.'

'I'm sure it is.'

'I'm going to invest in it. In fact, I'll be the only investor.'

'So?'

'It has a marvellous part in it for a woman. A beautiful woman of around your age...'

Lenore tried to contain her excitement. A lead role in one of Nathan's plays would set her on the road to real success. But Nathan would never give her the part.

'You...you'd suggest me for the role?'

'I'd insist you have it.'

'You're a wicked man.'

'I want Nathan to be happy, and, contrary to popular opinion, I want you to be happy too. Well, what do you say?'

'A makeover takes money, Byron. I might have enough but I'm not spending my own money starting up a new girlfriend for my ex-husband.'

'The girl has plenty of money herself.'

'Does she? How come?'

'I gave it to her for an opal that had come into her possession.'

'Well, well. OK, Byron, it's a deal. But has it occurred to you that Nathan won't marry this girl? He might just want her for sex.'

'Yes,' he surprised her by saying. 'But that's all right with me, if it makes him happy.'

'You shock me, Byron.'

'I almost died a few weeks ago, Lenore. Irene did die. Death has a way of making one reassess one's life and attitudes. I've been a fool in more ways than one but I mean to be different from now on.'

'How? By bribing me and poking your nose into Nathan's private life? You haven't really changed, Byron. You've merely changed your objectives. But no sweat. I'll do what you ask and God help you if you don't come through with your promise of that part. But I'll be giving Gemma some subtle warnings along the way. Because Nathan hasn't changed either. I have no intention of leading another lamb to the slaughter!'

Lenore spun on her high heels and strode quite angrily from the room. She marched down the highly polished hall, thumped the 'down' arrow of the lifts and was waiting there, fuming in silence, when the lift doors shot open and Zachary Marsden stepped out.

CHAPTER SEVEN

LENORE stared at him for a long, excruciatingly heart-aching moment, seeing nothing but the glittering lights of pleasure that danced in his midnight-blue eyes before he could stop them.

He's glad to see me, she thought with a wild rush of overwhelming joy.

But no sooner had she thought that than Zachary schooled his face once again into the mask of cool polite-ness he always adopted whenever he met her.

'Lenore,' he said with a small incline of his head, making no attempt to shake her hand in any way, or give her a kiss on the cheek. Yet it had been over two years since they'd seen each other, Lenore's divorce from Nathan having cut their social ties.

'Zachary,' she returned, ignoring the lift behind her, which eventually shut its doors and moved on.

How marvellous he looks, she was thinking as she stood there, his very male body encased in dark blue trousers and a pale blue short-sleeved golfing shirt. She was used to seeing him in business or dinner suits, not casual clothes, but it was clear that Zachary had kept his forty-five-year-old body in great shape. Perhaps he'd come to the hospital straight from the golf-course, because his normally neat and tidy thick brown hair was windblown, and there was a faint sheen of sweat on his high forehead that bespoke physical activity.

'I've come to see Byron,' he said brusquely.

'I've just left him.'

'Really? I'm surprised. You and he were never the best of friends.'

Lenore shrugged, her earlier fury with Byron seeming inconsequential now. All that mattered at this moment was finding some excuse to stay and talk to Zachary. Yet the girls were waiting for her in the car and it was so hot out in the open-air car park. She hoped they'd thought to turn on the engine and the air-conditioning!

'You're looking well, Lenore,' Zachary remarked, his eyes sweeping down over her own very casual outfit of apricot bermuda shorts and matching T-shirt. 'Divorce obviously agrees with you. How's Kirsty?' he added pointedly. 'I'd be surprised if she's as happy with the situation.'

Hurt by his sarcasm—and perhaps stung by guilt over Kirsty—Lenore lied outrageously. 'Kirsty's fine. She's not a little girl any more, Zachary. She's fourteen. Quite old enough to understand that her father and I were not happy together. Besides, it wasn't a bitter divorce. Nathan and I are still good friends. She's living with him at the moment in fact, at Belleview.'

'How very civilised of you,' Zachary drawled. 'Pity *all* people can't get over the pain of divorce so easily.'

Lenore looked away from his brittle blue eyes. How quickly her pleasure at seeing Zachary again had vanished. He was still the same man. Still inflexible in matters of morals and marriage, still intolerant of human failings. Didn't he know that not everyone was as strong as he was?

The lift doors opened again and people stepped out. Zachary and Lenore moved to one side to let them pass along the corridor.

'I haven't seen your name up in lights lately,' Zachary resumed. 'Are you still acting?'

'Yes. I start rehearsal next week for a new play. It's a comedy of manners. A real farce.'

'You usually go in for drama, don't you, not farce?'

Lenore shrugged. Her whole life felt like a farce right at that moment. Why was she making chillingly polite con-

versation with this man when what she wanted was to
throw herself into his arms and tell him how much he meant
to her, had always meant to her? For all she knew, he might
think she'd *loved* Nathan when she married him, that she'd
forgotten *him* as quickly as her actions had made it seem.

But she'd never forgotten him, never stopped loving him,
right from the first moment she'd seen him nearly fifteen
years ago, when she'd been a nineteen-year-old fledgling
actress, and he'd been a thirty-year-old rising star of a solicitor.

Lenore had just won a small role in the first play Nathan
had written. Zachary, as a friend and business colleague of
Byron's, had put up some of the money for the production,
and had dropped in at rehearsals one day to see how his
investment was faring. Lenore could still remember glancing down from the stage and seeing Zachary staring up at
her. It had been like a scene from the movies. Their eyes
had met and Lenore had known, instinctively, that this was
the man she wanted to spend the rest of her life with.

Zachary must have been similarly smitten with her,
whether he admitted it to himself or not, for he'd made a
beeline for her during a break and it was over a polystyrene
mug of coffee and a quite intimate little chat—mostly about
herself—that she fell even more deeply and hopelessly in
love. After Zachary left that day, the memory of him had
filled her thoughts and dreams, blocking out even her ambition to be a famous actress. All she wanted was
Zachary...

That night, Lenore broke off with her current boyfriend,
after which she had settled down to wait impatiently for
the handsome solicitor to visit the theatre once more. And
it was during this harrowing wait that she'd accidentally
found out he was a married man with two young sons.

She'd been devastated. And shocked. And angry. He
should have told her, she reasoned irrationally.

When Zachary finally returned to the theatre during the
last week of rehearsals, she'd done her best to remain cool

and distant, especially when he'd singled her out for his attentions a second time. And she'd managed quite well, yet when he finally left she'd felt utterly wretched, so much so that when rehearsals were over and she realised Zachary hadn't left at all, but had merely retreated into the dark recesses of the theatre to watch, she'd been overcome with a delighted relief.

The upshot was she had stayed chatting with him for far too long and missed her bus home. After a momentary hesitation, Zachary had offered to drive her, which was rather out of his way since she shared a small flat with another girl at Maroubra and he lived somewhere on the North Side of Sydney.

Lenore had known at the time that she should have refused the ride, but wild horses wouldn't have stopped her at that stage. Nevertheless, Zachary hadn't touched her or kissed her or said anything out of line on the way home, but she knew and he knew what was happening between them. The atmosphere in the car had been thick with tension and whenever the car had stopped at a set of lights she'd been hotly aware of his eyes slanting her way, coveting her, wanting her. She'd been more sexually aroused sitting there in that car with just Zachary's eyes on her than she'd been in bed with her boyfriend. Lenore had known, without a doubt, that if and when Zachary ever made love to her she would be transported to the heavens.

But Zachary didn't make love to her. He let her out of the car with a rather curt farewell and accelerated away as though the hounds of hell were after him. And maybe they had been, Lenore recognised. She had certainly reached the state where right and wrong had ceased to have meaning, and the devil himself had been whispering his wicked temptations in her ear.

She hadn't seen Zachary again till the party after the opening night of the play, thrown by Byron at Belleview. Zachary had attended—as he had the play—with his wife, Felicity. He'd studiously avoided Lenore all night, though she did catch him once looking her way, his eyes darkening with undoubted desire when they roved over the admittedly daring little black dress she was almost wearing.

Petticoat in style, it had had tiny shoestring straps holding up a short sheath of satin that slithered over the curves of her tall willowy figure, ending a few meagre inches past her buttocks, exposing a wide expanse of firm creamy thighs. Her hair, which had been even longer then, had completed her highly sensual image by tumbling halfway down her back in a riot of bronzed curls. Outrageous gold earrings had reached from her lobes to her bare shoulders.

Lenore's unrequited love for Zachary—along with several glasses of champagne—had sparked a wild recklessness in her that night, and when she'd seen his lone figure stroll out on to the back patio she couldn't resist following him. One part of her had still been angry with him for having played with her feelings, the rest had been on fire to be with him, no matter what.

But before she'd reached him, he continued down the patio steps, wandering off into the extensive gardens at the side of the house so that by the time Lenore caught up with him they were quite removed from the house and the other partygoers. In fact, they'd moved into the shadows of the trees, and were as alone as they would have been in the most private of bedrooms.

'Zachary!' she called out breathlessly from behind him.

He spun round, his eyes flinging wide with momentary shock before he could successfully gather himself. 'Good God, Lenore, what are you doing out here?' he said with cold anger. 'Go back inside.'

'No,' she panted, her small braless breasts with their erect nipples rising and falling in a ragged, unrehearsed rhythm. 'I won't go back inside and I won't keep pretending. I…I love you, Zachary. You must know that. And I think you love me. D—don't you?'

She was very close to him now, green eyes filled with a very enticing confusion as she gazed up into his face. 'Oh,

Zachary, don't torture me so,' she burst out. 'Tell me if you don't love me, for pity's sake.'

'For pity's sake?' His laughter was hard and bitter. 'What do you know of pity, you green-eyed temptress?' And with a sudden groan he swept her against him and kissed her till they were both struggling for breath. He might have drawn back then but Lenore was like a hunting tigress who had finally brought down her prey. She dug her claws in deep and drew him back into her den of desire, her mouth finding his again, her tongue inviting him with an erotic dance that sent a low growl of passion rumbling in his throat.

His mouth never lifted from hers as shaking fingers pushed the straps from her shoulders and the dress concertinaed at her feet. His hands were quite rough as they raked down her arms, and when they reached her thighs they gripped the soft flesh there with something like anger for a second before sliding upwards till they found her aching swollen breasts. She moaned softly as his thumbs rubbed roughly over her nipples, making them harden ever further. Her head was whirling madly, her conscience thoroughly routed, when suddenly, abruptly, he abandoned her.

She could not understand what had happened for a second as she stood there, limbs still trembling, eyes wildly dilated, till Zachary picked up her dress and practically threw it to her. 'No, Lenore,' he said harshly. 'No.'

'But…but you *love* me!'

'Yes, I love you,' he ground out. 'God forgive me, but I do. And perhaps you *think* you love me back. But you'll get over me, Lenore, if I let you. You're only nineteen. You'll soon fall in love with someone else if I have enough courage to turn my back on what you've just offered to me. God, but you're such an innocent, despite your womanly wiles! You've probably been thinking I might divorce Felicity and marry you.'

She clutched her dress in front of her and blinked up at him in disbelief. Surely, if he loved her, he *would* divorce

Felicity and marry her! How could he go back to his wife's bed, when it was her—*Lenore*—that he loved and wanted?

'I won't leave my wife and my sons for you,' he announced with a brutal frankness. 'I won't *ever* marry you. Oh, I could set you up somewhere and visit your bed on a regular basis. I could treat you with cool disregard when we run into each other in public, then ravish you behind closed doors. Believe me, I'm sorely tempted to do just that, and if you think you could stop me, then you don't know yourself very well. But eventually you'd grow to hate me as I would grow to hate myself. So let's forget we've ever said these things to each other, let's forget these stolen moments. Grow up, Lenore. Put your dress back on and we'll return to the party, where I'll dance with my wife and you'll dance with our handsome young playwright and we won't mention this incident ever again.'

Lenore had stood there in utter shock when Zachary had done just that. The pain when she'd seen him later in Felicity's arms, smiling into her eyes as though nothing had happened—*nothing!*—had sent a crazed need for vengeance stampeding through her veins. Oh, yes, she'd danced with Nathan all right, danced and drunk champagne, danced and flirted and generally been as irresistibly alluring as an up-and-coming young actress could be when she set her mind to it.

Nathan, in return, had danced her right home into his bed where he'd made love to her with a devastating thoroughness that had stunned and horrified her, for she had found herself responding to his amazingly expert caresses with a quivering pleasure which she'd been sure Zachary alone could evoke. When Nathan's body had finally fused with hers, he'd brought her inexorably to a climax she'd found shattering in more ways than one.

Lenore had woken the next morning, physically sated but mentally confused. Maybe she hadn't loved Zachary after all.

But she *had*!

It wasn't till after she'd been married to Nathan for a while that she learnt to her misery the difference between sex and love. One without the other left her feeling emotionally desolate. It had taken a chance meeting with Zachary soon after Kirsty was born to make her face the empty nature of her relationship with Nathan and make her realise Zachary would always have her heart.

And it had taken *this* chance meeting, today, to ram this fact home one more crushing time.

'Zachary!' she blurted out, determined to say something. Anything!

'Yes?'

'I…I…how's Felicity and the boys?' she finished, hating herself for her lack of courage.

'They're fine. Emery's at university now, in his first year of law. Clark's doing his HSC this year. Would you believe he wants to go into the airforce and become a pilot? I knew I shouldn't have let him watch *Top Gun* a few years back when he was only an impressionable thirteen.'

Lenore noticed he hadn't said anything specific about Felicity and she wasn't about to ask.

An awkward silence descended between them and Lenore was about to say she had to go when Zachary spoke.

'Have you seen the new play at the Royal?'

'*Women at Work*? Yes, I have. It's very good.'

'You wouldn't like to see it again, would you?'

Lenore stared at him.

'Felicity and I had tickets for tonight but she's been called away. Her sister is going through a divorce and breaks down with regular monotony and Felicity feels compelled to dash off and give sisterly succour. She told me to take someone else to the play but really, there was no one I could ask at the last moment, so I wasn't going to bother to go at all, but…'

'I'd love to,' Lenore said quickly, and held her breath.

He gave her a long look which could have meant anything. 'Just as friends, Lenore,' he warned curtly. 'Nothing more.'

'Of course. What shall I wear?'

His smile carried a wealth of self-mockery. 'Sackcloth and ashes?'

She laughed. 'Sackcloth and ashes coming up.'

'And you might leave off that tantalising damned perfume you always used to wear. The thought of sitting next to you in a darkened theatre with *that* on would be more than any man could bear.'

Lenore stared up into his blazing blue eyes and saw the blistering desire hiding behind the harshly delivered humour. Heat zoomed into her cheeks and a quivering started deep within.

Perhaps he saw her arousal, for a very real worry leapt into his face, though it was quickly hidden by a sardonic smile. 'I suppose you wouldn't let me take that invitation back, would you?'

'*Never*,' she said with far too much emotion.

'That's what I thought. Ah, well, perhaps it will have its pluses. There've been quite a few things I've wanted to know over the years, Lenore, my love, things that have eaten into me, things I couldn't very well ask in front of Felicity.'

'What things?'

'They can wait till tonight,' he bit out. 'I must get along to see Byron now.' He actually went to leave her.

'But…but…we haven't made proper arrangements for tonight. Don't you want my address? What time do you want me to be ready by?'

He turned back to face her, his smile bitter. 'My dear Lenore, I have no intention of picking you up at your home. Do I look a fool? I'm already walking a dangerous tightrope taking you to this play at all, a tightrope which you will undoubtedly enjoy rocking at every available opportunity. That's the nature of the beast. He reached out and traced a quivering finger down her cheek and across her mouth, his voice remaining hard but his eyes like the craters of an exploding volcano.

'I have you taped, Lenore. I understand you entirely. After all these years of cold common sense, I'll not play with fire now. It's one thing to sit together at a play, quite another to be alone with you in a car and have to drop you home afterwards.'

Her eyes widened with the understanding of how dangerous he would find that, how dangerous he found being with her except in the most public of places. She grabbed his hand in both of hers and held it. 'You still love me, don't you?' she whispered breathlessly.

Her open accusation startled him, his shock finding solace in a harsh rephrasing. 'I still *want* you. That's hardly the same.'

'You're a liar,' she said, and, opening the palm of his hand, she lifted it to her mouth.

Zachary stared, wide-eyed, as her lips pressed in blind passion to his flesh. Abruptly, he snatched his hand away. 'Stop it, Lenore. Good God, you haven't changed, have you? When are you going to grow up?'

Though shaken by her own actions of a moment ago, she looked him straight in the eye. 'I'm grown up enough to know what the truth is and to say it out loud. You love me and I love you. It can't be wrong to tell the truth, Zachary.'

'It *can* be wrong to tell the truth, Lenore,' he said fiercely. 'It can cause much more pain than lies. Always remember that.' He drew right back then, shaking his head at her with a rueful smile on his face. 'All these years and a moment's weakness could ruin everything. But I don't seem to have the courage to deny myself one miserable evening of your undoubtedly stimulating company. But do try to behave tonight, Lenore,' he warned bitterly. 'Give a man a break. That's all I ask...'

She nodded in silent acquiescence, totally unable to speak. Zachary loved her. Nothing else mattered.

'I'll meet you in the foyer of the theatre around seven-thirty,' he said. 'The play starts at eight.' And then he was spinning on this heels and striding away down the hospital corridor, not looking back, never looking back.

Lenore stared after him, her heart racing, her head whirling. And then his last words sank in. Behave, he'd said. She'd always had trouble behaving around Zachary. Would tonight be any different?

'Where on earth have you been, Mum?' Kirsty complained when Lenore hurried over to her car, her face flushed.

'I ran into an old friend at the lifts,' she admitted, 'and I simply couldn't get away. I'm sorry. At least you had the foresight to put on the air-conditioning.'

'Oh, that wasn't me, that was Gemma's doing. Not that *she* felt hot. She reckons compared to Lightning Ridge this is cool!'

'It is,' Gemma laughed. 'Anything under forty in the summer is cool.'

'My God, how did you stand it?' Lenore said, having difficulty concentrating on anything but where she would be in three hours' time.

'We didn't wear too many clothes, for starters.'

The mention of clothes reminded Lenore of her mission from Byron regarding Gemma's wardrobe, but it didn't seem the right moment to say anything about that. Nathan was away for the weekend and most of the shops were shut so it could wait till Monday, at least.

'What videos are we going to get?' Kirsty piped up happily.

Lenore frowned. She hated having to back out of their arrangements regarding tonight and hoped Kirsty wouldn't mind. She would stick almost to the truth, though giving the impression that the 'old friend' she'd bumped into was a woman and that she'd been talked into going to the theatre with her tonight.

Kirsty didn't mind at all, which gave Lenore another twinge of jealousy regarding Gemma's growing place in her daughter's life, till she realised she was being silly. Of course Kirsty preferred Gemma's company to her mother's. The girl was more her age!

Thinking of Gemma shifted Lenore's mind back to Nathan and her belief that he was going to seduce that girl. He might not consciously know it yet but it was as inevitable as the sun rising in the east and setting in the west. Gemma's only salvation would be if he got wrapped up in writing another play. Hopefully, he'd finished that play Byron had mentioned a while back, so that he'd be itching to start on another.

Nathan wrote an average of one play a year, the process involving him intensely for up to six months. During this creative period his need for sex was greatly diminished. Hopefully, Nathan was up there at Avoca this weekend, furiously writing away. Creating a new play and having to work at Whitmore Opals at the same time should really tire him out. Still, the last thing he needed was a revamped Gemma swanning around Belleview. Lenore vowed to hold back on her makeover promise for a little while longer, giving Gemma's undoubted virtue a fighting chance. She was far too nice a girl to be wasted on a unfeeling bastard like Nathan.

'Mum!' Kirsty complained with a disgruntled sigh. 'You've just driven straight past the video shop. Truly, you're becoming a real daydreamer when you drive these days.'

'Sorry. My mind was elsewhere, I admit.'

'What on?'

'Oh, nothing important…'

Lenore's stomach was beginning to churn with forbidden excitement by the time she dropped the girls off and headed for home. It was no use. She could tell herself a million times that this was just a platonic date with Zachary but she didn't believe it. Not after what he'd said. She knew that she would sit there beside him in the darkened theatre, fantasising the same things he was fantasising.

Thunder rumbled overhead and Lenore peered up through the windscreen. A summer storm was threatening, white thunderheads mixed with the grey of more ominous-looking clouds. It looked like being an electrical storm, a regular happening after such a hot sultry day.

Lenore wasn't frightened of the storm gathering in the sky, however. It was the storm gathering in her own body that was troubling her. She could feel the tingle of nerve-endings suddenly alert, feel the warm heat of desire igniting the blood in her veins. It had been a long time since she'd experienced the release of sexual satisfaction. Too long, perhaps.

Zachary didn't know the full extent of the danger he was placing himself in tonight. But Lenore was not about to tell him. She didn't appreciate the extent of it herself.

CHAPTER EIGHT

LENORE parked her car in the underground car park beneath the building that housed the Royal Theatre. By seventwenty on a Saturday night all levels were filling rapidly but she managed to find a spot. She kept repeating the 'yellow' colour-code of the level in the lift afterwards to imprint it on her mind. The last time she'd parked down there, she'd been distracted and forgotten what level she was parked on and it had taken her nearly an hour to find her car.

The lift doors shot open and she joined the passers-by in the curving arcade that went in all directions, one of them to the Theatre Royal. Anyone not knowing where they were heading could easily get lost, she thought, but she'd been to the Royal more times than she could count. She'd even performed there a few times, though only in minor parts.

Most of her acting career had been relegated to minor roles so far. Not because she wasn't a good actress, she believed, but because she didn't curry favour with the right people. Acting was the same as any other showbiz industry. You had to be part of the 'in' crowd to succeed. If you were 'in' you were at the head of the table, given first choice of anything on offer. Everyone else scrambled for the crumbs.

Sleeping with the right people might have helped, she supposed. But that just wasn't her style. Which was ironic, really. She'd slept with Australia's rising star of a playwright for years and it hadn't earned her a single decent role. But that had been deliberate sabotage on Nathan's part, in her opinion. He'd always said she wasn't suited to the women he created, but she knew he'd hated her not being home at night when and if he decided he needed her body.

God, but that man was a selfish chauvinist of the first order! She must enlighten Gemma of his true nature before it was too late.

Lenore gave herself a mental shake, astonished that she could be thinking of anyone other than Zachary at this point in time. But maybe she'd been deliberately diverting her mind from him in an effort to keep her emotions under control tonight. Right from the moment she'd dropped the girls off at Belleview she'd been fighting herself and the inevitable excitement growing within her.

When she'd arrived home, she'd been positively useless for a while, pacing mindlessly through the various rooms, unable to eat, unable even to think about what she would wear. Several times she'd contemplated ringing Zachary and telling him she had changed her mind. It would be the right thing to do.

Lenore knew that she wasn't as strong as Zachary. Normally. But from what she'd witnessed that afternoon, he was going through a stage where he wasn't so strong either. Maybe Felicity was neglecting him sexually. Maybe she was just neglecting him all round. He'd sounded resigned to her going off at all hours to be with her sister. Maybe the marriage was in trouble at long last.

Did Lenore want that? Did she want Zachary to turn to her chiefly because of his wife's neglect? Did she want him in a moment of weakness?

The answers to those questions had obliterated her conscience. Yes, yes, yes! She didn't give a damn what the reason was. She didn't care. All she knew was she wanted Zachary to take her in her arms at least one more time, have him tell her he loved her, hold her, kiss her, touch her. It didn't matter if they didn't go to bed. She was willing to settle for anything, for the crumbs.

Lenore had ground to a halt in front of the large lounge-room window and gazed up at the darkening sky.

I'm wicked, she had told the sky as it spat with lightning and rolled with thunder. I'm just plain wicked.

Yet I don't *feel* wicked, she puzzled now as she hurried across the hard floor of the arcade, her high heels clacking noisily. I feel like a young girl going off on her first date, like a virgin bride on her wedding-night, like a person going to a reunion with their best friend after not seeing them for many, many years.

If only Zachary could have been all of those things, she thought with a lump in her throat. Her first lover, her husband, her best friend...

I must not cry, came the swift edict, and she blinked madly. I've spent an hour doing this thirty-four-year-old face up to look like a rosy innocent young thing and I'm not going to mess it up!

Zachary was there waiting for her, as she'd hoped he would be, looking devastatingly handsome in a black dinner suit. Oh, God, she thought as she walked across the carpeted foyer of the theatre to where he was standing at one end of the bar, two glasses of champagne at the ready.

He watched her come towards him like a starved man, his eyes hungry upon her, his jaw and shoulders squaring in an effort, perhaps, to stop himself from rushing forward. She herself was finding it difficult not to run into his arms, though a sudden jelliness in her thighs would have made running a highly risky mode of movement at that moment. At long last, she was before him, a tremulous smile on her coral-painted mouth.

'Lenore,' he said with superb control, yet his gaze was still drinking in every inch of her slender form, encased that night in a cream suit with gold buttons which revealed nothing and hinted at everything. Her hair was up, tiny Titian tendrils curling around her face and neck. There were pearls in her earlobes and Arpège perfume drenched all over her. She'd remembered what he'd said about *not* wanting to smell her in the darkness of the theatre.

Now she shivered slightly at the thought. It was a shiver of the most sexual kind.

'Zachary,' she returned, and on impulse held out her hand to be kissed.

A wry smile touched Zachary's mouth, a mouth some women might have thought hard and uncompromising. But it was a mouth that had fascinated Lenore for years. Oh, to have that mouth on hers, to have it rove at will over her body...

She watched, dry-mouthed, as he lifted her hand to his lips, swallowing convulsively at the point of contact. She'd always known his lips would be warm, not cold. Soft, not hard.

'Is this an example of you behaving, Lenore?' he mocked as he let go her hand. 'First you arrive looking like the first breath of spring, then you have me kiss you before I've had a chance to recover my equilibrium.'

Green eyes glittering with arousal, Lenore found herself already on that merry-go-round to nowhere which Zachary put her on without any conscious effort. But she could have endured that willingly if it hadn't been for this unexpected shift in manner. His eyes had hardened with that kiss to a brittle blue, his expression becoming cold. Where had the desire-charged Zachary of a few moments ago gone to all of a sudden?

'I seem to remember you like champagne,' he said drily as he handed her a glass and picked the other up for himself.

'Do I?' She frowned for a second before realising what he was referring to. The night of the party at Belleview. A flush of guilt reinforced her already high colour.

'Ah, I see you've remembered the occasion to which I refer. Move over here a little, Lenore.' Taking her elbow, he guided her into a more private corner.

Lenore's thoughts stayed with that most unfair barb of

his and she could not remain silent. 'I needed to get drunk that night, Zachary,' she defended shakily. 'Surely you must appreciate that.'

'Did you need to jump into Nathan's bed as well?' he drawled. 'Tell me, Lenore, how do you think I felt when I received the invitation to your wedding less than three months later, when your baby was born nine months to the day from that night?'

Lenore paled. 'You mean you...?'

'Counted back?' He laughed, his mouth lifting in a travesty of a smile. 'Oh, yes, Lenore, I counted, and I found it...*telling*...that the night you told me you loved me you gave yourself to another man. But of course I appreciated in the end that you hadn't really been in love with me. A lot of young women become infatuated with older married men. It's something to do with such men being a challenge.

'The young women in question—who are invariably tantalisingly lovely—like to prove that they're irresistible. One such woman took my father away from my mother, and subsequently from his three children. I, being the eldest, witnessed most of my mother's pain, and ultimately my father's as well. His charming new wife decided after a mere eighteen months that he was, after all, too old for her. She left a trail of destruction behind, I can tell you.'

Lenore wasn't sure if she felt sorry for Zachary, or furious with him. She was sympathetic with the hell he'd gone through as a child, and she understood now why he was so strong on sticking with his marriage through thick and thin. But if he was placing her on a par with the woman who had destroyed his parents' marriage, if he thought her shallow and cruel...

'I was *not* one of those young women,' she insisted fiercely.

'Weren't you? Can you say that if I left my wife for you you wouldn't have grown tired of me after a while, that you wouldn't have felt the need eventually to flex your feminine power on some other unsuspecting male?'

Lenore's anger flared even further. 'You were never un-suspecting, Zachary. You sought *me* out in the beginning, not the other way around.'

A guilty colour slashed across his high cheekbones. 'I couldn't seem to keep away,' he muttered.

'Then blame yourself,' she snapped. 'Not me.'

They glared at each other.

Suddenly, the hardness around Zachary's mouth softened to a sardonic smile. 'You are so right, Lenore. So very right. It *was* my fault in the beginning. I knew you were forbidden fruit. I watched you on that stage, so beautiful and clever and fiery. And I told myself I only wanted to talk to you, that I could control what I was feeling. I played with fire and I got burnt.'

'I…I got burnt too, Zachary,' she choked out.

'Did you, Lenore? Or were you just scorched a little? I think perhaps I ignited you just enough for some other man to come along and quench your fire. That's what kills me the most, to think it was *my* fault you went to bed with Nathan. My God,' he groaned. 'I virtually pushed you at him.'

'Stop it, Zachary,' Lenore hissed. 'Just stop it! Blaming ourselves or each other for what happened is futile. What happened happened. But be assured I never loved Nathan. I slept with him, I married him, I had a child by him. But I never loved him. I divorced him, god-dammit, because I couldn't stand another night of lying in his bed and wishing it were you beside me!'

Zachary's face grew ashen as he stared at her. He uttered a brief obscenity then swept the champagne glass to his lips, gulping deeply. His hand was shaking and his eyes, when they lifted, looked bruised and haunted.

Lenore felt dreadful. Why, oh, why hadn't she kept her stupid mouth shut? Zachary had enough to bear without her burdening him with her own self-inflicted miseries. But at least he now knew she'd genuinely loved him. He hadn't been some passing fancy. For him to have kept on believing that was the case would have been intolerable!

They kept staring at each other in the most ghastly silence, and Lenore accepted that once again their love for each other was proving to be a highly destructive force. Its chemistry sizzled across the space between them, tormenting and tantalising, making them dissatisfied with their present existences, making them want what they shouldn't want. Both of them knew that to give in to their desires would ultimately render them wretched with guilt.

The buzzer announcing that it was time to be seated splintered the appalling atmosphere just in time. Zachary took the glass from Lenore's hands with a tight little smile and placed it with his on the bar before returning to take her elbow.

'Let's try and enjoy the play, shall we?' he said tautly. 'I expect it might be the last thing either of us enjoys for quite some time.'

Zachary behaved impeccably over the next three hours, not touching Lenore in the darkened theatre, not whispering anything suggestive in her ear, not putting a foot out of place. He played the role of platonic friend to perfection, making trite conversation when required, escorting her to the foyer at intermission where he secured her another glass of champagne before taking her back inside to see the second half of what was probably a riveting performance, if Lenore had been in the mood to be riveted.

She could not remember a single moment of either half, but she had seen the play before so could make suitable comments at suitable moments, such as when the curtain finally fell.

'It truly is a wonderful play,' she sighed.

'If you say so.'

Her sideways glance revealed a face like stone. The play was over and so was the night. He looked as grim as she felt.

'Where are you parked?' he asked as they made slow progress out of the theatre. The session had been packed.

'Underneath. Level Yellow.'

'I'm on Blue. I'll walk you to your car. I don't like these car parks much. Ideal places for women to be raped.'

'Really?' Lenore couldn't help it. She raised her eyebrows in black humour at Zachary, who tried to look reproachful but failed.

A rueful smile smoothed the frown from his forehead. 'If I did, you'd scream bloody murder.'

'Probably,' she laughed softly.

His eyes dropped briefly to her parted lips before he reefed them away, that steely mask clanging back into place.

Lenore sighed.

Several people exited from the lift on Level Yellow so that they were not strictly alone as Zachary walked her to her car. It seemed a very short walk to Lenore, she imagined as short as the walk from a murderer's cell down the corridor of death to the electric chair. Leaving Zachary's company was as horrifying a prospect as dying. In fact it *was* a little like dying.

Fumbling in her gold evening bag, she extracted her car keys and was just fitting them into the lock of the driver's door when she noticed the front right-hand tyre. It was as flat as a tack.

'Oh, no,' she groaned. 'Look at that.'

Zachary looked, and shrugged. 'It happens. I presume you have a spare? I'll change it for you.'

'Yes,' she said, a ghastly curl of guilt fluttering in her stomach as she recalled something. 'But…I—er—it's flat too.'

Zachary gave her a sharp, narrow-eyed glare.

'I…meant to get it fixed…'

'And how long has it been flat?' he asked curtly.

'Ages, I'm afraid. I—er—keep forgetting. Besides, I

didn't think I could possibly have two flat tyres in the one year. Before that I'd never had *one!*'

Lenore knew she sounded irresponsible, which was not like her at all, but in matters relating to cars she'd been more than happy for Nathan to take charge. Since the divorce, she'd been letting things slide where her car was concerned and she really would have to get her act together.

'I'm sorry, Zachary...'

'Are you? I doubt that, Lenore. I doubt that very much. I'll have to drive you home now, I suppose.'

'I could take a taxi...'

'So you could. Is that what you want to do?'

'No.'

'I didn't think so. Come along, then. We'll pick up the spare tyre as we drive past, drop it in at a garage on the way home and come back to pick up your car tomorrow morning.'

'Tomorrow? But...but...'

'Felicity won't be returning till tomorrow evening. We're in no danger of being caught, if that's what you're afraid of.'

Something in Zachary's tone sparked a flash of anger in Lenore. 'We're not doing anything really *wrong!*' she insisted.

Zachary laughed. The laugh was bad enough, but the wild glitter in his eyes unnerved Lenore completely. Was he in danger of going over some indefinable edge?

'Let's go, Lenore,' he said brusquely, and grabbed her upper arm.

He practically dragged her over to the lift, displaying a side of his nature she'd never encountered before. Or had she? He'd been a pretty tough character the night of that party.

'Hey! Cut out the rough stuff,' she complained as he shoved her into the thankfully empty lift. 'I happen to bruise easily.'

Savage blue eyes lanced the fair, faintly freckled skin of

her bare arm which was already showing fingermarks on the softer underside. 'How inconvenient for you,' he drawled, 'especially in the summer.'

'Meaning?'

'Meaning you must own some good body make-up, since I've never seen any marks on you. Or was Nathan an exceptionally tender lover? Somehow, I can't imagine you liking tenderness, Lenore. You're far too tempestuous by nature.'

She crossed her arms and fell sulkily silent. She didn't like Zachary in this mood. It wasn't *her* fault the tyre had been flat. Yet he was clearly furious at having to spend more time with her. Did he think she had planned it? That this was some devious ploy to get him to take her home?

Yes, of course that was what he thought!

She grabbed the sleeve of his dinner-jacket. 'I didn't plan this, Zachary. You must believe me!'

His sidewards glance was cold. 'Just leave it for now, Lenore.'

'No, I—'

'Leave it!' he spat out.

She left it.

Zachary's dark maroon Jaguar was a sheer delight to ride in but Lenore was beyond noticing, or caring. They swept in wretched silence up the ramp of the car park and into the night, only to find a southerly squall had blown in after the electrical storm, heavy rain lashing the windscreen and making driving hazardous. It took all of Zachary's concentration to negotiate the still busy city streets and get them safely over the Harbour Bridge and on to the Pacific Highway, heading for home.

A brief stopover to drop the tyre at a garage on the way brought Zachary back behind the driving wheel with water-spattered shoulders and damp hair. Lenore automatically glanced at him, her heart yearning for him to look back at her with some warmth, but he jerked his face away with a shudder and turned the key in the ignition.

Lenore fell into the deepest depression. He hated her. He despised her. He thought her manipulative and scheming and evil.

It wasn't till Zachary turned down a side-street and slid the car into the kerb right outside her villa home in Turramurra—without any directions from her—that Lenore snapped back to reality.

'How did you know where I lived?' she asked.

'Don't ask,' was his succinct reply.

'But I want to know.'

'Shut up, Lenore. Shut up and get out of this car.'

Oddly enough, he was already climbing out himself, which made nonsense of his attitude towards her. What was going on here?

'Lock the passenger door,' he ordered testily. 'I don't want to come out here tomorrow morning and find the damned thing stolen.'

She locked the door before his words sank in. Suddenly, her eyes snapped up, wide with shock and bewilderment.

'I can fight myself, Lenore,' he said with a raw, bitter passion. 'I can even fight you. But I can't fight fate. Yes, I'm going to spend the night with you. And if you say one word of protest, if you find one single solitary excuse why I can't, I swear to God I won't be responsible for the consequences!'

CHAPTER NINE

LENORE felt the blood begin to drain from her face. But she wasn't, and never had been, a fainting sort of female. So she pulled herself together and walked, with her whirling head held high, up the paved pathway that led round to the side-entrance of her quite luxurious and beautifully furnished two-bedroom town house.

Zachary followed.

She didn't look at him as she unlocked the door and stepped inside, keeping her eyes averted as Zachary brushed past her to stride ahead across the small entry hall and through the archway that led straight into the living-room. Although the room was in darkness, he found, as though by instinct, the lamps on the side-tables at each end of the sofa, switching them on to flood the room with their soft apricot light.

Lenore trailed after him to remain just inside the room to the right of the archway, watching with horrified fascination as Zachary discarded his bow-tie, stripped off his jacket, then started on the buttons of his white dress shirt.

'What...what do you think you're doing?'

His eyes mocked her from beneath their dark brows. 'I'm getting undressed, Lenore. I would have thought that was pretty obvious. Please don't be coy. I won't like you coy.'

A choked sound flew from her throat. 'I don't think you like me at all! Why must you reduce what we feel for each other to this?' she cried. 'It...it's disgusting. I won't have it, do you hear?'

'You won't have it?' He laughed and with a few appallingly quick strides grabbed her stunned body by the upper arms and drove her back against the wall. 'You'll have it any way I choose to give it to you,' he threatened. 'And you'll love it!'

She gaped into his passion-dark face and felt afraid of him for the first time in her life. Her fear must have been mirrored in her eyes for suddenly he groaned and drew her shocked body to his, cradling her head against his shoulder, and doing his best to stop the uncontrollable tremors that were racking her slender frame.

'I'm sorry,' he rasped. 'I didn't mean that. Dear God, I didn't mean it.'

Lenore finally began to cry, sobs tearing from her chest with dry, gasping sounds.

'I...I love you,' she blurted out. 'You must...believe me.'

'Yes, yes,' he crooned, and continued to soothe her while pulling the pins from her hair, stroking the gold-red waves down her back till her sobs were reduced to the occasional whimper and she was clinging to him.

'Yes,' he said at last with a return to steely resolve, and stepped back to rapidly undo the buttons of her jacket and drag it down off her shoulders till it fell into a crumpled heap in the carpet.

Her bra was nothing but a wisp of cream lace and satin designed to allure rather than support, for her small, firm breasts required no such foundation. Naked, they stood high and beautifully shaped, their long pink nipples invitingly tipped up as though soliciting a man's mouth.

When Zachary removed her bra he groaned and bent his lips to do their silent bidding.

Lenore gasped, her heart racing behind the breast he was so deliciously savouring. 'Oh, God,' she cried when his fingers started plucking at her other nipple at the same time, her desire flaring out of control.

She braced her palms against the wall beside her lest her knees give way entirely, giving herself up to Zachary's will with a blind, impassioned need that years of denial had created. The man she loved was finally making love to her and it was everything she envisaged. And more.

It was wild.

His mouth moved across to that other breast, sucking furiously now, his hand dropping to the waistband of her skirt, and soon it too joined the jacket and bra on the floor. Now only her panties, tights and shoes prevented her from being totally naked before him, and already the first two were being peeled down her body.

He gasped away from her breast to hurriedly complete the stripping away of her clothes, leaving her panting and nude against the wall. When he had scooped all her clothes out of their way, he straightened to stare at her, hot eyes feasting on her body for several arousing moments before lifting to meet her own wide, desire-filled gaze.

'I've thought about this moment for so long,' he said hoarsely. 'I've pictured it in my mind, imagined what I would do, how I would feel. But the reality is so different from my fantasies. I should have known... Hell, I should have known...'

His eyes held her in thrall as he ripped his shirt aside then proceeded to discard the rest of his clothes, never once letting his hypnotic gaze move from hers. And when he too was naked, he pressed his aroused body against hers, taking her hands in his, entwining their fingers and lifting them high above her head, squeezing tightly while he took her mouth in a kiss that was deceptively tender at first. But it built and built in power and passion till they were both beside themselves with longing to be one.

There was no question of going elsewhere, of finding some soft bed for their first union. Their need for each other was too strong and immediate for any further delay. Was it her own shaking hands that guided him inside, or was it his around hers? Lenore wasn't sure. She only knew she cried out as she felt his flesh fill hers and everything began to swirl in a black haze within her head. She felt hot and breathless and her hands were now miraculously gripping his shoulders and he was driving up into her with an impassioned rhythm that gave no thought to anything but achieving nature's objective.

Lenore was catapulted to a climax with amazing speed, her pleasure propelling Zachary into an equally tumultuous release, stunning Lenore with the sheer number of his shuddering gasps, and the length of time it took for his body to rest quietly within her. She'd never experienced anything like it.

'Oh, Zachary…darling…' she whispered when at last his head lifted and he started smoothing her damp hair back from her face.

'I know,' he groaned. 'I know…'

She laid her head on his chest and wrapped her arms tightly around him. 'Just hold me, Zachary. Hold me and never let me go.'

They were embracing each other in a state of mutual bliss when she felt his chest lift in a startled gasp. 'Dear God!' he exclaimed, very much shaken. 'You can't get pregnant, can you? I just didn't think.' His hands lifted to rake back his tousled hair in deep agitation. 'Hell, what have I done? I'm a bloody fool!'

She lifted a gentle hand to lay against his cheek, her smile rueful. 'No need to worry, dearest. Do you think I would let such a thing happen to me twice?'

He frowned down at her. 'You mean you came to the play tonight, prepared for this eventuality? Dear lord, yes, of course you did. Now I'm being naïve.'

A decided chill ran through Lenore. 'No,' she denied. 'I did not come prepared. I happen to be on the Pill. I have been ever since shortly after Kirsty was born. I kept taking it after the divorce because it gave me mental peace.'

'You've had other lovers since the divorce, I suppose,' he muttered.

'No!' she denied again, more forcefully this time. 'I have

not. And I don't think of you as a lover, Zachary. You're my love, my one and only love.'

There was reproach in her voice and hurt in her eyes. Zachary said nothing for a moment and when Lenore went to walk away from him he grabbed her and spun her back against him. 'I believe you,' he rasped. 'I must. Oh, my lovely Lenore, my beautiful, irresistible Lenore...' His hands were roving over her once more and she was powerless to stop their excitement. 'Don't let's argue. I want to make love to you all night. I want to put a lifetime of pleasure into a few hours. I want to do everything with you I've always wanted to do...'

Lenore groaned with a type of dismay when he swept her up into his arms and made for the bedroom. Logic demanded Zachary's words held no promise of a future together. But her love for him weakened any resolve to make an issue of his lack of commitment. She also pushed aside the worry that his feelings for her might be nothing but a sexual thing, easily burnt out now that he'd crossed the line which had kept them apart these many years.

But these doubts were quickly forgotten when she was in his arms once more. He must love her to want her so much, she reasoned. He must!

They lay in bed shortly after dawn, watching the rain beat against the window. The curtains were pulled back, their view that of an enclosed and very private courtyard, full of palms and other greenery.

'Did you know Turramurra has the highest rainfall of any suburb in Sydney?' Zachary remarked softly.

'Yes, I had heard that somewhere. It's good for the garden, though.' Lenore sighed the sigh of a sated woman, her body exhausted. She might have drifted off to sleep at long last if that same body hadn't felt the call of nature. 'I have to go to the bathroom,' she said. 'I'll probably have a shower while I'm there. *Alone*, this time,' she threw back over her shoulder.

He laughed and she pulled a face at him. But when she finally made it under the hot jets of water, she found herself recalling Zachary's insistence on having a shower with her earlier in the night, followed by his insistence on several other activities while in there. It really worried Lenore that this last night had been reduced to nothing more than a fulfillment of all Zachary's fantasies where she was concerned.

Lenore was fully awake by the time she snapped off the shower and dried herself, blowdrying her hair till it fluffed out down her back in a riot of waves. Inspecting her face in the mirror, she found her skin glowing, her eyes bright and her mouth a deep purple. Bruised, most likely, she decided.

She groaned when she looked at the rest of her body. Thank the lord it was raining. It would be long sleeves for her today. Wrapping a towel around herself sarong-style, Lenore left the bathroom and told Zachary that she was hungry and she might as well make some breakfast for them both, so what did he want?

He yawned and stretched, bringing her eyes to the rippling muscles in his broad chest and lean hard stomach. For a man of forty-five he still had an incredible body. 'You mean you're going to feed me as well?' he drawled.

'As well as what?' she retorted.

He totally ignored her, his eyes narrowing with that now familiar look as it raked over her. 'Take off that towel,' he said thickly.

'No. I'm making breakfast.'

'Then make it in the nude. I want you naked, Lenore.'

'Well, if that's all you want then I want you out of here!' she lashed back with such unexpected venom she shocked them both.

But reality had suddenly crashed through Lenore and she hadn't liked what she'd seen, either in Zachary or herself. All those encounters, those positions, those torrid matings.

They'd been nothing but sex, she realised with dawning horror.

Oh, she'd deluded herself by calling them love, but they didn't feel like love at this moment. They felt like lust. All of a sudden, she felt cheap and sordid and far, far worse than she had ever felt with Nathan. At least he'd been her husband. *This* man…why, he didn't love her either. Not the sort of love she craved. She could see that now.

'You don't mean that,' he rasped, clearly shocked.

'I most certainly do. Go back to your wife, Zachary. I don't want you any more. I…I…' Her voice broke, as did her heart. Sobbing, she turned to drop her head into shaking hands and cry tears of utter despair.

He was beside her in an instant, taking her in his arms, saying and doing anything to soothe her. But she would not be soothed.

'You don't l…love me,' she wailed. 'You just wanted to…to…'

'No,' he groaned. 'No!' he repeated in a pained shout, shaking her a little. 'That's not true. Maybe I was trying to exorcise you at first, when I took you up against the wall. But you'd sent me crazy with desire over the years, Lenore, whether you meant to or not. Then last night, when your tyre was flat, I couldn't believe that was an accident. I thought…the bitch has played me for a sucker. Old tapes went off in my mind and I thought you'd decided to win me through fair means or foul and yes, I lost my temper. Brother, I was so infuriated with you I thought I would explode. But my anger was simply another face of my love for you, just as my lust is another face of my love for you. I wallowed in both last night, Lenore, because they're far safer emotions than love. They can be controlled or superficially satisfied. Love can't. Love goes on and on and on and nothing can ever fill the empty place in my heart that yearns for you and you alone.'

'But you can have me, Zachary,' she burst forth. 'You can get a divorce. *Marry* me.'

'I can't.'

She stared at him. 'You mean you *won't*.'

'That's right,' he said firmly. 'I mean I won't.'

Lenore knew there was no point in arguing with him. His mind was made up. He was the same inflexible Zachary he'd always been, the same stubborn, proud, noble, decent man she'd fallen in love with.

'I see,' she said.

Shrugging his hands from her shoulders, she walked away, both to put a physical distance between them and to give her the opportunity to gather herself for what she was about to say. Finally, she turned, only to find that it might have been better to have remained where she was. To see him standing there in all his naked glory, clearly wanting her again, was hard on her resolve.

Swallowing, she embarked on the most important speech she had ever made in all her life. For she was fighting for her love, fighting for her future and her happiness. 'Yes, I really do see, Zachary. You have a code of standards or beliefs which demand that your marriage must be saved regardless of your feelings or mine. Your first loyalty—and priority—is to your wife and children. A very laudable commitment, and one which I appreciate and understand, especially now that you've told me about what happened with your parents.

'I admire you for your stance, Zachary. I always have. In the past, I would have said you did the right thing. Without question. But now...today...I believe you might be making a mistake to keep on throwing yourself on the sacrificial pyre of a marriage that can't possibly be making you happy. Your boys are nearly men. Your wife seems more interested in her sister's welfare than yours. Don't your own feelings rate here? Or mine?'

'No,' he said sternly. 'They don't. I made a vow, Lenore. I mean to keep that vow.'

'You broke it last night,' she pointed out, more in desperation than a desire to hurt him. But he looked pained all the same.

'That's my guilt to carry around. But Felicity will never know if we never tell her. Our marriage can go on as before.'

'You honestly believe that?'

'I do. As I said to you once, the truth can hurt, far more than lies. I would only hurt her by confessing our affair. I'd certainly hurt her if I divorced her. You don't know Felicity, Lenore. She's a sweet, gentle soul who needs a man to look after her. Oh, I admit she wasn't the right match for me all along, but I didn't know that till after she was pregnant with Emery and then it was too late. But she's been a good wife, and she's a damned good mother to my sons. I can't find happiness over her misery, Lenore. And I won't destroy my sons' good opinion of me.'

'But how can you go from my bed back to hers?' Lenore wailed.

'But you'll do it?' she gasped.

'Yes.'

'My God...'

'I could stand it, Lenore, if I knew I could see you from time to time.'

When he came towards her, she backed away in horror. 'No, don't you touch me. Don't you touch me ever again.' Tears began streaming down her face, tears of frustration and desolation. 'I...I want you to go. And I don't want you ever to come back.'

His face was grim, his eyes hollow and haunted. 'You would condemn me to that, Lenore? I thought you loved me...'

It was too much. His face. His words. The emptiness in his voice. With a cry of torment Lenore threw herself, weeping, back into his arms.

CHAPTER TEN

'How intriguing, Gemma,' Ava said as she stared at the old photograph, then at Gemma's birth certificate. 'What do you think, Melanie?'

'I think Gemma's assumption about her real age is probably correct,' was Melanie's considered opinion. 'But there *is* a slim possibility this is your mother pregnant with a child before *you*, Gemma, a child that might not have lived.'

Gemma frowned at this possibility, which had never occurred to her. It was a logical thought, yet everything inside her rejected it. She was convinced she was older than her birth certificate stated. This was *herself* her mother was pregnant with, not a dead brother or sister. She was sure of it.

'And I suppose there is also a slim possibility that your mother is still alive,' Melanie went on matter-of-factly, 'but I wouldn't like you to get your hopes up. On top of that, this birth certificate could be a complete forgery, full of all sorts of lies.'

Dismay filled Gemma as she picked up the document again and stared at it more closely. A forgery. Her heart sank even further.

'It would also be foolish to presume your parents were married at all. You said you didn't find any marriage certificate in your father's papers.'

'Do you have to keep saying horrible things?' Kirsty burst out crossly. 'Can't you see you're making Gemma unhappy?'

'No, no, Kirsty,' Gemma refuted. 'I wanted to talk about this. I appreciate hearing Melanie's thoughts. It's better I have realistic expectations rather than go round with my head in the clouds.'

'I can't imagine anyone less likely to have her head in the clouds than you, Gemma. What's this all about?'

All four female faces jerked round and up to stare at their unexpected intruder. They'd thought they were alone in the house that Sunday morning. Heavy rain had kept them indoors so they'd decided on a game of Monopoly on the living-room floor, and it was while playing that Ava had started questioning Gemma about her life in Lightning Ridge and soon Gemma had been telling her new friends about the mystery of her birth and her mother. The game had been temporarily abandoned while Gemma produced the photo and her birth certificate for the others to look at and comment on. Now it looked like she would have to show them to a fourth person. Nathan Whitmore.

'Dad!' Kirsty exclaimed with delight on her face. 'What are you doing here?'

'It's not much fun at the beach, sweetie, when it's raining cats and dogs.'

'Oh, *Dad*,' his daughter said with laughter and reproach in her voice. 'As if you ever go down to the beach much anyway. One quick dip and you're back, sitting at that computer of yours, creating away like someone possessed. You should see him, Gemma. Totally off in another world. I could go in and confess to murder and he'd say, "That's nice, sweetie".'

Ava laughed. 'That does sound like you, Nathan, you must admit.'

Melanie climbed gracefully to her feet. 'I'll make you some coffee and a sandwich, Nathan.'

'Thanks, Melanie. I could do with something to eat.'

'That's another thing he forgets to do when he writes, Gemma. Eat! He used to drive Mum up the wall once he got his nose into a new play. So how's it going, Dad? Another ripper for Hollywood to buy like the last one?'

'The only thing ripper about the play I'm working on at the moment,' he countered drily, 'is the amount of paper I'm ripping up. I don't know what's wrong with me. I can't seem to concentrate.'

He came forward, his eyes returning to Gemma who had once again failed miserably not to stare at him. But Nathan in tight blue jeans and a navy blue sweatshirt looked less formidable yet more devastatingly attractive than ever. He sat down in a nearby armchair and leant forward to pick up both the old photograph and the birth certificate which had been dropped back in to the middle of the Monopoly board.

'Has Gemma told you about her mysterious history, Nathan?' Ava asked as his eyes went from the certificate to the photo to the certificate again.

Steely grey eyes lifted to lock with Gemma's nervous brown ones. 'No,' he said. 'She also seems to have made a small miscalculation about her age. According to this...' he waved the birth certificate '...she's only eighteen.'

'That's probably a forgery,' Kirsty piped up before Gemma could fashion her own defence. 'If you turn that photo over, Dad, you'll see it's dated Christmas, 1973. Gemma believes that's her mother pregnant with her so that means she was born early in 1974 which makes her nearly twenty.'

Nathan stared at Gemma, then down at the photo for an elongated time, then up at Gemma once again. 'What do you mean, you *believe* this is your mother? Don't you *know*?'

She shook her head. 'My father refused to speak of her other than to tell me she died when I was born and to say I took after her, though whether he meant in looks or something else I'm not sure. After he died, I found this photograph hidden in his things. It *has* to be my mother. She has the same name. Who else could it be?'

'Who else indeed? Stefan and Mary…' He frowned and glanced at the birth certificate again. 'It says here your father's name is Jon, yet the photo says Stefan. Which one's right, Stefan or Jon?'

'Stefan, I think. He was definitely Swedish. I think the Jon is an alias. As far as the Smith part is concerned…it's likely that's an alias as well.'

'Mmm.' Nathan studied the photograph again. 'You seem to have similar colouring to your mother, and a similar shaped face, but it's hard to compare you properly with her wearing sunglasses. You don't seem to take after your father at all, except perhaps in your build. You're a much bigger girl than your mother.'

Gemma flushed when Nathan's eyes flicked to her full breasts which lay braless beneath her thin white top. Thinking he'd be absent from the house that day, she'd dressed very informally in jeans and an old T-shirt. Quite frankly, her bras were of a very cheap variety and they didn't fit all that well. She left them off whenever she could but in truth her breasts were the kind that needed some restraint. Left free, they jiggled alarmingly when she walked. Even when she sat as breathlessly still as she was sitting at that moment, they were an eyeful.

Nathan seemed to have difficulty dragging *his* eyes away from them, a fact which had the most embarrassing effect. Gemma knew if she looked down she would find her nipples poking at the thin material. The sensation was so alien to her—and so shameful—that she desperately wanted to cover herself with her hands. But how could she do that without looking ridiculous? All she could think of was to draw her knees up and lean forward to wrap her arms around them so that her breasts were hidden against her thighs.

Melanie's re-entrance with a small tray of food was a very welcome distraction. 'I see Gemma has shown you the photo and her birth certificate,' the housekeeper said as she placed the tray down on the small table beside the armchair.

'Perhaps you could make some enquiries about her mother for her, Nathan. She's anxious to find out if the lady might be still alive, or, barring that, if some of her family are.'

'Do you want me to do that, Gemma?'

Now she was forced to look back up at him again. 'Yes, I do, but…won't that cost a lot of money?'

'Only if you hire a private investigator. But I don't think that's necessary to begin with. I could get Moira to pop down to the births, deaths and marriages department during her lunch hour. And I have an acquaintance in the police department who could give me some pertinent information. But what makes you think your mother might be still alive? Do you have reason to believe your father lied to you about that?'

'I think my father lied to me about a lot of things,' she murmured, and dropped her eyes again.

'I suppose you're referring to the black opal,' Nathan said on a rueful note.

'What black opal?' Kirsty asked.

'Yes, what black opal, Gemma?' Ava joined in.

She told them about the opal.

'Good grief, Nathan,' Ava burst out after Gemma finished her tale. 'That has to be the opal that disappeared the day Byron married Irene!'

'Yes,' he admitted. 'The Heart of Fire.'

'What a passionate name for a mere opal,' Melanie remarked in her passionless voice. She hadn't rejoined them on the floor, having perched herself instead on the arm of an empty lounge-chair. 'To be honest, I've always thought opals rather cold-looking stones.'

'Not this one,' Nathan said.

'No, certainly not,' Gemma insisted warmly. 'It's the most beautiful thing I've ever seen.'

'I'll bet you were spitting chips when you found out it wasn't yours, Gemma,' Kirsty sympathised. 'I know I would have been.'

Gemma smiled. 'I wasn't too happy. But Byron's given me a lovely reward for bringing it back safe and sound.'

'But how did your father get his hands on the opal?' Ava re-entered the conversation, frowning. 'We always thought it had to have been stolen by one of the guests at the wedding. Or possibly one of the hired helps. Byron was planning to present it to Irene as a gift at the reception,' she told her intrigued audience. 'The opal was to be a token gesture to symbolise the healing of the rift between our two families. From what I can vaguely recall, the opal had something to do with the original feud between Byron's and my father and Irene's father, but I never did know what, exactly. Do you know what actually happened, Nathan?'

'No, I don't.'

'Well, I suppose it isn't too hard to guess,' Ava swept on excitedly, clearly in her element. 'I do know David Whitmore and Stewart Campbell were prospecting partners and best friends once, before they fell out, that is. It seems reasonable to presume their argument was probably over the opal. Maybe my father found it and refused to share it with Stewart Campbell.'

She heaved a melodramatic sigh. 'Whatever, they went their separate ways and became rivals in business, setting up opposing opal-trading companies here in Sydney, though Campbell's eventually branched out into other jewellery as well. Even when the original enemies passed away, their children were left a legacy of hatred and bitterness, especially on the Campbell side, which Byron has always claimed he hoped to heal by his marriage to Irene. But I still think—well, I find it hard to believe that—I mean…um—er…'

Her voice trailed away and Kirsty immediately jumped in. 'Don't stop there, Ava! We're all dying of curiosity. Dad, why haven't you told me any of this fascinating stuff before? Gosh, it's just like Romeo and Juliet!'

Ava slid worried eyes in the direction of Nathan, who

looked resigned. 'You might as well complete the saga now, Ava. I won't tell Byron, but don't paint him too blackly. I'm sure he meant well, and there wasn't a man in the world who could have made Irene happy.'

'Byron always means well,' Ava muttered. 'Still...I dare say he suffered enough for his greed. Everyone knew Byron asked Irene to marry him, not because he loved her, but because he wanted the two companies to merge. Campbell's marketing strategies with their new chain-type stores had been putting a big dent in Whitmore Opals' profits for quite a few years. We couldn't compete, especially when Campbell's kept targeting opals as the one gemstone they sold cheaply.

'Unfortunately for Byron, he didn't find out till after the wedding that Campbell's would never belong to Irene. She'd merely let him think that. In reality, when Stewart Campbell died the previous year, control had passed to his second wife, who was not fond of her husband's first-born daughter. Irene's mother had died when she was a baby and her father had quickly married again, a wealthy socialite named Adele who had two children by him—a daughter, Celeste, and a son, Damian. Adele eventually handed over control of Campbell's to her daughter, Celeste, who's proved to be one of the toughest, meanest, cleverest business-women ever to draw breath.'

'Beautiful, though,' Nathan inserted.

'Yes, but bad through and through. She has two pleasures in life, it seems. Scoring victories over Whitmore Opals and sleeping with younger and younger men as she gets older and older.'

'I don't think the young men mind, Ava,' Nathan chuckled drily. 'Would that all women looked as good as Celeste Campbell! Besides, she's not that old. I doubt she's even turned forty yet.'

Gemma told herself it wasn't jealousy that made her direct the conversation to other matters than this detestable-sounding woman whom Nathan felt compelled to compli-

ment. 'But what happened back at Byron's wedding, Ava?'
she asked abruptly. 'I want to know how the opal was stolen and what happened afterwards.'

'Didn't I tell you that? I didn't? Sorry.' She smiled. 'I
get muddled sometimes. Well, I was a flower-girl at the
wedding, and no one told me anything but when you're a
little kid in a mostly grown-up household you learn to keep
your ears and eyes open. The reception, for some reason,
was being held at Belleview—I think the second Mrs
Campbell refused to have it at Campbell Court.

'Anyway, if I recall rightly, Byron went into the library
just before the sit-down part of the meal started and the
wall safe was wide open and the opal gone. Boy, was there
a to-do. The police were called and people were searched
but the opal was never found. It totally spoilt the reception.
People say it was the opal that caused the marriage to go
sour, that it brought bad luck, which is hog-wash. Even if
Byron had adored Irene and kissed her feet every day, that
woman would never have been happy. She was totally—

'Oh, my goodness, Gemma!' Ava broke off abruptly
from what she'd been saying. 'An astounding thought has
just occurred to me. Maybe your father was an international
jewel-thief who came here from Europe and somehow wangled an invitation to the wedding, stole the opal, then spent
the rest of his life hiding out at Lightning Ridge so that
Interpol couldn't find him.'

'For pity's sake, spare us your romantic solutions, Ava,'
Nathan reprimanded impatiently. 'If Gemma's father had
been an international jewel-thief, he'd have sold the
damned thing to a fence and provided a better life for his
daughter than the back-blocks of Lightning Ridge. I doubt
very much if he had anything to do with the original theft.
Personally, I think he came across the opal quite accidentally and was too afraid to sell it or even show it to anyone.
He knew it had to be stolen property.'

'That's as much supposition as what I said,' Ava argued,
though feebly.

'Maybe,' he admitted, 'but since the original theft happened so long ago, it would be almost impossible to uncover the truth now one way or the other. Besides, Byron doesn't want it all dragged up again. It would only open old wounds between the Whitmores and the Campbells, and Celeste Campbell has enough knives ready for our backs already.'

Nathan returned to eating his snack and Ava subsided into chastened silence. Gemma felt sorry for her. She was such a dear, but did lack self-confidence. She allowed people to ride roughshod over her far too much. Her barb about Byron always meaning well was very telling, however. Still, maybe she had herself to blame if she allowed others to interfere in her life. She was thirty years old and should not be living in her brother's home off her brother's charity. What she needed was a job and a life of her own!

Thinking of jobs reminded Gemma of her own employment at Whitmore Opals. She was to begin Japanese lessons at a local business college in the morning, attending lectures every Monday, Wednesday and Friday for the next four weeks after which she was supposed to be able at least to make herself understood by a Japanese client. She hadn't said so to Nathan but she found the prospect daunting. If only she'd taken a language at school. But her father had steered her away from what he'd considered high-falutin' subjects.

'I'll keep this birth certificate with me,' Nathan said on finishing his sandwich and coffee. He handed her back the photo. 'Don't expect miracles,' he warned.

'I'm grateful for anything you can find out,' she said with sincerity, meeting his eyes now with far more ease. She'd grown used to his presence and thought her breasts were back to normal. Not that she was risking anything. Her knees would remain up till he left the room.

'I don't want to put you to any trouble for dinner, tonight, Melanie,' he went on when she came over to pick up the empty tray. 'I'll buy us all some Chinese takeaway.'

'Oh, goodie,' Ava said, clapping her hands delightedly.

'Yum,' Kirsty agreed.

Gemma said nothing. She'd never had Chinese take-away. Or takeaway anything other than the hamburgers and chips she'd been given free from the café. The housekeeping money had never stretched to such luxuries. She wasn't even sure if she liked Chinese food, though she'd always liked the smells emanating from the Chinese restaurant not far from the café she'd worked in.

'Not for me, Nathan, thank you,' Melanie said. 'I'm going to visit my brother and his family tonight for dinner.' Everyone watched as she carried the tray from the room with a quiet dignity. Gemma was beginning to admire her more and more.

'Then it's just the four of us,' Nathan said, smiling as his eyes travelled around the remaining three women to finally land—and stay—on Gemma. 'Do you like Chinese food?'

She found his gentle tone and direct gaze both disarming and disturbing. God, she hoped she wasn't blushing. 'I…I'm sure I will.'

He blinked disbelief at her. 'You've never had Chinese food before?'

Her laughter was self-conscious. 'I think, if I stay here long enough, you'll find out I haven't had a lot of things before.'

'Really.' Those lazy grey eyes glittered with dry amusement. 'I'll look forward to introducing you, then, to all those delights as yet untasted.'

Gemma stared at him. Was he laughing at her naïveté? Surely, he couldn't mean… No, no, he couldn't. *Could he*? Heat zoomed into her cheeks. 'I'm sure you'll find my reactions quite amusing,' she retorted, feeling flushed and flustered.

'Amusing?' His laugh was low and dark, seemingly vibrating with hidden meaning. 'Oh, no…not amusing. Refreshingly different, perhaps. And delightful, I'm sure. Our Gemma is delightful, isn't she, Ava?'

'Most assuredly.'

'Oh, my God, I just remembered!' Kirsty squealed and jumped to her feet. 'Dad hasn't seen my room yet.' She hurdled Gemma and grabbed her father's hand, dragging him out of his chair. 'Come on, Dad. Come on, Gemma.'

'Oh, no, you go ahead,' Gemma said, her attentions refocusing on her breasts once again. If her nipples were anything to go by, Nathan's cryptic comments had excited, rather than appalled her. Dear God, if he ever made a move on her would she have the strength to resist? 'I...I'll stay here and help Ava put this Monopoly away.'

'No, don't put it away,' Nathan called back over his shoulder. 'I'll challenge you all to a game this afternoon. I've given up the idea of writing anything this weekend.'

'Fantastic!' Kirsty exclaimed happily.

Gemma tried not to groan. She wondered if she could dash up and change without it looking odd. Yes, she would have to. She simply would. She could drag on a sweater of some sort. She would say she was getting cold.

'Gemma...'

'Yes, Ava?'

'I'm sorry if I upset you over what I said about your father being a jewel-thief.'

'But you didn't!'

'I must have. I can see it in your face.'

Gemma had to laugh. What Ava was seeing was concern over her swollen breasts and nipples. 'I'm not upset, Ava. But I am cold.'

'Cold?' She was clearly amazed.

'I'm from Lightning Ridge, remember? Anything under thirty-five is chilly. I won't be a sec.'

She dashed away.

What a pity Nathan and Kirsty had made slow progress up the stairs. They were just strolling along the corridor when Gemma, after taking the stairs two at a time, careered around the corner, her breasts in full voluptuous sway beneath her thin white top.

She saw Nathan turn, saw the direction of his eyes. She immediately skidded to a halt, but the rapid expulsion of air from her lungs did not help the situation.

'So you decided to join us after all,' he said with a cool composure she could only envy. 'I'm so glad. I've a feeling I'm going to need support once I enter this chamber of darkness.'

Kirsty laughed by his side. 'Chamber of darkness? What funny things you say, Dad. It's a gorgeous room!' And she flung open the door. 'Enter all who dare.' And she stood back against the door to wave her father inside.

'Shall we dare, Gemma?' he said, walking over to link arms with her before she could stop him.

'I don't think you're going to give me a choice,' she returned, a slight tremor in her voice.

'No,' he said, his tone as hard as his narrow-eyed gaze. 'I don't think I am.'

CHAPTER ELEVEN

GEMMA would never have believed she could be so grateful to Kirsty's room.

'Good God!' Nathan exclaimed on entering, his arm slipping out of Gemma's as his handsome and horrified face surveyed the walls.

'What do you think, Dad?' Kirsty asked, giggling.

'It's ghastly,' he said, and threw Gemma a reproving look. She didn't mind. Reproving looks were a welcome change from hard sexy ones, and shocked exclamations infinitely preferable to muttered comments which sounded suspiciously like sexual threats.

'Mum thought so too,' Kirsty agreed happily.

'Melanie let you do this?' he directed more at Gemma than his daughter.

'She even helped,' Gemma told him.

'Good God,' he repeated.

'Don't get your knickers in a knot, Dad,' Kirsty reassured blithely. 'The posters come off the walls easily enough, which is just as well. I can take them all home with me when I go.'

He swung round at this. 'Oh? You planning on deserting the ship already?'

'I might…after the Easter break. Gemma will be going to work by then and Pops is sure to be home. You know what he's like with teenage girls. He drove poor Jade out of the house.'

'Only after Jade drove poor Byron right up the wall!' her father countered caustically. 'That girl would try the patience of a saint. And for your information, madam, Jade left this house of her own accord. As for *your* going home...I think your mother might need a little more peace and quiet before you inflict *this* on her.' His hand made a sweeping gesture around the room, encompassing the eye-popping walls and bed.

'Nah. Mum misses me. I can tell. She misses you too, Dad,' Kirsty added, a catch in her voice.

'Let's not get into one of those arguments again, Kirsty. It's a no-win situation. Unlike Monopoly,' he swept on, his momentary grimness replaced by a teasing grin. 'I aim to whip your butt this afternoon, madam.'

'You and whose army?' Kirsty laughed, and ran from the room. Her father dashed after her.

'Coming, Gemma?' he threw back over his shoulder.

'I'll be with you shortly,' she hedged. 'I have to get something from my room.'

Five minutes later, with her traitorous body enveloped in a huge grey sloppy Joe, Gemma went down to the living-room where Nathan and Kirsty and Ava were all ready to play. Melanie had opted out since she had to leave mid-afternoon for her visit to her family. Gemma did her best to concentrate on the game, but after a while, whenever it wasn't her turn to throw the dice, her mind started drifting to thoughts of Nathan.

Was he still in love with his ex-wife? she puzzled. He'd certainly spoken of her with care and consideration up in Kirsty's room, and clearly been frustrated when Kirsty said her mother missed him. Gemma had wondered more than once since seeing Nathan kissing Lenore in the billiard-room if they were still sleeping with each other.

Probably not, she now decided, since he was showing such a sexual interest in *her*. Gemma might have allowed her own feelings for him full rein, if everyone hadn't warned her about him. First there had been Ma, then Jade, then Melanie. Even Kirsty's recurring theme that her father was still in love with her mother was a type of warning.

She didn't want to become involved with a man still in love with his ex-wife, whose only feelings for her were lust. The thought that Nathan would try to seduce her merely for sexual gratification brought such a stab of pain to her heart that she was shocked. Could she still be naïve enough to be falling in love with him? Dear God, she hoped not. She'd been doing her best all week to behave like a good, sensible girl. She'd heeded all warnings, kept out of his way and avoided staring when he came into the room.

Till today...

Today she'd stared at him again like an infatuated idiot, making him hotly aware of how attractive she found him, making her own body respond in a way she'd never felt before. But she could not deny there was a fierce underlying excitement in the feel of her flesh all aroused and a-tingle beneath her clothes.

She'd seen a video movie once where a man had sucked at a woman's breast. She'd found it repulsive at the time, thinking that the woman could not possibly have been enjoying such an activity. Now, she knew it would probably be very exciting.

'Your turn, Gemma.'

Her eyes gradually focused through the haze her thinking had evoked to find Nathan looking at her closely. Her heart, she realised, was racing madly, her lips parted slightly to let her softly panting breaths escape. His eyes fastened on those lips before lifting to narrow on her wide, unblinking gaze. It was impossible to look away, impossible to stop the heat that accompanied the mental image of Nathan bent over her bare breasts, taking one of the aching tips deep into those beautifully shaped lips of his.

His smile was slow, his voice wry. 'The dice, Gemma.'

She gulped then threw the dice, flustered with herself and furious with him. He knew. Maybe not exactly what she was thinking, but that she had been thinking of him, thinking of him and sex.

He had no right to know what she was thinking, she

stormed internally, anger her only salvation from total
shame. With agitated movements she hopped her token
along the board on to Mayfair, which was not only owned
by Nathan but had two hotels on it.

Her groan echoed a lot of things.

'Methinks Madam Smith here is in a spot of trouble,'
Nathan drawled.

Gemma refused to look at him, bending her head to start
counting out the remainder of her money.

'You haven't got enough money to pay him,' Kirsty said
with the satisfaction of a child glad to see one more opposing player go bankrupt. Ava had already gone broke and
was merely watching.

'Never mind, Gemma,' Ava said sympathetically. 'You
can help me make afternoon tea.'

'What a good idea!' Gemma plonked all her money and
properties down in front of Nathan and jumped to her feet.

By the time they returned with a pot of tea and plate of
biscuits, Kirsty and Nathan were in the throes of Nathan's
death rattle. Good, Gemma thought vengefully when she
saw he couldn't possibly win. Finally, he surrendered and
started helping Kirsty pack the game away.

'I might pop down to the hospital to visit Byron,' he
commented over tea. 'What time do you folks want Chinese
tonight? Seven-thirty do?'

'Yes,' Ava agreed. 'That way we'll be finished before
the Sunday night movie comes on. There's quite a good
one tonight. *Double Trouble*. Have you seen it, Gemma?'

'No, I don't think so. I—er—haven't seen all that many
movies, actually. We didn't have a television at home.' And
going to the movies was expensive.

'Didn't have a TV?' Kirsty gaped at her.

'Don't get me wrong,' Gemma explained. 'I saw plenty
of TV over the years at school and at friends' houses. And
there was one on the wall of the café I worked in, but Dad
and I lived rather—er—roughly, out in the opal fields. In
a dugout, actually.'

'A dugout?' Ava looked perplexed. 'You mean you lived in a hole in the ground?'

'In a way. It was dug out of the side of a hill.'

'How big was it, Gemma?' Nathan enquired, looking genuinely interested.

'Not big at all. One large room about twenty by ten, I guess. One end was the kitchen, the middle was where we ate, and our beds were down the other end.'

'But didn't you have your own rooms and bathroom?' Kirsty asked, still looking horrified.

Gemma smiled. 'Afraid not. We had a pit toilet in a wooden shed outside, and a water tank with a sort of shower rigged up under it. When it failed to rain we collected artesian water in drums and filled the tank that way.'

Gemma gradually realised they were all staring at her as if she was a little green man from Mars. Nathan's face was the first to change from shock to admiration. Gemma tried not to respond to his admiring look but she found it impossible to stop the wave of melting warmth that flooded through her under his appreciative gaze.

God, but this was more weakening than his desire, she realised, for it left her totally defenceless and quite limp. If he touched her now, she would definitely dissolve into mush.

Fortunately, that couldn't happen at the moment. Gemma vowed to always keep people around her when Nathan was home, and soon, with a bit of luck, this infernal infatuation would die a natural death.

'I don't know how you stood it,' Ava said, awe in her voice.

Gemma shrugged, the action feeling oddly heavy. 'I didn't know any different, then later you get used to it. You can get used to anything after a while.'

'I can't imagine any of the females I know ever getting used to living in such primitive conditions,' Nathan said testily. 'Maybe you'll appreciate what you have more now, madam,' he directed at Kirsty.

She pulled a face at him. 'You always have to turn everything into a lecture.'

'True. Which reminds me, time for your homework.'

'I should get back to my painting too, I suppose,' Ava sighed.

'And I have some ironing to do,' Gemma said, standing up. No way was she going to stay here so that Nathan could suggest she accompany him to the hospital. Not only did she not want to encounter the intimidating Byron again so soon, but the thought of being alone in a car with Nathan was highly unnerving.

'*Ironing*?' Nathan's frown was dark. 'What ironing? We have a lady comes in to do the ironing.'

'Not mine,' she countered crisply. 'I'll do my own ironing, thank you. *And* my own washing.'

'Then you can do it some other time. Come with me to the hospital. I'm sure Byron would like to meet you.'

'Oh, but I met him yesterday,' she quickly prevaricated. 'Lenore took Kirsty and me to visit him, didn't she, Kirsty?'

'Sure did, Dad, and Pops is still the biggest bossy-boots in the entire world. Heaven help us when he comes home here. When is he coming home here, by the way?'

'Next Friday, I think.'

Kirsty groaned. 'Can we go to Avoca with you next weekend, then?'

'If you like…' His eyes slid slowly across to Gemma. 'You probably haven't seen the sea, Gemma, have you?'

'No…no.'

'Gosh!' Kirsty exclaimed. 'How exciting to be able to show someone something like the sea for the first time. I can't wait!'

'Oh, but I…'

'Can't wait either, I'll warrant,' he finished for her, his eyes and voice firm. 'You'll love the sea, Gemma. And you'll love Avoca. I guarantee it.'

His steady gaze held hers a moment longer than necessary before he turned away to begin striding purposefully from the room. When Kirsty ran after her father, asking him to pick up something for her from home while he was on the road, Gemma wasn't really listening. She was, instead, staring after Nathan with a throat and tongue suddenly gone dry.

Gemma kept telling herself that he couldn't have, in that moment, made up his mind to show her something far more intimate than the sea up at Avoca. No man could be that presumptuous or that arrogantly confident of his own sex appeal, she reasoned agitatedly. No man could be that... wicked.

For it was wicked to deliberately plan a seduction, wasn't it? Wicked for a man of his age and experience to take advantage of a young girl's infatuation. Wicked to make her want him to do just that.

Totally besieged now by moral confusion, Gemma's mind turned to the down-to-earth advice Ma had given her in the letter she'd received on Friday in answer to *her* hurried, worried letter posted the previous Tuesday. She'd penned in a dripping Biro:

I did warn you about them city men, didn't I, love? They can be powerfully attractive, especially the rich handsome ones. But they don't marry poor little misses from Lightning Ridge. Go to bed with him if you must, love, by all means, but keep that loving heart of yours firmly in your chest and don't forget the condoms!

But would she keep her heart firmly in her chest if she allowed Nathan to make love to her? He only had to look at her and the blood started rushing around her body like a cyclist pedalling furiously round one of those circular tracks. Round and round they went, faster and faster, till they had to be as giddy as she was feeling.

Suddenly, Gemma realised she was standing in the liv-

ing-room all alone. Sighing, she turned to walk out through
the enormous kitchen and down the corridor to the equally
enormous laundry area, complete with automatic washers
and driers and a sewing-machine and ironing-boards all set
up. The first time she'd seen this set-up, Gemma had been
struck dumb, but it was amazing how quickly one got used
to luxuries, amazing how quickly one became corrupted by
money.

And other things...

Nathan's return from the hospital showed a totally different
Nathan from the one who'd left Belleview a couple of
hours previously. He was taciturn and preoccupied, snapping at Kirsty when she complained he'd forgotten to pick
up the book she'd asked him to get from her mother.

'You'll just have to do without,' he said sharply. 'I'll get
it tomorrow on my way home from work.'

'What about when you go to pick up the Chinese food?
Mum's place is only a couple of miles down the road.'

His jaw clenched down hard. 'Kirsty. Can you or can
you *not* do without this book tomorrow?'

'I suppose I can do without it,' she muttered irritably.
'But you'd better write me a note saying why I haven't got
it with me!'

'My pleasure.' And he stalked off.

'Brother, what's got into him?' she complained to both
Gemma and Ava. The three girls had regathered in the family-room, which had the biggest television Gemma had ever
seen, not to mention lovely comfortable squashy sofas just
made to curl up in. It was the most casual room in the
house—*and* the most modern—with one totally glass wall
overlooking the pool and tennis court. At the moment, however, the vertical blinds were drawn, shutting out the view
and the never-ending rain.

'He's probably in a bad mood because he's suffering
writer's block,' Ava suggested.

'Yeah, that's probably it,' Kirsty concurred. 'Writers! Never marry a writer, Gemma. They're impossible!'

'Maybe Mr Whitmore said something to upset him,' Gemma counter-suggested.

'Possibly,' Ava replied, 'though Nathan doesn't usually let Byron or anyone else for that matter get under his skin.'

'Mum gets under his skin,' Kirsty volunteered. 'She can get him mad as a hatter. There again, that's only natural. He's still in love with her.'

'Kirsty, dear,' Ava said with a sigh in her voice, 'you really must start accepting that your mother and father are no longer in love. You're lucky they've remained such good friends. Some divorces are very bitter. But their marriage is over. There won't be any reconciliation.'

'Fat lot you know!' Kirsty jumped to her feet, face flushed, green eyes glistening. 'They're going to get back together again. I know they are. Soon as Mum gets lonely she'll come and beg Dad to go back and we'll be a family again. You just wait and see. You're just jealous because you've never had a man at all, let alone a family of your own, and you want everyone to be as miserable and lonely as you are!'

So saying, Kirsty burst into tears and ran from the room. Gemma was torn between going after the noisily distraught Kirsty or staying with the silently distraught Ava. Finally, she stayed with Ava, because the poor darling looked so crushed.

'I'm so sorry, Ava,' she apologised for Kirsty. 'She didn't mean it, you know. Especially that last part...'

Ava nodded, her face pale and sad. 'She's a very mixed-up little girl. But she's wrong, about a lot of things...'

'What things?' Gemma probed gently.

'About her father for one. He's not in love with Lenore. He's *never* been in love with Lenore.'

Gemma blinked her shock at this remark.

'Nathan's incapable of loving like that,' Ava stated with chilling certainty. 'According to Byron, who knows him far better than anyone, Nathan was so damaged by his mother's irrational and destructive behaviour that he simply refuses to relate to any woman on an emotional level. Oh, he makes a charming dinner guest, and, from what I've gathered, a stunning lover. But as someone to have a close relationship with, he's an abject failure. That's why Lenore divorced him. She wanted more than he could give. Naturally, Kirsty isn't old enough to appreciate the finer points of what makes a marriage work.'

'What…what did his mother do to him?' Gemma asked shakily.

'The woman was deplorably irresponsible! Spoilt, of course. And beautiful, naturally. She came from a very wealthy family and got into drugs when she was only a teenager. Left home at eighteen, fell pregnant with Nathan at nineteen, and generally lived a very fast life. Lots of men and parties and drug-taking. She had quite a bit of money of her own so she could support this lifestyle without any trouble. Nathan was only eight when she first put him into boarding-school so that she could trip around the world with her new lover.'

'Dear heaven,' Gemma murmured.

'I don't think there was too much heaven in Nathan's upbringing,' Ava said drily. 'Every time his mother was dumped by her latest lover, she'd take Nathan out of boarding-school so she would have company. Then, later on, back he would go, often to a different school. This happened so many times his formal education was a disaster. In some ways, he was far behind the others in his class. In other ways he was far beyond them. He was always a voracious reader. But he refused to cooperate, refused to sit exams, refused to do anything. He was expelled from so many schools, his mother actually ran out of available establishments. When he was sixteen, she managed to find one more—in a different state—but he ran away within days and came home, only to find her dead of a heroin overdose.'

'Oh, my God!'

'Byron came across Nathan a few months later at King's Cross, living a life that would have made your hair curl. Not that he told me directly. I only know as much as I do because Irene liked to gossip.'

'Was Byron a family friend? How come he adopted Nathan?'

'No. He didn't know Nathan's family at all. Byron was a founding member of a charity organisation begun in the Seventies to help street kids. He'd helped lots of troubled boys before but something in Nathan touched a personal chord with him and he brought him home here. I was away at school myself at the time so this is all second-hand, I'm afraid.

'As far as the adoption is concerned... Who knows why Byron adopted him? Maybe he was the son he'd never had. Irene refused to have any children after Jade was born. Whatever, by the time I came home on my next school holiday, Nathan was very much installed, with little Jade running after him everywhere like an adoring puppy. I expected Irene to object to him, since she seemed to object to everyone and everything, but Nathan was the one person she never crossed. I think she was half afraid of him. He was quite frightening in those days.'

'In what way?' She couldn't imagine Nathan being seriously frightening.

'It's hard to explain. He had a lot of surface charm and was always gorgeous to look at. Goodness,' she laughed, 'I had quite a crush on him myself for a little while. But he could look right through you sometimes. Or you could look into *his* eyes and see nothing, just a cold emptiness.' A shudder convulsed her. 'I felt sorry for Lenore when she married him. I knew he'd make a rotten husband. He had no warmth in him.'

'But he's not like that *now*!' Gemma protested, perhaps far too vehemently, for Ava looked at her with surprise in her eyes.

'He *has* improved, I admit. Kirsty improved him.'

Gemma looked away, fearful that she had betrayed too much, fearful of what her automatic defence of Nathan kept telling her.

'Gemma...' Ava began hesitantly.

Her eyes jerked back. 'Don't say it,' she snapped. 'I'm sick of people warning me against Nathan. Sick of people telling me he's bad. I don't want to hear it any more, I tell you!'

Ava blinked at her, her sweet face quite shocked now. 'I...I was only going to suggest you come upstairs with me. I've got some clothes that don't fit me any more which I think would be very pretty on you.'

A fierce flush of embarrassment invaded Gemma's cheeks. 'Oh,' she said, then, 'Oh, God.' And she dropped her face into her hands.

A silence descended on the room.

'I know you don't want me to say this, dear,' Ava said gently at last, her hand on her shoulder. 'But I feel I must, in the circumstances. I didn't realise how you felt, which was very stupid of me. Aside from anything else I've just said, Nathan's way to old for you, dear. Way too old and way too experienced and way too...too...'

When Ava couldn't finish what she wanted to say, Gemma was compelled to look up. 'Way too *what*?' she demanded to know.

'I can't seem to find the right word. But something awful happened to Nathan either while he was growing up or after his mother died, something that twisted his ideas where women are concerned. He still desires them but basically he doesn't *like* them, let alone love them. That's not the kind of man for you, Gemma. You're warm and sweet and giving and you need a man who will appreciate you, who will love you back with his whole heart and soul. Nathan is not that sort of man.'

Gemma frowned. Every instinct inside her screamed denial of what Ava was saying. You're *wrong*, she wanted to argue. Nathan can love as strongly and deeply as any other man. He just hasn't found the right woman yet.

But if Ava was wrong, then so was every other woman who knew Nathan. They were all of the same opinion. She was the only one out of step.

'I do realise, Gemma,' Ava went on sadly, 'that Nathan must seem quite a glamorous, romantic figure to a young girl like you. But please...listen to what I'm telling you. I wouldn't like to see you hurt, because I like you, dear. I like you very much.'

Gemma was almost moved to tears by her concern. 'You're very kind, Ava. I won't forget what you've said, and I will try to be careful. But I can't promise not to find Nathan attractive. It's too late for that.'

Ava tut-tutted. 'That man has bewitched every woman at Belleview at some time or other. But who knows? Maybe he'll do the decent thing *this* time,' she bit out, 'and leave you alone.'

Gemma blinked. Who was she thinking about when she said that? Who were the women Nathan *hadn't* left alone?

Melanie? Jade, perhaps? Ava herself?

Gemma's blue eyes widened when her mind eventually moved to the one woman who had lived at Belleview, till recently. Byron's dead wife...Irene...

No, no, she instinctively rejected. He couldn't have done that. He wouldn't. Not her Nathan!

It was at that precise moment that Gemma accepted she was not merely infatuated with Nathan Whitmore any more. She was totally, blindly, irrevocably, in love with him.

CHAPTER TWELVE

BY the end of that week, Lenore knew she would never be cut out for the role of the 'other woman'. She and Zachary had snatched half an hour for a brief lunch together in the city on the Wednesday, but the whole time they were together she'd been in a highly nervous state, glancing around, afraid some mutual acquaintance would see them together. Yet, on the Saturday night previously at the Royal, she hadn't worried for a moment over such an occurrence.

Of course…they hadn't been illicit lovers then…

The same guilt poisoned any pleasure for her when she telephoned Zachary at his office. She'd agreed to ring him there, because she couldn't very well ring him at home and it was too awkward for him to contact her at the theatre during rehearsals. But by the third call she was sure she heard a sly, knowing tone in the secretary's voice once she gave her name. Zachary said she was imagining it, but nothing he could say soothed the ghastly squirming feeling in the pit of her stomach. She felt like a scarlet woman, a pariah, an evil scheming bitch who was trying to take a good man away from a virtuous wife and their innocent children.

Friday came and went without her calling Zachary at all. She simply hadn't been able to face the guilt. She drove home from the theatre, her spirits low, her depression deep. For she could see no happiness for herself with Zachary. Their relationship was as doomed as it had always been.

One night of passion had not changed that. *Nothing* would ever change that.

She turned into her street, and there was Zachary's car, parked at the kerb. And there was Zachary behind the wheel, waiting for her, a grim look on his face. That would have been bad enough, but a glance in the rearview mirror before she slid her own car into the driveway revealed Nathan's sleek navy blue Mercedes coming round the corner.

Lenore was almost sick on the spot.

Lurching to an unsteady halt, she sat in the car for a few seconds, her stomach churning. Not all the acting ability in the world was going to extricate her from this mess. There was nothing left but to brazen it out.

Lenore's mouth curved into a rueful smile as she climbed out of the car. Well, that was what Nathan had always thought she was. Brazen!

By the time she walked back down the driveway, Nathan had parked his car behind Zachary's and both men were standing on the pavement, facing each other like duellists at dawn. All that was missing was the pistols. Nathan caught the tail-end of Lenore's smile as he glanced over Zachary's shoulder at her and gave her a look that should have killed her at a hundred paces, pistol or no pistol.

But Lenore was used to Nathan's glares.

'I presume you've come for Kirsty's book at last,' she said with a blasé boldness that even astounded herself. 'She rang me last night to say you keep forgetting to pick it up.'

'I came by last Sunday for it,' he returned coldly, 'but you were otherwise occupied. Which reminds me…' Those cold grey eyes slid back to Zachary. 'If you intend sleeping with my ex-wife on a regular basis these days,' he said in the most insulting tone, 'then get yourself a less noticeable car. Or alternatively, go and do it in a sleazy motel room like most adulterers.'

Lenore's sharp intake of breath could be heard over the sudden stark silence. Her eyes swivelled to Zachary who,

as always, won her respect and admiration with his un-
shakable composure under fire.

'I appreciate your concern, Nathan,' he returned just as
coldly, 'but I think the operative word is *ex*-wife. Who
Lenore sleeps with these days is none of your concern.
She's not your wife any more.'

'Neither is she yours,' Nathan counter-attacked with the
thrust of a rapier-like tongue. 'As for Lenore's moral habits
not being my concern…then you're very much mistaken.
Unfortunately, she happens to be the mother of my fourteen-year-old daughter, who you will agree is at a very
vulnerable age. If her mother must screw around with another woman's husband, then I would appreciate she do so
with a little more discretion.

'I will not have my daughter exposed to depravity, do
you hear me?' he lashed out suddenly, stunning Lenore
with the savage emotion that blazed momentarily in those
normally implacable grey eyes.

But, as always, Nathan was quickly under control again,
only the shrugging of his shoulders under his suit jacket
showing the excruciating tension that had momentarily
seized him.

'I would have thought your own sons' welfare mattered
to you as much, Zachary,' he continued, his voice returning
to glacial. 'Clearly, I was wrong. There again, you do have
my pity. When Lenore decides she wants a man he just
doesn't stand a chance. Fortunately for me, she hasn't really
wanted me in years. I can only hope she grows bored with
you as quickly. But I doubt she will while you're married
to another woman. There's nothing so stimulating as someone society dictates you shouldn't have.'

Zachary's punch was conceived with his heart rather than
his head, so that Nathan saw it coming and ducked sideways. But Zachary still landed a glancing blow on one ear.
Nathan's fists clenched and flew up in defence, death in his
eyes.

'No!' Lenore cried, and jumped between them, facing

Nathan. 'Please don't,' she begged, tears filling her eyes. *'Please…'*

He stared at her for a few seconds, then frowned a bewildered frown. 'You really love him, Lenore?'

She nodded.

'And I love her,' Zachary declared, taking her by the shoulders and moving her to his side. 'We love each other.'

'You'll divorce Felicity, then?'

'No.'

'Why not?'

'I don't want to hurt her.'

Nathan's laugh was harsh and bitter. 'You think you're not hurting her now, you bloody fool?'

Nathan laughed again and whirled to leave.

'The book,' Lenore called after him. 'You've forgotten Kirsty's book.'

Nathan turned back, a mocking smile on his face. 'Now that's getting your priorities right, Lenore. Just don't forget your daughter *after* I'm gone, that's all I ask. And don't let Zachary forget *his* sons. They have feelings too, you know. The day you forget children are human beings with feelings is the day you condemn them to a living hell!'

Lenore stared at the man who had been her husband all those years and glimpsed, for the first time, the man he might have been, if he hadn't been warped and twisted by his childhood. He'd never revealed the horrors of his existence with his mother, her very basic knowledge of his upbringing coming from Ava via Byron. Whenever she'd tried to bring the subject up, he'd simply refused to discuss it, saying he preferred to forget a past that had little to recommend it in terms of the future.

Now she saw the depth of the damage, and was moved to real sympathy. Oh, Nathan…if only you'd let someone in, really in, there might be hope for you yet.

With an unhappy sigh, she turned and went to get the book. When she returned it was to find Nathan and Zachary talking quite civilly about some whizkid Byron was thinking of hiring to help him revamp Whitmore Opals. Nathan, it seemed, was intent on returning to full-time writing once Byron was back on his feet.

'Here's the book, Nathan.'

'Thanks, Lenore. At least now Kirsty will get off my case.' He turned back to Zachary. 'I dare say Byron will be in touch. He values your advice.'

'What do you personally think?'

'I think it's time for some new blood. And it's time Byron learnt to delegate more. He can't do everything himself. It's only since I've taken the reins for him that I've realised how much he used to do. The man's a workaholic. I know he *wants* to change, but it's hard to change at his age. Hard to change at *any* age,' he added drily.

Lenore stood by, listening to this interchange with growing irritation. It never ceased to amaze her the way men could keep the various parts of their lives separate. Work was work. Home was home. Affairs were affairs. Each had its own compartment and their own emotions, with lines firmly drawn between.

Women, by comparison, were not so capable of stopping everything from overlapping. This last week had been a perfect example. Her performance at rehearsals had been pathetic. There was no other word for it. Lenore knew the director was worried and if she kept up her abysmal standard of acting he would fire her and replace her with the understudy.

But her mind had simply not been on the play…

'Lenore,' Zachary said brusquely. 'Nathan's gone. Can we go inside, please? I have to talk to you.'

Lenore blinked back to reality, knowing that Zachary had shifted gears from 'work' to 'affairs', with its accompanying shift of emotions. His polite pragmatic face of a moment ago now mirrored a grim bleakness that made her shrink back in fear. 'You…you shouldn't take too much notice of Nathan,' she tried in vain. 'He doesn't understand love.'

'He understands children,' came the bitter reply. 'And he's right about my hurting Felicity.'

'F...Felicity?'

'She knows, Lenore,' he said in a tortured voice. 'She knows...'

Nausea rose in Lenore's throat but she gulped it down and somehow made it inside where she staggered out to the kitchen and poured herself a bracing drink before facing the subject of Felicity's knowledge once more.

'You want one, Zachary?' she called out as she slopped far too much gin into a glass.

'No. I have to drive home shortly.'

She topped the gin up with ice and bitter lemon then drank quickly and deeply, returning to the living area to find Zachary pacing agitatedly up and down.

'How does she know?' she asked.

'I have no idea. Maybe I gave myself away unwittingly somehow. Maybe I was too keyed up when she came home from her sister's last Sunday night. Maybe I've been acting like a guilty man all week. Hell, Lenore, I probably did a million things wrong. I've never had an affair before. Perhaps I tried too hard to act normally with her. God knows. I don't. I thought I was playing the role of innocent husband quite well. But she's been giving me the strangest looks ever since Sunday.'

'You never mentioned this on Wednesday,' Lenore reminded him curtly.

Her sharp tone brought him to a halt. 'Do you think I'm making this up?'

She shook her head in abject misery. 'No...'

'She hasn't accused me, but a couple of times, when I came home from work, I knew she'd been crying. I've been avoiding her in bed, you see, not going upstairs till I thought she was asleep. Last night, however, she came downstairs dressed in one of her prettiest nighties, and she actually tried to be...seductive. She probably thought she was doing the right thing but Felicity has never been an aggressive woman, sexually, and I'm afraid I must have looked shocked, or something, because suddenly she turned and ran from the room. When I followed her, she was sobbing on the bed. When I tried to take her in my arms she pushed me away, saying that it was hopeless, that it wouldn't be any good anyway and she would never lower herself like that again.'

'Oh, Zachary…'

'Yes, Lenore, that's exactly how I feel. Lower than the lowest.'

'But she doesn't *know*, my darling,' she tried to soothe. 'Maybe she suspects but she doesn't really know.'

'I can't live with her suspicion, or her pain. I can't live with myself if I do to her what was done to my own mother. I can't be happy over another person's misery.'

'What…what are you trying to tell me?'

'It's over, Lenore. I won't be coming to see you any more. Don't ring me. Don't drop into the office. And don't, for God's sake, even contemplate trying to force my hand by confronting Felicity and confessing all. If you do, I'll never speak to you again as long as you live.'

Shock and hurt rooted Lenore to the spot. She could not believe Zachary would think she would do such a thing.

'Oh, don't give me that injured innocent look, Lenore. You and I both know we crossed a line last Saturday night and it will be damned difficult for either of us to step back behind that line again. I'm doing it voluntarily, but I'm *forcing* you to do it. So it's quite likely that you'll come out fighting once you feel the bitter corner of loneliness again. But I beg you, Lenore, don't…don't take your pain out on my family.'

'I'd never do that, Zachary,' she said brokenly. 'I promise you, I'd never do that…'

'I didn't really think you would,' came his strangled reply before hanging his head a moment, his shoulders sagging as though a huge weight had been dropped on them. 'God, Lenore, I thought it was hell before, but now…' He looked up and took a halting step towards her, then checked himself. 'If I touch you…I won't be able to go through with this…'

Tears flooded her eyes, but her chin lifted. 'Then don't touch me, Zachary.' Her voice was surprisingly steady. And quite hard.

'So be it,' he pronounced bitterly, and with rapid strides carried himself out of the room, out of the house, and out of her life once more.

'You remembered at last!' Kirsty exclaimed delightedly when Nathan handed her the book. 'Only took you a week,' she added cheekily.

Gemma refused to look up from where she was sitting at the table in the family-room, pretending to study her Japanese. Her first awareness that Nathan was standing at her shoulder was that familiar pine smell teasing her nostrils, then she glimpsed a dark grey trouser leg out of the corner of her eye.

'Say something for me in Japanese,' he said.

She looked up, surprising herself with being able to stare into that handsome face and betray not a flicker of emotion. Still, she'd been practising hard all week. Clearly, practice did make perfect, she thought, despite still being bitterly aware that her pulse-rate had quickened alarmingly.

'*O genki desu ka?*' she said.

'*Hai O Genki Desu, O genki desu ka, Gemma san?*'

She gaped at him. 'You never told me you spoke Japanese.'

He smiled, pulling out an adjacent chair to sit down at the table with her. 'Saying that I'm fine and being able to ask how a person is won't make me fit to be ambassador to Japan. But I can hold a basic conversation. Byron, however, can chat away like a native.'

'I don't think I'll ever be able to do that,' Gemma sighed.

'I'll give you a hand, if you're ever stuck.'

Gemma stiffened slightly. 'Thank you very much, but

I'm sure I'll get the hang of it shortly. I've got little else to do during the day. Frankly, I'm not used to being so…useless.'

'Did she say she was being useless?' Ava called from the lounge where she was sitting, watching the television and eating chips. 'Don't you believe her, Nathan. She runs around here doing things all day. Insists on helping Melanie with the housework, bullies me into finishing my paintings, does her own lessons and homework. She even found time this past week to alter a whole lot of clothes I gave her. She makes me tired just watching her!'

Kirsty coming over to plonk down in another chair at the table was a welcome distraction. 'At least the rain has finally stopped,' she said. 'What time are we leaving for Avoca in the morning?'

'Early,' Nathan pronounced crisply.

'How early is early?' Kirsty asked.

'Six.'

'Six! I'm not even conscious at six.'

'Then stay behind. Gemma and I will go alone.'

'Not on your life! I've been looking forward to this all week. It's going to be such a ball, showing Gemma the beach and the rocks and everything. I'd get up even earlier if I had to!'

Gemma found her knuckles going white as she clenched her Biro harder and harder. She'd hoped to find some excuse all week not to go. But nothing had come to mind and now the moment was almost at hand. Seeing there was no way out of it, her only thought was to have the beach-house filled with as many people as possible.

'What about you coming too, Ava?' she suggested. 'I'm sure Nathan wouldn't mind, would you?'

This presumption on her part simply had to be accompanied by a polite glance his way, where she found to her consternation that he didn't *look* annoyed.

Yet there was something in his eyes—something watchful—that made her feel like a hunted animal who was slowly being forced into a smaller and smaller space where a net lay in waiting. Or a pit. Yes, she felt like she was balancing on the edge of a deep dark pit, where a sharp stake awaited at the bottom ready to pierce her heart.

'Yes, do come, Ava,' Nathan further surprised Gemma by saying. 'We'd love to have you. We could play Monopoly again on the Saturday night and have some more Chinese.'

'Thanks for the offer, Nathan, dear, but the beach and I are not on good terms. All that sun and sand.' She shuddered delicately. 'Besides, I don't have a swimming costume that fits me. No, I'll stay home here and keep Byron company.'

'Where is Byron, by the way?' Nathan asked Ava.

'Doing his leg exercises. He hasn't stopped since you brought him home this afternoon. The man's mad.'

'If it keeps Pops out of our hair, Ava,' Kirsty said, 'then don't complain.'

'Believe me, I won't, dear. By the way, Nathan, I've been meaning to ask, did you find out anything about Gemma's mother? I've been dying of curiosity all week.'

Gemma looked up, startled. She'd forgotten all about her mother, her mind consumed with none other than the man sitting next to her.

'The news is not good, I'm afraid,' he sighed, his voice full of sympathy. 'Your birth certificate isn't a forgery, Gemma.'

'*What*?' everyone exclaimed.

'I…I don't believe it,' Gemma rasped. 'I was sure I was older than eighteen. I was sure that was my mother in the photo.'

'You may very well be,' Nathan consoled. 'Legal does not necessarily mean accurate. Your father could still have supplied false details to the registry. In fact, it seems highly likely he did, since there is no birth, marriage or death certificate for a Mary Bell of about the right age in the whole of Australia. According to the records, your mother does not exist.'

'That's crazy!' Kirsty scoffed.

'It's also impossible,' Nathan said drily. 'So I suggest you give me that photograph you have, Gemma, and I'll have a good investigator look into it. And before you say anything, I'll pick up the tab.'

She stared at him and wished with all her heart that he didn't have some ulterior motive in doing such a thing.

'Poor Gemma,' he drawled, his hand reaching to cover hers. 'You look stressed. A couple of days relaxing up at Avoca is just what you need.'

'Same here, Dad,' Kirsty piped up with the innocence of a child. 'School has been hell this week. I hope you've got a swimming costume, Gemma. We're going to hit the beach as soon as we get there.'

'Yes, she has,' Ava answered for her. 'I gave her one I bought at a sale a couple of years ago in anticipation of my latest diet actually working. Needless to say, the poor costume has never seen the light of day.'

Kirsty gave Ava a worried look. 'What's it like? It's not—er—matronly, is it?'

Gemma almost laughed. There was nothing even remotely matronly about the shiny slinky purple maillot Ava had pressed upon her. If it hadn't had a roomy matching shirt to wear as a cover-up, she would probably never have the courage to wear it at all!

Her brown eyes stared deeply into Nathan's cool grey gaze, her throat turning dry at what she saw in its determined depths. There would be no hiding from him this weekend, she realised. Time had run out. She'd avoided him all week, keeping her eyes averted, her body under a tight control.

But the moment had come, the moment when he would take advantage of her love for him, when he would show her what she had never seen before, when he would invite her to taste the delights she had never tasted.

It was just a question of when.

CHAPTER THIRTEEN

LENORE sat in the living-room in the dark, dressed in nothing but a robe and drinking her fifth gin—or was it her sixth?—while she contemplated the future.

If Kirsty had been younger, she might have resigned herself to dedicating the rest of her life to her child. But in less than four years Kirsty would leave school and embark on her own journey through life. A smothering over-possessive mother would be the last thing her spirited stubborn daughter would want.

Which left Lenore nothing but her acting.

She sucked in then let out an emotionally exhausted sigh. Acting had lost its magic for her. Life had lost its magic for her. Without Zachary by her side, she might as well be dead.

Could one die from drinking too much gin? she wondered fuzzily. It would be good if you could. What a way to go! People made jokes about men who had heart attacks while having sex, but Lenore thought passing away in a haze of gin was infinitely preferable.

She stood up unsteadily and went to pour herself another, but most of the gin missed the glass.

'I'm drunk,' she told the ice-cube tray just before she dropped it. 'Damn,' she muttered and was trying to rescue the slippery cubes from the kitchen floor when someone rang the doorbell.

Lenore muttered another less ladylike word, abandoned the ice-cubes and weaved her way to the door.

'Who ish it?' she called out. Even drunk, she wasn't a

fool. It was ten o'clock at night and one didn't simply open one's door without knowing who was on the other side. 'If it's you, Nathan, get loshed.'

'It's me, Lenore. Zachary.'

'Z...Zachary?'

Fumbling, Lenore opened the door and promptly burst into tears. Zachary stepped inside, closed the door and gathered her in.

'Oh, Zachary, Zachary,' she sobbed, clinging wildly and pressing moist kisses to his neck. 'You came back... You came back...'

Suddenly, she pushed him away and slapped him hard, around the face. 'You barshtard!'

By this time, Lenore's emotional state was very fragile indeed. She was crying, angry, confused, despairing.

'Lenore,' Zachary said firmly, taking both of her hands in his. 'You're drunk.'

As if to underline this, she hiccuped.

'I'll put some coffee on,' he said, 'and before you give me any more trouble, you crazy adorable woman, then let me tell you that I'm not a bastard. I haven't come back here simply to go to bed with you again, although I won't say no to that...eventually. But because everything is going to be all right.'

She gulped. 'All...right?'

'Yes. *All right*. Felicity and I have agreed to a divorce, though for Clark's sake we've also agreed to keep it under our hats till he's finished his HSC.'

'A divorce...' Lenore's knees went from under her. Zachary scooped her up and laid her gently down on the sofa, tenderly pushing her hair back from her face and bending to kiss her several times on the lips.

'You...you wouldn't lie to an intoxicated person, would you, Zachary?' she whispered shakily.

'That depends,' he smiled, and bent to kiss her one more time. 'Must be gin. I can't taste a thing.'

'Don't tease.'

'With you? I wouldn't dare.' He stood up, still smiling. 'You just lie there and sober up while I get you some coffee.'

'Zachary, no!' She reached out her right hand, desperate fingers imploring him to come back to her. 'Don't go. I'm fine. Come back and sit beside me. Tell me what happened.'

He did as she asked, leaning over and kissing her once more before straightening. 'Very well. I'll start from the moment I arrived home after leaving you earlier this evening. I have to admit I was very distraught after our—er—parting, and had not managed to get myself entirely under control, so that when I walked in to find Felicity in floods of tears I was not at my most patient.'

'What did you do?' Lenore asked, finding it hard to picture Zachary losing his temper with Felicity.

'I guess I exploded. God, Lenore. I'd just made the most monumental sacrifice for that woman and there she was, weeping and looking at me like I was a monster or something worse. I…I demanded to know what was wrong with her. Guilt and rage made me totally irrational. I ranted and raved, told her I had been the best husband a woman could ask for. I demanded to know what more she wanted of me.'

'And?'

'She broke down and confessed that she'd fallen in love with another man, had started having an affair with him and now wanted to marry him.'

Lenore sat bolt upright. 'My God, Zachary! And you never suspected?'

'Not for a second. The symptoms were there, of course, but I was so caught up with my own feelings for you, Lenore, not to mention my own guilt, that I didn't see them.'

'What symptoms? You said she was trying to *seduce* you the other night.'

'Ah, yes…the famous, or should I say now infamous

seduction? You know those times she's been dashing off to see her sister?'

'Uh-huh.'

'She was seeing her lover and her sister was covering for her. Not sleeping with him, mind. Apparently that didn't happen till last Saturday night.'

Lenore's eyes widened. 'You mean the same night that we…we…'

He nodded. 'The very same. Ironic, isn't it? It seems, like me, she was so stricken with guilt by the end of the next day that she told her lover that she could never see him again and came home to try to make the best of things.'

'The poor love… But who *is* this mysterious boyfriend? Anyone you know?'

'Not at all. Apparently he met Felicity in a music shop when they were both enquiring about the same album. Felicity has always been large on music. Well, anyway they got talking, found they had a lot in common, he asked her for coffee and one thing led to another. He's a widower, apparently, with a grown family. Quite well off. Would you believe Felicity told me that she's always felt inadequate as my wife, but that Errol—that's his name, by the way—that this Errol makes her feel smart and needed? Do you know how that made *me* feel? To think I've crushed her self-esteem all these years. To think I'd made her feel… unwanted.'

Lenore said nothing because she could see some truth in Felicity's accusation. Zachary would not have meant to crush his wife's self-esteem, but he was an exceptionally clever, self-sufficient and strong-minded man. Any woman of Felicity's hothouse-flower make-up would have withered under the crushing force of his tough, slightly insensitive personality, whereas Lenore was not the easily crushable type. Besides, after Nathan's chilling idea of a relationship, she found Zachary positively warm and responsive.

When he continued to look bleak she leant forward and kissed him on the cheek. 'Don't start being hard on yourself, Zachary. You're a good man. The best. And don't you ever forget it.'

His smile touched her. 'You say the sweetest things sometimes.'

'Oh, go on with you. Now tell me the rest, and don't forget the bit about the night Felicity tried to seduce you.'

His smile widened. 'You would want to know about the sexy bits. Well, it seems that despite Felicity's best intentions to stick with our marriage she'd been trying to avoid having sex with me, going to bed extra early and pretending she was sound asleep when I came into the room. Another irony, considering I was staying up later and later for the very same reason. Finally, guilt got the better of her and she decided to take the bull by the horns.'

'Darling, what an evocative phrase!' Lenore said naughtily. She couldn't help it. Happiness was making her saucy and bold. Everything was going to be all *right*! 'You don't have to go on,' she said into his reproving face, all the while doing her best to keep a straight one. 'I get the picture.'

'I can see you need a strong man to keep you under control,' he rebuked.

'Am I going to get a physical demonstration of your controlling abilities?'

He groaned, sandwiching her face between trembling hands and taking her mouth in a kiss that just stopped short of an oral assault.

'Good lord!' she gasped when his head finally lifted. 'I think you'd better stop that and finish your confession before we get carried away.'

'Finish my confession?'

'You did tell Felicity about us, didn't you?'

'Yes, of course.'

'And?'

'I think she was relieved, though naturally, I didn't say I'd been in love with you all these years. That would have been cruel. I let her think I'd always found you attractive but that it wasn't till I ran into you last Saturday and asked you to go to the play with me that I realised I'd somehow fallen in love with you. I think she was so happy that I wouldn't be devastated by her own defection that she didn't stop to think we hadn't even seen each other in the last two years.'

'So we're to keep our relationship a secret till the end of the year, is that it?'

He reached out and picked up a stray curl and looped it back over her ear. 'Do you mind very much, my darling?' he said, continuing to smooth back her hair from her flushed face. 'We could go away for weekends, have discreet dinners. I could stay the night sometimes when Clark is at his friends' places, which is often. Look, I know it isn't ideal but it will come to an end and it's a small price to pay to secure everyone's happiness. Emery's mature enough to cope but Clark's desperate to be a pilot and he needs a good pass in his HSC for that. Neither Felicity nor I would be able to live with ourselves if we thought we'd somehow ruined his chances by our behaviour. Our divorce will still upset him, but once he's on his feet he's sure to be able to cope better.'

'I have a child too, Zachary,' she reminded him. 'She might be coming home to live next school term, which could put a stop to any nocturnal stayovers. I doubt Kirsty and Clark will be so co-operative as to go to friends' places on the same nights,' she finished a touch curtly before realising she was being both stroppy and selfish.

What was the matter with her? She'd gone fifteen years without Zachary at all! What did one miserable year of small sacrifices matter in the long run? It wasn't as though they wouldn't be able to see each other at all. Where there was a will there was a way!

Smiling softly, she smoothed the frown from his face with gentle hands, her lips following her fingers. 'I'm sorry,' she apologised. 'I'm being silly and selfish... We'll work it out… Oh, I do so love you, Zachary…' She kissed him full on the mouth.

He quickly took control of the kiss, pushing her back on the sofa and effortlessly reducing her to a trembling mess. She lay there in a daze of desire when he stood up and started tossing his clothes aside like a sex-crazed adolescent. His last sock flung aside, he bent over to reef the sash on her ivory silk robe undone, pushing the material roughly aside. When he ran his hands quite roughly down her quivering nakedness she arched her body in response and gave a voluptuous shudder.

'Women like you should be prohibited,' he groaned, and, without any further foreplay, joined her on the sofa and fused his flesh with hers. 'I don't think this is going to be one of my better demonstrations of my controlling abilities,' he rasped on setting up a desperate driving rhythm.

'Mmm,' was all Lenore could manage before tumbling headfirst into a wildly shuddering climax which precipitated Zachary's release even earlier than he'd anticipated.

After the storm had passed, they lay together in blissful peace, Zachary having pulled Lenore on top of him so that they could fit more comfortably on the sofa. He was happily playing with her back and buttocks under her silk robe, which slithered around their nakedness with a whispery sensuousness.

'Talk to me,' he said softly.

Lenore's head lifted. '*Talk* to you?'

He stroked her head back down on to his bare, hair-roughened chest. 'Yes, talk to me, tell me everything about yourself that you've never had a chance to tell me. I want to know it all, warts and all. I want to know what you were like when you were a little girl, I want to know when you decided to become an actress, I want to know…oh, I want to know the damned lot. Hey!' He suddenly jerked upwards and stared down his very damp chest. 'You're crying!'

Cupping her face, he stared into her blurred eyes, his

own bewildered. 'What did I say wrong? What did I do wrong?'

'Nothing,' she sobbed. 'You do everything so right that I can't stop crying with happiness.'

'God, you had me worried for a second,' Zachary said. 'I'm not used to a woman crying with happiness. I'm not used to a woman lying naked with me on a sofa, either,' he added thickly, a slight lift of his hips making Lenore hotly aware that things were on the move in his nether region. 'Do you—er—think we might leave our deep and meaningful discussion for just a few minutes?'

Lenore wiped her eyes, laughed and sat up.

'Now that's better,' Zachary growled. Then a few seconds later, 'God, yes, that's definitely better. Oh, you gorgeous beautiful wild creature... I do so love you...'

CHAPTER FOURTEEN

GEMMA didn't wait for seats to be assigned in Nathan's Mercedes the following morning. She immediately climbed in the back and belted up, leaving Kirsty happily to occupy the front passenger seat. Nathan made no comment on the arrangement, though his eyes did meet Gemma's in the rear-view mirror as he went to reverse out of the garage, and their expression suggested a dark amusement over her actions. She quickly tore her eyes away, annoyed to find her heart was beating madly.

A look, she thought despairingly. One miserable look...

'Well, we're almost away on time,' Kirsty said brightly. The clock built into the dashboard showed six twenty-five.

The dark blue sedan swung back in an arc once free of the huge garage door—it was a six-car garage—Nathan closing the door by remote control before he guided the car along the side-path and on to the circular drive which would lead them round to the front gates.

'Good God, Dad!' Kirsty burst out. 'That's Jade's car, isn't it? Look where she's parked it. It's almost in the fish pond!'

And sure enough, the white sports car Gemma had seen the day she arrived at Belleview had its bumper bar over the edge of the pond surrounds, skid marks on the grass where its driver had careered across the front lawn before coming to a precarious halt.

Nathan braked and just glared at the car. Everything about his very still body suggested sheer fury.

'I hope she'll still be here when we get back,' Kirsty added. 'Jade's fun.'

Nathan threw her a withering look. 'You've got a funny idea of fun, then, madam,' he ground out. 'If she's thinking of staying any longer than a day or two, then you'll be going back to your mother faster then the Bluebird crossed Lake Eyre. I'm not having you anywhere near that crazy female on a permanent basis.'

'Oh, Dad!' Kirsty wailed.

'What the hell's she doing back here anyway? She's got her own damned place up at Avalon now. Why doesn't she stay in it?'

'Maybe she's come home to visit her father,' Gemma suggested quietly from the back seat.

Kirsty spluttered into hysterics and Nathan muttered something marginal.

'I take it Jade doesn't get along with Byron?' Gemma asked, curious now.

'You take it correctly,' was Nathan's very dry comment, and continued driving round towards the gates, which were already opening.

'Why not?'

'To put it bluntly, she and he have different moral standards. He can't abide hers and she can't abide his.'

'In regard to what?'

'I don't think I care to discuss this any further right at this moment,' he said stiffly, and, turning the car into the main street, accelerated away with a sudden burst of speed.

'Oh, Dad, don't be silly,' Kirsty said in that bored tone teenagers liked to adopt when patronising their parents. 'I already know all there is to know about Jade. What Mum hasn't told me, Ava has. She's man-mad, Gemma. That's all. Dear old Pops just can't handle his little princess always having the hots for a different guy every week. She's not bad, she's just kinda wild and groovy!'

'Kirsty!' her father reproved. 'Does your mother let you go around talking like that?'

Kirsty shrugged. 'What did I say that was so bad?'

Nathan sighed. 'For one thing it is not healthy to be man-mad. Aside from the moral angle, it's downright dangerous. What if Jade ends up with AIDS? Have you thought of that?'

'She won't end up with AIDS, Dad. She's too smart.'

'Good God,' he muttered irritably. 'Can you talk some sense to her, Gemma? Maybe she'll listen to you.'

'I think what your father is trying to say, Kirsty,' Gemma said carefully, 'is that there is no fool-proof protection for the risk involved in having casual sex with a lot of different partners.'

'What about condoms?'

'They minimise the risk,' Nathan rejoined the discussion. 'They don't eliminate it. And who's to say a girl like Jade will always be in a fit state to think of protection? She drinks like a fish. And she's already been arrested once for possession of drugs.'

'Oh, Dad, it was only grass. That's nothing nowadays!'

'That comment perfectly demonstrates your immaturity, my girl, in matters of drugs as well as sex. Do you think people go to bed one night and wake up a heroin addict? They have to start somewhere and it pretty well always starts with marijuana. So don't understate its corrupting powers.' He slid a sharp glance over his daughter's way. 'You haven't been experimenting with drugs, have you?'

'Of course not!' Kirsty denied, but she was also blushing fiercely.

'You'd better not be. You're not too old to be taken over my knee and given a good paddle on the backside, and I'll do just that if I find you've been so foolish. Gemma, has Kirsty said or done anything to make you think she might be taking drugs?'

'No, Nathan, she hasn't.'

'Just as well.'

'See!' Kirsty pouted.

'Yes, I do see,' her father said very seriously. 'I see, and have seen, far more than you'll ever see!'

A tense, brooding silence descended on the car during which Gemma realised that not once in that brief discussion about Jade had her mother been mentioned. It was almost as though she had never had a mother, yet Irene had only been dead a few weeks. It was all very puzzling. But she supposed she would find out all about the Whitmore family over the coming weeks if Ava kept up her level of gossiping. That woman never shut up. Privately, Gemma thought she was a very lonely soul, filling her life with meaningless chatter and little else. Which was a pity, because Gemma believed she had real talent as a painter. Her watercolours were quite lovely, and would be even lovelier if she ever finished them!

It was hard, too, to think unkindly about Ava who'd so sweetly given her all those lovely clothes. Admittedly, most had still been slightly too large, though not the cream linen bermuda shorts she was wearing, nor the purple silk shirt that she'd teamed with it.

Thinking about Jade and Ava must have passed quite a bit of time for suddenly Gemma saw they'd left the suburbs far behind and were flying along a busy multi-laned highway with little on either side except stark, scrub-covered hills through which the road had been cut with bold disregard for the rocky terrain. A railway line followed a similar route, with Nathan's powerful car streaking ahead of the occasional silver train they momentarily drew parallel with.

The atmosphere in the Mercedes remained silent and slightly strained till the road angled down a steep incline and they burst on to a big bridge which crossed the most beautiful stretch of water Gemma had ever seen.

'Oh, how lovely,' she gasped in delight, swivelling her head from one side to the other. She didn't know which view she preferred. On the left, the river curved magnificently into the distance, an island in the middle, houses dotting the shore. Or on the right, where more than one vista boggled her eyes. Straight ahead, the already wide river grew even wider into a hugely impressive body of water, more islands and another bridge in the distance. But if she twisted around she could see the cutest little bay, full of boats, a tiny village hugging the hills that rose up behind.

'I've never seen such a pretty place,' she admired. 'Or such a beautiful river!'

'It's the Hawkesbury,' Nathan informed her. 'And that's Brooklyn you're looking at back there, where all the boats are moored. You can hire cruisers or houseboats down there for trips up the river. You can go for a day, or a weekend, or longer, if you wish.'

'Can you? Oh, I'd love to do that one day!'

'Then we will.' Again he caught her eye in the rearview mirror and this time, he was smiling at her without any hidden mockery or sardonic knowingness. Gemma felt a rush of such pure joy that tears pricked at her eyes, tears of the sharpest happiness. They blurred her vision slightly but she could not look away, and in that moment of bittersweet pleasure, that moment of mutual enjoyment, she pushed aside all her fears where this man was concerned.

He couldn't mean her any harm, she decided. He couldn't possibly be bad. Not the man who'd comforted her so kindly out at Lightning Ridge. Not the man who'd so generously looked after her since her arrival in Sydney. Not the man who obviously cared so deeply for the moral welfare of his daughter.

Such a man could not be a callous seducer.

The ice and her fears broken, the rest of the trip to Avoca was happy and cheerful, Kirsty busily pointing out the various spots of interest while Nathan concentrated on the driving. Despite their early start, the freeway was very busy in Gemma's opinion, though she was told the traffic was light for a summer weekend.

'That's where you turn off to go to Old Sydney Town.' Kirsty prattled away, rarely expecting an answer, though

Gemma did get to pop in a comment or a question occasionally. 'It's like a living museum of the olden days... We'll have to take Gemma there one day, Dad... And now we're going down the hill to Gosford... Isn't it a pretty town...? There's the League's Club... That big sheet of water? It's called the Brisbane Water, though God knows why, we're a long way from Brisbane... Yes, it's very green up this way, and the bush is real thick... High rainfall, isn't that right, Dad?... Sorta like a rainforest... Listen to the bell-birds...some bloke wrote a poem about them once... Dad will probably read it to you some time...he's a poem and play nut...a book nut too... Mrs Danvers? Never heard of her... Who's Mrs Danvers, Dad?'

'A housekeeper in a book called *Rebecca*. The house was called Manderley.'

'Who was Rebecca?' Gemma asked.

'The master of Manderley's first wife. She died mysteriously but was so powerful a personality that when the master married a second time—to a quiet, shy girl—his new wife felt her marriage was haunted by the memory of the first wife. The housekeeper, Mrs Danvers, loved Rebecca and hated the second wife. She made her life hell.'

Gemma shuddered. 'Poor thing.'

'I've got a copy of the book at the beach-house. You can read it if you like.'

'She hasn't come up here to read, Dad. She's going to go to the beach with me!'

'Not all day, she isn't. She'll get burnt.'

'Gemma? Burnt? She's already got a fantastic tan.'

'The sun at the beach can be very deceiving. It reflects off the sand, doubling the exposure. And we don't have an umbrella.'

'Just as well,' Kirsty said. 'I wouldn't be seen dead using an umbrella!'

'You might be dead in a few years if you don't start using one. Haven't you been listening to the ads on television about skin cancer?'

'Oh, not another lecture, Dad. I couldn't stand it.'

Nathan laughed, then grinned in the mirror at Gemma.
'Shall we give her a reprieve for the weekend?'

'Only if she promises to wear the sunscreen I bought
yesterday.'

'Done!' Kirsty agreed. 'Anything but the dreaded umbrella. Oh, look, we're here! The sea is over there, to the
left, Gemma. It's a bit hard to see from the road but you
can just glimpse it occasionally between the buildings and
the trees. Slow right down to a crawl, Dad. Now you can
see it!'

Gemma looked left where Kirsty was pointing across a
park. 'It's so blue!' she exclaimed.

'And very rough,' Nathan added ruefully. 'No walking
round the rocks today, Kirsty. And before you object, remember what happened to those poor people last year.'

'What happened?' Gemma asked.

'A family of foreign tourists were up here on holidays
and couldn't read the warning signs. There's a very interesting walk around the rocks, you see, near the base of the
cliffs, which on normal days is quite safe, but when the
tide is high and the sea's whipped up by a strong wind the
waves crash over the rocks. Mostly, that isn't really dangerous either, if you're not standing too close to the edge,
but every now and then a big wave comes that takes people
by surprise and washes them into the sea.'

'What happened to the family?'

'They drowned. Mother, father, and two children.'

'Dear God... You won't get me going on those rocks,
then, even in calm weather.'

'I'll take you when it's safe,' Nathan offered.

By this time they'd driven slowly past a funny old barn-
like building which Kirsty astonished Gemma by pointing
out as the local picture theatre. It looked like something
out of the ark, more fitting to Lightning Ridge than the
tourist mecca of the Central Coast.

She laughed her astonishment.

'Don't laugh. It's real interesting inside, isn't it, Dad, with all sorts of quaint old posters and pictures? It's not as bad as it looks, either. There's air-conditioning and free tea and coffee and on top of that, it's real cheap.'

'The seats are a bit hard on the derrière after a while,' Nathan admitted, 'but the kids love it. On Saturday nights in the summer, it has an all-night session.'

'Which I haven't been allowed to go to so far,' Kirsty pointed out drily.

'Maybe this year, if you've got someone to go with you. And don't look at me. My days of going to the pictures on a Saturday night with a mob of noisy teenagers are long gone.'

Kirsty twisted round and gave Gemma a hopeful look.

'Don't look at me either,' she laughed. 'I can't stay awake after ten-thirty.'

'Maybe Cathy's up here with her parents...' Kirsty frowned, then brightened. 'I'll find someone, never you fear. I'm not going to let a chance like this go by.'

Nathan groaned. 'Me and my big mouth. Well, here we are, folks. Everyone out.'

The beach-house was not Belleview. But it wasn't Gemma's idea of a beach-house either. Weren't they supposed to be rough-and-ready affairs? She should have known that any family used to living in Belleview wouldn't rough it. Hadn't Nathan said as much when she'd told them about the dugout?

It was up on the side of the hill that looked down on to the antique movie-house, cream brick and split-level with a front balcony that was larger than her dugout back at Frog Hollow and a back balcony that overlooked a private pool. The block was bounded by tall thick trees on three sides, giving them privacy from the neighbours while not impeding the magnificent view of the Pacific Ocean. Though not air-conditioned, each room had its own ceiling fans. The décor was modern and casual, with polished floors, cane furniture and assorted rugs for warmth and comfort. The kitchen was a dream and there were two bathrooms, three if you counted the shower and toilet downstairs near the pool.

Gemma finally shut her gaping mouth, trying not to shake her head as she wandered out on to the front decking a second time. If only Ma could see her now! Fancy clothes. Fancy cars. Fancy houses.

Glancing down over the railing, she spotted Nathan as he strode down the steep driveway and round to the back of the car again to collect a second load of luggage. He was wearing crisp bone-coloured canvas jeans and a caramel-coloured shirt which had an open collar neck and a sailboat logo on its single breast pocket. Sometime since arriving he'd slipped on a pair of expensive-looking sunglasses, the effect being to make him seem even more glamorous to her than ever.

A wistful sigh escaped her lips and she turned to walk back through the sliding doors into the large living area.

'Come on, Gemma,' Kirsty called out as she dashed down the hallway that led to the bedrooms. 'Get your cossie on. There's not a moment to waste. I have to get down to that beach and find someone to go with me to the movies tonight.'

Gemma walked down to stand in the doorway of the room Kirsty was proceeding to turn from tidiness into a tip. Clothes were being pulled out of her bag and thrown everywhere.

'Don't tell me I've forgotten my own cossie. Oh, there it is!' she sighed, and glanced up. 'Shake a leg, Gemma. Oh, you're waiting for your luggage, I suppose. Still, don't wait for Dad to come with us. He might pop down later but he's sure to hole up in his den, writing for the next few hours.'

'Are you bad-mouthing me again, young lady?' Nathan growled from just behind Gemma's shoulder.

'Who, me?'

'Yes, you. I've put your things in your room, Gemma.

By the way, there's plenty of beach towels in the linen press and if you're hungry the kitchen is kept well stocked. You look after Gemma, Kirsty. But you're right, I probably won't be down the beach till later. I have things to do.'

Gemma watched him walk down the hall and disappear into the furthest room which she'd peeped into only a minute or two before. It was clearly the room he wrote in, a combination of study, library, office and sitting-room. It was the only room in the house Gemma hadn't liked. The windows were covered with heavy curtains which blocked out the natural light and gave the room a dark claustrophobic feel. It had been cold in there too. She recalled shivering a little and quickly shutting the door.

The door shut behind Nathan with a definite click.

'Well, that takes care of Dad for today,' Kirsty grinned. 'Come on, Gemma, time for your introduction to the wide blue Pacific!'

CHAPTER FIFTEEN

GEMMA hated the sea. Well, not exactly *hated* it. But it frightened her, especially when she waded in and felt its power, pushing her towards the shore on top and sucking her back out underneath. Kirsty kept telling her it was extra rough that day, that the waves were all horrible dumpers, that there was an awful rip and that she shouldn't judge on this first unfortunate meeting, but Gemma knew she would never like placing herself at its mercy. The die had been cast.

In the end she begged off staying and Kirsty walked her back to the house where they made some toasted sandwiches, Gemma having a cup of tea while Kirsty drank a couple of the long-life milk drinks in the fridge. They each polished off an ice-cream from the freezer before Kirsty announced she was going back to the beach in search of some other starters for the movie marathon that night. The aforementioned Cathy had been found, but they were both keen to gather a large group.

'Why don't you read that book Dad was telling us about? *Rachel*, wasn't it?'

'No, *Rebecca*.'

'Yeah, that's the one. I'll go ask him where it is.'

'Do...do you think you should interrupt him?'

'Probably not. But if I don't, he'll forget to eat.'

Nathan emerged from the den with a scowl on his face and frustration in his body language. Finding the book in the book-shelves in the general living area, he tossed it on the kitchen counter and was striding back down the corridor when Gemma asked him if he'd like her to make him some lunch.

He swung round, that tight, tense look still in his eyes. She held her breath, aware that though the purple shirt was covering her costume from neck to thigh the buttons weren't done up and the gap between the free-falling sides revealed not only her substantial cleavage but the highly cut purple V between her thighs. When his eyes travelled from her face down her scantily clad body to focus on this spot, a wave of embarrassing heat swept right through her like a flash flood, making her suck in a startled breath. Suddenly, her throat felt as if it had been scraped with sandpaper.

His voice sounded raw too, when it came. 'It can't be lunchtime yet, surely.'

'Well and truly,' Kirsty informed him, fortunately not having witnessed their searing visual exchange. She'd walked out on to the balcony to hang the wet towels over the railing, coming back in time to hear his comment about the time. 'It's one-thirty.'

'Good God,' he muttered.

'The writing going well, I take it?' Kirsty teased.

'No, it bloody well isn't,' he snarled.

'Tch tch, Dad. Such language.'

'Why don't you do something useful like help Gemma make me some lunch, there's a good girl?'

'Oh, Gemma won't mind doing that by herself. I've got to go back down the beach. See yuh!' She was waving and tripping off out the door and down the front steps before Gemma could drag some air into her bursting lungs.

She looked at Nathan, eyes wide. He looked at her, eyes narrow.

Not a word was spoken. Not a breath breathed.

Slowly, and almost resignedly, she imagined, he moved towards her, grey eyes darkened to slate, one of those appalling smiles tugging at his gorgeous mouth.

'I thought I told you not to look at me like that,' he said

at last, his right hand reaching to tip up her chin, his gaze dropping to her softly parted lips. His smile faded as his thumb rubbed over her bottom lip. 'You should have listened to me...'

That tantalising hand drifted down the column of her throat, moving closer and closer to her aching, straining breasts with their aching, straining nipples.

'I'm sorry I wasn't able to give you good news about your mother,' he said, his matter-of-fact tone mocking what was happening between them. 'I was as surprised as you were that that birth certificate was legit. I could have sworn you were more than eighteen. Or maybe I just wanted you to be. Do you really want me to take it further, make more enquiries?'

She blinked up at him, baffled by his choice of conversation. How could he coolly talk about her mother and her age while his hands were tracing the curves of her breast, stroking the undersides, moving closer and closer to those tight aching tips pressing hard against the Lycra?

Somehow, she managed to nod a blank assent, her head feeling terribly heavy, her eyelashes drooping. Yet when his fingertips finally reached and brushed over her nipples, her head jerked upright as though she'd been stung. Wide brown eyes lanced his and she had the satisfaction of seeing that he was no longer looking so cool or controlled.

'I've been wanting to touch you like this since that very first day,' he whispered in a voice vibrating with passion. 'You've been wanting the same thing, haven't you?'

She nodded again, her tongue thick in her mouth. She would have admitted to anything to keep those hands on her breasts, to keep him doing what he was doing.

His eyes narrowed till they were dark slits of the most incredible desire. 'God, but you're the loveliest thing I've ever seen,' he rasped, and, parting the shirt further, he pushed it back from her shoulders, dragging it down her arms and letting it flutter away to the floor.

'You're a virgin, aren't you?' he asked, and peeled the

costume down to her waist, baring her breasts to his smouldering gaze.

She swallowed, and nodded again.

Maybe if he'd groped or pawed her, memories from that other experience might have risen to spoil things, bringing revulsion and fear. But his touch was so incredibly light and sensual that her mind was soon filled with nothing but the most heavenly haze.

Yes, run your fingertips over them again. Yes, mould your hands around them like that again. Yes, oh, yes, please kiss them...

A startled gasp fluttered from her parted lips when he did, and she swayed backwards. He caught her, lifted her and carried her down the hall and into his bedroom, laying her on the double bed and stripping her naked with firm but gentle hands. She watched, dazed, while he removed his own clothes, stunned by his smooth golden beauty, awed by the power of his desire.

Her head reeled when she felt his nude hard body cover hers, pressing her down into the mattress. His expression intense, he stroked back her dark hair on to the white pillows, then held her face and finally, finally, kissed her full on the mouth.

It was everything and more than she could have dreamt, bringing with it a dazzling explosion of desire that had her lips opening wide, inviting the most intimate of kisses. His groan as he filled her with his tongue was as arousing as the kiss itself, making her twist restlessly beneath him, making her wind her arms around his back and scrape his skin, ever so lightly, with her nails.

He broke off the kiss, his breathing heavy. Once more she felt the thrill of his lips on her breasts, though this time they were not so gentle. There was no more tender licking. He suckled at her like a greedy infant, drawing her nipples deep into his mouth, grazing them with impassioned teeth then tonguing them to an excruciating level of sensitivity.

A sigh of ragged relief burst from her lips when he aban-

doned her breasts to slide further down her body, burying
his face in the softness of her stomach. Gemma was astonished at how sensual it felt to have her navel licked, and it
was while she was marvelling at this highly erotic experience that his hand slid between her thighs.

From that moment on, she was delirious with pleasure.
Oh, God, yes, she thought. Yes, please. Oh, don't stop. Oh,
please, don't stop. Oh, God…

'Oh!' she cried aloud, and shuddered convulsively when
her body was racked by a series of the sharpest, most electric spasms. But just as suddenly it was over, and a draining
exhaustion washed through her, leaving her limp and
heavy.

When she sighed, he immediately retreated and she was
left experiencing a bewildering emotion that both puzzled
and upset her. There was peace, yet emptiness. Satisfaction,
yet resentment. This was not how it was meant to be,
surely?

Her eyelids fluttered open from where she'd been
squeezing them tightly shut only to find Nathan stretched
out beside her on the bed, his chest rising and falling as he
dragged in a series of deep, shuddering breaths.

'Nathan?' she said, her voice oddly husky. She tried to
lift her hand but it was heavy and languid, falling across
his still heaving chest.

He picked it up and pressed it to his lips, startling her
back to sexual awareness by sucking one of her fingers into
his mouth. When her head rolled sideways on the pillow to
stare at him, he shocked her even further by taking her hand
and carrying it down his body till he enclosed her fingers
intimately around him. With his hand still imprisoning hers,
he forced her to caress him, pressing her fingers tight, making her squeeze as well as stroke.

He groaned with a raw animal pleasure and with the
sound of his own mindless pleasure any hint of revulsion
vanished from Gemma. She became enthralled, her head
spinning with the intoxication of sexual power, her mind

thrilling to the way she could make him shudder and cry out. Soon, his hand dropped away from hers and he lay there gasping as she propelled him to a climax that left him shaking uncontrollably.

'God,' he muttered, and, shuddering one last time, rolled off the bed and strode into the *en suite*, shutting the door firmly behind him. There came the sounds of a tap running, then a cupboard opening and closing.

Gemma lay there, feeling suddenly awkward and embarrassed, but within seconds the bathroom door was reefed open and Nathan was back on the bed with her, slipping something under the pillow then gathering her back in to the warmth and security of his arms.

'Sorry about that,' he said ruefully. 'But it's some time since I've been with a woman, and I wouldn't have lasted long enough inside you to give you a hope of satisfaction.' His eyes glittered as they looked deeply into hers. 'Inside you...good God, even saying those words is enough to turn me on again.'

And it was, her eyes rounding as she felt his desire rubbing hard against her thigh.

'Don't worry,' he said. 'I keep a good supply of condoms in the medicine cabinet.'

Now her eyes widened further and he laughed softly. 'There's no obligation on our part to use them all. But I think one is definitely in order.'

She watched, half curious, half shy, as he retrieved a small plastic envelope from under the pillow and, with obviously expert fingers, extracted then drew on the seemingly inadequate protection. In no time he was back, cupping her face and kissing her hungrily. 'Now I can love you properly, my darling. I can concentrate on giving *you* pleasure, beautiful unselfish gorgeous sexy creature that you are.'

Gemma was dazzled by his words, by his calling her his darling, by his overwhelmingly confident sexuality. There were no fumbling moves, no furtive actions, no feeble excuses for what he'd done earlier. He'd had a plan in mind and he'd executed it boldly.

'I don't think you know how irresistible you are,' he went on. 'How you've tormented me these past two weeks. I tried to put you out of mind, but I see now that was an insane solution to what you've done to me. There is only one solution. Only one…'

He was kissing her again, and the explorations of that erotic, demanding tongue excited her unbearably. Soon, she was writhing beneath him, panting and pressing her flesh into his, her lush, nubile young body arching upwards in a driving need for closer contact. When he slid down her body to suckle her breast, her arousal flared to frustration. She moaned, shaking her head from side to side on the pillow.

'No,' she cried huskily. This was not what she wanted. She wanted what *he* wanted. Him, inside her. 'Do it,' she urged. 'Just do it!'

His head lifted. 'Patience,' he exhorted gently. 'I don't want to hurt you.'

'I don't care if you do,' she insisted wildly.

His smile was dark. 'Oh, yes, you would…if I did. Now just lie here and be still,' he ordered, 'and leave this up to me.'

Be still! Was he mad? She wanted to move, to…to touch him, to…

She froze. For he had slipped a pillow under her buttocks and was pushing her knees right up, opening her body to his gaze. Her face flamed and she might have shut her legs but already he was between her thighs and God, he was rubbing himself against her and…and…it felt so heavenly, so *glorious* that any protest, verbal or physical, died in her suddenly dry throat.

Gemma swallowed, closed her eyes and gave herself up to what was happening to her. And once she surrendered the last shreds of her defences, her mind spiralled out into a dark erotic wasteland from which there seemed to be no returning.

'Yes,' she moaned in agreement when he stopped the increasingly frustrating rubbing to probe the velvet depths of her stunningly aroused flesh. Only a shallow penetration at first, but steadily more and more, till he was filling her completely.

'Oh, yes,' she groaned, and blindly reached out her arms for him.

He came to her. They clung together, and for a few seconds Gemma was overwhelmed by a feeling of intense emotional love. But when Nathan braced his body with his elbows on either side of her and started a deep and powerful rhythm she was spun back into that wasteland, where nothing existed but a black haze and what was happening deep inside her.

There was a gathering of heat and tension and pleasure that wasn't really pleasure. It was a yearning, a longing where everything twisted tighter and tighter, and only seconds before she thought she must surely disintegrate she did, her flesh shattering around his in a series of stunning sensations that scorned her first climax as nothing but a sip at the cup from which she was now drinking her fill.

'Oh, Nathan,' she cried out beneath his own shuddering body. 'I love you so much.'

Finally, he collapsed upon her and they clutched at each other, gasping and still trembling with the ebb-tide of their pleasure. Gradually their breathing quietened and Nathan left her to make a brief visit to the bathroom. When he came back to lie down beside her on his back, thoughtful grey eyes on the ceiling, a quite appalling silence descended on the room and Gemma suddenly found herself down in that pit, that stake through her heart.

He doesn't love you, you fool, came the cruel voice of reality. He's one of those handsome city devils Ma warned you about. He wanted you and now he's had you. End of story.

'Gemma...' he said at long last, sounding worried.

'It's all right,' she rushed in. 'I...I shouldn't have said I loved you. It was silly. I don't expect anything from you. I know you couldn't possibly be in love with me. I understand. You still love Lenore and...'

His head and shoulders shot up then, his eyes stunned as he turned to her. 'Lenore!' he exclaimed. 'I don't love Lenore. Good God, whatever made you think such a stupid thing?' Abruptly, he dragged her into his arms. 'It's you I want, you silly little ninny. Why do you think I haven't been able to write? You've been obsessing my mind and my body. All I can think about is having you, and God forgive me, I'm going to.'

'You...you are?'

'Yes, damn it, I am,' he muttered. 'I'm going to have you in my bed every night, and at my breakfast table every morning, and in my life every damned day.'

Abruptly, he rolled over and pulled her on top of him. 'Gemma,' he said with steely eyes.

'Yes?'

'We're going to be married. As soon as possible.'

Gemma could not believe what she was hearing.

'You...you can't be serious.'

'I am. Deadly serious. What's the matter? Don't you want to marry me?'

'Yes, of course, it's what I want more than anything in the world, but...but what is everyone going to say?'

'A lot, I would imagine. But we won't tell them till it's a *fait accompli*.'

'Nathan, I...I'm not sure that—'

He pulled her mouth down on his. 'Just say yes,' he growled a minute later. 'Just say yes and let me worry about the rest.'

She just said yes and he kissed her again, and soon her head was back in the clouds. Nathan loved her and wanted to marry her. He didn't love Lenore. He wasn't a callous seducer. He was her hero, her Prince Charming who promised to fix all her problems.

It all seemed a little incredible.

But as he carried her further into the abyss of ecstasy, Gemma became blissfully certain that she would be happy with Nathan for the rest of her life. He filled her mind and her heart and her body. In the end, nothing else mattered, not the possible problems back at Belleview, or her lost heritage, or even the mysterious black opal that had first propelled her into Nathan's life. They were trivial and insignificant at that moment. They were consigned either to the past or the far distant future. All that mattered for her was the moment, and the moment was, indeed, miraculous.

She sighed, and surrendered to its pleasure.

seducer. He was her help, her fiancé, Christophe who promised to fix all her problems—

It all seemed a little incredible.

But as he carried her farther into the abyss of ecstasy
it came before the foggy curtain that she would be happy
with Joachim for the rest of her life. He lifted her head and
her heart and her body. In the end nothing else mattered,
not the possible problems, her a believers, or her past
heritage, or even the miraculous black opal that had first
propelled her into Joachim's life. They were crystal and re-
significant at that moment. They were obliterated quite to
the past of the far distant future. All that mattered for her
was the moment and the moment was indeed marvellous.

She relaxed and surrendered to its pleasure.

DESIRE & DECEPTION

CHAPTER ONE

JADE woke to daylight and confusion.

Where on earth am I? she wondered fuzzily, her head thick with the after-effects of sleeping tablets.

And then she remembered.

She was back in her old bedroom at Belleview. Back home.

'Oh, God,' she groaned, and rolled out of bed, clutching her pounding temples while she staggered, naked, across the white shag carpet and into her white and gold *en-suite* bathroom.

'Oh, *God*,' she groaned again when she saw her reflection in the mirror. Her short white-blonde hair was sticking out in all directions, her dark blue eyes like black holes in her pasty face.

But it was her bruised breasts that drew and held her attention. She hadn't realised...

Jade stared at them for a long moment before shuddering violently. Suddenly, the full horror of what she'd narrowly escaped hit her, and she sank down on the side of the bath, her head dropping down between her knees as the nausea rose from her stomach. For a few seconds, the room spun, but the moment passed. Jade braced herself with hands on knees and slowly lifted her head. She still felt a little clammy and decided to sit there for a while longer.

Her thoughts kept going round, however. Regretful, recriminating thoughts.

She shouldn't have agreed to let Roberto use the spare

room of her unit till he could find a place of his own. She definitely shouldn't have agreed to his holding a small party last night.

But in truth, she hadn't seen any danger. After all, Roberto was gay. And so were all his friends. Jade had always found gay men not only sweet, but kind and gentlemanly and very interesting to talk to. They made good friends for women. Safe friends.

But one of Roberto's friends had not been safe.

The horror washed in again, bringing another wave of nausea.

Jade stood up abruptly and walked over to the shower, snapping on the water and standing there testing till it was hot enough. Stepping into the steaming spray, she shut her eyes and turned her face upwards, closing her mind to everything but the steady beating of its cleansing, reviving heat.

It was a mental trick she had learnt long ago. When things got too painful, she just clicked off her thoughts to everything but the most immediate and superficial needs. Washing. Eating. Sleeping.

For the first time, it didn't work. She couldn't seem to forget that hand over her mouth, that steely arm clamped around her breasts, those filthy words whispered in her ear. If she hadn't managed that lucky kick to her assailant's groin, God knew what would have happened.

But she had, and unexpectedly she'd been free. Snatching up her car keys from the hall table, she'd bolted for the door, wearing nothing but a silk robe, driving home to Belleview at a speed which owed thanks to its being three o'clock in the morning, with the streets of suburban Sydney almost deserted. Heaven knew what would have happened if she'd been stopped by the police. God, she could see it now, being arrested for dangerous driving and hauled, half-naked down to the police station. Then a sour-faced Nathan arriving the following morning with the family solicitor in tow. Like the last time.

Only the last time her arrest had been for possession of drugs. Zachary Marsden had defended her on that occasion as well.

Of course, it hadn't been *her* marijuana in the glovebox of her car. She detested drugs. It had belonged to a so-called friend who'd vowed she'd given up the habit. Luckily, Zachary was a top defender—would her father employ any other kind?—and he'd soon proved her innocence to the satisfaction of the magistrate and the charges had been dropped. Zachary had really believed in her innocence, too, which was more than could be said for Nathan.

What a hypocrite her adopted brother was!

He pretended to be holier-than-thou, just like her father. But she knew what he'd been up to before Byron found him on the streets of King's Cross. Yet he had the hide to judge her over her supposedly loose lifestyle, to criticise her for being sexually provocative.

Jade had to laugh at that. Nathan oozed sex. Why, there wasn't a woman within fifty feet of him who hadn't wanted him at some stage, her own mother included.

Immediately, Jade's mind closed in on the subject of her mother. In her opinion, she hadn't had a mother. End of story.

Back to Nathan.

Jade switched off the shower, her generous mouth curving into a bitter smile. She had that cold-blooded devil taped, all right. People felt sorry for him because of his supposedly unfortunate background. Well, *she* didn't. No way. He'd loved every minute of his decadent existence with that crazy mother of his.

Yes, Nathan was as hard as nails and an opportunist of the first order, conning his way into her father's heart, getting Byron to adopt him, securing a cushy lifestyle and a fantastic job that he wouldn't have had a hope of winning with his pathetic education. People said he was clever and perhaps he was—not many people could whip off an award-winning play every year in their spare time—but he didn't even have his HSC, let alone a university degree, which was what her father had said *she* had to have before she was allowed to set one foot inside Whitmore Opals.

Nathan's cleverness, for want of a better word, lay in his ability to psychoanalyse people and play on their weaknesses.

From the word go, poor Byron had believed Nathan had turned over a new leaf where his morals were concerned. Pity her father hadn't kept his eyes open to what had happened around his own home from the moment he brought that walking phallic symbol into Belleview all those years ago.

But Byron hadn't, perhaps because he'd rarely been home himself. The head of Whitmore Opals was a workaholic of the worst kind, meaning well, but invariably neglectful of his family except in short bossy bursts. He was also totally ignorant of their true feelings and real natures. Even when it came to Nathan's marriage, Byron had a tendency to blame Lenore for everything from its shotgun beginning to its inevitable demise. As if any woman other than the most martyrish could endure marriage to a machine. Yes, Byron was blind to the real Nathan.

But that was understandable. Nathan could make others believe he was something he wasn't if it meant achieving one of his selfish ends. Look at how she'd adored him for years. Hero-worshipped him. Loved him.

She'd thought he'd at least liked her back. What he'd liked was wallowing in her unthreatening adoration, the adoration of a little girl. Now that she was a woman, with a woman's needs and desires, he'd turned on her. Not because he didn't desire her. She knew he did. My God, he'd had to scrape up every ounce of that amazing willpower of his to stop making love to her that afternoon a few months ago. But he'd managed, because an affair with her would have endangered what he desired more: Whitmore Opals. The Whitmore fortune.

With Jade being Byron's only natural-born child and a

female to boot, Nathan probably figured he had a good chance of inheriting at least control of Whitmore's. Byron was a chauvinist of the first order who believed a woman's place was in the home, most certainly *not* in the board-room of a company! His tirades against women like Celeste Campbell were never-ending.

Jade secretly admired the female head of Campbell Jewels. The woman was bold and beautiful, and more than a little brazen in the way she conducted her private life. But so what? If she'd been a man, there wouldn't be a whimper of protest or criticism. Alas, however, Celeste was a woman, and the old double standards applied. Her usually younger lovers were denigrated as toy-boys. She was slyly called a slut.

Which was what Nathan had said *she* was in danger of becoming, Jade recalled with a twisting inside. Now that was the pot calling the kettle black in her opinion! And not true, either. She could count her so-called lovers on one hand, and still have enough fingers left over to play 'Chopsticks'!

An angry indignation had her grabbing a towel from the nearby rail. But when she started vigorously rubbing her-self dry, her bruised breasts moaned a protest. Looking down at them again, she suddenly burst into tears.

It took quite a while before Jade felt sufficiently in con-trol to leave the sanctuary of her bedroom and face her family.

The house seemed unnaturally quiet as she made her way slowly down the huge sweeping staircase. Where was everyone? Sighing, she headed for the kitchen and laundry wing, where Melanie was sure to be located.

Jade was right. Belleview's highly efficient housekeeper was filling the dishwasher, looking her usual stark self, and quite out of place in the newly renovated all-white kitchen with its bright shiny surfaces. One could well imagine Melanie, with her solemn Madonna face, prim black top-knot and severe black dress, as the housekeeper in a Gothic novel, gliding silently through dimly lit rooms, the only lights in those dead black eyes of hers the flickering reflection of the candle she was holding.

Jade gave a little shiver at this highly evocative and almost frightening scenario.

Melanie straightened, turned and saw her. 'Hello, Jade,' the housekeeper greeted her in that expressionless voice of hers. 'I put your car around in the garages for you. You seemed to have a little trouble finding them last night,' she finished drily.

'What? Oh…oh, yes. Thanks, I was a little—er…'

'Blind?' Melanie suggested.

Jade laughed. If there was one thing she could count on at home, it was everyone's bad opinion. There would be no sympathy here, no understanding. Her reputation was totally shot around Belleview. What would be the point in telling Melanie that the sight of home with its solid safe walls had flooded her eyes with tears last night, making her run off the circular driveway, across the front lawn and into the cement surrounds of the large, lily-filled pond? Or that, still terribly shaken from her ordeal, she'd left her car there and staggered inside, taken more sleeping tablets than was good for her and crashed into blessed oblivion?

'Will you be staying for dinner tonight?' the housekeeper asked.

'If it's all right with you.' She was hoping to inveigle Nathan into going back with her to her unit tomorrow to see if Roberto and co were still there. Big brothers—even adopted ones who despised you—had to be good for something.

Melanie shrugged. 'Whatever. I have tomorrow off, though. You'll have to do for yourself or get Ava to cook for you.'

'Good God, no. Auntie's cooking is even worse than her watercolours. I'll rustle something up myself. Where is the old dear, by the way? And everyone else, for that matter? This place is like a morgue today.'

The housekeeper looked up with those dull black eyes of hers, giving Jade a droll glance before turning away to start loading the dishwasher. The clock on the oven said two-fifty, Jade noticed. The sleeping tablets had knocked her out for nearly twelve hours.

'Nathan's not here, if that's who you've come looking for,' Melanie informed her. 'He's taken Kirsty and Gemma with him to the beach-house at Avoca for the weekend.'

'Gemma?' The name was vaguely familiar but she couldn't place it. 'Who's Gemma?' Jade asked, ignoring Melanie's assumption she'd come visiting just to see Nathan.

'Kirsty's minder. Kirsty's living here for a while.'

'Oh? Why's that? Lenore found herself a lover at last?'

Jade suspected that after twelve years married to Nathan Lenore might find it hard to replace her husband with another man. From what she'd heard—and her own limited experience with him—the man was dynamite in bed.

'I have no idea what Lenore's private life is like,' Melanie said with cool rebuke in her voice. 'She was simply fed up with Kirsty's behaviour and thought a few weeks with her father might do her good. But with Nathan working late at Whitmore's every day, he felt he had to hire someone to personally supervise Kirsty before and after school.'

Jade laughed. 'I'll bet Kirsty just loves having a minder at fourteen.' Suddenly, the penny dropped on where she'd heard that name. 'This Gemma person wouldn't happen to be a lush young thing with big brown eyes, would she?'

Melanie's eyes snapped round, confirming Jade's intuitive guess.

'I happened to drop by a couple of weeks back,' Jade elaborated wryly. 'Nathan was just getting out of his car with the aforesaid nymph sitting in the passenger seat,

looking as if butter wouldn't melt in her mouth. Nathan
was doing a good imitation of a protective father figure
but he didn't fool me for a second. I take it she's living
in?'

Melanie nodded, and so did Jade. Slowly. Cynically.

'I'll bet she's not the same innocent young thing today
that she was a couple of weeks ago.'

'I wouldn't bet too heavily on that,' Melanie said.
'Gemma's a strong-minded young woman with a wealth
of character.'

'She'll need to be,' Jade muttered, surprised by
Melanie's defence of this Gemma. *And* her confidence in
the girl's will-power. Despite her deadpan exterior,
Melanie was still a woman. She couldn't be ignorant of
the magnetism of Nathan's sex appeal, even if only as an
observer. The answer to the housekeeper's high opinion
of the girl had to lie in the girl herself.

'So tell me about her,' Jade resumed, her curiosity
piqued. 'Where did Nathan come across this gem of a
Gemma?'

Melanie looked up. 'Careful…your claws are showing.'

Jade laughed, recognising the truth of this statement.
Her feelings for Nathan perhaps weren't as vanquished as
she'd thought they were.

'OK, OK,' she agreed. 'I sound like a jealous cat. So
where does she come from?'

'Lightning Ridge.'

'The opal town way out back of Bourke?'

'That's the one. Nathan was out there buying opals for
Byron and Gemma sold him some. It seems her father had
just been accidentally killed—fell down a mine shaft—
and she was selling up everything to come to Sydney.
Nathan made her the offer of a job if she ever needed
one.'

'Which she took him up on, of course,' Jade said ruefully. 'What girl wouldn't, after meeting Nathan? Say no
more, I get the picture entirely.'

The housekeeper's sigh sounded exasperated.

'You can sigh, Melanie, but I saw the way that girl looked at Nathan the other week. Are you telling me she's *not* smitten by our resident Casanova?'

'All I'm saying is that she's not a pushover.'

'Meaning I am?'

Melanie gave her a sharp look. 'Don't go putting words into my mouth, Jade. You know better than anyone what sort of girl you are. I wouldn't dream of making such a judgement. I've only known you two years, six months of which you haven't even been living in this house. You weren't home much, even when you *were* living here.'

Jade's laugh was wry. 'I don't need to live here in person for you to have found out all the dirt on me. My mother used to adore telling everyone how bad I was. And it's all true. The climbing out of windows to meet boys in the middle of the night when I was only fifteen. Everything! I'm a bad 'un, Melanie. No doubt about it.'

'You and I both know you're not nearly as bad as you pretend to be, Jade,' Melanie astonished her by saying. 'Your teenage rebellions were revenge on your parents for their supposed lack of love, as well as some other imagined—or even real—transgressions.'

'My,' Jade returned caustically, 'What are you? The resident psychoanalyst around here?'

'I've had my share of experience with analysis,' Melanie said with not a flicker of retaliatory emotion.

Sympathy for this sad, soul-dead creature replaced Jade's anger. She knew about Melanie's past, how her husband and baby son had been killed in a car accident right before her eyes. It had been a horrific tragedy.

Yet while Jade could appreciate the numbing effect that would have on any wife and mother, it had been years now, for heaven's sake. Time to live again. Either that or put yourself out of your misery and throw yourself off a cliff or something.

Jade knew she herself would never commit suicide. She

refused to let life get her *that* down. Life was meant to be lived, and, goddammit, she was going to live hers. To hell with her father, and Nathan, and even what had happened last night. And to hell with her mother. Irene was already probably in hell, anyway!

'Are you all right, Jade?' Melanie asked.

'Yes, of course.' She blinked rapidly, then tossed her head in memory of when her hair had recently been long and brown. After Nathan's rejection she had gone out and had most of her hair cut off, the remainder dyed whipped-cream blonde, shaved at the sides and spiked on top. Oddly, the outrageous style and colour suited her. Men now pursued her even more than they had before. 'I'm fine,' she lied blithely.

'You don't look fine. You look terrible.'

'Oh, that's just because of the sleeping tablets I took last night. They always leave me dopey the next day.'

'You shouldn't be taking sleeping tablets,' Melanie reproached seriously. 'You shouldn't even have them in your possession. They're like having a loaded gun around. People say they never mean to shoot anyone but if they didn't own a gun they couldn't. Same thing with sleeping tablets.'

Jade stared at the housekeeper, and wondered if she had once overdosed on sleeping tablets. Unexpectedly, Jade felt the urge to try to make friends with this woman whom she'd always pitied but never really liked. Now, she wanted to extend the hand of friendship, to see if she could help her in some way. But what to say, how to start? They were hardly of the same generation. Melanie had to be over thirty. If not, she sure looked it!

'Let's not talk of nasties,' Jade started up in her best breezy voice. 'How's things going with Auntie Ava? I presume she's up in that studio of hers, fantasising about Prince Charming sweeping into her life on a white charger. Has she finished any of those infernal paintings of hers, yet?'

'I would have thought your first concern would be your father, Jade, not your aunt.'

'I said no nasties, remember. Hopefully, Pops will stay put in that hospital a while longer. I can just about tolerate visiting him there. It's rather amusing seeing him trussed up in that pristine white bed with his leg in a sling. Of course, I haven't seen him for over a fortnight. We had the most frightful row over my appearance and that was that. What's he done? Has he been a bad boy? Banged up his leg again trying to seduce one of the nurses? He certainly wouldn't have tried it on the matron. What a tartar that woman is!'

Melanie smiled at Jade's ravings, shocking Jade. Why, the woman was quite striking when she smiled, with dazzling white teeth and eyes like glittering jet jewels. Not only striking, but sensual. The mock scenario of Byron trying to seduce the nurses seemed to have tickled the housekeeper's fancy, lending a decidedly sexy flavour to her smile.

Now Jade was floored. Melanie... *Sexy*? The idea was preposterous. And yet...

Jade looked at the housekeeper, really looked at her, mentally stripping away that shapeless black dress, trying to see the real woman behind the sexless façade. Her slender shoulders were broad, her breasts full, her waist and hips trim. And when she bent down over the dishwasher, her buttocks showed shapely and firm through the black gabardine. Her knees—what Jade could see of them— were very nice indeed. As were her ankles. Those ghastly thick beige stockings distracted from, but not entirely hid, the slender coltish lines of the legs inside them.

Jade tried to imagine what Melanie would look like in a slinky black dress, scarlet gloss on that sultry mouth of hers and sexy earrings swinging around that long white neck she had. Everyone's eyes round Belleview would fall right out of their sockets, her father included. He wouldn't recognise his prim and proper housekeeper.

A sudden memory stabbed at Jade's heart before the corner of her mouth lifted in a cynical smirk. It was just as well, perhaps, that Melanie was as she was, considering what had happened between the last housekeeper and the master of Belleview. Catching her father with that woman in his arms had come as a dreadful shock to Jade. Her god of a father, high on his pedestal—or was it podium?— always preaching about character and control and moral standards. Her father, having an affair with his house- keeper while his manic depressive wife was safely in- stalled in a sanatorium somewhere.

He'd tried to explain everything away, saying he hadn't actually slept with the woman, saying he'd kissed her in a moment of weakness. Jade had not accused. She'd sim- ply stood there, not listening, refusing to understand, un- able to forgive, regardless of the circumstances. She couldn't abide parents who had the policy of 'don't do as I do, do as I say.'

She'd been just twenty at the time. Her father had dis- missed the unfortunate woman—another injustice, she be- lieved—and hired Melanie. But Jade had never looked at her father in the same way again. Neither had she taken a blind bit of notice of anything he tried to tell her. She went her own way, did her own thing. She had her own code of right and wrong, and had never hurt anyone as she was sure *he* had. He, *and* Nathan. *They* were the hurt- ers, the despoilers.

Jade frowned as her mind shifted uncomfortably to her mother.

No, she decided abruptly. I will not make excuses. For either of them. For *any* of them!

An alien tap-tapping sound click-clacked somewhere in the house. Not recognising it, Jade swivelled on the kitchen stool she was perched up on, only to see her father making his way across the family-room, a walking cane in his right hand.

Their eyes met simultaneously through the open doorway, Jade's widening as Byron's narrowed. He looked hopping mad.

'You didn't give me a chance to tell you,' Melanie said quietly from the other side of the breakfast bar. 'Your father came home from the hospital yesterday.'

CHAPTER TWO

'YOU'VE changed your mind, it seems, about darkening this doorstep again,' Byron barked at his daughter.

'And hi to you, Pops,' Jade said with a flipness she fell into when at her most stressed. What on earth was her father doing home from hospital? A fortnight ago they'd said his leg wasn't mending properly and he'd be stuck in there for another month at least. She should have known he'd prove them wrong. 'You thinking of auditioning for the part of Long John Silver?' she quipped airily, waving at the walking cane.

Byron hobbled into the kitchen, still scowling at his daughter. 'One day you'll use that sassy mouth of yours on the wrong person. I hope I'm around to see it. Melanie, I'm expecting a visitor shortly. A Mr Armstrong. Show him into my study when he arrives, will you? And we'll be wanting coffee. Or tea, if he prefers. Ask him.'

'Certainly, Bryon. Will this Mr Armstrong be staying to dinner?'

'Maybe. Maybe not. I'll have to let you know.'

'And who is Mr Armstrong?' Jade asked, the name not at all familiar.

Byron's hard blue eyes swung back to his daughter. 'No one you know.' He looked her up and down, his upper lip curling with disgust at her appearance. 'Good God, girl, don't you ever wear a bra?' And, spinning round on his good leg, he limped off.

She pulled a face at his disappearing back. She *did* wear a bra...once every hundred years or so.

Admittedly, the ribbed pink vest-top she was wearing moulded her well-rounded breasts like a second skin, her nipples outlined and emphasised. But she hadn't brought any clothes with her and all that was in her wardrobe were things she hadn't worn for years, most of which were a little tight on her. She'd gone through a semi-anorexic stage back in her teens, till the loss of half her boobs had brought her up with a jolt. Horrified, she'd quickly eaten up till she was back to her shapely self, substituting the dieting with aerobics and weight-training. Her figure had steadily gone from gaunt to good to great. She was quite proud of it and had no intention of hiding her hard-earned shape under dowdy matronly clothes. Lord, she was only twenty-two, not fifty-two!

Sliding from the kitchen stool, however, reminded her that the jeans she had on were close to obscene, they were so tight. Maybe she should hunt out something of Auntie Ava's to put on. The old dear was always buying things in sales that were several sizes too small.

Jade was on the way through the family-room, heading in the direction of the front hall when the doorbell rang. 'I'll get it, Melanie,' she shouted back over her shoulder. 'It's sure to be the mysterious Mr Armstrong.'

'Find out if he's staying to dinner, will you, Jade?' Melanie called back. 'And if he wants tea or coffee.'

'Will do.'

She was whistling when she opened the door, her whistle changing to a low wolf-whistle as she took in the man standing there. God, but he was gorgeous! Tall, without being too tall, black curly hair, olive skin, lean saturnine features and piercing black eyes. His thick dark eyelashes were curly too, the bottom ones resting on high cheekbones that looked as if they'd been carved in stone.

He looked as if he'd been carved in stone, so still was he. And so totally unaffected by her none too subtle whistle.

Jade thought she detected the slightest flicker of something when his hard gaze raked over her eyecatching form. But if he was in any way impressed by what he saw he certainly didn't show it. Instead, there was a fractional lifting of his already sardonically arched eyebrows before he spoke in a voice reminiscent of Melanie's for its lack of emotion.

'Good afternoon,' he said coolly. 'Mr Whitmore is expecting me. Kyle Armstrong.'

I wonder if there's a *Mrs* Armstrong, was Jade's first thought, not at all put out by the man's apparent indifference to her charms. Nothing like a good challenge. It would make for a pleasant change. But she never tampered with married men. That was one of the lines she drew.

Pity other people didn't, she thought bitterly.

Her attention returned to the man before her. He wasn't wearing a wedding-ring but he was too good-looking not to be married. Taking a wild stab at his age, she came up with somewhere between twenty-eight and thirty-two. She was always hopeless at ages. She'd thought Roberto around thirty and he'd been closer to forty!

'Good afternoon, Mr Armstrong,' she greeted, holding out her hand and flashing him one of her most winning smiles. Her dentist had every reason to be proud of the perfectly even white teeth she displayed. 'Yes, my father mentioned he was expecting you. Do come in. I'll take you to him.'

Her smile turned slightly smug at Mr Armstrong's startled reaction to her announcing her relationship with the man he'd come to see. Possibly, he expected any daughter of the wealthy Byron Whitmore to be dressed a little more classily. Or maybe he hadn't known Byron *had* a daughter?

Now that was an interesting speculation. Still, Jade appreciated her father wouldn't go round proudly showing her photograph to every Tom, Dick and Harry. He was probably terrified one of them might recognise her as the little bit of fluff they'd had one night. After all, if she'd slept with as many men as her father and Nathan presumed, Byron was bound to come across one sooner or later!

Jade brushed aside the jab of dismay this thinking brought and wondered for the first time what business the gorgeous Mr Armstrong was in. He had to be calling on business. Why else would he be dressed in a dark grey suit on a hot Saturday afternoon? Besides, her father was not one for male friends of the personal kind. He *was* close to Nathan, and had a type of friendship with Zachary Marsden. But that too was partly business. Zachary had been the Whitmores' legal advisor for as long as she could remember.

Jade shut the front door and turned to their guest. He was no longer looking at her but was glancing around the house. Assessingly, she thought.

'This way...' She waved him along the downstairs hall that went under the staircase. Byron's study being the second last door on the right. 'Mr. Armstrong...' She began as they walked side by side.

'Kyle,' he returned coolly. 'Call me Kyle.'

'How nice. Kyle, then.' She smiled over at him. 'And I'm Jade.'

'Jade,' he repeated, but said nothing more. He didn't smile back, either.

Jade felt a momentary irritation. She didn't like men she couldn't read, or who didn't react the way she expected them to. It came to her abruptly that she didn't like men who were challenges after all. She much preferred men who fell victim to her charms immediately, and who pursued her doggedly. She enjoyed leading them a merry dance, making them almost beg for her favours, favours she did *not* bestow left, right and centre, *au contraire* to popular opinion.

She slid a sidewards glance over at the man beside her. In profile, he was not as pretty. His nose was sharp. His chin jutted stubbornly. He was not a man to beg for any-

thing, of that she was certain. He was also staring steadfastly forward as they walked along the hallway together.

But if Jade's mind found Mr Armstrong's rude indifference highly offputting, her body did not. Just looking at
him was making her stomach curl with a quite alien sensation. Dear God, but she would give anything to have him
want her as she was suddenly wanting him.

Jade only managed to stop herself gasping in shock. For
she had never really wanted a man like that in her entire
life!

Oh, yes, she'd once been mad about the opposite sex,
thriving on the dizzying excitement of being desired and
needed and loved. But she'd been very young then, a teenager desperately looking for love and attention and approval, finding substitutes for all three in the kisses and
arms of her boyfriends.

But she'd only had two actual lovers during her teenage
years, not a zillion, her last serious relationship breaking
up well before Nathan came back to Belleview to live after
his separation from Lenore. That was when Jade's hero
worship for her adopted brother had flared to a full-blown
infatuation, and, while her feelings for Nathan had seemed
part sexual at the time, she could see now that they hadn't
touched the surface of real desire. Real desire was what she
was feeling at this moment.

Yes, she'd tried to seduce Nathan, but not looking for
sexual satisfaction—frankly, she'd never found intercourse
at all memorable—but as a way to recapture his love and
attention, the love and attention he'd once bestowed on her
as a child and which had made her young life bearable.
Admittedly, after that first bold kiss of hers, he'd quickly
turned the tables on her, taking the initiative and managing
to arouse her quite stunningly before he'd abruptly terminated the encounter. Her body had undoubtedly been left
aching with physical frustration, which might explain why
she'd raced precipitately into the arms of a new admirer a
couple of days later.

The next morning, however, she'd felt ashamed of herself for the first time in her life. She'd only met the man the previous night at a party, where admittedly she'd had too much to drink. Not that that was any excuse. At least, she hadn't gone out with him again.

There had been several admirers since. But none had persuaded her into his bed.

Jade conceded, however, that Kyle Armstrong would not have much trouble doing just that.

Suddenly, she hoped he was married. That would put an end to this amazingly intense desire he'd somehow managed to spark in her. Her whole body felt tense and tingling by the time she stopped outside the study door and knocked.

'Yes,' boomed her father.

Opening the door, she popped her head inside. 'Mr Armstrong is here.'

'Well, bring him in, girl. Don't stand there looking ridiculous.'

Gritting her teeth, Jade threw open the door and waved their visitor inside.

He went, not giving her a second look. She was disgusted to find her heart was still racing and that her eyes were clinging to the back of that dark grey suit, to the way it fitted his nicely shaped shoulders like a glove. Jade had been on the end of undressing eyes from men before, but she'd never been guilty of doing such a thing herself. She was very definitely undressing Kyle Armstrong in her mind at that moment, however, and the results were unnerving. How was he managing to exude such a potent sexuality without even trying?

'Don't get up, Mr Whitmore,' Kyle said when Byron started struggling to his feet behind the huge desk. Striding over, he outstretched his long arm to shake Byron's hand. 'I'm so glad to meet you at last, sir. Talking on the telephone is not the same, is it?'

Jade saw her father look his guest up and down. Clearly, he liked what he saw almost as much as she did.

'It certainly isn't, my boy,' he said.

Jade dropped his age down to twenty-six or -seven. Her father would not call a man close to thirty…my boy.

'You were just leaving, Jade?' Byron snapped, making her seethe inside. How dared he dismiss her so rudely?

She delivered a saccharine smile his way. 'Melanie asked me to ask if Kyle was staying for dinner. Also, if he preferred tea or coffee.'

'You *know* Kyle here?' Byron ground out.

'Not till a minute ago,' she replied sweetly. And make of that what you will, you horny old hypocrite.

'Ah…'

His obvious relief infuriated the life out of her. 'Well?' she said sharply.

'What about it, Kyle? Can you stay for dinner? I'd like you to. I doubt if we'll have finished our discussions till then.'

'I'd love to stay,' he replied politely, still not looking at Jade. Suddenly, she felt like slapping his coolly supercilious face. Though poisoning would be better. She might slip some hemlock in his wine tonight.

But then she thought of a better vengeance for this snooty pair. Her father wanted her to wear a bra. Well, she would! At dinner tonight. A quite spectacular bejewelled corselette number that she'd bought for a fancy-dress costume a few years back and which would undoubtedly be at least one size too small. By God, if those unflappable dark eyes didn't fall out of their sockets when she walked into the dining-room wearing *that*, then she wasn't the girl voted most likely not to be a virgin in her last year at St Brigit's girls school.

'Tea or coffee?' she asked with the simpering sweetness of a Southern belle, fluttering her eyelashes when Kyle turned to glance her way at last.

'Coffee. Black, no sugar.'

Not a twitch. Not a flicker, either of irritation or amusement or anything. The man was a robot, she decided. A cold lifeless sexless robot. How could she have possibly thought he was sexy a moment ago?

But he was, she groaned silently. He most definitely was. God!

It struck Jade quite forcibly then that he couldn't be married. Married men always showed interest in her. *Always*.

She stared at him for a long moment with angry eyes, then, whirling, left the room, slamming the door behind her. 'Pompous fool!' she muttered aloud. 'Arrogant bastard,' she amended as she marched along the hallway. By the time she reached the kitchen, various other unprintable descriptions had found favour, the last one bringing Melanie's eyes snapping up with startled surprise.

'Goodness! Who are you referring to? Surely not your father!'

'No. Kyle Armstrong. Mr. Cool-as-a-cucumber.'

'Oh, I see. You found him attractive and he didn't respond accordingly.'

When Jade glared outrage at Melanie, the housekeeper actually laughed. Once again, Jade was struck by the transformation in the woman once she abandoned her icy façade. What Melanie needed to snap her out of the past was some man to come along who could make her smile and laugh again. Laughter made life bearable.

Jade wagged a finger at Melanie. 'I haven't given up yet,' she warned. 'Mr Armstrong's staying for dinner.'

'Is he, now? And what are you going to do, come down to dinner in your birthday suit?'

'Not quite.'

'Has it ever occurred to you that some men just don't like women who are obvious in their pursuit of them?'

Jade declined telling Melanie that it didn't work if you dressed like a nun and acted like a corpse, either. 'I don't intend chasing the man. I simply want him to see what he could have if *he* chased *me*!'

'And what if he doesn't choose to chase you? What if he likes more subtle women whose clothing hints at their charms rather than shoves it in their faces?'

'I don't shove my charms in men's faces!' Jade protested.

'Don't you?' Melanie's eyes slid drily over the skintight jeans and top. 'Look, Jade, you can get away with things at university that the more mature world won't tolerate kindly. How old is this Mr Armstrong?'

Jade shrugged. 'Late twenties, I think. But he acts like he's pushing forty.'

Melanie smiled. 'In that case, if you want to attract his attention, perhaps you should adopt a more mature fashion sense and attitude.'

'I'd rather be dead than dress and act like some snobbish society bitch,' she pouted. 'They all look the same, as if they've been poured out of a mould. If Mr Kyle Armstrong doesn't like the way I am then he can drop dead. I won't play ice princess for any man.'

'Then you'd better resign yourself to losing out this time.'

'We'll see,' Jade bit out, and went to leave. 'Oh, by the way,' she added, stopping to look back over her shoulder. 'He likes coffee. Black, no sugar. Same as me.'

With that, she stalked from the kitchen, determined strides carrying her across the family-room to the front foyer, up the stairs two at a time and along the picture-lined gallery down to Ava's studio. Bursting in without knocking, she threw a greeting at her startled aunt before plonking herself down on the much used divan. With a disgruntled sigh, she rearranged the many pillows and lay down, stretching out her long legs.

'I've had it with Pops, Auntie,' she grumbled. 'Really had it!'

'Tell me something new, Jade, dear.' Ava put down her paintbrush and wandered over to stare down at her niece. She took one look at the dark smudges under the girl's eyes and felt a surge of sympathy. She'd always liked Jade, felt the girl had got a raw deal in life with Irene as a mother and Byron as a father. Things hadn't improved much with Byron bringing Nathan home, either. Having someone like Nathan as an adopted brother was no help at all. Ava had been relieved when Jade finally left home. Nothing like having to do for oneself to make one grow up, and grow.

Ava silently wished she had the courage to buck her big brother's controlling hand and do the same. But it was too late for her. Far too late…

'At least you don't have to stay, if your father annoys you, dear. Why are you here, by the way? Melanie told me at breakfast that you'd come home during the night.'

Ava was shocked by the haunted, almost horrified look that zoomed into her niece's dark blue eyes. But the fear vanished almost before Ava could be sure that was what she'd seen, replaced by one of Jade's nonchalant *c'est la vie* expressions. Ava had always admired the girl's courage and spirit, but it worried her that she buried far too many problems behind that good-time-girl persona. Clearly, something had happened last night to send Jade running for home like a frightened child. But she knew Jade too well to hope she'd confide in her stuffy old aunt.

'Oh, just thought I'd drop in and see how the old family was doing,' Jade said, waving an airy hand. 'I didn't know Pops was home, of course. Or that Nathan had escaped to Avoca with his daughter and his girlfriend.'

Ava frowned. '*Girlfriend*? Oh, you mean Gemma. She's not Nathan's girlfriend, Jade, she's—'

'Kirsty's minder,' Jade broke in drily. 'Yes, I gather that's the occupation she goes under. But you and I both know, Auntie, that she'll be providing some extra services before long.'

'I think that is Nathan and Gemma's business, don't you?' Ava rebuked gently. 'After all, Nathan's divorced and Gemma's single.'

'Single! She's barely out of nappies.'

'She's nearly twenty, Jade, only two years your junior. You didn't seem to think Nathan was too old for you a while back.'

'Auntie!' Jade mocked. 'Have you been spying on me?'

'One hardly needs to spy on you, Jade, dear. You flaunt your feelings for all to see. You flaunt your other attributes as well,' she added, casting an acerbic eye over the girl's eyecatching and obviously braless figure.

For once, her niece seemed bothered by criticism over her appearance. Normally, she responded by being even more outrageous.

Jade sat up, glancing down at her body with a frown on her face. 'Melanie was saying much of the same a minute ago,' she muttered unhappily. 'But honestly, Auntie, I don't like stuffy clothes. And I don't like stuffy people, especially stuffy men!'

Ava laughed. 'What man's been putting your nose out of joint?'

'Some nerd Pops is holed up with in his study. Do you know him? He goes by the name of Mr Kyle Armstrong.'

'Ah…the whizkid from Tasmania.'

'And?'

Ava walked back over to sit down at her easel. She picked up her paintbrush and started dabbing before she satisfied Jade's curiosity. 'Can't tell you much. He's a marketing expert your father is thinking of hiring to jazz up Whitmore Opals.'

'Jazz up? That man couldn't jazz up anything. If Pops wants someone to jazz up Whitmore Opals why doesn't he hire someone with a bit of flair, someone modern and really young? Someone like me! I'm specialising in marketing at uni this year. I'll have my degree in November. God, I don't believe this. I'm so mad I could spit.' She jumped to her feet and started pacing the room.

'One is hardly likely to hire an undergraduate for head of marketing, Jade,' her aunt advised logically.

But Jade didn't feel logical. Fury and resentment were

firing her blood. Not only did she have Nathan coveting control of the entire Whitmore fortune—the family had fingers in many pies besides opals—now she had her father overlooking his own daughter to hire some pompous upstart into the very job she'd been going to invent herself after she'd gained her marketing degree. Up till this point, Whitmore Opals didn't even *have* a marketing section, let alone a head of it. Byron had been only too happy to be head of everything: managing, selling, marketing, buying, advertising.

Jade's temper was reaching boiling point when she suddenly realised this could be turned to her advantage. Why, if she played her cards right, she might be able to get the super-cool and undoubtedly ambitious Mr Armstrong on her side. By reminding him on the sly that she was the boss's daughter and a marketing undergraduate, she might be able to con him into letting her work part-time in the office, so gaining some valuable training. Maybe once she showed her father she could be as clever and competent as any man, he would relinquish that stupid old-fashioned idea that a woman had no place in business.

Of course, to achieve such an end, she would have to present a slightly more conservative image, as Melanie had suggested. Any thought of wearing that ridiculously provocative corselette would have to be abandoned. She might even have to wear a *normal* bra.

'Auntie,' she said slowly, 'you wouldn't mind if I looked through your wardrobe, would you? I might borrow something for dinner tonight. Mr Armstrong is dining with us.'

'I think you'll find it a bit depleted, dear. I gave everything that didn't fit me to Gemma.'

Jade couldn't believe it. What kind of girl was this Gemma person that everyone was so taken with her? No doubt her own father thought she was just the ants' pants, not like his own cheap, vulgar tramp of a daughter. God, she hoped Nathan hurried up and corrupted that girl. And she hoped everyone found out about it, including her father.

Grumbling under her breath, she decided there was nothing else to do but go downstairs and throw herself on Melanie's mercy. The woman had to have something in her wardrobe besides those hideous black dresses she always wore.

Before she left, she wandered over to look at her aunt's painting.

'Hey,' she said, surprise in her voice. 'That's rather good. You must be improving, Auntie.'

'Either that, or your taste is,' Ava countered with uncharacteristic wit. She and her niece exchanged startled glances.

'Goodness, Auntie,' Jade laughed. 'That was quick.'

'Yes, it was, wasn't it?'

Jade gave her a considering look. 'You seem happier, do you know that?'

'You could be right. The whole house has been happier since Gemma came to live here.'

'God, not that girl again! I'll have to meet this paragon of perfection soon or I'll explode with envy and irritation!'

Now Ava laughed. 'She'll have you eating out of her hand in no time, just as she has everyone else.'

'I wouldn't bet on that if I were you, Auntie.' And, thinking darkly jealous thoughts, Jade marched from the room.

Gemma propped herself up on one elbow and looked down at the naked man sleeping beside her. He was so beautiful.

Her eyes caressed his perfect profile, his gorgeous golden hair, tousled at the moment, and that glorious mouth, full-lipped and sensual but not at all feminine. There wasn't a feminine bone in Nathan Whitmore's beautiful bronzed body.

Hard to believe he was thirty-five.

Hard to believe that less than an hour ago she had been a fear-filled, quivering virgin.

Hard to believe he wanted to marry *her*, a silly little country girl not yet twenty. She couldn't believe her luck.

'You're making me self-conscious, staring at me like that,' he murmured, his left eye flicking half open.

'Oh! I...I thought you'd fallen asleep.'

'Just resting,' he whispered, and reached for her.

Gemma gave herself up momentarily to the excitement of his kisses, but as soon as he lifted his mouth to take a breath, she wriggled out of his arms and away from further temptation.

'We have to stop, Nathan,' she said breathlessly. 'Kirsty might come back from the beach at any moment. She's been gone over an hour. It's nearly three.'

It was only by chance that Gemma wasn't down at the beach with Kirsty. But she hadn't liked the sea; hadn't liked it at all.

'Kirsty never leaves the beach till the sun goes down,' Nathan reassured her. 'Still, it's possible, I suppose, and I wouldn't want her to catch us together like this.' He trickled a hand over Gemma's breasts, smiling softly as an involuntary tremor rippled through her. 'My own lovely little Gemma,' he said, and bent to flick a moist fingertip over the nearest erect nipple. 'Do you realise we'll have all night together now that Kirsty's going to that movie marathon?'

Gemma tried to dampen down her excitement at such a prospect to focus on Nathan's daughter. 'I'm not sure Lenore would be happy with Kirsty going to an all-night movie session, Nathan. She's only fourteen, after all. Not only that, she's supposed to be grounded for another week.'

At the mention of his ex-wife, Nathan scowled and rolled away, planting angry feet on the floor beside the bed. 'I'll make the decisions for my daughter while she's under my roof. Lenore can go jump.'

Gemma was taken aback by Nathan's burst of temper, so unlike his usual cool self. Her mind flashed to that kiss she'd witnessed between him and his ex-wife less than two weeks before, on the very first night she'd come to Belleview. It had been one of the main reasons she'd fought her attraction for Nathan, thinking he was still in love with

Lenore. The passion of the last hour had deflected her mind away from any earlier doubts, but now the possibility that the man she loved still harboured strong feelings for the woman he'd been married to for twelve years raised its ugly head again.

'She's Kirsty's mother,' Gemma argued unhappily. 'I think her feelings have to be considered.'

Nathan started pulling on his clothes, his actions jerky. 'As if that selfish bitch has got any real feelings,' he muttered.

Gemma stared at him. When Nathan saw her shocked expression he leant back over the bed to cup her chin and kiss her lightly on the mouth. 'Not like you, my darling girl. You have more feeling in your little finger than Lenore has in her whole body.'

Then why were you kissing her less than two weeks ago as if you wanted to devour her? she was dying to ask. Instead, she said tremulously, 'You do love me, don't you, Nathan?'

'*Love* you? I *adore* you.' His mouth returned to hers, demanding and hungry. He groaned and pushed her back on the pillows.

'Nathan, we can't!' she gasped.

'There's no such thing as can't, Gemma,' he growled. 'Only won't.' He buried his face between her breasts, then slowly slid downwards.

'You...you shouldn't,' she managed in a weak whisper, both embarrassed and fascinated by what he was now doing. For a while the embarrassment won, her face flaming, her hands fluttering helplessly by her sides. But then sheer physical pleasure triumphed over any shock or shame. Her fingers started grasping the sheets on either side of her, and her mind spun out into a void of endless delight.

CHAPTER THREE

JADE surveyed her reflection in the mirror with mischievous satisfaction. Melanie had come through with a navy linen suit that would have looked ghastly if Jade had worn the white silk blouse with the tie at the throat that went with it. Instead, she'd filled the deep V neckline with a lacy pink camisole rescued from the depths of Auntie Ava's wardrobe. The dear old thing had also produced a pair of dainty pink sandals with outrageously high heels, a relic from her partying days.

Digging deep in her own drawers, Jade had come up with some pink multi-disc earrings which she'd adored as a teenager but which hadn't seen the light of day since. Oddly enough, they looked very effective with her new short blonde hair.

The combination of the sedate and the saucy produced a highly tantalising whole, which hinted—as Melanie and Ava had suggested—but was still sexy at the same time. Of course, Jade couldn't resist the naughty little added touches, such as painting her toenails a vibrant pink, then leaving off tights. She'd also turned over the waistband of the knee-length pleated skirt a couple of times so that the hem swirled mid-thigh when she turned around. She made a mental note to turn around often.

Only once during her dressing did Jade's mind whip back to the distressing events of the previous evening. Melanie had lent her a bra—they were around the same size—but Jade found her bruised breasts too sore to tolerate the constriction. For a moment, as she was forced to face her phys-

ical damage, fear swept in again, but this was swiftly followed by a bitter fury. Being a quivering victim was not
Jade's style. She gritted her teeth and vowed she would not
let some pervert damage her mind. He could damage her
body—that would heal!—but not her mind. Her mind was
her own. She refused to have it warped or twisted. If she
did, she might end up like her mother. Now there was a
warped and twisted mind if ever there was one!

So with her freshly shampooed and moussed hair teased
to its maximum height on top of her head, and enough
Spellbound perfume on to cast a thousand spells, Jade
swanned downstairs and along to the formal drawing-room
where Melanie said her father was having pre-dinner drinks
with his guest. The grandfather clock in the hall donged
seven-thirty as Jade passed. Dinner had been ordered for
eight.

Both men were sitting down when she sashayed in, her
father on the green velvet sofa that faced the fireplace,
while Mr Cool occupied one of the overstuffed brocade
armchairs that flanked the marble hearth. There were no
guesses which one drew her attention first.

Hell, but he looked as lethally attractive sitting there,
sipping his drink, as did the drink he was sipping. By the
colour, it had to be straight Johnny Walker. Jade conceded
she could have done with a stiff drink herself right at that
moment, her courage in danger of failing her. What was it
about this man that rattled her so—the fact that she fancied
him so badly, or that *he* didn't fancy *her* at all?

She resisted licking suddenly dry lips and kept moving
into the room, her skirt swishing around her bare legs, her
eyes still on Kyle Armstrong, waiting for—no, hoping
for—a favourable reaction to her vastly changed appearance.

His eyes lifted as she approached, locking with hers.
They remained perfectly steady, showing nothing in their
coal-black depths that she could read. But he didn't turn
his eyes away and oddly she gained the impression he was

challenging her, no, *compelling* her to keep looking at him. Suddenly she felt the power of his mental strength, and her knees almost went from under her. This most uncharacteristic weakness unnerved Jade, unnerved then annoyed her.

Gathering herself, she shot him a bold smile, hoping to ruffle his equilibrium as much as his gypsy-eyed stare had ruffled hers. But he didn't smile back, merely lifted his drink to his lips again, keeping up his cool assessment of her over the rim.

Jade found her smile fading and an amazing blush heating her cheeks. Totally rattled now, she wrenched her eyes away from him to land on her frowning father, who couldn't seem to make up his mind whether he liked how she looked or not. She appreciated his ambivalence, and found amusement in it, thank heavens. She needed *something* to break this awful tension that had been invading her since entering the room.

'Good evening, Father, dear,' she said, abandoning her usual address of Pops. 'Kyle,' she added, inclining her head their guest's way without actually meeting his eyes.

Both said good evening back as she continued over to the rosewood drinks cabinet, where she mixed herself a triple Scotch and ginger ale, taking a deep swallow before returning to make the twosome a far from cosy threesome.

Her father clicked his tongue impatiently when he had to move his cane for her to sit down next to him. 'Did you finish whatever it was you had to finish?' she enquired casually, crossing her legs and tucking her ankles back toward the base of the sofa.

'I think we tied up everything to our mutual satisfaction, wouldn't you say, Kyle?' Byron conceded, his reply not really telling her anything.

'Yes, indeed,' came Mr Cool's equally uninformative remark.

Piqued, Jade decided to put this chauvinistic pair on the spot. 'Auntie Ava says Kyle is going to be the new head of marketing at Whitmore Opals—is that right?'

'Damned woman,' Byron muttered under his breath.

Jade laughed. 'Did I hear right, Father, dear? Are you calling me a woman at last?'

His hard blue eyes turned her way. Clearly, he would have liked to tear strips off her for her impudence, but the presence of a guest stopped him. With a great effort of will, Byron relaxed back on the sofa and found a smile that should have warned her what was coming.

'A real woman is more than a set of curves, daughter, dear,' he said with poisonous pointedness.

'So true, so true,' she returned airily after taking another deep swallow of her drink. 'And a real man is more than an impressive set of—er—muscles. Don't you agree, Kyle?' she finished, flashing him a mock-innocent smile.

Good God, was she imagining things or was that actually a twinkle of amusement in those implacable dark eyes of his? His mouth, however, maintained its habitual straight line, though he did cover it slightly by lifting his drink to his lips once more.

The glass retreated and yes, his mouth was as unmoved as before. 'I most certainly do agree, Jade,' he said smoothly. 'And you're right about that other matter as well. Byron has offered me the position as marketing manager and I have accepted.'

Most Australians didn't move their lips much when they spoke. Kyle Armstrong, however, had a surprising mobile mouth when he talked, his voice clear, cultured and well enunciated, like an actor. It drew one's attention to his mouth, and his lips.

Intriguing lips, those, Jade realised, her gaze fastening on them, the top one thin and cruel, the bottom soft and sensual. Which was the real man? God, she just had to find out. But *how*? He wasn't at all impressed by her. Or interested.

Or was he?

Her eyes lifted to that enigmatic gaze of his, only to find it fixed on the expanse of tanned thigh she was showing.

Jade's heart began to beat faster. Maybe he *was* a little interested. Maybe he was just good at hiding it. Maybe it was only her father's presence that stopped him from showing any interest. What was he wondering while he looked at her legs? Was he speculating what it might be like to get lost between them?

Jade found herself pressing her thighs tightly together, appalled by the escalating explicitness of her thoughts.

So this was lust, she thought dazedly.

This was one of the seven deadly sins.

No wonder people fell prey to its seductive power. She'd never felt so excited, so *driven*.

Once again, she started hoping that Kyle might be married, so that she had a good reason to fight this alien force that was possessing her.

'Are you married, Kyle?' she asked abruptly.

'No,' he said, his brows drawing slightly together as his eyes lifted to hers. 'Why do you ask?'

Perversely, she was relieved by the news, which didn't augur well for her future behaviour. Jade suspected she was about to embark on a course of action even more outrageous than any she'd ever been accused of. 'I was just wondering what your wife—if you had one,' she added with a husky laugh, 'might think of her husband moving interstate for a job.'

'How did you know that…?' The corner of his mouth tipped up into the tiniest of rueful smiles. 'Ah…your Auntie Ava again?' he suggested drily.

'Of course.'

'I'll never tell that infernal woman another damned thing!' Byron pronounced testily from the other end of the sofa.

'Poor Auntie,' Jade muttered before rounding on her father, her voice sharp. 'Why all the cloak and dagger stuff, anyway? Who'd care if Mr. C—?' She broke off, her eyes widening. My God, she'd almost called him Mr Cool out loud! Clearing her throat as a cover, she said 'excuse me', then sipped her drink. A fit of mad giggles sprang to her throat but she managed to stifle the urge and continue in a surprisingly normal voice. 'I was going to say why shouldn't other people know about Kyle's appointment?'

'Because I don't want Celeste Campbell to get wind of it, that's why!' Byron snarled.

Jade raised her eyebrows. She often wondered what had happened between her father and Celeste Campbell to make their relationship so vitriolic on his side, and continuingly vengeful on hers. Celeste was, in fact, Jade's aunt, being her mother's half-sister. Her mother, Irene, had been Stewart Campbell's first-born child, but his wife had passed away within weeks of Irene being born and the widower Campbell had subsequently remarried and had two more children, Celeste and Damian.

Jade found the antagonism between her father and Celeste Campbell quite perplexing. The ancient feud between their fathers, David Whitmore and Stewart Campbell, was well known, though not the reason behind it. Something to do with an opal, she had heard once, a very valuable one which had disappeared or something.

Whatever, after the two men passed away, her parents' marriage had seemed to heal the rift between the families to a degree. Enough, anyway, for the old animosity to die down to nothing but normal competition between business people who shared a common trade. Apparently, however, when Celeste had taken control of Campbell Jewels about ten years ago, she'd found cause to resurrect the old feud between the Campbells and Whitmores.

It was a mystery all right and one which she didn't think she'd ever solve. Her father was not about to confide in her. Neither was Celeste Campbell. Maybe they just hated each other's guts. Or, more likely, Jade's mother had stirred up some trouble. Irene had bad-mouthed Celeste every chance she got.

'I doubt Ms Campbell could do much more to Whitmore's than she's been doing,' Jade commented wryly.

'You don't give an enemy any advantage,' her father snapped.

'But *why* is she your enemy, Father? What did you do to her, or vice versa? I've always wanted to know.'

'I do not wish to discuss this topic at this juncture, thank you, Jade. Kyle doesn't want to hear our family dirty linen aired, I'm sure.'

Dirty linen? That sounded intensely personal and far darker than anything she'd been imagining.

Jade stared at her father for a second before recovering. 'I'm sure Kyle would like to be acquainted with the nature of the competition between Campbell's and Whitmore's. He needs to know what he's up against.'

'He already knows what he's up against. Celeste Campbell is a conniving, ambitious, vengeful bitch who will stop at nothing to ruin me. There's no more to be said!'

Melanie's entering the room at that precise moment to announce dinner was a frustration to Jade. For there was a lot more to be said. The frown on Kyle's face showed he agreed with her. Maybe he was even having second thoughts about the difficult job he was taking on. Jade suspected that if the family had had to rely on the profits from Whitmore Opals over the past few years they would be in deep financial straits. Fortunately, during the good years, both Grandfather Whitmore and her own father had diversified their investments into property and blue-chip stocks and shares.

Not that Jade had to rely on her family—or her father— for money any more. When she'd turned twenty-one last year, she'd inherited a substantial income from a trust her grandmother had set up for her before she was even born. This had been added to with her mother's recent estate, which included a lot of valuable jewellery.

Unhappy about taking anything from her mother, Jade had left the jewels to languish in the family safe. Thinking about them now, she decided she would give them all to Auntie Ava. The poor dear had to ask Byron for every single cent, her big brother having been made executor of her inheritance till she married, a most unsatisfactory arrangement for any self-respecting female. No wonder she buckled under his will all the time. She would advise Ava to sell some of the jewellery and do something with the proceeds. Go to a proper art school. Or take off on a world cruise. Who knew? Maybe she'd even meet her Prince Charming if she got out and about. And maybe she'd lose some weight!

'This way, Mr Armstrong,' Melanie was directing their guest in her cool, slightly imperious manner. 'I hope you like lamb...'

Jade was left to help her father struggle to his feet. 'Here, lean on me, Pops,' she offered.

'So it's "Pops" now, is it?' he frowned. 'What happened to "Father dear"? Or was that only to impress our visitor?'

'Naturally,' she grinned, and hoisted her father's arm around her shoulders. He grunted with real pain when his weight shifted across his bad leg.

'I'll bet you signed yourself out of that hospital too soon, didn't you?' Jade accused.

'Bloody hospitals should be banned. Torture chambers, all of them.'

Jade laughed.

'You have a nice laugh, daughter, do you know that?'

'*You* certainly haven't told me before. Watch the edge of that coffee-table!'

They watched it together as she manoeuvred Byron into clear territory. The drawing-room was rather cluttered with a myriad antiques and expensive knickknacks.

'You're strong, aren't you?' Byron commented with surprise in his voice. 'You have broad shoulders. Must take after your father.'

'Part of what you're feeling is shoulder pads,' she said, not sure how to take this shift in the conversation. If she didn't know better, she might think her father was trying to make up with her after their last row, not to mention his earlier rudeness.

'I can manage by myself now,' he said curtly, as though embarrassed by his conciliatory behaviour and taking it back. 'Hand me my cane.'

She did. Smiling.

He caught the smile and smiled back.

Jade's heart contracted. Why did she love him so much when he was such a cantankerous bastard, and when he lived his life by typically male standards? Did he honestly think she believed that one incident had been his one and only transgression with other women while her mother was alive? Good God, just look at him! Fifty years old with a bung leg and a scowling face and he'd still stop most women dead in their tracks at a single glance. His body was still hard, his head still full of hair. And those hard blue eyes were so damned sexy it was sinful.

'You're a good girl,' he said. 'Underneath. And you look very nice tonight.'

Jade's smile widened.

'What's the private joke?' he demanded to know.

'It was the underneath part. I still haven't got a bra on, you know.'

'No, I didn't know. And neither would any other man looking at you in that rig-out, which is exactly how it should be. The only man who should see a woman's bare breasts is her husband!'

'I'll keep that in mind, Pops.'

Jade resisted telling her father that the last thing she was ever going to have was a husband. Marriage, in her books, was not the key to eternal happiness. She couldn't deny men filled a necessary niche, every once in a while. But as a daily diet?

Good God, no. Marriage was not for her. No way. She did her own thing, ran her own race, thank you very much. Imagine being married to someone like Mr Cool. In no time, he would be telling her what to wear, how to act, how

to *vote*, even! Men like him couldn't seem to help taking
on the role of bossy-boots. The poor darlings actually
thought they knew best, that the world would stop spinning
if they didn't spin it personally.

No, she was not interested in marrying Kyle Armstrong.
She simply wanted to sleep with him. There! She could
admit it now and not tremble with shock. And if she could
wangle a position for herself at Whitmore Opals at the same
time, then so much the better!

The grandfather clock slowly and sombrely donged eight
as they passed, as though giving her a grave warning about
something. Jade ignored the omen. She didn't believe in
such things.

Eight o'clock found Gemma finding a temporary sanctuary
in the swimming-pool. She stroked up and down, up and
down, wishing she could recapture the euphoria she'd felt
earlier that afternoon in Nathan's arms. But reality had
come back with a rush and it was impossible to stop all the
doubts and fears from crowding her mind.

What was everyone in Belleview going to say when she
and Nathan announced one day in the near future that they
were married? Maybe Byron wouldn't be too surprised—
she had an odd feeling he already knew there was something between herself and Nathan. Neither would Ava or
Melanie be too shocked. But they wouldn't be at all
pleased. They might start thinking she was a little schemer,
that she'd inveigled her way into Belleview in order to
entrap Nathan into marriage.

She could perhaps endure that. Kirsty's reaction, however, loomed as a major problem. Nathan's daughter was
going to feel betrayed. Gemma had become the girl's
friend, more than her minder. How was Kirsty going to
react when she found out Gemma had married her father,
the father she still hoped would be reconciled with her
mother?

Gemma hated even thinking about it. She also hated having to pretend there was nothing between herself and Nathan till they were safely married. She'd always believed honesty was the best policy. Deception and lies were wrong.

But Nathan insisted they keep their relationship a secret till after the event. He wanted no fuss, he said. No arguments. People would try to talk them out of marrying if they knew beforehand.

Which people? she'd asked as soon as Kirsty had left the house to go to the movie marathon with her friends. Was he talking about Byron? Ava? His daughter? His ex-wife? Was it *himself* he feared could be talked out of the marriage. Or *herself*?

Nathan hadn't really answered her. He'd diverted her questions by making love to her yet again. Afterwards, while he was in the bathroom, she'd slipped on her swimming costume and fled to the pool, anywhere where she could think. The suspicion that Nathan might deliberately have used sex to silence her arguments was now teasing the edges of her mind, and, while she automatically shrank from the idea, Gemma found it wouldn't let go. If anything, it was growing.

A splash behind her had her feet searching for the bottom of the pool. But she was at the deep end, so she was madly treading water when Nathan swam underneath her feet and surfaced in front of her.

'I couldn't find you,' he said, slicking his hair back from his handsome but angry eyes. 'Why didn't you tell me where you were going? I wouldn't have known where you were if I hadn't looked out of the study window.'

'I...I needed some air,' she answered breathlessly, already feeling tired. She wasn't the strongest swimmer in the world. If there hadn't been a learn-to-swim programme at school she never would have learnt at all. Lightning Ridge did not abound in water.

'Have you changed your mind?' he asked coldly. 'About getting married.'

'No, of course not. It's just that it isn't going to be easy. I…I'm worried about what Kirsty's going to say.'

'Kirsty will adjust. So will everyone else. Just do as I say and everything will be fine. Here, you're sinking. Put your arms around my neck and wrap your legs around my waist.'

She went to do so but jerked back as though stung. 'You're…you're naked!'

'Uh-huh. And so will you be…once I get you out of this strait-jacket.'

Gemma gasped as her breasts burst free of her costume, Nathan peeling the purple maillot downwards till it was dragged right off and let go of, to float away. For a while she trod water again, her flapping arms and legs making her even more aware of her abrupt nudity. She glanced nervously around, happy to see that the trees and shrubbery around the edges of the garden gave them privacy from neighbors. The sun had not long set but the evening was warm. Stars twinkled overhead in a clear sky. A half-moon bathed the water in its soft glow.

'I…I'm not used to this kind of thing,' she babbled.

'I know,' he said, and caught her to him.

His mouth was wet and warm and wild. Gemma wanted to push him away, to say she had things she needed to talk about, but she soon ran up the white flag. Making love with the man she loved was too new and too wonderful and too exciting to replace with serious discussion. That could wait, she supposed. After all, they did have all night.

With a sigh, she moved to fit her body to his, to entwine her arms and legs around his hard lean torso. Nathan groaned deep in his throat and clasped her even closer. Gemma's head whirled and she pushed all thought of Kirsty aside. It was a night made for love, a night made for lovers. She would worry about tomorrow…tomorrow.

CHAPTER FOUR

JADE watched Melanie steering their dinner guest into the dining-room ahead of them, her conversation obviously finding favour with Mr Cool, since he was smiling over at the housekeeper. A pang of jealousy was quickly followed by a surge of annoyance. What was wrong with her today, becoming fixated on a man who obviously did not return her interest? A challenge was all very well but when it started affecting her total equilibrium then it was time to call a halt!

Besides, she couldn't possibly be wanting Kyle as much as she thought she did. Sex for sex's sake had never held any fascination for her. How could it when the physical act left her unmoved? It was male attention she occasionally craved, not male bodies.

Nathan was the only man ever to have really aroused her. But then Nathan was an enigma in that regard. Men like him should be banned from female company. They were far too dangerous.

As for men like Mr Cool…Jade was at a loss to understand why she was finding him so physically fascinating. One would think that after last night her susceptibility to the male sex would have to be at an all-time low. Yet here she was, being plagued by feelings she didn't want, and desires that were so alien to her that she didn't really know how to handle them.

Feeling irritated and somewhat bewildered, Jade fell uncharacteristically silent. Too bad her father wasn't similarly content.

'Well, what do you think of him?' he demanded to know
as they made slow progress together towards the dining-
room.

Jade suppressed a sigh. 'I think I'll reserve judgement
for now.'

He threw her a knowing look. 'You don't like him.'

'I didn't say that.'

'You don't have to. I picked up your vibes back in the
drawing-room.'

Jade was astonished. If there'd been any vibes to pick
up, they certainly weren't dislike. Or were they? Maybe
she would instinctively dislike any man who endangered
her need always to be in control of her life, regardless of
whatever other feelings he evoked in her. And Kyle Armstrong was doing that. Somehow...

'What do you know about him?' she asked.

'Enough.'

'How did you find him?'

'Through one of those head-hunter agencies. His creden-
tials are second to none.'

'Naturally,' she muttered.

They turned into the dining-room, where their guest was
already seated next to a pink-faced Ava, who was never at
her best with strangers. Still, this particular stranger was
apparently being as charming to her as he had been with
Melanie, Jade noted tartly, since her aunt was smiling prettily at him.

'So there you are, Ava,' Byron roared. 'I've got a bone
to pick with you!'

Jade was furious with her father for hollering at his poor
sister like that and making her jump nervously in her seat.
To give him credit, Kyle didn't look all that impressed with
Byron either, though he was quick to hide his annoyance.
Jade didn't feel at all disposed to hide her own irritation.

'Don't be such a bully, Pops. Auntie, take no notice of
him. He's out of sorts because his leg hurts and he's got
no one left to boss around, now that I've left the nest. One

would think he'd be on his best behaviour with a guest in the house.' This with a sardonic lifting of eyebrows Kyle's way. 'But of course, wealthy men don't bow to such niceties. They forge on regardless, being rude and trying to intimidate everyone around them.'

Jade was startled to note Kyle looking at her with an expression akin to admiration in his eyes. Admiration, and something else. Was it amusement at last? Hard to tell behind that inscrutable face of his. Whatever, it egged her on to more outrageousness.

'Money and manners don't often mix, I've found,' she continued, a saucy smile teasing her wide, pink-glossed mouth. 'Sit down, Pops, and I'll put some mood music on.'

'None of that modern garbage,' Byron muttered, though doing his daughter's bidding and sitting down meekly enough.

'I'll bet that's just what Beethoven's father said when his son produced his latest symphony,' Jade quipped. 'What kind of music do you like, Kyle?' she asked, sending another bold smile and bright eyes his way. This time, however, his stony reaction disappointed her, as did his reply.

'Mozart,' he said. 'I like Mozart.'

'A man of taste,' Byron affirmed gruffly.

'Mozart,' Jade pouted. '*God*!'

What a pompous jerk, she thought as she whirled away. I'll bet he just said that because he thought it would please Pops. I'll give him Mozart!

Shortly a heavy-metal number reverberated through the high-ceilinged room, turned up so loud it shook the chandelier overhead.

'Turn that infernal rubbish off!' Byron shouted.

'Sorry,' Jade apologised carelessly over her shoulder. 'Wrong CD. I don't have my glasses on.'

'You don't *wear* glasses,' her father bit out.

'Don't I? I'm sure I should. Big thick ones! Then I wouldn't be able to see all the cruelty in this miserable rotten world of ours.'

'*Jade*,' her father warned through gritted teeth.

Mozart floated through the room and Jade found her chair, opposite Kyle's. She went to throw him another saucy smile, but suddenly it changed to a very bleak one. Her own cynical words of a moment ago had brought memories of the newsflashes she'd seen all week on television about the starving children in Africa, their emaciated bodies tearing at her heartstrings.

What kind of world was it that allowed such misery, such suffering? She'd sent the Save The Children Fund some money but had still been left feeling depressed. Why was it always innocent children who suffered the most? Her eyes suddenly misted over and she looked down very quickly, blinking rapidly.

She was just getting herself under control when their guest went into a fit of coughing, forcing her to look up before she was fully composed. Her reaction was a most unsympathetic irritation.

What on earth was wrong with him? It didn't seem likely that Mr Cool was having an attack of asthma, or was allergic to the flowers on the table.

'Are you all right?' the others asked.

He flicked open his serviette and pressed it briefly against watering eyes. It annoyed Jade that, even watering, his eyes were gorgeous. The man was a menace, projecting sex appeal in waves even when he was coughing and spluttering like a smoker on his last inhale.

'I'm fine,' he choked out. 'Something went down the wrong way.'

What? she thought crossly. He hadn't started eating yet.

The soup arrived at that moment—another of Melanie's famous home-made varieties. The first of Byron's wines was poured and soon everyone was as mellow as Melanie's superb cooking and the best of Australia's vineyards could make the stressed inhabitants of the twentieth century. Jade, of course, drank far too much, too quickly. Consequently, she became more and more naughty as the night wore on.

Not so much in what she said, but in the way she looked at the man seated opposite her.

Drunks often said the bartender got better looking as the night wore on. Kyle Armstrong definitely became more attractive as the night wore on, yet at the same time more unattainable. He was like a mirage, or the spectre in a dream that kept scooting away, out of her grasp. More and more he avoided her eyes and deflected her attempts to chat him up.

'When do you start work for Whitmore Opals?' she persisted over dessert, a mouth-watering chocolate pudding with lashings of cream.

'Monday,' came his cool reply.

'*This* Monday?'

'Mmm.'

'I've always wanted to work for Whitmore's in marketing,' she muttered into her wine. Frustration and alcohol were propelling Jade to a point somewhere between depression and aggression.

'Not that again, Jade,' her father sighed. 'If I've told you once, I've told you a thousand times. When you've attained your degree, I'll think about it.'

Jade's glassy blue eyes shot up. '*Think* about it! What do you mean, *think* about it? You told me if I got my degree you'd definitely give me a job. Are you trying to go back on our deal?'

'You know my feelings on women in business, Jade,' he said. 'Besides, I've employed Kyle now and I can't see him wanting some green assistant who'd probably hinder more than help.'

She pushed the rest of her pudding away, really upset now. 'But you *promised*!' she burst out.

'Jade, for God's sake, not now!'

'If I may speak, Byron?' Mr Cool inserted smoothly.

'Of course, Kyle. I'm just sorry you have to be exposed to our family squabbles like this.'

'I've worked for family companies all my life. I'm used

to the occasional squabble. Might I say, however, that if things at Whitmore Opals are faring as badly as you've told me then I will need as many new marketing ideas as I can muster. A young, innovative brain like Jade's here would be an invaluable asset, even on a part-time basis. Not only that, we can be assured she would have Whitmore's best interests at heart. Since we have a formidable foe in Celeste Campbell, then there is always the chance of an employee being bribed or corrupted. We wouldn't have to worry about loyalty with your daughter, Byron. Frankly, I was thinking of hiring someone young to assist me and Jade would be the perfect person.'

He turned that implacable dark gaze on to her startled blue eyes and, once again, she felt the power of his mind. Here was a man who could not be forced into doing anything he didn't want to do, but likewise, who would be unstoppable once he'd made up his mind to achieve some end. It underlined the futility of her throwing herself at him when it was patently clear he wasn't interested in her in that way. Suddenly, she felt ashamed of herself for continuing to try after he'd made his feelings quite clear. It was beneath her. It was belittling. And cheap.

Jade sucked in a startled breath. *Cheap*? My God, she was beginning to sound like her own father!

'You must have some days off from lectures, Jade,' Kyle was saying. 'At least a morning or afternoon here and there. If not, there's always the weekends.'

A surge of excitement rushed through her. What Kyle was offering was better than the satisfying of her passing fancy for him. It was the career she'd always wanted, the life she'd always secretly coveted. Who knew? In a few years, she might give Celeste Campbell a run for her money.

'I...I have Wednesdays off,' she said eagerly. 'And Friday afternoons.'

'Good. Then I will expect to see you at head office next Wednesday morning. Nine, on the dot.'

Jade blinked several times, then turned to her father, who rolled his eyes. 'Pops?'

His sigh was resigned. 'I promised Kyle a free hand. If he wants to risk the likes of you, then so be it. I can only say I admire his fortitude.'

'Fortitude, Byron?' An odd smile crossed the new marketing manager's face. 'Fortitude has nothing to do with my hiring your daughter. Destiny is more like it.'

'Destiny?' Ava piped up, frowning. 'Whose destiny, Mr Armstrong?'

'Why, Jade's, of course,' he replied silkily. 'She stands to inherit Whitmore's at some future date, does she not, Byron? Or did I get my wires crossed this afternoon?'

Both women's eyes turned to Byron, Jade's the most round. So she *was* going to inherit Whitmore's. Nathan hadn't wangled the company for himself yet.

'No, you didn't get your wires crossed. Jade inherits the family business, though if we can't do something to turn the tables on our competition in the next year or so it won't be worth much.'

'Then it's about time she learnt the business,' Mr Cool pronounced. 'Time you took your future into your own hands, wouldn't you say, Jade?'

'Yes.' She beamed agreement and excitement at him. 'Oh, yes!'

Byron laughed. 'Don't give her too many ideas, Kyle. She's likely to run with them.'

'That's exactly what I want her to do.'

'What if she runs right off a cliff, like one of those lemmings?'

'Then I'll be there to catch her, Byron. I wouldn't let anything bad ever happen to your daughter. You can be assured of that.'

Jade bristled at the dry flavour she heard in that last statement. She didn't doubt he meant every word. The boss's daughter would always be cosseted and protected and pandered to. Pity he wasn't the type who was prepared

to go even further to curry favour, she thought with a re-
surgence of pique. But he was too prim and proper for that.
Too damned conservative and holier-than-thou. Trust her
father to employ a prude!

'I don't want any special treatment,' she said sharply.
'I'm not doing this just to amuse myself, you know. I'm
dead serious about learning everything you can teach me.'

'And I'm dead serious about teaching you everything I
know,' Kyle returned, an odd note in his voice. Irony, perhaps?

Jade stared at him. A small warning prickle at the back
of her neck made her sit up straight. She rolled her shoulders in an effort to dispel a sudden tension between her
shoulder-blades. Had she missed something here? Why did
she suddenly suspect there had been more to this exchange
than appeared on the surface?

Melanie's drifting in to take the dessert plates away and
ask who wanted tea or coffee obliterated the moment and
Jade dismissed it as an aberration of her fuzzy state of
mind. By the time everyone was on their second round of
coffee she'd sobered right up, her revitalised brain already
harnessing all sorts of marketing ideas for Whitmore Opals.

I'll have to start writing them down, she told herself, her
earlier wild burst of excitement having been replaced by
the calmer realisation that she must not waste this wonderful chance. And while a slight nervousness crept in at the
prospect of working with and for Mr Cool, she resolved to
do her very best.

Which meant she would have to ignore this unfortunate
physical effect he had on her. OK, so he was gorgeous-
looking and irritatingly sexy and even intriguing, in a way.
But trying to seduce one's boss was not the way to impress
him with her business acumen. This was her one chance to
show her father she could be an invaluable asset to Whitmore Opals and she wasn't about to muff it by letting a
little thing like sexual desire get in the way.

So what if she wanted the man to make love to her? So

what if she wanted to make love to *him*? So what if the thought of either possibility was sending goosebumps all over her skin? So damned what!

Jade clenched her teeth down hard in her jaw, thankful that the jacket she had on was lined. Thinking such thoughts was doing scandalous things to her breasts. Dammit, but this wasn't going to be easy, not easy at all. The man had cast a spell on her. He was a Svengali, with dark powers to enslave and compel. Thank the lord he didn't realise it!

Good God, why was he getting to his feet? Surely he wasn't *going*! What had he just said to her? *Had* he said anything to her? Had she answered? She'd been off in another world, her body working on automatic pilot whilst her mind had been dancing with the devil.

He was looking at her as though he were expecting her to say something. Well, *say something*, you little nincompoop.

'I'll see you Wednesday, then?' she tried.

Everyone stared at her.

'What's the matter with you, girl?' Byron snapped. 'You just agreed to walk Kyle to the door and open the gates for him.'

Her laughter was self-mocking as she stood up and moved across to the doorway. Kyle was right on her hammer.

'Call me from the office on Monday morning, Kyle,' Byron called after him.

'Certainly.'

Jade tried very hard to be the epitome of social grace as she walked Kyle towards the front door. It was as though this was her first test in controlling herself and acting like a mature young lady. She didn't walk too fast, she said all the right things—wonderfully polite inanities she would not recall later. She even remembered to press the remote control on the wall that opened the gates before she escorted their visitor through the front door and out on to the well-lit front patio. Why, there wasn't anything she couldn't do, Jade decided.

Her faith in herself was a little premature.

The moment Kyle turned to her and took her hand in his—no doubt only as a gesture of goodbye—she lost the plot entirely. Did he really squeeze her fingers? Did those dark eyes darken with desire for her? Surely it wasn't her imagination that his stillness was suddenly projecting a sexual tension that was so palpable she could feel it in every pore of her body.

'Kyle,' she whispered in automatic response, his name a husky plea of raw arousal.

She could have sworn his fingers tightened even further for a second, that his mouth dipped slightly toward hers. But then he was saying goodnight in cold clipped tones and was walking away, away from her parted panting lips, away from her madly pounding heart.

Jade watched, dry-mouthed and stunned, as he drove off in a silver-grey sedan, a super-cool car for its super-cool driver. He hadn't given her a backward glance, or a wave, or even a smile. He'd given her nothing but his hard cold back.

I hate him, she decided. And flounced inside.

CHAPTER FIVE

NATHAN directed his navy blue Mercedes through the gates of Belleview shortly after seven-thirty on Sunday evening. Kirsty had slept most of the day, exhausted by her movie marathon the night before. Gemma and Nathan hadn't been much brighter, equally exhausted with their own marathon. The trip home had been slow, the freeway choked with cars returning to Sydney from a weekend up on the coast.

Gemma locked eyes with Nathan in the rear-view mirror as he directed the car round to the garages.

Keep your head, his steely glance seemed to say.

She looked away, all her insides tightening into tangled knots. She hated having to pretend to people she liked, hated to think that one day soon Kirsty and Melanie and Ava—and even Byron—would look at her with shock and disappointment in their eyes. She shuddered to think what Lenore might say as well, still not sure how Nathan's ex-wife felt about her ex-husband. Nathan might not love *her*, but did she still love *him*?

'Home at last,' Kirsty yawned. 'I'm really bushed. Just as well I don't do that every weekend.'

'I think it might be wise if you didn't tell your mother about last night, Kirsty,' her father warned.

Kirsty grinned. 'What she doesn't know won't hurt her, eh, Dad?'

Gemma groaned silently. Out of the mouths of babes…

'Everyone carry their own bags,' Nathan directed crisply as they all climbed out of the car.

'I'm going straight to bed,' Kirsty said with another yawn.

'I've got a bit of Japanese study to do before tomorrow,' Gemma admitted.

Kirsty frowned at her. 'I thought that was what you were doing all day today.'

Gemma could feel the heat gathering in her cheeks, which was crazy since she and Nathan hadn't done a thing today. They hadn't dared, with Kirsty in the house. There again, if she admitted to resting most of the day that might lead Kirsty asking what she'd been doing the previous night to make her so tired. 'I...I couldn't seem to concentrate,' she hedged. 'I had a headache.'

'You might have got a touch of the sun yesterday,' Kirsty said, lifting out her bag which was on top of the pile in the boot. 'That can give you a headache sometimes. You should drink a lot of water and take a couple of aspirin before going to bed. Well, I'm off. Thanks heaps, Dad, for letting me do you know what. You're a cool dude. See you in the morning, Gemma.'

Kirsty kissed her father on the cheek then was gone, using the internal door that connected the garages with the laundry and kitchen wing of the house. Gemma was still standing there beside the car when Nathan banged down the boot, then slid her a drily amused look.

'A headache, eh?' he drawled. 'I hope that isn't going to become a standard excuse of the future Mrs Whitmore.'

Before she could fashion a reply, he leant over, cupped her chin and kissed her—not at all lightly—on the mouth. He'd just lifted his head when the sound of hurried footsteps had them both whirling to stare at the still open doorway that Kirsty had gone through.

Jade didn't have to be Sherlock Holmes to guess what she'd just missed seeing. If their guilty movements hadn't given them away, then she only had to look at the flush on the girl's face and the frustration in Nathan's eyes to know there'd been some surreptitious canoodling going on.

Not that she cared.

Jade sucked in a sharp breath. My God, she didn't care. She actually didn't. How marvellous!

Her smile carried a startled delight. 'So there you are, Nathan. I've been sweating on your getting back. I have a favour to ask of you.'

Nathan's scowl was predictable, but the girl's fiercely jealous glare took Jade by surprise. So things had gone that far already, had they? Sympathy for the poor thing's predicament soon replaced any shock. Jade had been in the same position not that long ago, hopelessly besotted with the man and hating any woman who so much as looked at him, let alone took up his time.

'Hello there,' Jade said sweetly. 'You're Gemma, aren't you? Do you remember me? I'm Jade, Nathan's sister.' Maybe if she dropped the adopted part, the girl would stop looking so threatened.

'Of course she remembers you,' Nathan ground out. 'You're not easily forgotten, Jade. What do you want? You aren't going to move back here to live, are you?'

'No, darls,' she said automatically before she could snatch back her usual meaningless endearment. The girlfriend didn't realise how meaningless, of course, and was looking none too happy. Beautiful, though. God, yes, she was a stunner all right. Jade just managed not to feel envious, concentrating instead on the improvement her own life would make next Wednesday. Hating Kyle Armstrong didn't change the fact that he'd hired her as his marketing assistant and she just couldn't wait to start!

But her more immediate problem was getting Roberto out of her unit. Hopefully, by now, his so-called friends—including her attacker—had gone back to their own caves. But she couldn't be sure of that, and returning to her unit on her own was just too scary, even for her.

'Look, I know you're probably tired and I hate to ask,

but I need you to go with me back to my unit. I have to evict a friend who's turned out to be a problem and I'm afraid he might need some persuasion.'

'Is it Roberto? Or someone new?' Nathan added in a nasty tone.

'Roberto.' God, but she was going to enjoy enlightening him about Roberto's sexuality. She was getting sick and tired of Nathan pointing a moral finger at her when he was obviously racing off this sweet young thing under everyone's noses. How dared he judge her, the cradle-snatching lecher?

Nathan sighed. 'I supposed we might as well get this over and done with and go now.'

'Really? Gosh, thanks.' She beamed. For all his faults, Nathan usually came through if one asked nicely. 'I'll just get my car keys.'

She scuttled away, thinking magnanimously that this would give the lovebirds a chance to say a proper—or improper—goodnight. When she got back, Gemma had disappeared and Nathan was leaning against the driver's door of his car, an impatient glint in his eye.

'I hope you don't expect me to rough up this boyfriend of yours, Jade. I gave up that sort of thing when I was seventeen.'

'I doubt anything of that kind will be necessary with Roberto, Nathan. He's basically a gentle soul. Unfortunately, one of his friends wasn't.'

Nathan frowned and stood up straight. 'Meaning?'

For some reason Jade couldn't quite meet his eye. A trembling started deep within and, try as she might to stop the memory of the assault from unnerving her, she found that all of a sudden she was very jittery. 'I...I...'

'What? Spit it out, for God's sake.'

His impatience infuriated her. 'I was almost raped!' she blurted out, shaking now, though whether from anger or fear, Jade wasn't sure. 'Luckily, I got away from the filthy creep and I...I came here.'

'On Friday night?'

'That's right.'

'At least that explains the car in the fishpond,' he muttered, shaking his head at her as though it were *her* fault she'd been attacked. 'I knew this would happen one day. I hope you've learnt your lesson, and stop inviting every Tom, Dick and Harry to move in with you at the drop of a hat.'

'I don't do that! I've *never* done that. I'll have you know that Roberto is not my boyfriend, *or* my lover. He was just a friend in need of a room for a while. He's also gay. He had a few friends over on Friday night for a party. Not that I attended. I went to bed. Later in the night, I got up for a drink of water. I…I thought everyone had gone home. Apparently not, however.'

Nathan stared at her for a few moments before speaking. 'Was this man who attacked you also gay?'

'I'm not sure, but he certainly led me to believe he hated women. You should have heard the things he said he was going to do to me while he was trying to drag me from the kitchen to the bedroom.' She shuddered violently.

'But you got away before he really hurt you?' Nathan asked, anxiety in his voice.

'My breasts were bruised.' She undid a couple of buttons of her shirt and showed him some of the black and blue marks.

'Good God.' His eyes showed real shock and Jade found it hard not to dissolve into tears.

'I presume you haven't told Byron any of this?' he asked more gently.

'Of course not. Do you think I'm stupid?'

A wry smile crossed his handsome face. 'I think you're crazy. But I also think you're very lucky, *and* very brave.'

'Not really, I've spent the whole weekend trying to pretend it never happened. If I didn't have to go back to that flat, I wouldn't. I doubt I'll ever be able to go into the kitchen again without reliving it all.'

'Then don't go back.'

Jade gaped at him.

'You're only renting, aren't you?'

'Yes.'

'And the unit came furnished?'

'Yes.'

'So you only have to remove your clothes and give back the keys to have done with the place.'

'Not really. My lease won't be up for another few months.'

'That's just a matter of money, Jade. I'll fix that up.'

'But I can't allow you to do that! It would run into a couple of thousand dollars. Surely you've got enough expense what with paying Lenore alimony and…and—'

'Jade,' he interrupted. 'I think it's time you knew I'm no longer the deprived stray from the streets your father brought home. I do not have to make ends meet on the salary your father pays me, or via the iffy financial rewards that my plays occasionally bring in. My maternal grandparents, despite refusing to have anything personal to do with me after they disinherited my mother, still saw fit to make me their heir. A few years back I inherited a considerable estate, so I think I can well afford to extricate my favourite adopted sister from a sticky situation, don't you?'

'F…favourite adopted sister?' Jade repeated, a lump in her throat.

Nathan's smile was rather sad. 'Favourite and only adopted sister. I wish you'd go back to filling that role, Jade. I rather liked being your big brother. Anything else felt all wrong, even if you were an incredible temptation there for a while. You'd be an incredible temptation to any man.'

Jade hid her pleasure behind a dry laugh. 'I know one particular man who wouldn't agree with you.'

Now Nathan laughed, and it was just as dry. 'Not another man, Jade. Good God, doesn't anything turn you off the opposite sex? Still, I'm relieved I've been taken off the list, but I pity the poor sod—whoever he is. No, don't tell me, just give me the keys to your flat and I'll go sort Roberto out and come back with your clothes.'

'You…you'd really do that for me?'

'I'm your big brother, aren't I?'

Her heart contracted. 'Forever and ever.'

Gemma was sitting on the side of her bed, feeling woebegone and abandoned when there was a knock on her door. Going to answer it, she found Jade standing there, looking as raunchily sexy as ever, skin-tight jeans and a man's white shirt doing little to disguise that spectacular body of hers.

'I thought I'd better warn you,' Jade said. 'Nathan might be a good while. He's gone to get my clothes from my unit at Avalon. I'm going to be staying at Belleview here for a while.'

Gemma felt totally confused. 'But I thought you said that…that…

'That I wouldn't be moving back home,' the girl finished with a sigh. 'Yes, I know, but I had this problem with a man last Friday night which was rather serious and Nathan feels it would be safer if I stayed here for a while. I dare say I'll find another place in the near future, but I have to admit it feels good to be home in the meantime.'

Gemma's heart sank. What was it about the women in Nathan's life that he castigated them to her in private, but then his actions didn't match his words? Lenore got under his skin, but he'd *kissed* her. He was highly critical of Jade and said he would not have her under the same roof as his daughter but here he was, helping to bring that about. In fact, it sounded as if it was *his* idea.

She was startled when Jade suddenly put a gentle hand on hers. 'Please don't think I'm a rival for Nathan's affections,' the girl said softly. 'I admit I had a crush on him once, but I'm over that now and quite frankly I would like

nothing more than for him to fall in love with a really nice
girl like you.'

Gemma was taken aback by the girl's compliment, and
her intuitive comment about her and Nathan. 'How…how
would you know if I'm a nice girl or not?' she asked tentatively.

Jade smiled. 'I've been listening to Ava and Melanie
singing your praises all weekend. To be honest, I was quite
prepared to hate you on sight, but I don't seem to be able
to rustle up the necessary emotion. Maybe I'm all out of
hate or maybe this weekend has made me grow up a little.
In the space of two days, I've fought off a rapist, survived
being rejected by a man I *did* fancy and then was spectac-
ularly hired for a job I've always coveted. I'm feeling too
good to hate.'

She grinned at Gemma, who shook her head. 'You're
crazy.'

Jade laughed. 'Crazy is as crazy does, darls. Let's go
down to the kitchen and have some hot chocolate, and then
you can tell me your life story.' Linking elbows with
Gemma, she started railroading her from the room. Surrender seemed the safest course of action.

'I think yours might be more interesting than mine,'
Gemma said.

'Nah. Mine's been miserable, but it's looking up. Yes.
It's very definitely looking up.'

'You really fought off a rapist?'

'Yup. Kicked the creep in the balls.'

'Good lord! Weren't you afraid?'

'Scared to death. But madder than a meat-axe at the same
time.'

'And who was this man who rejected you?' Gemma
asked, finding it hard to see any man daring to reject this
wildly attractive creature.

'Some stuffed shirt named Kyle Armstrong. He's the
new marketing manager at Whitmore Opals and he came
here to dinner last night. Talk about scrumptious-looking!

But batting my baby blues at him just didn't work. Still, he knew what side his bread was buttered on, my being the daughter of the boss and all. So he's hired me to be his part-time assistant till I finish my business degree this year which is what I've always wanted.'

'You're doing a business degree?'

'Well, you don't have to sound so surprised, darls. I'm a smart cookie underneath the bleached hair and big boobs.'

Gemma stared at her hair.

'Yes, the hair's fake but the boobs aren't. They're all mine.'

'I...I...'

'Close your mouth, darls, or you'll start catching flies. Now tell me, how did a nice girl like you get to be living in a den of iniquity like Belleview? No lies now, I want the truth, the whole truth and nothing but the truth!'

By the time Nathan returned over an hour later, Gemma had just got to the part where Nathan had told her the disappointing news about her mother, though she had, naturally, omitted her personal involvement with him. Nathan would be furious with her if she let the cat out of the bag, especially to Jade. That girl didn't know how to shut up!

'I thought you'd be in bed by now, Gemma,' Nathan said on entering the kitchen via the door that led to the laundry and the garages.

'She was waiting for you, darls,' Jade said naughtily before adding, 'To come back, that is. We've had the loveliest long chat about Gemma's colourful life up till now. Fancy all that business about her father's having that opal belonging to Pops. You know...the one called the Heart of Fire.'

'I know the one.'

'But what a coincidence! And what a shame her birth certificate is packed full of lies. Poor Gemma probably won't ever find her mother's family now, will she? Or even know her mother's real name? Are you sure you can't do something about that? Hire a private investigator or some-

thing? They have access to all sorts of information us ordinary people can't tap into.'

'I intend doing that, Jade. Don't pre-empt me. Don't you
want to know what happened at your unit with Roberto?'

'Not if you did anything violent?'

'Didn't have to. Once I pointed out what might happen
to him and his friends if he stayed one minute longer, he
left like a lamb.'

'Poor Roberto…'

'Keep your sympathy for someone who deserves it, Jade.
Now how about you two girls coming along to the garage
and help me empty my car of madam's gear?'

'You make it sound as if I've got tons!' Jade complained.
'I don't have that many clothes. I live in jeans and shorts.'

'I brought all the linen as well. I've got a bootful of
towels and sheets and quilts and God knows what. Most of
them need washing so we'll just pile them into the laundry
and you can help Melanie sort them out tomorrow.'

'I have lectures first thing in the morning,' Jade said.

'I could help after I get home from my Japanese lessons,'
Gemma offered.

'Would you?' Jade smiled her appreciation. 'Oh, you are
a dear. She's a dear, isn't she, Nathan?'

'Yes, she is, so don't take advantage of her.'

'Talk about the pot calling the kettle black,' Jade muttered under her breath after Nathan had whirled and stalked
back down the corridor towards the garages.

Gemma pretended she hadn't heard, but she had, and the
reasoning behind the remark worried her.

Jade knew about them. Not only knew but had made her
judgement. Nathan had once again been cast in the role of
callous seducer. Wasn't there anyone around Belleview
who had faith in his ability to love a woman? Anyone besides herself?

Gemma frowned, mulling over the thought that all these
other people had known Nathan a lot longer than she had.
Was she being naïve believing he meant to marry her? Was

he stringing her along merely to have sex with her? Was that why he wanted to keep their engagement a secret?

Her head told her she had reason to worry, but her heart was strong in Nathan's defence. He loved her and meant to marry her. She felt sure of it.

Still…it wouldn't do any harm not to be too easy when it came to letting Nathan make love to her, especially here at Belleview. He said they would be married within a month, five weeks at the most. A man genuinely in love could wait that long, couldn't he?

Gemma hoped so. She herself would find such a sacrifice quite hard. Nathan making love to her was the most wonderful experience in the world. But they had all their lives ahead of them if his intentions were honourable and true, and Gemma would not want to marry any other kind of man. She wasn't so besotted that every ounce of her common sense had flown out the window.

Her mind made up, she picked up her empty mug and glanced over at Jade, who seemed lost in her own thoughts. 'You finished with your mug, Jade?' she asked.

'What? Oh, yes…yes, I have. But you don't have to wash it up for me. I'll do it.'

'It's no trouble.' Gemma swept the other mug up off the counter and made for the kitchen sink.

'Gemma…' the other girl began tentatively.

'Yes?'

'Oh…nothing. I…I'd better get to bed or I'll be wrecked tomorrow. Goodnight. And thanks again. You're a doll.'

Gemma watched Jade walk away, still amazed at how much she liked her. If Jade had once been in love with Nathan she certainly wasn't now, which was a relief. The girl was a walking sex symbol.

Maybe she was one of those girls who fell in and out of love a lot. Gemma had known a few like that at school. A good-looking boy only had to smile at them and they were crazy about them, their previous boyfriend forgotten. Then the following week there would be someone else.

Gemma had never been like that. There again, she'd found most boys at school boring and immature and highly unattractive. She'd never even had one serious boyfriend.

Gemma had always suspected she found the opposite sex unappealing because of that awful night as a young girl when that drunken miner had sexually assaulted her, his attack only falling short of rape because he'd been too drunk to do it.

But now, looking back, she could see not having a boyfriend had more to do with her real age than wariness. She'd been two years older than her classmates. Emotionally, she'd been even older.

Nathan's news that her birth certificate was a legitimate one had not changed her mind about her true age. She wasn't eighteen. She was nearly twenty, or already twenty by now. That photo of her mother and father proved it, as it proved her father a liar. The more she thought about her father, the more she was convinced he was not only a liar but a thief. He'd stolen that black opal. That was why he hadn't sold it, why he'd hidden it away.

How he'd managed to execute the original theft here at Belleview all those years ago she couldn't fathom. Maybe he'd had an accomplice. Whatever, she was sure he'd been criminally involved, which was why he'd been so secretive about everything, why he'd lied about things.

Thinking of her father and the opal reminded Gemma that she must give that photo of her parents to Nathan. But not tonight. Going to his room at night was courting disaster. No, she would give it to him at breakfast. And she wouldn't be going to Avoca with him any more either. Not till after they were married. Gemma had a point to prove to herself and she was going to prove it, come hell or high water!

Having washed up the two mugs, she made her way upstairs, thinking to herself that Ma would be very proud of her.

CHAPTER SIX

BY THE following Wednesday morning Jade was in a state of nervous agitation which wasn't entirely due to her starting work that day. Living at home was proving to be a trial of the first order.

She found it hard to resume the role of daughter of the house, especially with her father in such a frustrated mood. She'd become used to running her own race, without having to put up with any criticism, especially about what she wore or the hours she kept. Even Ava's well-meaning pieces of advice began to grate after a while.

Frankly, Jade felt extra irritated with her aunt, who had refused her offer of Irene's jewellery, saying she wouldn't feel right about it. Clearly, there was no hope for Auntie Ava. She seemed determined to grow old playing the part of the unattractive, eccentric spinster of the family, stuffing her face with cream buns while dreaming of imaginary beaux that got away.

On top of all those irritations, Jade felt uneasy with what was going on between Nathan and Gemma.

They were certainly putting on a good act with their platonic conversations and avoidance of any telling eye contact, but Jade's bedroom was opposite Nathan's and she'd heard the soft sound of his door opening and shutting very late the previous night.

Because she'd been too excited about starting work to sleep, she'd still been awake when, even later, she'd heard more sounds. Slipping from her bed, she'd snuck over and opened her door an inch or two just in time to see a scantily clad Gemma high-tailing it back into her room. And she hadn't been coming from the direction of downstairs!

Jade had found it even harder to go to sleep after that, because like everyone else around Belleview she'd found herself growing very fond of Gemma with her country-sweet and very caring ways. Despite her own reconciliation with Nathan—and a new appreciation of her adopted brother's strength of character—Jade still felt the girl deserved better in life than to get involved with a man as emotionally screwed up as Nathan was, not to mention as sexually dangerous.

Did he himself appreciate how infatuated a young girl like Gemma could get in double-quick time? She was sure to think she was madly in love, especially with her limited experience with men. She probably thought Nathan was in love with *her*. God forbid, he might have told her he was, for who knew what a man might say when in the throes of a new passion?

Jade didn't like to judge Nathan too harshly—he hadn't turned out to be as heartless as she'd once imagined—but he did still have his limitations when it came to relationships with women. Lenore had confided to Jade shortly after their divorce that all Nathan wanted from a wife was an elegant partner on his arm and a willing body in bed. No true intimacy or companionship. He'd even told her once that if she hadn't fallen pregnant with Kirsty he would never have married her at all, nor any other woman for that matter.

Lenore had confessed that she might have been able to put up with all this—Nathan was apparently so good in bed that the woman was almost prepared to put up with any-thing!—but it seemed that when he was consumed by a creative burst with a new play Lenore had found herself denied even the small consolation of a good sex life. Writing, it seemed, involved Nathan to the exclusion of every-one and everything else.

Jade suspected that there was an element behind Lenore

and Nathan's divorce that still remained hidden, but the main thrust was pretty straightforward. Nathan had made a lousy husband.

Thank the lord Jade didn't have to worry about Nathan rushing Gemma off to some altar somewhere. He'd always made his feelings on remarrying quite clear. Still, that didn't mean Gemma wouldn't ultimately get hurt, and this upset Jade. The poor darling had had a rough time of it so far in life and she deserved a break. Hell, there she'd been, thinking she'd inherited a fantastic opal from that rotten dead-beat father of hers and what had happened? It had turned out to be stolen from none other than Jade's own father. Pops might have given Gemma a nice reward for the opal's return, but what was a hundred thousand dollars compared to a million? One was a nice little nest egg, but the other would have set Gemma up for life.

Jade was mulling over all these thoughts as she headed downstairs for breakfast, resolving to drop a few subtle hints to Nathan when she got the chance. Maybe he didn't realise how naïve and impressionable Gemma was.

Or maybe he did, came another far more disturbing, darker thought. God, if Nathan did anything to really hurt that girl she was going to tear strips off him! Come to think of it, she would accept his offer of a lift to work this morning. She'd been going to drive herself, liking her independence, but riding into town with Nathan would give her a great opportunity to find out how things stood.

'All ready for your first assault on the business world?' the man himself said when Jade walked into the morning-room. 'You certainly look the part in that outfit. I've never seen you looking so—er...' He broke off, frowning. 'What have I said to make you glare at me like that? I wasn't making fun of you, I swear. That black suit looks fantastic on you.'

Jade wiped the scowl off her face and rewarded him with an insincere smile. Hypocrisy never did come easy to her. If she was angry with someone it showed on her face, not the best thing if she was going to become a businesswoman. No doubt Celeste Campbell had the best poker face in the whole of Australia.

'Sorry,' she said. 'I'm a bit out of sorts this morning. Guess it's nerves. Where's Gemma? Sleeping in, is she?' Oh, dear, did that sound as pointedly sarcastic as she thought it did?

'How would *I* know?' His shrug was superbly nonchalant and Jade's level of worry increased.

Damn, but he was a clever devil. And too darned handsome for his own good. He and Kyle Armstrong made a good pair.

Kyle Armstrong...

Jade's mind was suddenly filled with that brooding gypsy face and those glittering black eyes. She would be seeing him today, would be spending most of the day with him. Hell.

Reminding herself of Whitmore's new marketing manager blocked out all thought of Gemma and Nathan for the rest of breakfast. In fact, Jade was so distracted she almost forgot to tell Nathan she'd decided to accompany him into the city. Only Gemma and Kirsty coming downstairs reminded her to speak up.

Gemma looked unhappy with the news. Surely she's still not worried I'm interested in Nathan, Jade frowned to herself.

Whatever, the girl's jealous reaction underlined the very things Jade had been worrying about earlier. Gemma might think herself mature at nearly twenty, but she was light-years behind a city born and bred girl of the same age. And a *zillion* light-years behind Nathan!

'Gee, Jade, you look smashing,' Kirsty said as she pulled out a chair and sat down.

'Yes, Jade,' Gemma agreed, though not quite as enthusiastically. 'You certainly do.'

Jade hoped her smile was as soothing as her words. 'How nice of you both to say so. I was thinking I was a bit overdressed. Lenore directed me to a boutique that specialises in the smart working-girl look and I splashed out on three suits. One black, one white and one red, all of which I can mix and match.'

'Really? Where is this boutique?' Gemma asked, her interest quite genuine. 'I'm going to need some clothes for work.'

'Chatswood. I could take you there tomorrow night if you like.'

The girl frowned. 'Tomorrow *night*?'

'It's late-night shopping. I suppose you didn't have that up at Lightning Ridge.'

'No, we didn't.'

'I'll get Lenore to come with us,' Jade suggested. 'She knows heaps about fashion and what suits a person.' It was slowly coming to Jade that it was her super-smart appearance that had troubled Gemma, who admittedly still looked very young in her clothes, even the ones Ava had given her. Ava's taste had always leant towards the cute and pretty rather than the elegant or sophisticated.

'Gemma looks fine as she is,' Nathan said in a voice and with a look that totally betrayed his feelings for his daughter's minder. Not only possessive, but fiercely protective of the person she was right at this moment. He didn't want her tampered with in any way, or changed, or made over.

Jade resolved to do all three as quickly as possible, for only by widening the girl's horizons and opening her eyes a little could she be saved from Nathan's selfish male desires. Even if he imagined he loved the girl, it was not a healthy type of love if it didn't allow Gemma to grow, if it tried to imprison her in a narrow world where all that was to exist for her was his wishes. Jade hated the way men liked to dominate and control the women they supposedly loved. Real love didn't have reins.

'That's for Gemma to say, surely, Nathan,' Jade retorted, seeing the girl's instant frown. 'She's not a child. Even if she was, you're neither her father nor her big brother, so your opinion doesn't count.' She threw Gemma a dazzling smile. 'I'll get in touch with Lenore today, Gemma, and we'll make a date to buy you some working clothes to-morrow evening. When do you start being a super salesgirl, anyway?'

'In about a month.'

'The time will fly by.'

'I hope so.' The wistful tone in the girl's voice didn't escape Jade and she vowed to take the girl out and about a lot more. Gemma needed a girlfriend, that was clear, someone she could perhaps confide in. Jade had loads of advice for any unfortunate female infatuated with Nathan. After all, she had first-hand experience of the disease. With a bit of luck, Lenore might drop the odd antidotal remark about her ex as well.

By the time Nathan angled his car out of the driveway and into the traffic heading for the city—Jade firmly belted in the passenger seat—she was feeling quite angry with him. Though determined to tackle him on the subject of Gemma, she knew better than to simply blurt out a tactless accusation. Nathan would simply close up shop and tell her to mind her own damned business. She decided a comment about the weather was always a good place to start.

'Nice day,' she said.

'It's rather chilly in this car,' Nathan returned drily. 'Is it something I've done, or shall we blame first-day nerves?'

'Chilly? I don't know what you mean.'

Nathan laughed. 'Come now, Jade, I've known you far too long not to pick up your airwaves. You're spoiling for a fight but just aren't sure where to start.'

Jade's mouth thinned. If there was one thing she detested more than male chauvinists, it was when the devils were right! 'I admit I have a delicate problem which requires some subtlety of approach,' she said archly.

'Which lets you out, sweetheart. Subtlety is not your strong hand.'

Jade bristled. 'In that case, I'll bypass subtlety in favour of blunt honesty.' She dragged in a deep, courage-filling breath. 'I know you're sleeping with Gemma on the sly, Nathan, which is not only reprehensible considering Gemma's obvious inexperience with men, but in appalling bad taste with your fourteen-year-old daughter just down the hallway.'

The stillness and the silence in the car was mind-numbing. After a minute had passed Jade could not stand the strain another second.

'Say something, for heaven's sake!' she burst out.

His sidewards glance would have killed a brown snake at a hundred yards. 'I am still recovering from your gall,' he said in a voice dipped in liquid nitrogen.

'*My* gall!' Jade squeaked. 'At least I climbed out of the window for *my* assignations. I didn't have any of my boy-friends sleaze their way into my room in the dead of night.'

Nathan's inward breath sounded like a bellows with em-physema. It came to Jade she just might have overstepped the mark.

'My God,' he snarled. 'If I hadn't heard it with my own ears I would not have believed it. Jade Whitmore, lecturing *me* on matters of morals. I'll have you know, Madam Lash, that I have spent the majority of my adult life stopping the women of the Whitmore family from sleazing their way into *my* bedroom in the dead of night. They've all made the offer at one time or another. But I did the right thing, every damned time. Even with you, who came along when I was sexually vulnerable. You, who draped herself all over me in a semi-naked state. *You*, who used every one of your considerable womanly wiles to seduce me! And yet here you are, with the effrontery to make a moral judgement on *me*!'

Guilt and confusion rattled Jade for a moment, but then she recognised Nathan's argument for what it was—a clever ruse to deflect her from the real issue at hand here. Which was the reality of his association with Gemma.

'I know I've been silly in the past, Nathan. But I'm not

nearly as bad as either you or Pops think I am. I could count my lovers on the fingers of my left hand and still have a finger or two left over. But that's immaterial to what's going on between you and Gemma and you know it.'

Another silence descended on the car but this time it was Nathan who broke it, though his voice was no warmer than the last time.

'I'm only going to say this once, Jade. If there is something going on between Gemma and myself then it is nobody's business but Gemma's and mine. When you grew up, Jade, I accorded you the rights and privileges of being an adult, one of which is privacy. What you do in your own private life is your business, and what I do in mine is mine. Do I make myself clear?'

'Absolutely.'

'I sincerely hope you haven't been voicing these scurrilous suspicions of yours to others around Belleview.'

'Not as yet, but they may have already jumped to the same conclusions.'

'I doubt that very much.'

'Are you saying you haven't been sleeping with Gemma?'

'What makes you think I have?'

'I saw her leaving your room late last night.'

'We were just talking. She was worried about something.'

'I don't believe you.'

'It's the truth.' And he looked her straight in the eyes. Damn it, but she believed him.

'You mean you're not having an affair with her?' she quizzed, and watched his face some more.

'No,' he said solidly. 'I am not.'

'Well, I'll be blowed! I could have sworn you were.'

'If you say anything of the kind to Gemma she'll be horribly embarrassed. She's not as sophisticated as you,

Jade. She'll want to curl up and die. She might even leave Belleview, and we don't want that, do we?'

'No, of course not. I won't say anything if you promise never to hurt that girl, Nathan. She's much too sweet for the likes of you.'

His laughter was dark. 'I promise never to hurt Gemma. There, will that do?'

'I suppose so. But watch it, I think she has a crush on you.'

'Do you, now?'

'Yes, I do.'

'One more thing while we're discussing Gemma, if you don't mind, Jade.'

'What?' she responded warily.

'This clothes-buying expedition you'll be going on with her. Don't let Lenore turn her into a clone of herself, will you? Gemma's charm lies in her being herself, in being unspoiled. Why change an original mould in favour of a mass-produced variety? Women like Lenore are a dime a dozen around Sydney.'

Jade stared over at him. 'I didn't realise how much you hated poor Lenore.'

'I don't hate her.'

'You could have fooled me.'

'Divorce is an ugly thing, Jade. It leaves scars.'

'Lenore carries a few of her own.'

Nathan laughed. 'You women always stick together.'

'So do you men.'

'You've become a feminist.'

'What do you mean...*become*? I haven't worn a bra in years.'

He slanted her a rueful smile. 'At least you can't tell under that jacket,' he said, his comment startlingly close to Byron's last time she'd dressed up.

'It wouldn't matter if you could,' came her dry reply. 'Braless breasts don't raise an eyebrow on the man I'll be working with today.'

'Is that so? Sounds as if your nose is out of joint a little. I didn't realise you'd met the inimitable Mr Armstrong.'

'I was home when he came visiting Pops last Saturday. He stayed for dinner.'

'But he didn't want you for afters?' Nathan mocked.

'Didn't even want a little nibble,' Jade admitted with a melodramatic sigh.

Nathan laughed. 'There's no accounting for bad taste, I suppose. Or maybe he's gay, like Roberto.'

Jade's head whipped round. 'Good grief, I never thought of that.' But when she did every feminine instinct within her screamed in protest. 'No,' she said confidently. 'He's not gay.'

'How can you tell?'

'I can tell, believe me. My female antennae wouldn't have worked so well if he had been. I dare say he has a girlfriend or lover stashed away somewhere. That's the problem. Our sexy new marketing manager is just not on the market.'

'You really found him sexy, Jade? I'm amazed. I thought he was rather cold and arrogant when I met him on Monday. But first impressions can be deceiving, I would also have said he'd been born with a silver spoon in his mouth and was no stranger to being sucked up to. Which shows how wrong one can be. His résumé revealed a more than ordinary background. A state school education, a business degree at the Hobart University, followed by seven years straight with the marketing section of an international food company, the last three as head of the division. A successful enough career but one which I didn't think matched his personality.'

'I couldn't agree more,' Jade drawled. 'The man's insufferably egotistical. But I have to admit he was clever with Pops. Called him sir and kowtowed beautifully without being at all obsequious.'

'Is that so? Mmm. Perhaps our Mr Armstrong bears close watching for a while.' Nathan was pensively silent for a minute then brightened, throwing Jade one of his double-sided smiles. 'But you'll have to do the watching, Jade. I'm finishing up at Whitmore's this week to write full time. Your father will be back at the helm next Monday.'

Jade liked nothing more than the thought of watching Kyle Armstrong closely. She was still as besotted, beguiled and bewitched by the man as she had been last Saturday. But the news that Nathan was permanently leaving Whitmore's came as a surprise, though not an entirely unwelcome one. She'd always been jealous of his relationship with her father and relished the idea of becoming closer to Byron herself, and proving she was every bit as clever and competent as her adopted brother.

'You're really leaving, Nathan?'

'Yup.'

'Will you stay living at Belleview?'

'Can't say that I will.'

Now this *was* good news. He could hardly seduce Gemma when they wouldn't even be under the same roof. Unless he planned to take both Kirsty and Gemma with him...

'I suppose you'll move up into the beach-house at Avoca,' she suggested sneakily, knowing that would mean Kirsty would have to go home to her mother to live. 'You've always been keen on that place and you seem to write well there.'

'Yes, that's definitely where I'll go.'

'What about Kirsty?'

Now he frowned. 'She'll have to go home to her mother, I suppose.'

'Well, that's where Kirsty is best off, surely. And Lenore loves her dearly, Nathan. She probably only wanted a break from her. Teenage girls can be a right pain in the neck, as you well know.' She grinned over at him in memory of her own hair-raising escapades.

Nathan grunted.

'Maybe Lenore will let Gemma live with them, since

Kirsty's grown so fond of her minder. Actually, that might
not be such a bad idea. I suppose you know Lenore's rehearsing a new play which starts in a couple of weeks. With
her out most nights, she might like someone at home with
Kirsty.'

'Lenore has a pensioner lady neighbour who sits with
Kirsty whenever she has to be out at night. I doubt she will
want a third person living in the house with them. Lenore
values her privacy these days,' he finished with an acid tone
that astonished and irritated Jade. Surely it was Nathan who
had always valued privacy.

'Which rather leaves Gemma like a shag on a rock,
doesn't it?' she retorted. 'You know the poor little thing
doesn't have any friends or relatives in Sydney. Which reminds me, have you found out anything more about her
mother or her folks?'

'Gemma gave me a photo she had and I've asked
Zachary to hire an investigator he knows to make enquiries.
As for Gemma herself, there's no reason why she can't stay
on at Belleview indefinitely. Melanie and Ava like having
her around.'

'Are you sure it's not you who likes having her around,
Nathan?'

His smile sent icicles up and down Jade's spine. 'You
don't give up easily, do you?'

'I'm not one to underestimate a man's sexual needs, Nathan,' came her cool reply, her mind flying to a mental
image of her father and Mrs Parkes embracing and kissing.
'I haven't noticed you taking out any ladies lately. Yet
you're not writing at the moment.'

His grey eyes hardened as they slid her way. 'My, you're
an observant little thing, aren't you? Or has my darling ex-
wife been telling you stories out of school?'

'Women talk. You know that.'

'Well, men don't,' he snapped. 'Certainly not about their
personal lives. Stop prying into mine, Jade,' he warned. 'I

don't like it. Stick to your own. I'm sure it's colourful enough to amuse you.'

'One day, Nathan, you'll believe me when I tell you I'm not the promiscuous little tart you seem to think I am.'

Again Nathan smiled. It projected scepticism with a capital S.

Suddenly, Jade could not wait for Nathan to leave Whitmore's. *And* Belleview. He was far too judgemental of her for her liking. She also had the awful feeling that Gemma would not be safe till he was way out of sight and out of mind. Yes, everything would be much better without him being around!

CHAPTER SEVEN

As NATHAN drove across the Harbour Bridge Jade realised she hadn't been into the head office at Whitmore's for ages—maybe two or three years—but she knew her father pretty well and she was sure nothing would have changed. Pops was not a man who liked change.

Whitmore Opals occupied half of the seventh floor of a conservative rather than glamorous office block, tucked in behind the taller larger flashier buildings that faced Circular Quay. Therè was no view worth looking at through Whitmore's windows, unless one wanted to inspect the backs of other buildings or windswept alley-ways.

The reception area was presentable enough with black leather seating, bluish carpet and the inevitable rented pot-plants. The reception desk itself was functional, however, rather than showy, as was the woman who'd sat behind it for a dozen years or more. Moira had been hired for her superb secretarial skills, not her looks. Jade's father did not believe in putting glamorous blondes on the front desk whose only talents lay in answering the telephone in sing-song voices or smiling seductive smiles at visiting clients and sales reps.

The head of Whitmore's also didn't believe in wasting money on unnecessary staff or housing them in overly lav-ish accommodation. Management had reasonably plush of-fices, but none, other than Byron, had his own personal secretary—if one could call Moira that. The other execu-tives shared the secretaries and typists who all resided in one large room with 'Administration' on the door.

All the other sections had similar open floor-plan accommodation. Exports, Accounts, Sales, Personnel and Design were each housed in the one large room on either side of a central corridor, Design being the only section where individual workers were given the privacy of cubicles to help them create the quality pieces that were the hallmark of Whitmore Opals.

Some of the more individual designs were never duplicated or reproduced, though these were usually ones commissioned for a particular opal that Byron had bought. Neither did Whitmore's make doublets or triplets, which were thin slices of opals adhered to a black backing to make the opal look bigger and brighter, the triplets having a glass or crystal cap further to enlarge the opal's appearance. Whitmore's only used solid opals in their jewellery—an uncommercial and snobbish decision, Jade thought.

Doublets and triplets might not increase in value, but they could still look beautiful and brought pleasure to people who could not afford the much more expensive solids. People didn't always buy opals for investments, Jade reasoned sensibly. If she were running the company, Whitmore's would make a much wider range of opal jewellery. They could supply the cheaper items to souvenir and gift shops all over Australia as well as export them to similar shops overseas.

Yes, Whitmore's had become an old-fashioned, stodgy company in Jade's opinion. It was to be hoped that with the employing of a young marketing manager like Kyle change was at last on the way.

Nathan's car crawled off the bridge and along the already jammed city streets before turning down a narrow lane which was refreshingly empty, though bleak-looking. He whizzed along for half a block before abruptly turning down the well-disguised ramp that led into the basement car park. There, after a couple of neatly executed corners, he slid the Mercedes into a reserved spot alongside a silver-grey sedan.

'Can I have your parking place when you're gone?' Jade asked Nathan once he'd turned off the engine.

'Sorry,' he said. 'No can do. This is Byron's spot. Mine's already been allotted to your Mr Armstrong.' And he pointed to the Magna alongside.

'He's not my Mr Armstrong. Yet,' she added, more to irritate Nathan than any real desire to pursue the man. Jade was not one to set herself up for further humiliation or rejection, and Kyle had made it quite clear the other night that he was not interested in her in that way.

'In that case, soon you won't have to worry about a parking place,' Nathan returned drily. 'You'll be able to ride in with *him* on the necessary mornings.'

'Very funny,' Jade remarked, ignoring Nathan and swinging her long legs out of the car. Standing up, she eased the straight, rather short skirt back down over her hips then straightened her sheer black tights. Bending to peer into the car's side-mirror, she checked her make-up, readjusted her black and gold earrings, ruffled her blonde hair up on top and patted it down at the sides before last, but not least, moistening suddenly dry lips. Taking a deep breath, she slung the gold chain of her black patent handbag over her shoulder and strode round to join Nathan, who was standing there watching her with a sardonic expression on his face.

'The poor bastard,' he muttered, looking her up and down.

Jade might have shot back some suitably caustic comment but Nathan had already turned away to walk towards the basement lift where two more people were standing waiting. Neither of them was a Whitmore employee, since they didn't speak to Nathan, who remained silent during the ride up to the seventh floor. Jade did likewise, her nerves returning. Her mind was not on attracting Kyle, as Nathan might have thought, but on the job facing her.

What would her work consist of? Would she be able to

make an intelligent contribution to the company? Would she make a fool of herself?

'Where have you put Kyle?' she asked once they stepped out of the lift and were alone in the corridor.

'In my old office. I've been occupying Byron's.'

'And where will I be located, do you know?'

'Kyle had another desk moved into his office yesterday.'

Jade did a double take. 'You mean I'm to be in the same room with him all day?'

Nathan ground to a halt outside the double glass doors that had 'Whitmore' in black lettering on one and 'Opals' on the other. 'Why the panic, Jade? That should surely play right into your hands. Nothing like being with a person constantly to create an atmosphere of intimacy. I would have thought you'd be ecstatic at the arrangement.'

'Do you know what, Nathan? You're getting to be a bore!' And, sweeping past him, she pushed the door open and marched inside.

Moira glanced up from Reception, managing to look both surprised and pleased at sighting Jade. 'Well, if it isn't little Jade, all grown up and very glamorous-looking. I almost didn't recognise you in that suit and with that blonde hair, but it suits you.'

'Thanks, Moira. You're looking well, too.'

The woman's smile was slightly sheepish. 'I have to admit it's been less harrowing working for Nathan here than your father. But I gather that situation will come to an end next Monday. Still, perhaps Mr Armstrong's arrival will take some of the load off Byron's shoulders and he'll be less stressed. What do you think, Nathan?'

'I think everyone might be in for a big surprise. A close brush with the grim reaper has a tendency to make one sit up and take stock of one's life. I wouldn't be surprised if Byron comes in here next Monday a changed man. You mark my words. I almost regret not being here to see it. I'll have coffee in ten minutes, Moira.' And, so saying,

Nathan strode into Byron's office and closed the door behind him.

Both Moira and Jade stared after him, Moira in startled shock, Jade with dry scepticism.

Her father hadn't changed. Her father would never change. Black was still black in his eyes, just as white was white. Right was right and wrong was wrong. People were good or bad. There could be no grey. Except, of course, when it applied to his own private and personal life. Then things could be very grey indeed.

Moira cleared her throat and swivelled round in her chair to face Jade. 'That's telling us, isn't it? Still, Nathan's never been one to mince words.' Her face showed she admired him for that. 'So! You're going to be getting the feel of things by helping Mr Armstrong out a couple of days a week, Jade, is that right?'

'Uh-huh. He's a brave man, isn't he, taking on a troublemaker like me?' Jade was aware Moira probably knew all about the various problems she'd caused over the years. Byron had a tendency to talk very loud on the telephone when he was lecturing.

'A lot of teenagers go through a difficult time,' the woman said with sweet generosity, 'but you're all grown up now and very lovely, if I may say so.'

'Why, thanks, Moira, that's really sweet of you. Well, I suppose I'd better go and beard the lion in his den.'

'Jade, before you do, I just want to say I'm sorry about your mother and to apologise for not coming to the funeral. Someone had to hold the fort here and, to be honest, I never did get to know Mrs Whitmore very well. She didn't come to any of the staff functions and...well...'

'And she never invited any of the staff to Belleview,' Jade finished for her, hating the way she felt when she had to talk about her mother, not to mention the guilt that consumed her because she couldn't bring herself to feel grief or loss over her death. Regret was the closest to either she could summon up, regret that the woman had made it impossible for people to love her. 'It's all right, Moira,' she sighed. 'I understand.'

The door of Nathan's old office opened and Kyle stood there, staring over at her. His coldly black but strangely sensual gaze hit her between the eyes—and in the stomach—as forcefully as it had the first time. She gulped and tried telling herself he wasn't that good-looking, or that sexy, even if he *was* wearing a magnificent pale grey lounge suit which would have looked well on any man, let alone one as elegantly built and attractive as he was. Jade just barely stopped her own eyes from eating him up the way a hot, tired trucker might eye a cold frothy beer. He, of course, was surveying her back with his now familiar cool style, showing not the slightest hint of either the surprise or admiration Moira had afforded her, let alone any real interest or desire.

It quickly came to Jade that working closely with this man would take considerable control on her part. Still, she supposed she should be getting used to personal rejection by now!

Plastering a bright smile on her face, she walked towards him. 'Hi, there!' she greeted breezily. 'I'm here in good time. Look, it's only ten to nine.'

'So it is. You're going to be working in here,' he said. 'With me.'

'Yes, Nathan told me on the way in this morning.' Jade kept smiling as she brushed past him on her way into the office where immediately she saw that her desk had been placed at right-angles to his. She would be working even closer than she'd imagined. God!

She whirled round just as Kyle closed the door. 'Before I forget,' she said a little breathlessly, 'do you think one of those reserved parking spots in the basement could be arranged for me?'

'No,' he said bluntly, and strode over behind his desk.

She followed to stand on the other side, facing him. 'Why not?'

His expression was so bland she felt like hitting him. 'It would cause trouble with other members of the general staff who don't have the privilege of a personal parking space. Only management has that perk, certainly not a part-time assistant.'

Jade frowned her instant disgruntlement. She was more than a part-time assistant, surely. One day she'd own the damned company. 'Surely, as Byron's daughter, I should be able to—'

'I don't believe in blatant nepotism,' he interrupted curtly, his face turning hard. 'A person should earn privileges, not have them handed to him—or her—on a silver platter.'

Jade felt her control slipping. 'If you don't believe in nepotism then why give me this job in the first place?' she snapped. 'If you did it just to suck up to my father then you pulled the wrong rein. My father doesn't believe in women holding executive positions. The only position he likes them in is the missionary position!'

Jade regretted this last comment the moment it slipped out of her mouth but to her surprise Kyle laughed. 'Let me assure you, Jade, I didn't hire you hoping to score brownie points with your father, though he may be grateful to me in the end. I saw qualities in you that perhaps your father is incapable of seeing with those undoubtedly biased eyes of his.'

'What qualities?' she challenged, highly sceptical of this seeming about-face. 'Name one.'

'Boldness.'

Now Jade laughed. 'You find boldness a quality? My father finds my boldness a pain in the butt.'

'I can appreciate that,' he admitted drily. 'But, as I've already pointed out, I am not your father.'

'Boldness, eh? Name another of these mysterious qualities of mine.'

His smile, when it came, took her breath away. Go back

to your other face please, she wanted to tell him. I can almost cope with that one!

'I think you've had enough flattery for one morning,' he drawled. 'Let me just say I think your various qualities can translate into tangible assets for the marketing section of this ailing company, *provided* you can be stopped from going over the top. Your qualities need a firm hand, Jade. And direction.'

'And *you're* going to be my firm hand?' she mocked.

'I would prefer the word "director".'

'Then direct me to where I can park within walking distance of this place.'

'I said director, Jade, not babysitter. Find your own parking place. If you can't, then catch the train or the bus like everyone else. Or alternatively, ride in with your father. He'll be coming in from next Monday.'

Jade gritted her teeth and counted to ten. Underneath, she was grudgingly impressed by the man's stand—and almost pleased by his highly unexpected though rather backhanded compliments—but she'd be darned if she was going to give in without a fight.

'What about this Friday afternoon?' she argued. 'I'll be coming here straight from university. I can hardly leave my car behind.'

'Can't you catch a train that day?'

'I could, but my lectures don't finish till one. It would take me ages to get here by public transport in the middle of the day. By the time I arrived it would almost be time to go home again.'

'Not really, I always work late on a Friday and so will you as my assistant. But I'm not an unreasonable man. You can have my parking spot on Friday, *if* you agree to drive me home afterwards.'

Jade blinked. She hadn't expected him to capitulate. She certainly hadn't expected him to offer her his own spot. As for driving him home afterwards... Her heart fluttered wildly at the thought. Damn, but she'd resolved to ignore this unwanted desire, yet here she was, thinking all sorts of scandalous things.

'Where's home?' she asked, trying to sound casual while her insides were doing the fandango.

'Northbridge. Not that far out of your way.'

'It's a deal,' she said, knowing damned well she would have agreed even if he'd said the Blue Mountains. Or Timbuctoo.

'Right,' Kyle said brusquely. 'Now let's get to work. Do you like tea or coffee?'

Her eyes widened in surprise that he was offering to get *her* a drink, not the other way around. Clearly, he was no Nathan. 'Coffee,' she said. 'Black, no sugar.'

'Ah, yes, I remember now. Same as myself. Get yourself settled and start looking over the sales figures I put on your desk while I get the coffee. I won't be long.'

Jade's eyes followed him as he strode from the room, his walk elegant, the carriage of his head as arrogant as Nathan had said. But it was not an arrogance that grated, Jade realised. There was something eminently appealing about a man being as cool and self-possessed as Kyle was, who could stand up to the daughter of the boss one moment, then get her a cup of coffee the next. It came to her then that there was no chauvinism in Kyle Armstrong. God, but she liked that, she liked it a lot!

Shaking her head, Jade turned and walked over to the corner of the room where she hooked her handbag over a peg of the coatstand. The man was an enigma all right, not easily read. A man of mystery. So he liked her boldness, did he? Now that was a surprise! He certainly hadn't the other night. Still, that had been on a personal basis. Maybe it *was* an asset in marketing to be bold. A bold thinker might produce some new innovative daring strategies. Whitmore's could certainly do with them.

As for his declaration that she needed direction… Jade supposed he was right about that too. It was time to tone down her wild, tempestuous nature, high time to stop acting the rebel. Since she wasn't interested in embracing marriage and motherhood—lord preserve her from following her own mother's wonderful example—it was also time she put her head down and showed her father that she could make a real contribution to the family company, that she meant business!

Jade was still in front of the coatstand, smiling at her own pun when Kyle re-entered the room and threw her an exasperated glance.

'Something amusing you over in that corner?' he said curtly, kicking the door shut behind him and walking over to put a steaming mug on each desk. He glared down at the untouched sales reports. 'Don't tell me you haven't even sat down yet. Look, Jade, there's no room around here for any dead weight. You're either serious about this job or you aren't. I was hoping by your appearance this morning that you were!'

Jade bit her bottom lip and hurried over. 'I've never been more serious about anything in my life!' she pronounced. 'I'm sorry, Kyle. It won't happen again.'

'Make sure it doesn't. I've stuck my neck out hiring you, Jade. Don't make me look a fool.'

'I won't, Kyle. I'll be a model assistant from now on, I promise. I won't even breathe till I've read every single page here.' And she buried her face in the first report, not even touching the coffee.

'There's no need to get carried away,' he said drily.

The telephone on his desk rang then and he picked it up. Jade couldn't help but overhear his side of the conversation. After all, he was only a few feet away and the sales reports weren't *that* involving.

'Kyle Armstrong…'

A short tense silence was followed by a frustrated sigh.

'Look, I've told you not to ring me here. Couldn't this have waited till tonight?'

Jade's ears pricked up. One didn't need to be imaginative to get the drift. A girlfriend was making a nuisance of herself, ringing Kyle at the office when he'd told her not to. Despite her having suggested as much to Nathan, the thought of Kyle actually having a girlfriend brought an intense stab of jealousy. How dared he have a girlfriend? He'd hardly been in the state long enough to *meet* women, let alone snaffle one up for himself.

Oh, my God, she thought. Had he brought one with him over from Tasmania? A live-in kind?

I do not care! she told herself furiously. It means nothing to me. He's just my boss, nothing more. And a chauvinist after all, from the sounds of things. He's talking to that poor girl like dirt. I couldn't possibly fancy a chauvinist. I most definitely would not want to go to bed with one.

'I'll be home around nine,' he was saying sharply. 'Yes, do that, and don't—I repeat *don't*—ring me here again.'

He muttered something as he hung up. Jade looked up and their eyes met.

'Girl trouble?' she said between clenched teeth.

His gaze didn't waver but she could have sworn it turned a fraction smug. 'Something like that,' he drawled.

Jade's teeth clenched ever harder in her jaw.

I hate him, she decided once again.

CHAPTER EIGHT

JADE was still poring over sales reports and profits and loss statements when another mug of coffee materialised on her desk. Startled, she looked up to find Kyle standing there with a steaming mug in his own hand.

'It's gone eleven,' he said.

'Really?' she gasped, only then realising how absorbed she'd become in the figures. Absorbed and appalled.

'Yes, really,' Kyle said drily, and perched on the corner of her desk, sipping his coffee. 'Drink up. I'm sure you're in need of resuscitation after looking at those figures.'

She certainly was. 'I didn't realise things were that bad,' she said, and picked up her mug.

'Half of the problem is stagnation. The other half is Campbell Jewels, who have a stranglehold on the opal market, though it's not clear why. Admittedly, they undercut Whitmore's prices in their chain stores, but not in their duty-free shops around Sydney. In fact, their duty-free opal prices are actually dearer than Whitmore's. Yet their sales are still higher, a matter I'm investigating at the moment. Meanwhile, it might help if you tell me what happened between Celeste Campbell and your father to cause such a savage vendetta on Ms Campbell's part.'

Jade's shrug carried true confusion. 'I wish I knew. I think it goes back a long way.'

'Tell me what you do know.'

She did.

'Mmm. Since things settled down between the Campbells and Whitmores after your father's marriage to

Irene Campbell, then something else had to have happened afterwards. Do you think there could have been some personal involvement between Byron and Celeste around that time? An affair turned sour?'

'I have to admit that has crossed my mind,' Jade conceded. 'My parents' marriage was not a happy one.'

'Your father doesn't strike me as an adulterer, Jade,' Kyle commented thoughtfully.

'I'm sure he wouldn't be in normal circumstances,' she said, stunning herself with this new sudden insight. 'But my mother was...difficult to love.' Oh, Pops, she thought with an unexpected rush of emotion and understanding. Forgive me for taking such a holier-than-thou narrow-minded stand. We all need to be loved, and if we sometimes look for love in the wrong arms then who is to blame for that? Certainly not the unloved one.

Tears of remorse and something else stung her eyes, and she quickly dropped her lashes, hiding her distress as she sipped her coffee. A silence descended upon the room, Kyle seemingly giving her time to gather herself. Finally, she looked up, and those beautiful eyes of his were watching her closely, sympathy in their normally inscrutable black depths.

Sympathy was something Jade wasn't used to. For some reason, it annoyed her, Kyle's job was marketing, not probing into the private life of his employer.

'Now that I've had time to think about it,' she said sharply, 'I'm quite sure that's not the answer. Father would not do anything of the kind. He's an exceptionally moral man. Who knows? Maybe Celeste made a play for him and he turned her down. She's a real man-eater, that one. Though she usually prefers younger men. You'd better watch yourself, Kyle,' Jade flung at him a touch acidly. 'You'd be her type, and once she finds out you're working for us you'll become her prime target.'

His eyes glittered with dark amusement. 'How kind of you to warn me. But let me assure you, Jade, I'm not the sort of man who responds well to being a target of the opposite sex. *I* fire the bullets where women are concerned, not the other way around. That's the way mother nature made the beast, and that's the way I like it.'

Sliding off her desk, he walked over to the door where he glanced back over his shoulder at her, his mouth stopping just short of a smile. 'Excuse me for a moment,' he said with cool politeness. 'I have several things I wish to discuss with Nathan. Take a break till I get back, then we'll put our heads together and see what we can come up with to put Whitmore's back on the map.'

Jade sighed audibly once the door shut behind his exit. That man! He had a way of fascinating and irritating the death out of her at the same time. Had that been a slap on her wrist, the comment about *his* wanting to fire the bullets where the opposite sex was concerned?

As for putting their heads together...

Jade groaned as the image of Kyle kissing her flashed into her mind, bringing with it a definite curling of her stomach. Dear lord, never had a man affected her like this before. It was utterly, utterly amazing. And utterly, utterly futile. Kyle already had a female in town, panting for him so much that she had risked disobeying orders and ringing him at the office.

Jade frowned over that phone call for a moment. Kyle had been arrogant and quite rude to the person on the other end. Funny, she wouldn't have thought that was how he'd treat a woman-friend. She would have imagined him being a suave charmer, always doing and saying the right thing.

Damn, but he was really getting under her skin. Why was she getting the sickly feeling that there was something not right about him, something not quite real?

Something Nathan said in the car came back to haunt her, something about Kyle bearing close watching. What had he meant by that? Did he think there was a chance Kyle was some kind of industrial spy? A saboteur, maybe, from Campbell Jewels?

Her mind flashed back to that phone call. Maybe it wasn't a woman who'd called him. Or maybe it was? Could Kyle be already involved with Celeste Campbell? Was that the solution to all these niggling concerns?

It didn't seem possible. In fact, it was a crazy idea, Jade finally accepted. If he was Celeste's spy, he would not be asking questions about her, would he? She was becoming paranoid.

Jade was glad when she suddenly remembered her promise to Gemma to get in touch with Lenore about going shopping. Anything to distract her from that infernal man! After a quick dash to the ladies' room, she elicited Lenore's number from the highly efficient Moira and returned to her desk to dial. An answering machine told her that Lenore would be at the Drama Theatre at the Opera Hall all day rehearsing. Jade hung up, thinking she might walk over there during her lunch-hour. It wasn't far.

The door opened and Kyle came in, looking pensive. 'I hope,' he informed her with a worried look, 'that I haven't bitten off more than I can chew here.'

Jade was privately astonished that he would admit to any doubts about his abilities. Yet, in a way, his expressing even the smallest degree of apprehension came as a relief. This wasn't the action of a dastardly con-man, intent on inveigling his way into everyone's confidence in order to cause trouble for Whitmore's. Such a bounder would be all bluff, displaying not a chink in his armour.

Jade found herself warming again to Kyle. God, would she never stop this see-sawing of emotions where this man was concerned? Still, she much preferred liking him to hating him. Though both made her heart race like that of an adolescent schoolgirl.

'I have every confidence in you, Kyle,' she praised. 'After all, you can't do worse than Father has been doing. Besides,' she added with a cheeky grin, 'you have me by your side and that has to be worth something. Not much, perhaps, but I'm a trier. And bold, remember?'

Kyle blinked at her for a few moments before throwing his head back and laughing.

'I didn't think what I said was *that* funny,' she said stiffly, all the while trying not to stare at the man. Laughing, Kyle was more devastatingly attractive than ever.

He flashed dazzling white teeth at her, his laughter slowly being reduced to a wide smile. 'You are the most entertaining female I have ever come across.'

Jade bristled. 'Is that why you hired me? To be your court jester?'

'No,' he said, his smile now a mere quirk at the corner of his mouth. 'Nothing could be further from the truth. My reasons for hiring you were deadly serious. So let's get to work, Ms Whitmore. We have a company to save!'

By two o'clock, Jade's head was reeling. What a task-master! What a slavedriver! She'd heard of *think* tanks. Well, she'd just drowned in one!

'Kyle,' she said at last when her stomach started grumbling. 'I'm awfully hungry.'

He glanced at his wristwatch, which, if she wasn't mistaken, was a most expensive one. Clearly, Kyle spent a good proportion of his salary on his personal appearance, if his clothes and accessories were anything to go by. His grey suit had 'Italian' written all over it. His white shirt was the finest lawn. And his dark red tie with the black dots and matching kerchief were silk. A diamond sparkled in the corner of the gold and ebony ring he was wearing on the middle finger of his right hand.

'I didn't realise it was so late,' he muttered. 'You should have said something earlier.'

'And stop our brilliant flow of ideas?'

His smile curled her stomach. 'They *were* pretty good, weren't they? You're right of course about starting a cheaper line of opals. That's only common sense. And I loved your idea of an annual ball with the belle of the ball being presented with a solid opal pendant. The free advertising that will get us from the society pages and women's magazines will be invaluable.'

'Well, I adored your idea of an auction at the ball,' Jade countered enthusiastically, 'not to mention Whitmore's sponsoring a major horse-race. That's what we desperately need. Some exciting promotion and exposure. Opals have too staid an image.'

'Whitmore's won't have too staid an image if *you* ever get your hands on the reins,' Kyle said drily.

'Do I take that as a compliment?'

'I'm sure you will.'

'Meaning?'

'Meaning I've never known a young woman to be as impregnable to criticism and disapproval as you are. Do you ever care what people think of you?'

Jade's laughter was slightly bitter. 'Oh, I see. You've been talking to Nathan about me. You know, Kyle,' she said, standing up and straightening her skirt, 'you shouldn't believe half of what people say about me. For one thing, I don't change my men-friends every other week at all.'

'Only every month or so?' he taunted as she walked over to get her handbag from the coat-stand.

She unhooked the bag before turning, her dark blue eyes flashing angrily. Was she to be plagued with male hypocrites for the rest of her life? Her smile was a cover for her fury.

'Every month?' She pretended to consider the concept seriously. 'Well, perhaps that is going too far. I doubt any of my relationships have lasted *that* long. I have to confess, Kyle, that I have a low boredom threshold when it comes to men. Once they show their true colours—and they invariably do—I quickly lose interest.' This she delivered while looking him straight in the eye.

'And what true colours are those?' he demanded to know, his voice clipped and hard.

'Oh, the usual,' she retorted airily.

'You mean they only want sex from you?'

She laughed. 'Don't be silly. That goes without saying. No, it's their need to control everything that drives me mad. Just because you go to bed with them, they think they can start running your life!'

'How naïve of them,' he drawled. 'Maybe some women can be controlled by gaining a sexual upper hand, but I would imagine that would never work with you, Jade. A man would need a far greater lever when it came to capturing and holding *your* interest.' He smiled at her, a darkly cool and disturbingly enigmatic smile. 'Now hadn't you better toddle off for lunch? I want you sitting back at that desk no later than three.'

Jade stared back at him for a few electrically silent moments, her heart racing. Then she turned, and left the room, hating herself for allowing Kyle to continue to intrigue her. If she kept this up, next thing she knew she'd really fall in love with him. And that would never do.

Jade had once enjoyed playing at falling in love, but her recent experience with Nathan had taught her that really falling in love could bring considerable heartache. Creating a career for herself, she decided, was far more important than surrendering to an emotion fraught with such dangers. She wanted to succeed at Whitmore Opals, wanted quite desperately to show her father she could be as businesslike and successful as Nathan.

But she wouldn't do that if she started mooning over Kyle or going all gooey every time he threw a smile her way. No wonder men thought women had no place in business. Jade didn't doubt a lot of them let personal issues get in the way of their better judgement. Well, no more. From now on she would be all business. In fact, she would be as cool and controlled as Mr Cool himself!

The day had turned bleak and windy. Or was it just the narrow city street, sandwiched in between the tall buildings, blocking out the sun and forming a natural tunnel that accentuated any air movement? Whatever, Jade shivered as she hurried along, sighing her gratitude when turning the corner brought back the sunshine and no breeze at all.

The takeaway sandwich place she found a couple of doors along was empty. And why not? she thought tartly. It was no longer lunchtime!

With a salad sandwich, a low-fat chocolate milk drink and an apple in a paper bag, she strode quickly across the pedestrian crossing and into the quay area where there was no shortage of people dashing for trains and ferries. Finding a spare seat in one of the harbourside parks, she devoured her sandwich and drink, refusing even to think about Kyle Armstrong. Much nicer to watch the ferries chugging into and away from the piers, or the other craft that was cruising the blue water of the harbour.

Her craving for food temporarily satisfied, Jade wandered down towards Bennelong Point and the Opera House. Synonymous with Sydney, it was a building you couldn't help but admire, but Jade decided she could well do without the myriad steps one had to mount to reach the front doors and foyer.

Having explained at Reception who she wanted to see, she was allowed to slip into the back of the theatre without any trouble. Rehearsal was in progress, with Lenore on stage. Jade sat down in the back row of seats and was soon absorbed in the play which was funny in both a witty and farcical way.

Jade loved the theatre, and went often, though she had always avoided Nathan's plays, after seeing one a few years back. It had been an emotive drama about family relationships, hitting too close to the bone for her taste. Jade wanted to be entertained when she went to the theatre, not put through an emotional wringer.

Her mind and eyes back on Lenore, she found herself admiring the woman's acting ability. She was quite brilliant and exquisitely beautiful as well. Jade envied her willowy elegance and that glorious red hair which was so vibrant under the spotlights. She could well understand Nathan not wanting a divorce from so desirable and lovely a woman.

When the group on stage abruptly broke off and Lenore moved down some side-steps and started walking down one of the aisles towards her, Jade was surprised. She was in shadow at the back of the theatre and would have thought Lenore couldn't possibly see her from the stage. Jade had been prepared to wait for a natural break in the rehearsal before letting her presence be known. All she could think was perhaps the lady who'd let her in had somehow got a message to Lenore.

Jade was about to stand and meet Lenore halfway when a dark figure did exactly that from a row of seats on the other side of the aisle. It was a man, Jade quickly realised, a tall well-built man with dark hair and wearing a dark suit. As he hurried towards Lenore, he came into better light and Jade's eyes rounded. *Zachary Marsden*? They widened even further when the couple clasped hands together like long-lost lovers and Zachary started swiftly to draw Lenore towards the back of the theatre.

'What is it, darling?' Lenore was saying as they approached the row where Jade was sitting like a statue. Impossible for them not to see her now that they were facing her way. No amount of shadow could hide Jade's white-blonde hair from that distance.

Lenore's gasp when she noticed Jade was full of shock and guilt. Jade herself was dumbstruck. Zachary was, after all, a married man with two children, a *happily* married man, she'd always thought. Jade's heart hardened towards this woman who'd always had her admiration and sympathy. Suddenly, she felt sorry for Nathan. So *this* was what had caused the divorce!

Lenore whispered something to Zachary, who threw Jade a worried glance before reluctantly leaving. Jade, at this point, still hadn't moved. Lenore came over and sat down next to her, sighing as she did so.

'Before you say a word,' she began immediately, 'this is

not as bad as you think. Yes, I'm having an affair with Zachary, but no, it wasn't going on while I was married to Nathan. Zachary and his wife have agreed to divorce but they want to wait till their last boy, Clark, does his HSC exams at the end of this year. Not only that, Felicity was the one who asked for the divorce. She's fallen in love with another man.'

Jade stared at Lenore. 'Felicity? I don't believe it. She *adores* Zachary.'

Lenore shook her head. 'Felicity would always look as if she adored whatever man she was with. She's the clingy adoring type. But she certainly hasn't adored Zachary for quite some time, whereas I've loved him for years. Nathan and I were never in love, Jade. We only married because of Kirsty. I tried to make it work. Dear God, I tried for twelve long years, but Nathan…he…he should never have married at all. You know what he's like. He keeps all women at a distance. Emotionally, not sexually. He's mad about sex,' she finished with a caustic laugh.

'Yes,' Jade admitted drily. 'I can appreciate that.'

Lenore looked startled. 'Nathan hasn't been coming on to you, has he?'

Jade laughed. 'No, though I did throw myself at *him* once. It was quite interesting there for a minute or two but once he remembered who he was getting carried away with he stopped and gave me an enormous lecture. Sometimes, Lenore, I'm not sure what to make of Nathan. Is he a saint or sinner?'

'Maybe he's neither,' Lenore sighed. 'Maybe he's just human.'

Both women fell silent for a few seconds.

'You've met Gemma, haven't you, Lenore?' Jade resumed.

'Yes, I have. She's lovely, isn't she? I hope you're not here to tell me Nathan's seduced the poor girl already. Not that I didn't see it coming.'

'Oh? So he's been that obvious, has he?'

'Maybe not to everyone but certainly to me. You can't be married to a man as long as I was and not know the signs of sexual frustration.'

'He swears he isn't sleeping with her, you know. I tackled him about it this morning in the car on the way to work. Wednesday is one of my days in the office with that irritating Mr Armstrong I told you about on the telephone. Anyway, I don't want to talk about him—pompous man!—or Nathan for that matter. Believe it or not, I actually believed Nathan when he said he wasn't sleeping with Gemma.'

'I think it's just a question of time.'

'I couldn't agree more, which is why I'm here, Lenore. I've promised to take Gemma shopping tomorrow night at Chatswood to help her choose a working wardrobe and I was hoping you might come along, since you're so up on fashion. And I thought at the same time we both might drop a few hints about Nathan not being the right man for her, and...what are you laughing at?'

'Nothing much. Something just tickled my fancy. I can't tell you, I'm afraid. It concerns a little secret between your father and myself.'

Jade frowned. 'I hate secrets.'

'It's nothing to do with you, Jade. Truly.'

'If you say so. Well, will you come?'

'I'd love to.'

'Oh, goody. We'll have Gemma all glammed up and clued up at the same time. Look, I'd better fly. I have a feeling if I get back to the office even a minute late there'll be hell to pay. My boss alternates between being a new-age sensitive man and an even worse chauvinist than Pops, with the leaning towards the latter.'

'He sounds charming.'

'Oh, he is. That's the problem.'

Lenore's smile was wry. 'And good-looking?'

'Leaves Tom Cruise for dead.'

'You're not going to fall in love with him, are you, Jade?'

'Not if I can help it. The last thing I want is to stuff up this chance, Lenore. You know I've always wanted to learn the family business.'

'Yes, I know, but you have a habit of falling in love with the wrong man, don't you?'

Jade had to laugh. '*You* ought to talk.'

Lenore coloured guiltily. 'You won't tell anyone, will you, Jade?'

'Not a soul.'

'Thanks. I'd better go and call Zachary. He'll be worried. Now when and where shall we meet tomorrow night?'

Before they parted, Jade grabbed Lenore's hand, her face suddenly serious. 'I...I hope you'll be happy with Zachary, Lenore. I really do.'

There was a catch in her voice which squeezed at Lenore's heart. Happiness had been an elusive thing for Jade, she realised sadly. The girl tried so hard to be happy and outgoing all the time, but one didn't have to look far beneath the surface to find a troubled soul. The poor darling. If only she would stop flitting from boyfriend to boyfriend. If only she could find a good solid man like Zachary, a man of character and depth and sensitivity.

Too bad she was obviously attracted to this boss of hers. He didn't sound at all the right type for Jade. Besides, office romances could be very messy, especially with her being the boss's daughter.

A sudden thought came to Lenore and she grimaced. Dear lord, she hoped the new marketing manager at Whitmore's wasn't one of those cold ruthless bastards who'd do anything to get ahead. He wouldn't be the first good-looking man who thought he could either sleep or marry his way to the top. Maybe she should warn Jade.

And maybe I should just mind my own business, Lenore sighed. I have enough problems of my own.

CHAPTER NINE

AT PRECISELY one-thirty on the following Friday afternoon Jade zipped her natty white Ford Capri down the ramp of the basement car park, wondering if Kyle had remembered his promise to leave his reserved parking place empty for her, not to mention his condition that she drive him home later. She hadn't spoken to him since leaving the office at five the previous Wednesday. In fact, she'd had little opportunity to talk to him that afternoon at all after returning from her lunch break with Lenore.

Within minutes of her walking in the office door, Kyle had sent her out again to inspect their two retail outlets in Sydney with an eye to finding ways to update and improve their operation. She'd taken copious notes, her mind whirling with ideas to relate to him, but when she hurried back to work shortly before five Nathan had announced he was leaving straight away, if she wanted a lift home.

Kyle had seemed glad to see the back of her, she thought, and quite frankly she was at the end of her tether as well, both physically and emotionally. Some breathing space away from him would do her the world of good. She had been quite sure that, by Friday, she would have this unwanted reaction to his baffling sex appeal well and truly under control. Lust, she had found to her annoyance, was very distracting and not at all conducive to concentration. If she meant to succeed at Whitmore Opals, she would have to conquer it.

And the two days away from him seemed to have done the trick. She felt superbly composed and ready for the fray.

She'd reorganised the notes she'd taken on Wednesday and couldn't wait to impress Kyle with her ideas. But her reaction to seeing the empty parking place quickly put a dent in her confidence. She started thinking about having to drive him home that night, and hoping he'd invite her in, hoping he'd...

Hoping he'd *what*? she berated herself sharply as she snapped off the engine. Make a pass at you? Take you to bed, even? As if he would. He doesn't even like you that way. Besides, he's already got a girlfriend. Why are you even *thinking* like this, damn you? Where is the new, cool, sophisticated, career-woman Jade?

She was smouldering with self-disgust by the time she reached the lift, folding her arms and standing in a corner for her ride up to the seventh floor. But, despite all her self-criticism, her mind would not let up on that rotten girlfriend.

Was she a live-in variety, or just a passing fancy? A sexual stop-gap, so to speak.

The lift doors shot open and Jade made her way out, walking slowly along to Whitmore Opals while she continued to torment herself over the relationship Kyle might have with his mystery girlfriend. It didn't seem likely any woman would have moved in with him so soon, not unless he *had* brought her over from Tasmania. But would a lover of such long standing tolerate the way he'd spoken to her on the telephone the other day? Jade didn't think so.

Still frowning, Jade pushed open the glass door.

Nathan, who was standing at the reception desk chatting to Moira, looked round immediately, his grey eyes cool upon her. 'I'd like to speak to you for a moment, Jade,' he said brusquely. 'Come into my office.'

'But...but...'

'I'm sure Kyle won't mind,' he said drily. 'Moira, contact Kyle on the intercom and tell him I've kidnapped his assistant for a few minutes, will you?'

Nathan waved Jade to a chair once he'd shut his office

door but she declined, walking over to stand near one of the viewless windows.

'What do you want to talk to me about?' she asked impatiently.

'You and Gemma came home rather late last night,' he began as he sat down behind his large desk. Leaning backwards, he placed his elbows on the padded armrests, his long, elegant fingers linked in an arch in front of him. 'The shops closed at nine, yet it must have been eleven-thirty by the time you got in.'

'So?' she shrugged. 'We went for a drink afterwards. Is that a crime?'

'Gemma's not used to alcohol,' he said coldly. 'Or the sort of city dives you frequent. It's bad enough your changing the way she looks and dresses. Don't try to change the way she thinks and acts.'

Jade gave him a long, considering look. 'You know, Nathan, you keep claiming you have no ulterior motives where Gemma is concerned. And she certainly has been well briefed not to give anything away. So how come I continually get the feeling something is going on between you two?'

His smile carried too much cynical irony for Jade's peace of mind.

'What do you think of Gemma's new look?' she asked abruptly.

'I haven't seen Gemma since dinner last night.'

'Really? Well, you're in for a surprise.'

'A happy one, I hope.'

'That depends.'

'On what?'

'On what role you've cast yourself in where she is concerned. She looks really beautiful and a lot older. Very much a mature woman in every way.'

'And how large a hand did Lenore have in this transformation? I hope you didn't let her turn Gemma into a clone of herself. I asked you not to.'

'Why do you care?'

'I promised myself to look after the girl's welfare. I wouldn't like to see her spoiled. Or corrupted.'

Jade laughed. 'Then I suggest you look to yourself, darls, and not to me or your ex-wife. Lenore genuinely likes Gemma, as we all do, and she's just as concerned as I am over what stake you have in a girl of only twenty. You're thirty-five years old, a divorcee and a cynic. Gemma's a sweet innocent young thing who undoubtedly still believes in true love and marriage and playing happy families. Surely you can find other outlets for your male needs, brother dear, and leave her alone.'

Nathan glared at her for a moment, then grimaced. It was an odd expression for him, for it betrayed an inner turmoil that Jade found both bewildering and disturbing. Nathan was not given to moments of obvious emotional anguish. Anger, yes. And frustration. But not this black torment.

'I wish I could,' he muttered darkly.

Jade stared at him, horrified. 'Nathan, you *haven't*, have you?' Dear God, you lied to me the other day, didn't you?'

His cloudy grey gaze cleared to one of cold steel. 'I did not. Gemma is a lot safer with me,' he ground out, 'than she would be with a host of other men in this deplorable world.'

'Does…does she love you?'

'She thinks she does.'

Jade gasped her shock. Nathan's wording betrayed so much. 'And does she think you love her? No, don't answer that,' she rushed on, shuddering violently. 'I already know the answer. Oh, Nathan…you might not have seduced her body yet, but you've seduced her heart. She's far too young to know if she loves you or not. How could you be so wicked?'

He stiffened, his face hardening further. 'You don't know what real wickedness is,' he scorned. 'Besides, I certainly don't need you to lecture me on sexual morality. Or love, for that matter. You're the one who's always called any activity of your hormones "love". You claimed to be in love with me, remember? Am I to take it you've changed, along with your appearance? Poor Mr Armstrong,' he mocked. 'There I was, thinking you only lusted after him. If it's true love that has stirred your once fickle heart then I really pity him. You'll eat him alive!'

Jade felt an uncomfortable heat rushing through her making her heart beat faster and turning her hands hot and clammy. 'I am not in love with Kyle Armstrong,' she denied fiercely. 'I hardly know the man.'

'You think falling in love takes time? Or knowledge of character?'

'Apparently not, since Gemma loves *you*,' she lashed out blindly before being overtaken with guilt and remorse. But pride, and a degree of confusion, had her chin lifting, her nose sniffing with indignation. 'I'm not going to stay here and trade insults. I have better things to do.'

She strode over and reefed open the door. 'And before you make some unsavoury crack,' she threw back at him 'I'll have you know that any interest of mine in our new marketing manager is strictly business. I was only teasing you the other morning when I pretended to be after him Do you honestly think a man like that would be my type? You'd have to be joking. I like my men to have blood in their veins, not ice!'

Head held high, Jade marched from the office, just managing to slam the door shut before she collided smack bang with Kyle Armstrong's very hard and surprisingly warm chest.

'Oh!' she cried out, blushing fiercely when he cupped her shoulders to steady her, all the while peering down into her highly flustered face. There was no doubt in Jade's mind that he must have heard every single word she'd just said. A swift glance over his shoulder revealed that Moira had temporarily deserted the desk, so at least there was no one else to witness her humiliation. Which was just as well since she was practically dying from embarrassment.

'I…I didn't really mean any of that, Kyle,' she babbled.
'Nathan was needling me about you and I…I had to say
something.'

God, but she wished he would let her go. He was so
close and his hands felt so strong and all of a sudden her
knees were going to water. This lust business was *hell*, she
groaned silently.

'Which part didn't you mean?' he drawled.

'W…what?'

His hands fell from her shoulders back to his sides and
she almost sighed aloud with relief. As it was she took a
staggering step backwards, gulping when his cold black
gaze drifted slowly down over her tailored red suit. It had
a double-breasted jacket, the skirt straight and conservative
in length. So how come his sardonic scrutiny made her feel
she was wearing something highly erotic?

'Never mind,' he grated out. 'I take it you're now ready
for some hard work?'

Jade somehow pulled herself together. 'Yes, of course.'

'Good. Because I'd hate to think you were just amusing
yourself around here,' he snapped. 'I was talking to your
father on the telephone earlier and I think you should know
he's not expecting much from you. Quite frankly, Jade, no
one seems to expect much from you.'

She sucked in a pained breath. Despite being no stranger
to people's low expectations, they still hurt. Terribly.

'But I'm here to tell you that I do,' he stated sternly. 'I
expect everything from you.'

'E-everything?' she stammered.

'Yes, everything. Dedication. Imagination. Inspiration.
Perspiration. But above all, loyalty. I do not want to ever
overhear you discussing your feelings for me, either personal or otherwise, with anyone else in this company, and
that includes your brother. Because, in here, you're not Byron Whitmore's daughter, you're my assistant. Now get
your butt into our office so we can get to work!'

So saying, Kyle took hold of Jade and gave her a propelling push along the corridor, landing a decisive smack on her bottom as she went. For a split-second she contemplated murder, but killing Kyle didn't seem worth twenty years' imprisonment, so she kept going, stomping along the corridor a few strides ahead of her rapidly following boss. There were many ways to skin a cat, she thought vengefully. Or freeze a Mr Cool!

But if Jade thought she was going to get away with giving Kyle the cold shoulder for the rest of Friday, then she was sadly mistaken. His formidable business hat now on, he brushed aside any feeble attempts of hers to make him suffer her frosty silence, jabbing at her pride by calling such tactics the childish display of a spoilt juvenile, as well as an easy cop-out because underneath she felt she couldn't make the grade as a real employee worth her salt.

In the end, stung by his insults, she was forced not only to speak, but actually to work with him.

By six, Whitmore's was deserted except for Kyle and Jade. At seven, he had a pizza delivered and Jade made their third batch of coffee. By eight they'd almost finished mapping out a comprehensive strategy to rescue Whitmore Opals. By nine, they had!

The hours had been long and hard, but oddly enough, Jade didn't feel at all exhausted. Exhilaration was closer to the mark. Not that she would ever admit such a thing to Kyle! But for the first time in her life another person had told Jade something she'd said or done was clever, that *she* was clever. Beneath her outer prickliness Jade was thrilled, her self-esteem soaring to new heights.

'I think we'll call it a night,' Kyle announced shortly after nine. 'Come next Wednesday you can start organising the ball, Jade. I'll have fixed up the sponsorship of the horse-race by then. I have connections with the Sydney Jockey Club. My main concern is getting that new cheaper line of jewellery into production and on the market. And I must remember to ask Byron if he has an opal that would be suitable for auctioning.'

'You could ask him about the Heart of Fire.'

'The Heart of Fire?'

'Yes, it's a large solid opal still in the rough that was stolen from Whitmore's many years ago but which turned up again recently.'

'How did it turn up?'

'You won't believe it. Some alcoholic old miner out at Lightning Ridge was accidently killed and his daughter found the opal in his belongings. She brought it to Sydney to us to have it valued, thinking she'd inherited a fortune, only to find it was stolen property. Now isn't that the most incredible story? Another interesting sideline…it's the same opal that is supposed to have caused the original feud between the Whitmores and the Campbells.'

'Mmm, that *is* interesting, but bad luck for the daughter. Do the police think her father was the thief?'

'I really don't know, but I doubt it. The opal disappeared on my father's and mother's wedding-day twenty-three years ago, during the reception at Belleview. It was in the safe in the library.'

'It's certainly a colourful story. And is it a very beautiful opal?'

'I've never seen it, but I'm told it is. It's supposed to be worth over a million.'

Kyle whistled. 'Such a story would get Whitmore's a lot of free publicity.'

'Oh, I doubt my father would sanction that,' Jade said quickly, worried that she might have spoken out of turn. 'He doesn't even like talking about that old feud within the family, let alone in public. Besides, the—er—miner's daughter has become a close family friend since coming to Sydney. We wouldn't want to embarrass her or hurt her feelings,' she went on, thinking to herself that the Whitmores had already caused Gemma more than enough heartache, with possibly more to come.

'It sounds as if you think highly of this girl, Jade.'

'Yes, Gemma is very sweet. Unlike me,' she added drily.

'You don't think you're sweet?'

She threw him a caustic look. 'Do you?'

Those black eyes glittered with a dry amusement as they looked her over. 'I've never liked sweet much. Give me spicy any time.'

Jade froze, her breathing suspended. Surely that was a flirtatious remark he'd just delivered? Surely he was looking at her with something approaching desire?

'Time for you to drive me home, I think,' he said brusquely, and looked away.

Jade stared at him while he stood up and turned to unhook his suit jacket from the back of the chair, her startled eyes riveted to the play of muscles beneath his shirt. She'd noticed, when he'd taken the jacket off hours earlier, what a nice body he had, that he didn't need false padding in his shoulders. But she'd been so annoyed with him at the time that any physical reaction to his male appeal had been blocked by anger. Now, with that disarming compliment just delivered, Jade found herself more than susceptible to the blinding sexual attraction that she'd felt for Kyle right from the first moment she'd seen him.

Her mouth was dry as she watched him shrug into the dark blue jacket. After pulling down his shirt cuffs and straightening his pale blue tie, he started to tidy his desk, throwing her a sharp look when she still hadn't moved.

'What's the matter? What are you still sitting there for? Surely you remembered to bring your car in, didn't you?'

'Yes,' she managed to get out, her dismay acute. She'd obviously been wrong about the desire in his eyes. *Very* wrong.

'Then what's the problem? I would have thought you'd have liked to get rid of me so that you could go out on the town. That's what most young people do on a Friday night, isn't it?'

His patronising tone propelled her out of the depression that was threatening. As did his indifference to what she did tonight after she dropped him off. She stood up and started clearing her desk with snappy movements, her reply just as snappy. 'Anyone would think you were old, the way you talk! You're only twenty-eight, for heaven's sake.'

When she looked up to glare at him, he was smiling over at her. 'Someone's been peeking at my résumé.'

'So?' she scoffed, doing her best to ignore her guilty colour. 'I was curious. What's wrong with that?'

'Absolutely nothing. Don't be so defensive. I'm flattered.'

'Don't be.'

His smile widened, if anything. 'All right, I won't. Now, can we go home?'

'We aren't going home,' she snapped. '*You're* going home.'

His smile faded. 'Meaning?'

'Meaning I'm glad you reminded me that young people go out on the town on a Friday night. Because after the week I've had I could certainly do with some relaxing.'

'You shouldn't drink and drive, you know,' he warned.

'Who said anything about drinking? I don't *drink* to relax, Kyle. Perhaps you'd like to ask me what I do do?' she taunted, knowing that she was being outrageous but unable to stop. Kyle certainly brought out the worst in her.

His face became a stony mask. 'I don't think so. I too have had enough for one week. Now get your keys,' he bit out.

'Say please.'

He simply stared at her, disbelieving of her defiance. Her chin tilted upwards and she smiled at him. Boldly. Irreverently. 'Go on. It won't kill you.'

Suddenly, he smiled back, a most peculiar smile that sent the hairs standing up on the back of her neck.

'All right, Jade. You win. *Please* get your keys and take me home.'

CHAPTER TEN

'I CAN'T get over how much different Gemma looks with her new hairstyle,' Ava commented towards the end of dinner that Friday night. 'That feather-cut around your face is so flattering, dear, yet your hair's still lovely and long. You'll have to get the name of the hairdresser for me from Lenore. I'm fed up with this frizz of mine.'

Gemma tried to smile at Ava's compliments, but Nathan's continued silence over her new look had already spoiled any pleasure the previous night's makeover and shopping spree had given her. Personally, she'd been *thrilled* with the co-ordinated wardrobe of skirts, trousers, jackets and blouses that Lenore had chosen for her in creams and tans and greens, even if it had cost a small fortune. But since she knew she was marrying Nathan the outlay seemed worth it. After all, she wanted him to be proud to present her as his wife, which he could do now. She no longer looked like a country bumpkin, but a smart sophisticated woman.

Lenore had shown her not only how to mix and match the various items, but also how to make up her face in a way complementary to both her new clothes and hairstyle. Tonight, she'd chosen to wear tan trousers and a cream cashmere sweater, the evenings having turned cool this past week. Her dark brown eyes were enhanced by subtle eye make-up in natural and brown tonings, her full lips glossed with a deep bronze lipstick. She'd shampooed and dried her thick brown hair, amazed and pleased when it simply fell into place around her face and shoulders. Clearly, the outrageous price charged for her haircut had been worth it!

The mirror in her room had told her she looked good before she came downstairs for dinner. So why didn't Nathan like her new appearance? Everyone else did, even Byron. In fact, he'd fairly gushed over her, saying she looked utterly scrumptious and very grown up. Even when she tried not to take the credit, explaining that it had only been achieved with Jade's and Lenore's help, he'd still been very sweet.

'They had good material to work with, my dear,' he'd said warmly. 'Excellent, in fact. You were wise to take Lenore along with you. The woman has a splendid eye for fashion. Jade's my daughter and I love her but her taste is sometimes questionable, though there has been some improvement lately, I'm thankful to say. Though I think Lenore had a hand in that as well. I must ring her and thank her.'

Yes, everyone had said nice things earlier that day.

But not Nathan, who from the moment he'd arrived home from work this evening had been taciturn and obviously disapproving. Not that he'd actually said anything. He'd been annoyingly silent on the matter. But she'd caught him looking at her a few times and he hadn't looked too happy.

'What do you think, Nathan?' Ava said abruptly, and Gemma's eyes snapped to the man she loved more than life itself.

'About what?'

'About Gemma's hair, of course. Are you being obtuse or just plain difficult to get along with?'

Gemma waited for his answer with bated breath. Slowly, those beautiful grey eyes eyed her across the table, their scrutiny brief and cold. 'I'm sure it is very stylish, but I've always thought Gemma's face and hair were beyond compare. How can one improve on perfection?'

Everyone stared at Nathan, even Melanie, who was topping up Byron's coffee-cup at the time. Gemma began blushing, thankful that Kirsty wasn't present. Nathan's daughter was staying at a girlfriend's that night. Lord knew what the girl would have made of her father's saying such a thing to her.

Byron, Gemma noticed, was surprised though not displeased. Melanie was startled but Ava was looking almost bewildered.

Nathan chose that moment to wipe his mouth with his serviette and get to his feet. 'That was a great dinner, Melanie,' he said smoothly. 'But then your cooking is always superb. Please excuse me, everyone, I have some pressing personal business I must attend to.'

He strode from the room, his walk as elegant as his person. Gemma's eyes clung to his back till he disappeared.

'Nathan's in an odd mood tonight, isn't he?' Ava mused. 'From brooding silence to extravagant compliments to an abrupt disappearance all within seconds.'

'He's not an easy man to understand,' Byron admitted. 'But he's not given to idle flattery.' This with a close look Gemma's way. Ava began looking at her as well, a speculative expression on her face.

She busied herself sipping the last of her coffee.

'Well, he certainly made *me* feel good about my cooking,' Melanie said. 'I spent hours on dinner tonight. What was the general verdict? Is beef Wellington to have a regular appearance on the menu this winter?'

'*Winter*?' Byron growled. 'It's only autumn.'

'Same thing in my book. My cooking is divided into summer dishes and winter dishes.'

'It was delicious,' Ava said. 'I'll vote for it.'

'Yes, indeed,' Gemma agreed, grateful for the change of subject. 'Though I think the same as Nathan—all your cooking is superb.'

'I see we have two flatterers in the house,' Melanie said, smiling wryly.

Gemma felt her woman's heart stir with pity for the

housekeeper, who, even when smiling, still looked incredibly sad. She was a lovely-looking woman but what kind of life was she leading, keeping house for a family not her own, and having no social life whatsoever except for a weekly visit to her brother? Would she never get over the tragic deaths of her husband and baby, and embrace love and marriage again? In ten years she would be forty, then fifty, then sixty… Gemma wished Melanie would make the choice to try life again, but she couldn't see that happening while she hid herself away in Belleview, never meeting new people, especially eligible men.

Gemma stood up and started clearing the table. Melanie let her do this nightly chore nowadays without protest, knowing Gemma would do it anyway. Ava raced away to catch the Friday night movie on television and Byron took himself off to the library to read. He was moving around a lot better, though still with the help of a cane. Gemma could see the improvement in both his leg and his temperament, though Kirsty was still threatening to go home to live with her mother, mainly because Byron refused to let her watch the soaps on television on school nights.

Gemma suspected that was the reason for her staying the night at her girlfriend's house. Nathan was going to pick up both girls in the morning and take them to Avoca for the weekend. Gemma, knowing she wouldn't be able to resist Nathan's sexual advances in the setting of his initial seduction, had declined to accompany them, much to Nathan's obvious irritation.

Was that why he was in a mood tonight? Gemma wondered as she went about the clearing up. It couldn't be his finishing up at Whitmore's. He'd told her a few times already that he wanted nothing more than to write full time, and would be glad to see the end of working in an office. He'd only stayed on out of gratitude to Byron, not because he either wanted to or needed the money. Gemma assumed he meant by this that he was earning a good living from his plays.

They hadn't discussed money, as such. Or where they
would live after they were married, she realised with a
frown. Or children...

They hadn't discussed much at all, really.

Gemma was gnawing at her bottom lip as she stacked
the plates in the dishwasher.

'Did you get that letter that came for you, Gemma?'
Melanie said on joining her with a pile of cutlery. 'I put it
on your dressing-table.'

'No, I must have missed it. I wonder who could be writing to me here?'

'I think it's from your old lady-friend out at Lightning
Ridge.'

'Ma?' Gemma was astonished. 'I only got a letter from
her on Tuesday. I wonder what prompted another one. She
hates writing letters.'

''Why don't you pop upstairs and read it? I'll finish this.'

'Thanks, Melanie. I'll do that.'

Gemma hurried upstairs, curious and pleased. She would
never have dreamt she would ever be homesick for Lightning Ridge, and she certainly wasn't for the way of life.
What young woman could prefer living in a primitive dugout in hot dry outback conditions to her existence in this
beautiful Sydney home with its luxurious privacy and
swimming-pool and lovely gardens?

But she did miss the feeling of belonging. No matter how
nice everyone at Belleview was to her, she didn't really
belong here. This was not her family. Her family—what
she'd known of it—was buried in Lightning Ridge. So was
her dog, Blue, who'd been her best friend.

She still missed Blue very much. And she missed Ma.
Gemma was only now appreciating how kind Ma had been
to her over the years. How many times had the old lady
saved her from her father's foul temper? How many times
had she lied for her, protected her, soothed her? Not only
that, she gave good solid advice, full of homespun philos-
ophy but not in any way old-fashioned. Ma was a realist.

Gemma hurried into her bedroom and snatched up the letter, ripping it open and sitting down on the side of her bed to read the contents.

Dear Gemma,
Just a short note to let you know a man's been around asking questions about you and your dad. He said he was doing some Government census survey but I didn't believe him for a moment. He's one of them private eyes, I'll bet. He was specially interested about when you both came to live here but of course I didn't tell him anything. Anyway, I sent him off to Mr Gunther who was the closest thing your dad had to a friend around here. I hope I did the right thing. By the way, you didn't say anything about Nathan Whitmore in your last letter. Is that good news or bad? You don't have to worry about shocking me, love. Old Ma ain't shockable. Write soon and give me the drum. And fancy you learning Japanese and going to work in one of Byron's opal shops. I'm real proud of you, love. Write soon. I sure love getting your letters.

Your old mate, Ma.

Gemma folded the letter, a deep frown on her face.
'Trouble?'
Startled, Gemma's head whipped round to see Nathan standing near the open doorway, looking as impossibly handsome as ever. The light from the chandelier above was giving his flaxen hair a softly golden glow. He'd also abandoned the business suit he'd worn at dinner for casual beige trousers and a cool green silk shirt which was open at the neck. A thin gold chain lay around that neck, drawing her eyes to the smooth tanned V on display.
Before she could answer his query, he walked in, shutting the door behind him.
Gemma swallowed. The physical chemistry between them was so strong that just being in the same room with

him was agitating, even with other people present. Being alone with him in the bedroom was murder.

'Ma says a man's been asking questions about me around Lightning Ridge,' she blurted out, jumping to her feet. Fortunately, Nathan stopped his advance at the foot of her bed, his right hand curving over one of the ceramic bed-knobs that decorated the brass bed. Relieved, Gemma sat back down on the side of the bed. 'I suppose that's the man you hired?'

'I guess so. I instructed Zachary to handle the matter for me.'

'Zachary?'

'Zachary is the Whitmores' solicitor. Among other things,' he muttered.

'Oh. Has...has he found out anything concrete yet?' Gemma didn't like to get her hopes up about finding her mother alive, or even contacting her mother's family. But it was hard not to.

'No. Zachary said with so little to go on it could take months.'

Gemma's frown returned. 'That will cost an awful lot of money...'

When Nathan came round to sit beside her on the bed, taking her hands in his, she froze inside. Dear lord, if he started kissing her, she would have no hope of keeping to her resolve not to sleep with him again till they were married. He'd been fairly good about her decision to save further lovemaking for their wedding-night, but Gemma suspected that, underneath, he was as intensely frustrated as she was. She shivered when she recalled what a virile man he was, and how often he could make love in one night, not to mention the ecstasy she felt when he was doing so. But the urge to make him prove his love, to ensure that he *did* marry her, was almost as strong as her desire to be in his arms once more.

Only *almost*, however. He could tip the scales in his favour very easily, she suspected.

'I think there's something you should know about me, Gemma,' he said softly, 'and then I won't have to hear any more nonsense about money. I am a very rich man, my wealth totally independent of my adopted family. My maternal grandparents made me their heir and I inherited a considerable private income a few years back. I do not have to work. I do not have to write plays. If I wished, I could spend my entire waking life doing nothing but make love to you...'

Gemma tried to draw her hands away from his suddenly tightening grasp but his hands were like steel traps and for some unaccountable reason his refusal to let her go frightened her. When his mouth started to descend towards hers, her head jerked back. 'No, Nathan, don't!' she cried. 'Please...you promised.'

He eyed her with a small, dry smile. 'What did I promise? Only that I wouldn't sleep with you again before our marriage. Does that mean I can't even *kiss* my fiancée? Which reminds me...' Letting her hands go, he drew a wine-coloured velvet box from his trousers pocket and snapped it open, showing her the most magnificent solitaire diamond engagement ring.

She simply stared for several seconds, before lifting blurred eyes to his. 'Oh, Nathan... It's so beautiful...'

'Not beautiful enough,' he said, 'for my extremely beautiful lady.'

She took the box and dropped her eyes back to the diamond, rubbing a fingertip over the sparkling gem, a lump in her throat. 'I...didn't think you thought me beautiful any more when you came home tonight,' she murmured.

He sighed and tipped her chin up till she was looking into rueful grey eyes. 'I acted like a jealous fool,' he admitted. 'And I apologise. Of course you look beautiful, so beautiful that it's killing me not to kiss you and touch you. God, Gemma,' he groaned, and before she could do a thing he was crushing her to him, his mouth feasting on hers like a starving man. She couldn't help but respond, her heart and body leaping. But when he bent her sideways on to the bed and his hands began a fevered journey down her back, she started struggling. When she dropped the ring box and it rolled off her lap on to the floor, she cried out in dismay.

'My ring!' she wailed.

They sat up, both breathing heavily.

'I'll find it,' Nathan offered resignedly, dropping down on to his knees and sweeping the floor with his hands till he found it. 'Here it is. I guess we'd better check to see if it fits, not that you can wear it openly as yet. But I thought you might like a ring as a token of my commitment and love.'

A strangled sob broke from Gemma's throat. 'You make me feel awful.'

'Not as awful as I'm feeling at this moment.' He laughed before picking up her left hand and sliding the ring on her ring finger.

It was a little too large.

'Oh, what a pity,' Gemma murmured, content to stare down at her hand. The whole incident had really upset her, mostly because she really wanted to give in to Nathan. His giving her the ring should have reassured her of his love, but still her trust lacked something. Maybe everyone around Belleview was to blame with their warnings and their innuendoes about him. Maybe her own past had set up a basic mistrust of the male sex. Her father had been a cruel, hard man. Then there was that other awful time when another miner had sexually assaulted her. That *must* have dented her faith in men, even if she wasn't consciously aware of it.

'I'll have it made a size smaller,' Nathan said, putting the ring back, snapping the box shut and slipping it back into his pocket. His eyes ran over her mouth, a dark passion reflected in their gaze. 'I presume there's no chance of starting up where we left off?'

'I...I'd rather not...'

'That sounds wonderfully indecisive. Are you saying you could be persuaded?'

Gemma's chin shot up. 'I've no doubt you could persuade me into just about anything, Nathan, as you very well know. But if you love me, please don't try.'

She flinched when his hand reached out to trace a highly tantalising fingertip along her jawline, around her mouth then down her neck to linger on the pulse at the base of her throat. His eyes, narrowed and hard now, remained on her parted lips, her rapid breathing betraying her already dangerous state of arousal.

'I'm glad to see that the fancy hairstyle and clothes haven't changed the girl you are,' he said in a low, husky voice, 'but once we're married there'll be no more of these testing games. You will let me make love to you whenever I want.'

'Don't worry...' That tantalising hand travelled down to where her breasts were pressing their swollen contours against the soft cashmere of her new cream sweater. Slowly and insidiously, with a strangely mesmerising rhythm, he played with her right breast, all the while talking to her in a calm, extremely hypnotic voice. 'You won't find my demands any hardship, my beautiful Gemma, because I aim to love you as no woman has ever been loved before. We will be so finely attuned, you and I, that when you see me looking at you a certain way your body will automatically respond. We'll be one as no two people have ever been one and you'll never want any other man. Of course, if you ever so much as *look* at another man, I might strangle you with my bare hands...'

He bent to press feathery lips to hers, his hand returning to her throat where it slid around its slenderness in what might have been a threatening gesture, if Gemma had been capable of feeling threatened at that moment. She was, however, totally enthralled, her body revved to a state of high sexual excitement, her dazed mind eager for what sounded like a relationship so intimate and fiercely loving that she could hardly wait.

When his head lifted, she swayed towards him, lips parted, heart pounding. 'Nathan... Oh, Nathan...'

He kissed her once more, a deep drowning kiss that demonstrated his power to reduce her will-power to water in no time flat. But then he put her aside, a dark mocking smile on his mouth. 'This next four weeks is going to be hell,' he rasped. 'But, oddly enough, I have to agree with you. It will be much better all round if we deny ourselves till we're legally joined. You'll feel much more secure then, and much more willing to surrender yourself totally to my love.'

He left her then, left her to suffer as she had never suffered before, left her to lie down on her bed, wide-eyed and aching for him. She tossed and turned, her need to totally surrender herself to his love already a tangible thing that tormented her body with a restlessness just short of screaming point. She wanted to go to him and tell him she'd changed her mind about going to Avoca with him this weekend, about a lot of things. She wanted to beg him to put her out of her misery.

But some inner instinct told her Nathan would not change *his* mind again. The moment for savouring his love-making had passed. She had rejected him one time too many and the offer had been withdrawn.

Four weeks, she groaned.

It seemed an eternity away.

CHAPTER ELEVEN

'TURN right at the next set of lights,' Kyle said.

Jade did not reply, just did as he instructed, her mind still on that peculiar smile he'd delivered back at the office while saying she had won. Won what? His meekly saying please? That was a laugh! She had seen the mocking behind the pretended meekness. As well as the arrogance. Kyle Armstrong would never be a yes-man. So what had he meant?

'Pull over,' he said abruptly, startling her out of her reverie.

'Here?' she queried, guiding the car into the kerb outside an all-night chemist.

'Yes. I have to buy something,' he said, opening the passenger door and climbing out almost before she'd cut the engine.

He was back in less than a minute, a small paper parcel in his hand. She declined showing any curiosity over what he'd bought and he declined telling her, merely slid back into the car and snapped his seatbelt back into place. 'Turn left at the next intersection,' he ordered, 'then second on the right which will take you down to a small bay. Home's not far from there.'

After checking the oncoming traffic, she pulled away from the kerb.

'You drive well,' he complimented as she swung round the corner, as per instructions.

'Thank you,' she murmured, trying not to sound as ridiculously pleased as she felt. But compliments did not come Jade's way very often. At least, not about anything other than her looks and her body.

And she *was* a good driver—if a little too fast sometimes. She certainly had to brake sharply when the road suddenly dropped down a steep incline. 'Sorry,' she muttered, then stayed silent, having to concentrate on the narrow, curving road that was taking them down to the small bay Kyle had mentioned.

'Where to now?' she said, finally having reached the bottom of the hill where the road flattened to run alongside the edge of the cove. It was a very pretty place, with a small marina housing various crafts and a line of trees between the road and the shore.

'Just pull in here,' Kyle said, and pointed to a small parking bay beside a long wooden pier that stretched a fair way out into the water. At the end of it sat what looked like a permanently moored houseboat. It seemed far too big to be the kind that put-putted around the harbour.

'That's where I'm living at the moment,' he said, seeing the direction of her eyes.

'In that houseboat?' She was astonished. Such a dwelling didn't come cheap, especially in this area of Sydney. Middle Harbour and its surrounds were top drawer.

'It belongs to a friend,' he explained before she could ask.

The penny dropped immediately. He had a rich girlfriend, a *very* rich girlfriend.

'No,' he said drily. 'A male friend.'

Irritated by his mind-reading ability, she threw him a caustic look. 'Did I say anything?'

'You didn't have to. Your face is an open book.'

'Is it, now?'

'Yes,' he said, and laughed. She didn't like the sound of that laugh. It was far too arrogant and far too knowing.

When he went to get out and she didn't, he slanted sardonic eyes back over his shoulder. 'Don't you want to come in?'

'Not particularly.'

He sighed and slid his legs back into the car, slamming the door shut again. Now his eyes carried exasperation. 'I know women are contrary by nature but honestly, Jade...'

'Honestly what?'

'God,' he muttered, and, twisting abruptly in his seat, he reached over, snapped off her seatbelt then slid a cool firm hand around the back of her neck, turning her to face him. Jade was so stunned that she simply stared at him, her lips slightly parted in shock.

'That's better,' he rasped, his gaze dropping to her mouth. 'Oh, yes, that's much better...'

His fingers tightened around her neck and he pulled her ever so slowly closer, his own body shifting forward so that their mouths were destined to meet over the gearstick.

Jade's heart was thudding madly in her chest by the time his lips actually made contact with hers, her blood roaring, her head whirling. He was going to kiss her, she thought dazedly. Kyle was going to kiss her. Kyle *was* kissing her. Oh, God...

She moaned softly deep in her throat and his fingers tightened further, biting as deep into her flesh as his tongue was sliding deep into her mouth. Both her hands fluttered up to rest against his shirt and she could feel his own heart slamming against his chest wall.

I've died, she thought. Died and gone to heaven.

Suddenly heaven vanished, and she was back in the real world, Kyle's mouth deserting hers. Automatically, she straightened to sag back into her seat, but her wide eyes never left his. He was shaking his head at her and smiling that peculiar smile again, although this time she thought she understood it better. It was self-mocking.

'I was right,' he said cryptically, and not that happily. 'Damn and blast. Who would have believed it?'

'Right?' she repeated blankly. 'About what?'

He took both her hands in his and lifted them to his lips. 'You do want me, don't you, Jade?'

He was kissing her fingertips and she could hardly think. 'I...I...'

'Why can't you say it? You got your message across loud and clear last Saturday night. Don't be coy now, Jade. That's not your style. Say it,' he rasped, yanking her over so close that her panting breath was mingling with his. 'Tell me you want me,' he urged huskily. 'Tell me you've been wanting me all week. Tell me *I'm* the man you want to relax with tonight.'

His hot, erotic words had set her head reeling and her blood on fire.

'Say it, damn you! I want to hear you say it!'

'I...I want you,' she blurted out. 'Want you,' she moaned as his mouth fused with hers.

Jade had been kissed many times in her life before but never like this. She trembled beneath his devouring lips, his fiercely demanding tongue. Trembled and moaned.

Both of them were panting raggedly when Kyle finally brought the kiss to an end. 'Glad to see you won't disappoint me, Jade,' he said ruefully. 'This is not what I intended, you know. But I can't fight you—or your body—any longer.'

He flicked open the top two buttons of her jacket and slid a surprisingly cool hand inside, caressing a single taut breast, making her gasp when he started rolling the nipple around in his fingers, bringing it to a peak of such exquisite arousal that she cried out.

'How responsive you are,' he muttered thickly, then, quite abruptly, withdrew his hand and did up the buttons. 'But enough of that for now. A car is hardly the place to adequately pursue our mutual desires. I'm sure you gave up such adolescent activities years ago, as did I. There is a perfectly comfortable bed inside the houseboat, as well as champagne, music and other mod cons. Let's adjourn, shall we, and take advantage of them?'

He was out of the car in a flash and coming around to open her door, which was just as well since she was sitting

there in a rather dazed state. When he reefed the door open
and shot a hand down to help her out, she stared up at him.
My God, was that her Mr Cool, peering down at her with
eyes like hot black coals? This was another man, a roused
impassioned creature who wanted her maybe more than she
wanted him, who would not be denied.

She placed a quivering hand in his and allowed him to
draw her forth from the car, allowed him to draw her body
hard and close against his so that she could feel his need.
Groaning, he cupped her head and kissed her briefly again
before dragging his mouth away with a dark laugh. 'You'll
be thinking I haven't had a woman in years if I keep this
up. Not true, I assure you. But I have to admit I haven't
had too many quite like you, Jade. Come...'

He started hauling her along the pier, walking so fast
that Jade had trouble keeping up on the uneven planked
surface. Kyle's kisses and caresses had brought her to a
pitch of arousal she'd never known before and while she
longed to have him really make love to her—dear lord,
hadn't that thought tormented her since meeting him?—
alongside the desire lay a churning feeling of panic.

For when it came down to the reality of real sex, when
the kisses were left behind and the nitty-gritty begun, she
was hopeless, absolutely hopeless. Kyle was in for a big
disappointment.

Jade had never worried about such inadequacies before.
It hadn't been necessary because she hadn't cared. Her two
fumbling teenager lovers hadn't commented on her lack of
enthusiasm or expertise. They'd been only too happy to find
a pretty and willing female, and hadn't given ratings as long
as the desired end was reached. Her only other experience
had been with that man after Nathan had rejected her and
quite frankly she'd been too intoxicated to remember much
of it. But she suspected she hadn't set the world on fire
with her technique.

Yet Kyle seemed to expect her to set him on fire with
her technique. The way he'd spoken about her—as though

she was a right raver—was both unnerving and dismaying. My God, he probably thought she was a slut, just like Nathan had!

The pain of such a thought ground her to a halt. When her hand ripped out of Kyle's he swung round, almost glaring at her.

'What is it now?'

'I can't,' she choked out.

Kyle's fury was of the speechless variety.

'You don't understand,' she went on, her voice shaking. 'I...I haven't done this sort of thing nearly as much as you—and everyone else—seem to think. And I just can't...can't go to bed with you, especially with you thinking I'm nothing but a...a...'

She couldn't say it, her eyes dropping to the pier as a wave of shame hit her. For honestly, what had she expected him to think with the way she'd dressed and acted last Saturday night, not to mention the outrageous things she'd said all week about her men friends and such? If he thought she was cheap and easy then she damn well deserved it!

A firm finger tipped up her chin and Kyle was looking at her with a dark frown on his face. 'How often is not often?' he said. 'You said you changed lovers at least once a month.'

Her blush was fierce, her mortification acute. She wished she could go back and cut her tongue out. 'I...I was exaggerating.'

'OK, I can accept that. Then give me a ball-park figure. Approximately how many lovers *have* you had? Five? Ten? Fifty?'

'I don't have to approximate,' she muttered, her eyes dropping again. 'I know the exact number. It's three.'

The silence was electric and she didn't dare to look at him for fear of seeing his scornful disbelief. 'I'm not lying,' she insisted shakily. 'The first two were when I was a very silly mixed-up teenager. The other was a one-night stand a few months ago when I was...unhappy.'

Finally, she felt compelled to look up, only to find that Kyle was no longer facing her. He had turned away and was staring out over the water.

'Kyle?' She reached out and touched him lightly on the arm. 'You do believe me, don't you? I'm not lying, I swear.'

His face was totally unreadable as he turned to gaze down at her. 'Have you always used protection when you had sex?'

'Yes, always.'

'And have you ever enjoyed sex with a man, Jade?'

She didn't know what to say. She'd enjoyed Nathan kissing her, but surely that was not what Kyle meant.

'Tell me,' he ground out. 'I need to know.'

'Not really,' she admitted. 'But I...I'm sure I will with you,' she added, fearful now that *he* would be the one to back out of tonight. Suddenly, she didn't want that. She wanted...oh, she didn't know what she wanted any more, except that she wanted him to keep on wanting her the way he'd wanted her a minute ago.

But maybe he'd only been wanting her because he thought she was a woman of experience, she realised wretchedly. Someone who knew all the sexual tricks, who could pleasure him in sophisticated ways unknown to her, who wouldn't be hesitant or nervous or just plain stupid.

No, no, I'm not stupid, she denied fiercely to herself. I'm not, I'm not!

Tears blurred her eyes as those old feelings of failure swept in. Dear heaven, she'd fought hard all her life to throw off the crippling effect of her mother's relentless criticisms by telling herself over and over she was a great person, by developing an extrovert personality, by pretending that nothing and no one could get her down for long. Where was her so-called boldness now when she needed it most?

'Don't,' Kyle said on a raw whisper.

The emotion in his voice startled her into blinking back the tears and staring up at him.

His smile squeezed her heart. 'That's better,' he said. 'The Jade I know doesn't cry over spilt milk. She picks herself up and goes bravely forward, especially when she's got nothing to be ashamed of, except perhaps a little naïveté.' He reached out and laid a tender hand against her cheek. 'Do you trust me, Jade?'

She nodded, his unexpected tenderness bringing a lump to her throat. At least if he was going to reject her, he was going to do it kindly.

'Then I'm going to take you inside, where we're going to have a drink, listen to some music, and then, when the time is right, we'll let nature take its course.'

Her eyes widened, her heart leaping. 'You...you still want to make love to me?'

His laughter was dark and very, very sexy. 'Silly Jade. I've been wanting to make love to you since the moment you opened your father's front door.'

She gasped her surprise.

He chuckled again. 'You've led me a merry dance this past week. One which I hope I'll never have to live through again.'

'But you...you never showed anything,' she said, almost accusingly.

'Perhaps you weren't looking in the right places,' he said drily. 'But enough of such talk. If I'm to be your first successful lover I need all the control I can muster.' He crooked his arm and adopted a po-faced expression. 'Would madam like a grand tour of the houseboat? And perhaps some refreshments after her arduous week?'

Jade giggled before smoothing her face into a parody of his super-cool façade and linking her arm with his. 'I can think of nothing I'd like better.'

The houseboat was one of only a few allowed around Sydney, Kyle told her, adding that he was houseboat-sitting for a Mr Gainsford, who'd gone away on business and wasn't expected back for many months.

'Lucky you,' Jade said with feeling. She couldn't imagine anywhere more delightful to live. In fact, from the moment Jade stepped aboard she was entranced, so much so that any lingering nerves about the night ahead were momentarily distracted by her surroundings. Never had a place taken her eye so much before. And she'd seen plenty of beautiful homes in her privileged life.

It couldn't have been because of the design, which was basic and simple, the A-shaped frame having one huge open-plan room downstairs, surrounded by verandas, and a wooden staircase leading up to a loft which housed the only bedroom.

Maybe it was because everything was made out of wood. The floors, walls, ceilings, fittings, furniture—all were beautifully fashioned and polished, from rich red cedars to light golden pines back to a warm comfortable teak, their shining expanses broken only by thick fluffy cream rugs on the floor, and cool turquoise-coloured cushioning on the sofas and chairs. The downstairs living area contained a huge kitchen and breakfast bar down one end, with a partitioned-off dining section to one side, the rest being devoted to a sitting area and various entertainment equipment.

'Your Mr Gainsford has plenty of money,' she said on seeing the huge range of CDs and videos arranged on shelves beside the CD player. 'And he doesn't like Mozart,' she added teasingly.

'No, he doesn't,' Kyle agreed with a wry smile.

'What does he do?' she asked, curious to know more about this mysterious friend.

Kyle shrugged carelessly. 'He's a businessman. You know the type. Sits on numerous company boards, flits around the world all the time and beds beautiful women left, right and centre. He also has excellent taste in champagne,' he smiled, walking over to open the refrigerator from which he extracted a bottle of the French variety. 'Shall we?'

'Why not?' Jade wandered over to perch up on one of the kitchen stools, having to undo the last button on her jacket to manage it. 'Will he mind, do you think?'

'Not at all. I have permission to use whatever he's left behind.'

'Including the beautiful women?' she asked, thinking of the mystery woman who'd telephoned him.

The bottle popped and Kyle expertly filled two fluted glasses to the brim without any fizzing over. It came to Jade that he'd poured champagne for women he was about to bed many times before, and the thought bothered her. Which was crazy. She didn't mind him being experienced, did she?

When he finished the pouring and looked up, his expression was amused. 'What a loaded question! I refuse to answer on the grounds it might incriminate me.' Walking round the breakfast bar, he handed her a glass before joining her on the closest stool. 'What shall we drink to?'

'To the generous Mr Gainsford?' she suggested, a touch tartly.

Kyle laughed. 'Very well. To Mr Gainsford. May he stay absent.'

They clinked glasses and drank, Jade almost emptying her glass. Champagne was one drink she could guarantee to make her tipsy in no time flat, especially on a near-empty stomach, and with the thought of the inevitable outcome of the evening reviving her earlier nerves she decided a little intoxication might be on the agenda. Reaching over, she picked up the bottle and refilled her glass, topping up Kyle's as well.

'So tell me, Kyle. How did you get to meet this super-richy in the first place? Did you work for him at some stage?'

'No. We—er—went to university together.'

'Really?'

'Most assuredly. He wasn't very popular, I'm afraid. A terrible snob. And spoiled to boot. Thought his money could get him anything he wanted.'

Jade wrinkled her nose. 'I don't think I like him very much.'

'I don't think I did either. Back then. But he's not such a bad chap nowadays. I'm growing to like him more and more.'

Jade laughed. 'That's because he's not here. Still, he must like and trust you to let you stay in his house. Or is he just using you?'

'Must we keep talking about Gainsford? I'd rather talk about you. No, quite frankly I'd rather not talk at all. Bring your glass. I'll bring the bottle. We're going to bed.'

Jade gasped. 'Just like that?'

'Just like that,' he said, and, picking up the bottle, slid off the stool.

She slid off her stool as well. 'But you said...'

'I know what I said. I was wrong. I have to make love to you now, Jade. I can't wait any longer.'

The breath hissed from her lungs, her own desire flaring. She stared at his mouth and thought of how it had felt on hers, how it might feel on other parts of her body. Coming forward, he lowered his mouth and kissed her without touching her. It was a soft, lingering erotic kiss that made her shiver uncontrollably.

'You don't really want to wait either,' he said on straightening. 'We don't need hours of foreplay, Jade. This whole week has been foreplay. You and I are as turned on as we're going to get with our clothes on. Any more damned arousing and I won't have a hope in Hades of realising your fantasies about having sex with me.'

'I don't want to *have sex* with you,' she protested. 'I want you to *make love* to me!'

For a moment, he looked taken aback, then he smiled, a highly satisfied smile. 'How silly of me to make such an elementary mistake,' he murmured. 'I'd forgotten the semantics had changed. Make love. Yes, I like that a lot better than having sex. I really do.'

He actually sounded surprised and, brushing past her, walked over towards the wooden staircase in the corner. There he stopped abruptly on the first step, his black eyes glittering and narrowed as he peered back over his shoulder at her. 'Are you in love with me, Jade?'

Her own eyes blinked wide. 'I...I don't know.'

He smiled softly. 'What a lovely honest answer. I do so admire it. And I do so admire you. I won't tell you I love you either, because I too have a problem with that term. Is it enough that I admire you, lovely Jade? Will that do for now?'

Her nod was slow, her head heavy, her thoughts awhirl.

'Are you coming, or are you going to torture me some more?' he said in a drily teasing voice. 'I have a feeling you like seeing men suffer.'

When she stayed standing there, as though frozen, he put down the bottle and the glass and walked back to take the glass from her suddenly trembling hand, draining it with a single swallow. 'You've had enough of this. Let's see if we can't satisfy your other cravings.'

Bending, he swept her up into his arms, smiling ruefully down into her wide-eyed face. 'Who would have thought the outrageous creature who whistled at me last Saturday night was a closet *ingénue*! How intriguing you are, Jade. And how exciting. I'm going to enjoy teaching you to like making love. Not that I think I'll have any trouble. Half the battle is in the wanting to. And you've already confessed to that.'

He carried her as if she were a feather, his strength amazing her. Though tall, he wasn't an overly big man, his muscles lean rather than bulky. But strong he was. Strong and male and totally in command of the situation. Jade was entranced.

'The name suits you,' she whispered on the way upstairs. 'What name?'

'Mr Cool.'

'Mr Cool? Who calls me that?'

'I do.'

'You *do*?' He chuckled his amusement. 'What a minx you are.'

'And a tease.'

'That too. But not for much longer.'

'I'm a little nervous, Kyle.'

'No, you're not. You're excited.'

He set her down on her feet beside the king-sized bed but her knees went from under her and she had to cling to the lapels of his jacket to stop herself from falling back on the bed. Her swaying action reefed the suit jacket wide open.

'What a quick learner you are, darling. I had no idea you'd want to undress me.'

'U-undress you?' she repeated blankly, her heart having leapt wildly with his calling her darling.

'That's the opposite to dress,' he mocked, but not un-kindly. 'You know…you undo all the little buttons and zippers and things, instead of doing them up? And when you're finished you haven't got any clothes on. Making love is much easier when in the nude. Not necessarily more exciting, mind. The idea of making love to you with se-lected clothing on has an exquisitely erotic appeal but I think we shall leave that for future encounters. For our first time, I think a certain primitive simplicity is called for.

'Ah, I see you're getting the picture,' he chuckled when she pulled the jacket off his shoulders, dragged it down his arms and tossed it aside to fall she cared not where. Her heart was going at fifty to the dozen as her fingers began fumbling with his tie.

'I think you need some help,' he said, and, with one sharp tug, the tie was loose enough for her to lift it over his head. It joined the jacket on the floor. The shirt went in a similar fashion once he'd undone the cuffs and the top button, over his head and fluttering away.

Now he was naked to the waist and Jade could not believe how exciting she found that. Quite instinctively, her hands reached out to touch him, to rove over the dark curls that covered the centre of his chest and ran down to where they were terminated abruptly by his trousers. She could actually feel his heartbeat beneath her exploring touch, telling her he wasn't nearly as cool as he pretended.

Jade didn't try to pretend anything. The wanting had become a need so sharp that she had to resist the urge to dig her nails into his flesh. As it was, her fingers started to splay upwards, over his hard male nipples, and up over his strong, smooth shoulders. Her eyes were glittering blue pools of desire when they looked up, her lips falling apart in a silent invitation for him to kiss her.

He moved so fast that it was a blur, his mouth crashing down on hers, his arms crushing her to his naked chest, a tormented groan rumbling deep in his throat. The realisation that he'd been right about foreplay was echoed in the rush of heat between her thighs. Jade knew that this last kiss had brought her to a pitch of need previously unknown to her. She didn't want to be kissed any more. She only wanted him.

Tearing her mouth from his, she pressed feverish lips to his throat and whispered her desire in the most explicit terms. The uttering of her need in such a way didn't shock her. It only inflamed her further. She said the words again, biting him this time. She heard his sharply indrawn breath, felt his body flinch, then shudder.

'All right, damn you,' he rasped. 'But don't complain afterwards.'

Any further slow, measured undressing was out of the question. Kyle tore the clothing from her body. Literally tore. Once she was nude, he stopped briefly to stare at her, his breathing ragged. Then suddenly, he pushed her back on to the bed and crushed his body down on hers, spreading her legs, opening her to his desire. Jade had no thought of nerves, or technique or anything, her whole being con-

sumed with nothing but her awareness of his flesh entering
hers, filling her totally, making her gasp. His rhythm, when
it began, was ruthless and powerful. He went on and on,
on and on, till she was clinging to him, writhing with him,
moaning with him. She could not believe how it felt. The
pleasure, the excitement, the exquisite tension. Till suddenly, it was unbearable.

'Kyle!' she cried out, then groaned in a type of agony.
But the agony abruptly shattered into ecstasy and she
caught her breath. Her nails dug deep as her body began
to spasm, her heart seemingly bursting in her chest. 'Oh,
God…Kyle…'

She felt his body begin to shudder, pulsating deep within
her, and as she listened to his raw groans of animal pleasure
she knew at last what it meant to be primitive woman, what
it meant to be sexually satisfied. *And* what it meant to lose
her head.

Jade was lying there, still dazed with wonderment at the
experience, when she realised they hadn't used anything.

CHAPTER TWELVE

JADE might have bolted up into a sitting position if Kyle hadn't been sprawled across her, his weight pinning her to the bed. But her body must have done something because Kyle lifted his head, opened a sleepy eye and said, 'What?'

'We...we didn't use anything,' she whispered.

He nodded then slumped down again. 'I realised that halfway through.'

Jade was shocked by his casual admission. 'Then why didn't you stop?'

Again his head lifted. This time both eyes were opened and their expression was sardonic. 'You have to be joking. After what you said to me? You're lucky I remembered where the bed was.' He sighed wearily. 'I'm sorry, Jade. Believe me when I tell you that the only misfortune that might befall you is pregnancy. What's the odds of that, do you know?'

'I...I can't think... Oh, God, I don't want to have a baby. I...' Her relief at finally calculating the date of her next period brought a huge sigh. 'I'm due Sunday, thank the lord. For a second, I thought it was the next Sunday. Still, come tomorrow I'm going to the doctor and going on the Pill!'

Kyle rolled from her so abruptly that she gasped. From feeling all warm and cosy she suddenly felt empty and abandoned. He settled himself beside her on his back, staring up at the ceiling. 'Would it have been such a catastrophe, Jade? Having my baby?' His voice was coolly re-

proachful and it flustered her. As if he would really want
her to fall pregnant, anyway.

'Not *your* baby particularly, Kyle,' she explained. '*Any*
baby. I'm in my final year at uni and I've just started work
at Whitmore's. Do you know how long I've wanted to do
that?' She didn't add that she didn't think she'd make a
very good mother and hadn't intended to have children.

His head turned on the pillow to stare thoughtfully over
at her. 'What do you want out of life, Jade? Besides my
job.'

Her laughter was slightly embarrassed. 'So you know
about that, do you?'

'Of course. I told you. Your face is an open book.'

'I'm quite happy to let you have the job a while longer,'
she said teasingly. 'Till I've learnt all I can from you.'

He slanted her a mocking look. 'Are we still talking
about work here?'

Realisation what he was inferring brought a fierce blush
to her cheeks. 'Surely you don't think that I…that I…'

His smile was reassuring as he rolled on to his side. 'I
do love it when you're flustered like that. It's so sweet.'

'I'm not sweet. I'm spicy, remember?'

'Mmm.' His fingers started feathering over her breasts
and she caught her breath, still amazed at how his touch
made her feel. 'You have a beautiful body,' he murmured.
'Your mother must have been a beautiful woman.'

Jade flinched inside. 'Yes,' she said stiffly. 'She was.
Physically.'

His fingers stilled, his eyes thoughtful upon her. 'What
do you mean by that?'

She shrugged, trying desperately to ignore the pain jabbing at her heart.

'Didn't you get along with your mother, Jade? Look, I
know she died recently. Byron told me. If you're feeling
guilty about something then perhaps you should talk about
it.'

'*Me*, feel guilty?' she scorned bitterly. 'That would be a

laugh. I've nothing to feel guilty about. My only regret is that death allowed my mother to escape before I had the courage to tell her what I thought of her, to tell her what an evil, wicked witch she was!'

Her tirade finished, Jade lay trembling in the bed, till Kyle gathered her close, his strong warm body soothing her, as his words soothed her. 'You're wrong, Jade. Her death was a blessed release. For everyone around her. She must have been a terrible person and a terrible mother to make you feel about her like this.'

'I think she hated me, Kyle,' she cried. 'And I keep asking myself why. She used to hit me a lot when I was little. Not when my father was around, of course. If Nathan hadn't come to live with us…' Jade broke off, a lump filling her throat.

'Nathan stopped her?' Kyle asked gently.

'I don't know,' she choked out. 'Maybe. Or maybe his just being there stopped her. Auntie Ava was away at school at the time. After that, it was just verbal abuse. I couldn't do a thing right. She even made Pops believe I was bad. Bad and worthless. Why would she want to do that? Mothers are supposed to *love* their children.'

'I don't know, Jade. She must have been sick in the head, or just plain mean. There are people like that. Mean and sour and cruel. But she didn't succeed in turning your father against you, darling. Your father thinks the sun shines out of you. He does worry about you—you are a little wild, darling, and totally outrageous at times—but all in all, he's coming around to my way of thinking.'

'Your way of thinking?'

'That his daughter is an exceptional girl. Talented and bright, if a tad provocative. You might benefit from wearing a bra occasionally. Though I won't complain at the moment.' He laid her back on the pillow and slid an outstretched palm back and forth across the tips of her breasts, making her lungs expand with an inward rush of breath. Soon, her mother was forgotten and she was breathless with desire and need again. She started touching him back, more boldly than she'd ever touched a man before.

'I've never wanted a man the way I want you,' she whispered, all the while caressing him. 'Why is that, do you think?'

'Maybe you've fallen in love for the first time,' he suggested thickly.

'Would it worry you if I told you I loved you? A lot of men would run a mile.'

'*Do* you love me?'

'I'm still not sure. I've thought myself in love in the past and now I can see I never was. Not once. Have you ever been in love, Kyle?'

'Never.'

Was that a pain deep in her breast when he said that? Could that be a sign of true love, when it hurt if the man you were touching so intimately said he didn't love you? No, no, she'd been hurt when Nathan rejected her. That couldn't be an infallible sign.

'Whatever I feel,' she whispered, 'I know I loved it when you made love to me. I love the feel of your body. I love everything about you…'

He grabbed her hands and held them up over her head, looming over her with dark glittering eyes.

'And I love everything about you, my darling Jade. Every…single…thing…'

He kissed her, very slowly, as though he were savouring something delicious but didn't want to rush. First just her bottom lip, then her upper, then both. When his tongue finally slipped into her mouth, her breath caught. She'd never been kissed so lasciviously before. His tongue swept sensuously around the soft well of her mouth, before slowly withdrawing. Her own tongue followed as though magnetised. Now it was deep in *his* mouth and her excitement soared. He groaned, his hands cupping her head while he regained control of the kiss. By the time he stopped, her whole mouth felt all swollen and tingling.

'Might as well be hung for a sheep as a lamb,' he muttered, and he rolled them both on to their sides, hoisting her left knee high on his hip, his flesh slipping inside her very easily. Jade sighed her pleasure as his hips moved gently back and forth, creating the most delicious feelings. His fingers started feathering over her nipples at the same time and she moaned softly.

'Would you like to be on top?' he asked in a desire-thickened voice.

'I...I don't know,' she said breathlessly. 'I've never been there.'

His smile was rueful. 'Don't get too used to it.'

'Thank God it's Friday!' Jade exclaimed to Moira as she hurried in to work shortly before two, letting the glass doors swing shut behind her. The doors weren't the only things that were swinging. The skirt of Jade's white woollen suit was finely pleated and quite short.

'Amen to that,' Moira sighed. 'This last week has been very trying.'

'You can say that again,' someone muttered from just behind Jade.

She whirled round to find Kyle striding towards her. He must have come from the direction of the design rooms. Or the gents'. He looked tense and almost angry, strain giving his leanly chiselled features the sort of primitive, brooding look she found insidiously attractive. The black suit and crisp white shirt he had on didn't detract from his appeal either, making his black eyes seem even darker and more intense.

Jade stared at him as though he were a chocolate éclair and she were a compulsive eater. It had been a whole week since he'd touched her, and she was on fire for him. Working with him all Wednesday had been an ordeal, sleeping at night since then a problem. She hadn't realised her frustration was so intense till she sighted him again in the flesh.

Kyle glared at her, his facial muscles tightening. Taking

her elbow, he ushered her towards their office. 'You're just
in time, Jade,' he ground out. 'I've had nothing but hassles
all day and now another problem has come up.'

'Not the date with the ball!' she groaned. 'That PR
woman at the Regency doesn't want to change it again,
does she?'

'No, that's not it,' he ground out once they were alone
and the door shut. Reefing her bag from her arm, he threw
it in the corner, took her by the shoulders and yanked her
against him, kissing her savagely. A shocked Jade did nothing when he urged her back against the solid wooden door,
but she soon realised that if his marauding tongue was anything to go by she was dealing with an even more frustrated
individual than she was.

'You're late,' he growled after the most arousing minute
she'd ever endured.

'You're the one who wouldn't let me bring my car,' she
reminded him breathlessly, before curving her hand around
his neck and dragging his mouth back to hers for another
dose of erotic torment.

This is crazy, she was thinking all the while. We can't
do anything here. Why torture ourselves?

Jade was underestimating her Mr Cool, however, who
was far from cool at this moment.

'I like you in white,' he rasped into her mouth while
busy fingers flicked open the buttons of her jacket. 'But I
like you better in nothing.' Jade stiffened against the door
when he started kneading her bare breasts. When he bent
to draw a rock-like nipple into his white-hot mouth everything inside her contracted fiercely, desire bursting like a
firecracker in her head.

'Kyle, don't,' she groaned. God, if he kept that up she
was going to go mad! Her sigh of relief when he deserted
her breasts was short-lived. Kyle was merely homing in on
a more intimate destination.

The scrap of white silk and lace she was wearing was
highly inadequate protection against an impassioned man.

He simply tore it aside. Jade bit her bottom lip some more, though a small cry did escape her lips when Kyle achieved what he was bent on achieving. But dear heaven, he felt fantastic. A flush of heat zoomed into her cheeks and she just had to lick her lips, they were so dry.

'What…what if someone wants to come in?' she asked, her voice shaking.

'Can't think about that right now.'

'N…neither can I. Oh, Kyle…'

No one wanted to come in. Thank God.

Afterwards, Jade couldn't believe what they had just done. But she had plenty to remind her. Half-wrecked panties for one.

'You…you do realise we're supposed to take added precautions for the first month I'm on this Pill,' she reminded him shakily after she slumped down in her chair behind the desk.

'Yes,' he said, striding round to sit at his own desk, looking so cool and unruffled now that Jade felt a fierce flash of resentment.

'Well? You didn't just now. *Again.*'

His glance was wry. 'You do seem to have a bad effect on my normal precautionary nature.'

She wasn't at all mollified by his amused tone. In fact, she was rather rattled by the whole encounter. 'I…I hope this isn't all our relationship is going to be, Kyle. Sex in the office on Fridays.'

'I certainly hope not. I'll add Wednesdays to the agenda in future. And when did it become sex instead of making love?' he asked with an arched eyebrow.

'You can ask that with me sitting here at my desk with wrecked panties?'

God, but he was sexy when he smiled like that. But so damned arrogant, so damned sure of himself.

'I don't want our relationship reduced to just sex,' she argued.

'I couldn't agree more,' he countered drily. 'I already

asked you to move in with me last weekend, if you recall. But you said no. You also wouldn't go out with me this past week, simply because you had a period. That's rather reducing our relationship to just sex, wouldn't you say? I wouldn't have minded simply spending time with you.'

Jade winced under the interpretation he'd put on her actions. But it hadn't been like that at all. When she'd woken last Saturday morning to find Kyle bringing her breakfast and calmly suggesting she move in with him, she'd been consumed with panic, and an intense desire just to get away from him. Perhaps it was her natural tendency to resist others organising her life which gave rise to her sudden desperate need for personal space. Or perhaps she'd been frightened by how much she kept wanting him, how tempted she'd been to just say yes to everything and anything.

Which was why she was uncomfortable with what had just happened in the office. She hadn't meant to let him go so far but she'd simply lost control. She didn't like losing control like that! And yet…it had been incredibly exciting. Was this what happened when lust got its claws into you? Did it make you vulnerable to the point of losing your own identity? Bewilderment brought irritation. And a rise of temper.

'It wasn't just my period,' she reiterated crossly. 'I had to finish an assignment.'

'You could have finished it at my place.'

She laughed. 'Oh, yes? I don't think so, Kyle. You're far too distracting.'

'If you lived with me all the time, we'd soon settle into a less distracting mode. And then I wouldn't have to rip your clothes off against office doors. I certainly can't cope with working in the same room as you, my darling Jade, if you're going to put me on rations.' His smile was wickedly seductive. 'Come now…you usually live away from home, don't you? Byron said you did.'

'Not with a man, I don't,' she said, all the while horribly

tempted. 'I think single women are crazy to live with men they're not married to.'

'So *that's* the problem. All right. Name the date.'

'Oh, don't be ridiculous, Kyle. You don't love me. Why would you marry me? Besides, I have no intention of ever getting married, or having babies for that matter! Now I really must go to the ladies'.'

Jade dashed for the door before she threw herself at him and just said yes to whatever he wanted of her. But while she hurried along the corridor, she kept thinking about the look she'd glimpsed on Kyle's face. He'd seemed quite put out. Surely he hadn't meant that off-the-cuff proposal, had he? No, he couldn't have, she dismissed, though not without a sharp contraction of her heart. He didn't love her. It was 'making love' to her he loved. He'd made that pretty clear on Friday night. Not to mention just now.

She was drying her hands after a visit to the loo when a sickening thought struck. Maybe he *had* meant it. But not for reasons of love...

She was the boss's daughter, wasn't she? A lot of ambitious men married the boss's daughter to get ahead. Her own father had married her mother with one eye on the Campbell fortune.

Another, even more appalling thought invaded her stunned brain. Twice, Kyle had not taken precautions when having sex with her. Twice, he'd risked her getting pregnant. Yet he was a very clever, cool individual who wouldn't make silly mistakes or take silly risks.

Her heart squeezed even tighter. God, could he do something as wicked as that—seduce her, make her pregnant, then marry her simply to further his ambition? She recalled Kyle looking assessingly around Belleview, and the way he'd ingratiated himself with her father.

I'm being paranoid again, she finally decided. Kyle's not like that. I just know he's not!

But she was not entirely convinced as she slowly made her way back to the office, her mind racing over everything

she knew about him, which was…not very much. She
didn't even know anything about his family.

A grim-faced Kyle was on the telephone when she re-
entered the room.

'I see,' he was saying as she sat down at her desk. 'So
that's how she manages it. Clever bitch. But unless we give
the tour companies and guides kickbacks as well, our stores
will keep on being bypassed in favour of Campbell's. And
Byron won't do that… What's that? No, I can't see how
we can take legal action, but I might leak the story to a
few of the television stations. Campbell Jewels won't smell
too good by the time I'm finished, and neither will Celeste
Campbell… Yes, well, you're welcome to her. She's not
my type, I can tell you. I like warm, loving women, not
bloodsucking vampires… Yes, thanks, Peter. You've done
wonders.'

He hung up, his expression pensive as he leant back and
fiddled with a Biro. Jade couldn't tell if he was deliberately
ignoring her, or was genuinely preoccupied. She decided
the only way to handle her nervous curiosity about him
was to be upfront and honest. He said he liked that about
her.

'Kyle,' she began somewhat hesitantly.

His black gaze drifted her way, finally focusing on her.
'Yes?'

'Do you have any brothers or sisters?'

He snapped forward in his chair. 'No. I'm an only child.'

'And are your parents still living?'

'What is this? Twenty questions?'

'No. I…I realised while I was in the ladies' that I didn't
know much about you. On a personal basis, that is.'

'What's prompted this sudden need for more details?'

'You won't get mad if I tell you the truth?'

'I'll try not to.'

'I…I began wondering if you could have been serious
about asking me to marry you, even though you don't love

me. I even started worrying you were *trying* to get me pregnant…'

'Now why would I do a silly thing like that?' he returned coolly.

'To marry the boss's daughter?' she suggested, trying to keep her voice teasingly light.

His smile sent an odd shiver rippling down her spine. 'If that was my intention then why would I have stopped off at the chemist to buy protection the other night on the way home?'

'You did? Well…well…you didn't use it, did you? Just tell me straight, Kyle,' she persisted bravely. '*Is* that your intention?'

'What?'

'To make me marry you?'

'Good God, no.'

'You don't have to sound so appalled! I'm not that bad, am I?'

'No, of course not, but any wife of mine will come to me willingly. Which reminds me, I take it you'll be coming home with me tonight?'

'Maybe. Maybe not.'

He laughed. 'That won't work a second time, Jade. Now come over here. I have a mind to…'

A tap on the office door was followed by a barked 'come' from Kyle and Moira popping her head inside.

'Byron wants to see Jade for a tick.'

'I…I wonder what he wants?' Jade asked, her head still whirling from what Kyle had had a mind to do. God, but she was like putty in his hands. All that garbage she'd told herself about not wanting him to make love to her in the office had been just that: garbage. It was clear he could have her any time he wanted. And the thought excited her unbearably.

In a way, she was happy to flee his seductive presence, even if meetings with her father were also fraught with danger. Nathan's prognostication that he might have mel-lowed had been way off track. He was as difficult and demanding as ever.

'Ah, there you are,' he gruffed on her entering his office and closing the door. 'I just wanted to ask if you needed a lift home tonight.'

'Oh—er—no. I think I'll go out after work.'

'All night again, I suppose,' he bit out. 'Like last Friday night.'

Jade declined to answer. She was not a child and refused to be treated like one. Her father heaved a ragged sigh.

'Well, sit down while you're here and tell me how you and Kyle are getting along. He speaks warmly of you, says you have a sharp business brain and a flair for marketing.'

'That's generous of him.'

'Kyle's not generous. He's got one of the toughest and best business brains I've ever encountered. You must be doing something right to impress him as much as you do.'

Heat zoomed into her cheeks. Say something, for pity's sake, she told herself swiftly, before he guesses the truth!

'By the way, Pops, did Kyle mention our plans for the ball? And did he ask you about the Heart of Fire?'

'Yes, he did. A ball like that will cost a lot of money, you know. Still, I promised to give Kyle his head for a while. As for the Heart of Fire, do whatever you want with the damned thing. Frankly, I'll be glad to see the back of it. That opal's brought Whitmore's nothing but bad luck and heartache. Far better it finds another owner. Of course, I would like to see it bought by a collector, not someone who's going to have it cut up. Gemma would have my hide if we allowed that to happen.'

Jade smiled to herself. Fancy her tough businessman of a father caring what Gemma felt about an opal she didn't even own. The girl had a way with her, there was no doubt about that.

'It would bring far more if sold as a collector's piece, anyway,' Jade said. 'We'll advertise it as such and display it in the window of the Regency Hotel store. A lot of wealthy people pass that way and I'm sure its auction at the ball will draw a lot of avid collectors. And if it brings what it's worth, believe me it'll bring *good* luck to Whitmore's, not bad. A million dollars will finance some of the changes we're going to adopt. Nothing like some cash flow to soothe the bank manager's hesitancy to give us any loans we want.'

Byron stared at her. 'You sound as if you know what you're talking about, daughter.'

'I do, Pops, I do. Now when can I have a look at this treasure?'

'No time like the present. I'll get it for you and you can show Kyle.'

It was magnificent, there was no doubt about that. And huge! Though unless one turned it over to the side where the rough stone had been sliced away to reveal the opal inside, it looked like a useless piece of gray potch.

'What happened back in the olden days with this opal, Pops?' she asked as she turned it this way and that, dazzled by the pinfire flashes of changing colour. 'Did Grandfather find it and refuse to share it with Mr. Campbell? Is that what started the original feud?'

'I have no idea,' her father said, so curtly that Jade knew for certain he *did* know the truth. It had to be something really awful, she decided, something that made David Whitmore look very bad. She also knew there was no point in keeping on asking her father about it, because his handsomeness was only exceeded by his stubbornness.

Byron Whitmore's main failing in life, his daughter believed, was his maniacal clinging to the family's good reputation, at all cost. That was why he hadn't divorced his wife, why Jade herself had been such a trial to him as a teenager. Nothing was to sully the good name of the Whitmores. Which was why Jade had been so upset—and shocked—when she'd caught him kissing their last housekeeper.

Not that she cared about that so much now. She wasn't

so shocked any more, either. Heavens, if she couldn't appreciate how her father could turn to another woman after being married to her mother for all those years...

'Pops,' she said abruptly. 'Why was Mum the way she was?'

Byron shook his head, sighing. 'She was a very unhappy woman, Jade. Very...disturbed.'

'Yes, but *why*? Tell me the truth. It's important to me and I'm old enough, surely.'

His taut face told her he didn't agree. 'I don't like to talk ill of the dead.'

'Pops, I think she *hated* me. I want to know why.'

'No, Jade, it wasn't *you* she hated.'

'Well, it wasn't *you*. She was crazy about you.'

Jade used to be amazed at the change in her mother when Byron came home. If ever there was a Jekyll and Hyde character, it was Irene Campbell Whitmore.

'She loved me and she hated me,' Byron said grimly.

'But why? Was it because she found out you didn't love her?'

His face paled with shock. 'How did you know about...?'

'Everyone knows, Pops,' she cut in drily.

'*Everyone*?'

'Well, everyone in the family.'

'What...what do they know?'

'That you married Mum because you thought she was going to inherit Campbell Jewels.'

He stared at her hard, then dropped his eyes and shook his head. 'I had no idea...'

'It's all right, Pops. I forgive you. It's all water under the bridge now. I just needed some answers.'

His eyes lifted, eyes as blue as the sea and just as unfathomable. 'Well, now you have them. Believe me, if I did wrong, daughter, I suffered for it.'

And so did I, Jade thought ruefully. But at least it wasn't my fault. It wasn't that I was unlovable but that my mother was not right in the head. Jade felt as if a huge weight had been lifted from her soul.

She stood up, the opal in her hands, keen now to take it back to show Kyle.

'Is that to hit me with?' the younger man mocked on seeing the opal, which did look like a chunk of stone.

'Do you deserve hitting?' she teased, walking over to slide up on to the corner of his desk, crossing her legs and placing the opal before him. 'There it is. The Heart of Fire. What do you think of it?'

He dragged in then exhaled a ragged breath. 'I think…that if you don't want to have sex in the office…then I suggest you get off my desk immediately.'

His eyes were fixed on her thighs and Jade felt the thrill of real sexual power. It compelled her to push things further. She began swinging her leg in a slow, tantalising fashion, and watched in fascination as his fists curled over, his knuckles going white.

'I just might have changed my mind about that,' she husked. 'I've decided I like having my own toy-boy on tap.'

'Get off this desk, Jade,' he bit out. 'Now!'

Startled by his angry outburst, she slipped off the desk, laughing nervously. 'Sorry. I…I didn't realise you were so lacking in control.'

Jade scuttled back towards her desk, a glance back over her shoulder stopping her in her tracks. Never had she seen Kyle look like that. Was he shocked, or in pain?

'What?' she gasped. 'What is it?'

His expression slowly hardened to one of cold fury. 'I can see I've damaged my Mr Cool image in your eyes, Jade,' he said with icy disdain. 'I doubt you even respect me as a man any more. How perverse… Still, the situation is not irretrievable. We will simply have to abandon our affair and return to our previous *status quo*. Yes, I really do think that would be best. This isn't going to work.'

Initially, Jade froze with shock. But once she accepted

that Kyle meant every word he said, her legs went to water.
She had to lean on the desk for support. 'You...you don't
mean that, Kyle.'

His expression was so aloof, she shivered.

'I'm afraid you don't know me very well, Jade. Except
in the biblical sense,' he added with a sardonic twist to his
mouth. 'But I can assure you that, as of now, any physical
intimacy between us has ceased. We will revert to boss and
assistant, unless, of course, you only came to work with
me for sexual gratification,' he finished derisively. 'In
which case you can quit right now.'

'You know that's not true!'

'Do I?'

Jade's hands lifted to her temples which had begun to
pound. 'Why...why are you doing this?' she cried. 'A little
while ago you wanted me to move in with you. What's
changed? What have I said or done?'

'I don't have to explain myself to you, Jade. Neither do
I have to keep risking my position here simply to get my
rocks off.'

Jade felt the nausea rising in her stomach. 'Is that what
you were doing earlier? Getting your rocks off?'

'What else?'

She stared at him, horror and hurt in her eyes.

'I have to go out now, Jade. I suggest you get on with
your promotional work regarding the ball. Oh, and you'd
better ask your father for a lift home. You're going to be
needing it.'

Jade managed to hold herself together till he left, then
she collapsed, sobbing, at her desk.

CHAPTER THIRTEEN

'I'M GOING to miss you,' Kirsty wailed, and threw her arms around Gemma.

'Me too,' Gemma whispered, tears pricking her eyes. This would probably be the last time that Kirsty would look at her with such affection. By this time next week, she would be Nathan's wife and Kirsty's new stepmother. God knew what the shock was going to do to their friendship. Gemma didn't like to think about it.

'We're only down the road, for heaven's sake!' Lenore complained. 'Gemma can visit whenever she likes, and so can you, Kirsty. Anyone would think you were going overseas, not a suburb away!'

Both girls looked at each other and laughed. They were in Kirsty's bedroom, which had been transformed back to its previous pink and white prettiness, the rock posters and geometric quilt now installed in her bedroom at home, much to Lenore's disgust.

Jade wandered in, looking far from her usual perky self. 'We're going to miss you, darls,' she told Kirsty, and gave her a hug.

'Come along now, Kirsty,' Lenore pleaded. 'I have a performance tonight. We have to go.'

It was Easter Thursday, the last day of the school term, and the last day in March. Kirsty's school had only had a half-day of classes and Lenore was using the free afternoon to get her daughter moved home.

They all trailed downstairs, and after a flurry of further

goodbyes they were gone. Gemma watched Jade turn to walk slowly upstairs, head down, shoulders slumped.

There was definitely something wrong with her. But Jade was a hard person to talk to about personal matters. Her bright, extrovert personality formed a barrier against people even *thinking* she had problems, let alone asking her about them. Gemma had tried the other night, and what had Jade done? Brushed her query aside with a laugh and an excuse.

'I'm just tired, darls,' she'd said. 'This working business is a lot tougher than I thought it would be. I think I'd better have an early night.' With that, she'd gone to her room.

In her own way, Jade could be as difficult to pin down and discuss something with as Nathan could be.

Gemma's frown deepened as her mind shifted to the man who would become her husband within seven days. She loved Nathan deeply—in fact was crazy about him—but they still hadn't discussed basic issues such as children, not to mention where they would even live. Nathan's announcement that he would be moving permanently to Avoca after Easter had startled her till she realised he'd said that to ensure Kirsty went home to live. He couldn't really mean to live there, not when she was supposed to start work at the Regency Hotel store, four days after their planned wedding on the Thursday afternoon.

But she hadn't been able to discuss anything private and personal with Nathan since that interlude in her bedroom three weeks before, simply because they hadn't been alone together since, except for a couple of times briefly in the hallway, and on the stairs. On each occasion, someone had come along to interrupt their conversation and they hadn't been able to talk at length. Tonight, however, she was determined to find out what Nathan's plans were, even if she had to go to his bedroom.

This thought immediately unnerved her, not because she thought Nathan would try to make love to her, but because she knew he wouldn't. The waiting leading up to her wedding night had been as nerve-racking as she'd envisaged.

She wasn't sleeping well and when she did her dreams were disturbingly erotic. On one occasion, they'd been quite frightening.

She'd dreamt she was naked and tied to a chair in Nathan's den at the beach-house. She'd been freezing cold and was begging Nathan to untie her. But he'd sat at his computer, writing and ignoring her pleas. Finally, he'd looked up at her and coldly told her that he didn't like little girls who begged, that she was to shut up and not say a word till he decided he wanted her again.

She'd awoken from the dream, sobbing. It had been the last she had slept that night.

Thinking about that dream now sent a *frisson* of fear rippling down her spine, and she quickly decided against going to Nathan's room tonight, or asking him anything. She knew it was weak of her, and silly. She had every right to know these things. But somehow, that dream had undermined her faith in Nathan's love for her, as well as her faith in her own judgement.

Suddenly, she bolted upstairs and ran into her room, shutting the door and turning the lock.

'He wouldn't hurt me,' she whispered out loud to herself. 'Not my Nathan.'

But she started to shiver uncontrollably, and, no matter what she did, an inner chill remained. Finally, she sat down and wrote a long letter to Ma. It was a light, newsy letter which not once mentioned Nathan or her coming marriage. It was as though if she wrote it down it might not come about. Or was she afraid that Ma would advise her against the marriage, would make her face things she didn't want to face, things buried so deep in her subconscious that they only surfaced in her dreams?

'*Married*!' Ava squawked, her plump face going pink.

'Married?' Jade repeated, as though she'd never heard of the institution.

'Married,' Byron said slowly, nodding with quiet satisfaction at his adopted son.

Melanie, who'd been standing at the dining-table, serving the entrée, when Nathan and Gemma walked in, simply stared at them both.

'Yes, married,' Nathan said, and tightened his grip around Gemma's shoulder. 'We didn't say anything before because we didn't want any fuss. And we don't want any now,' he added, his tone and eyes whipping round the gathering at the dining-table. 'In fact, we're about to leave on an extended honeymoon, first at the Regency over the weekend and then at Avoca. I'm afraid Gemma won't be starting work next week after all, Byron. That will have to be delayed for a while.'

'Of course, Nathan, of course. A new bride won't be wanting to work.' He stood up and came forward, all magnanimous smiles.

The three women did not move, their eyes no longer shocked, Gemma thought, but pitying. Strangely, she didn't find their pity annoying, but disturbing. They're afraid for me, she realised, and trembled.

Nathan's head jerked down, his expression concerned. She looked up into his eyes and was sure she saw real love there. Or was she just hoping?

Suddenly, Byron was upon them and Nathan had to let her go to accept his adopted father's congratulatory hug.

'I can't tell you how pleased I am, Nathan. You've chosen well this time. And Gemma, my love...' He turned to her and took both her hands, bending to kiss her on the cheek. 'I couldn't ask for a lovelier daughter-in-law. I know you'll make Nathan happy, my dear.'

'We must away, Byron. I have a limousine waiting.'

'A limousine, no less,' he chuckled warmly. 'I'm impressed. You've finally learnt the way to a woman's heart, have you?'

'I think so,' Nathan said with an odd little smile.

Gemma shivered again, and Nathan slid an arm around

her waist, giving her a little squeeze. 'Say goodbye to everyone, darling.'

She said goodbye to everyone, and was about to let Nathan guide her firmly from the room when she broke free from his hold and dashed back to kiss each woman in turn, thanking them profusely for everything and saying a whispered 'forgive me' in each ear. Tears in her eyes, she fled back to her husband's arms and was quickly spirited away.

The limousine swallowed her up, the heavily tinted windows giving her an even more claustrophobic feeling which she found smothering and depressing. A great feeling of sadness suddenly overwhelmed her. Tears were streaming down her face by the time Nathan climbed in beside her and the car moved off. He took one look and gathered her against his chest, stroking her hair, while she cried and cried.

'Let it all out,' he soothed. 'You'll be better soon. Much better. It's the tension, you see...'

He talked to her gently and kindly, his embrace sweet and tender. Gemma hardly noticed the moment when the privacy partition slid upwards and the seduction began. It was all done so slowly, so smoothly, and so expertly that she didn't stand a chance from the start. And when it was over, and she lay replete and totally relaxed in her husband's arms, she could hardly remember those few moments of panic when she'd realised what Nathan was going to do. Or those other earlier fears. That all seemed irrelevant now, and far, far away.

'Happy, Mrs Whitmore?' came the husky query, moist lips pressed against her throat.

'Mmm,' she sighed.

'We'd better get you dressed, then. We'll be arriving at the hotel soon.'

Jade lay on her bed, staring up at the ceiling.

Married.

Nathan and Gemma were married.

She couldn't believe it. He'd actually *married* her. Suddenly, she sat up.

Lenore! Did she know? And what about Kirsty? Oh, the poor kid. She had set her heart on her parents eventually getting back together again. Of course, everyone else had known that would never happen, but they'd also all thought Nathan would never marry again either. Kirsty having to face the reality of her father having a new bride would be shattering to her. Having that bride be Gemma would only make things worse. Gemma had been Kirsty's friend, more than her minder.

Jade jumped up and ran downstairs to find her father. He was in the library, reading.

'Pops,' she said abruptly, startling him. 'Does Lenore know?'

He frowned. 'I don't know.'

'I think someone should tell her, don't you?'

'Surely Nathan would have told her.'

'What if he hasn't?'

'Mmm. I need to speak to Lenore anyway. Look, I'll call her straight away and find out, then I'll come and tell you what the situation is.'

'OK. I'll be in the kitchen, having some hot chocolate.'

Byron heaved a troubled sigh as his daughter left the room.

Damn! What if Nathan *hadn't* told Lenore and Kirsty? It would be darned irresponsible if he hadn't. And inconsiderate. There again, Nathan could be like that sometimes.

Byron brooded for a moment, remembering the mess Nathan had been in when he'd found him all those years ago up at King's Cross. There were times when Byron wondered if he'd done the right thing, adopting Nathan, bringing him into his own home. But he'd been compelled to try to rescue the boy from the corruption and depravity surrounding him. How could he leave him there in the clutches of that evil woman? She had been screwing up his mind, as well as his body. Byron shuddered to think what she'd already made the boy believe about the male sex.

Byron had been proud of what he'd made of the lad. Why, he'd turned him round from a potential lost soul to a man of good character and moral strength. A decent man. Admittedly, he did worry sometimes about Nathan's tendency to withdraw emotionally from those around him, yet one only had to read his plays to know that he had more emotions within him than a hundred men. But perhaps writing was the only way he could express it. Maybe when it came right down to his relationships with people—especially women—he could only operate on the level he'd been taught, first by example, and then by experience.

No, Byron thought with sudden venom. I refuse to believe that. He's changed since those days. Grown. Matured. And Gemma's right for him. I knew that from the start. Her very innocence will be his salvation. He wouldn't dare try to corrupt that. Or take advantage of it. At least...I hope not.

'Damn! Damn! Damn!'

Byron levered himself to his feet, cursing more colourfully when a sharp pain shot through his thigh. Would this bastard of a leg never get better? Limping slightly, he made his way over to the desk and the address book he kept next to the phone. Flicking over the pages, he looked up Lenore's number and dialled. She'd probably be home, he knew, because the play she'd been in had folded at the weekend after a very short run. Comedies never did as well as dramas, in his opinion.

Lenore answered on the second ring.

'Byron here, Lenore. I have some news for you which you may or may not already know.'

'If you're referring to Nathan's marriage to Gemma,' she said with a disgruntled sigh, 'I already know. Nathan rang me earlier.'

'Have you told Kirsty?'

'Yes.'

'How's she taking it?'

'Badly.'

'Is there anything I can do? Or Jade? We were worried.'

'Not really, Byron. At least Kirsty's now coming to terms with our divorce being permanent, but she's cut up about Gemma. I've tried explaining that she should blame her father, not that unfortunate child, but I guess she feels betrayed.'

'Why do you say unfortunate child?' Byron snapped.

'Oh, for God's sake, Byron, don't you have any idea what Nathan's like? He doesn't see a female as anything other than a sexual partner, to be manipulated and programmed to his needs.'

'That's not true this time, Lenore. He loves the girl!'

'If he does then I only pity her the more. He'll leave no stone unturned till he's made her his to the exclusion of everything else. I was lucky because I *didn't* love him. Despite that, he didn't do a bad job of enslaving my senses, since I stayed married to him for so long. But in the end, Byron, sex alone just wasn't enough. I needed love. Real love. Gemma will too.'

'Nathan really loves Gemma, Lenore. I'm sure of it.'

'But does she really love him? Or is she just infatuated by Nathan's glamour and sexual sophistication? If so, then you'll have another divorce on your hands once she starts growing up.'

'She's grown up already,' he pronounced stubbornly, unwilling to accept the sense of what Lenore was saying.

'Oh, Byron, don't be ridiculous. She's just a child.'

'I don't like you talking like this!'

'You don't like anyone telling you how it is, Byron. You never have.'

'Humph! And you've always had an acid tongue, Lenore. You won't find yourself another man if you don't learn to curb it.'

'Oh, really?'

Byron heard the smugness in her voice, and frowned.

'So that's how the land lies, eh? Who's fallen into your clutches this time?'

'That's my business.'

Lenore's uneasy tone of voice sent a ghastly suspicion popping into his head. 'Who is he, Lenore? I want to know.'

'As I said, it's none of your business.'

'Maybe. Maybe not. If you don't tell me, our other deal is off.'

'But you promised!'

'A verbal contract with no witnesses is no contract at all.'

Lenore muttered something very uncomplimentary. 'All right, though why you want to know I've no idea. It's Zachary Marsden. There! I hope you're happy.'

'*Zachary*?' Byron was astonished. He'd been worried that maybe Lenore had become mixed up with Damian Campbell. He'd seen that snake hanging around her at parties a few times, oozing his brand of charm. The younger of the two Campbell heirs, he was sinfully handsome and had turned plenty of women's heads, most of them married. He was a lecher of the first order.

Still, lechery ran in the family.

Byron stiffened and dragged his mind back out of the cesspool that started swirling in his mind. God, would he never get that damned woman out of his mind?

'Might I remind you, Lenore,' Byron lectured, 'that Zachary is a happily married man?'

Lenore sighed her frustration. 'I hate to disillusion you about *two* members of your sex tonight, Byron. But Zachary is far from happily married. In fact, Felicity recently asked him for a divorce and when it comes through next year we will be getting married. Till then we're keeping our relationship a secret. I'm only telling you this because you've forced it out of me, but if you mention it to a soul, I swear, Byron, I will come round and impale you with that walking stick of yours!'

Byron only just managed not to chuckle. He had to give Lenore credit for courage and spirit. As for Zachary... maybe he even envied him a little. Lenore was a beauty all right, and a very passionate woman, if he was any judge. She reminded him a little of...

Byron clamped his teeth down hard in his jaw.

'I won't tell anyone, Lenore,' he bit out. 'And you'll have the lead role in Nathan's new play, as promised. Nathan doesn't want any say in the production, I asked him. I'll contact you next week once I've lined up a director and a theatre.'

Byron hung up before she could say another word, taking a while before he remembered the original purpose of the call. Rising, he went in search of Jade. At least Nathan had done the right thing and told Lenore himself, but after what Lenore had said he had to admit he was worried about Nathan's marriage to Gemma now, which was a shame. He'd been so happy about it before, had really felt they were made for one another. Who knew? Maybe *his* gut feelings would be proved right in the end, and not Lenore's. She had to be biased, after all. Nathan had not loved her. But he did love Gemma. Byron was sure of it.

'How's Kirsty bearing up?' Jade asked Lenore as they wandered together through the shopping arcade. A week had passed since Nathan's and Gemma's marriage, a week during which hardly a word had been spoken at Belleview about the hopefully happy couple. Everyone seemed to be reluctant to give voice to an opinion, adopting a more wait and see attitude. 'Pops told me she was upset,' Jade added.

'She's a little better. A letter arrived from Gemma which made her cry again, but with more understanding this time, though no real forgiveness. I read the letter myself and to be honest I cried too. That poor girl sounded terribly upset to think we might not like her any more because of her marrying Nathan. She's so sweet, Jade, but so naïve. Nathan deserves to be shot for marrying her.'

'I don't agree. I'm rather proud of him.'

Lenore's green eyes snapped round. '*Proud*?'

'Yes. He didn't have to marry her to have her, Lenore. We both know that. He could have simply used her, as so many men do young girls, then tossed her aside. Even if the marriage doesn't last, this way her rights are protected by law. Gemma will at least be financially secure for life.'

'Financially secure and emotionally destroyed,' Lenore said acidly.

'We'll see...'

'What exactly are we shopping for tonight, Jade?' Lenore asked after a minute's awkward silence.

'An outfit for me to wear to the races on Saturday. Whitmore Opals are sponsoring one of the races at Rosehill and it's my job to sash the winning horse. I have to look the part. Kyle says I'm not to embarrass him or the company by wearing something outlandish.'

Jade avoided Lenore's penetrating look, turning her head to window shop. 'This boutique has some nice things in it,' she said, stopping. 'What do you think, Lenore? Do you think that blue dress would suit me?'

'Not if you're dressing for a man.'

'I'm not,' Jade snapped.

'So what happened between you and the marketing manager? Or aren't you ever going to tell me?'

Jade shrugged, her heart sinking as it did whenever she thought of Kyle these days. If only he'd been nasty to her these past few weeks. But no, he'd been exceptionally decent and polite. Remote, though. And strictly business. Her one attempt really to talk to him had been given short shrift, and she hadn't tried again.

'Didn't he fancy you?' Lenore asked gently.

Jade laughed. 'Oh, he fancied me all right, but I was my usual stupid self and gave him the impression that I only wanted him for sex...which perhaps I did at first. I can see now that his male pride had trouble with that,' she went on shakily. 'Looking back, I think he also became worried that his career at Whitmore's might be jeopardised by sleeping with me. So he cut dead our affair before it had hardly begun.'

Jade had to stop for a second, an enormous lump filling her throat. 'I only realised afterwards,' she choked out, 'how much I...really loved him, and *needed* him, and... and...oh, God, I'm so miserable.'

Jade dissolved into tears right then and there, her shoulders shaking uncontrollably as her head dropped into her hands.

'Oh, you poor love,' Lenore sympathised, putting her arms around her and leading her away to a quiet corner till she could compose herself. Which she eventually did.

'Would you like to marry this man, Jade?' Lenore asked carefully.

Jade nodded.

'Goodness, then you do love him, don't you? You always said marriage was for the birds. And babies? Have you changed your mind about that as well?'

Jade's thinking hadn't carried her that far as yet. She'd always feared she'd make a terrible mother. Now, her mind and heart filled with the images of having Kyle's baby, of holding it in her arms, caring for it, loving it. Something moved deep within her, something warm and strong and elemental.

Oh, what a fool she'd been to think she would not make a good mother. She'd make a *great* mother, because she knew exactly what a child needed most of all. Love.

Her eyes glistened with new tears. 'I'd love to have Kyle's babies. But that's just wishful thinking. He doesn't love me or want to marry me. He never did.'

'You can't be sure of that, Jade. Male pride makes liars out of the best men. Why don't you tell him how you feel and see what happens?'

'Oh, no.' She shook her head vigorously. 'I...I couldn't do that.'

'Why not? What have you got to lose?'

'What have I got to lose?' Her smile was infinitely sad. 'His respect. I think, oddly enough, I might have gained some of that in his eyes lately. If I tell him I love him, he'll think I'm trying to blackmail him back into a sexual relationship. I am the boss's daughter, after all. No, Lenore, Kyle's the sort of man who makes his own decisions where women are concerned. If he ever wants me back, he'll let me know.'

'Maybe so,' Lenore returned a little drily. 'But there's no reason why his wanting you back can't be helped along a little, is there?'

'And how can I do that? I have no intention of being obvious, Lenore. *Or* bold. That won't work a second time.'

'My dear, there is no need to be obvious, *or* bold, to be desirable. Come along. We have some shopping to do.'

CHAPTER FOURTEEN

'MY GOD, Jade, what have you done to yourself!' Ava exclaimed. 'I've never seen you look so...so...'

'Exquisite?' Melanie suggested, walking into Ava's studio with the vacuum cleaner in one hand and a duster in the other.

'Yes,' Ava agreed, throwing the housekeeper a ready smile. 'That's the word. Exquisite. And what a sensational figure she has. I'd give my eye-teeth for one half as good.'

Jade was truly taken aback by their compliments. When Lenore had selected an ultra-feminine white lace over organza dress from the racks, her immediate reaction had been negative. Demure clothes didn't suit her, and this dress was demure, with a high neck and long sleeves, not to mention a mid-calf gored skirt.

'You really think it looks all right?' Jade asked, still unsure.

She'd bought the dress on Lenore's say-so, not at all convinced Kyle would like such an old-fashioned looking outfit. Though he had said once he liked her in white. Perhaps it was the white organza picture hat she was uncomfortable with, not to mention the pearl choker and matching earrings. She felt like a member of the royal family going to Ascot, or one of those garden brides at the turn of the century.

'I hope I don't have to walk far,' she muttered. 'These new shoes are going to kill me by the end of the day.'

'They look lovely.'

'They should at the price. In fact, this outfit has set me

back a pretty penny, which is ridiculous since I'll never wear it again.'

'You never know,' her aunt soothed. 'Is that a new perfume I can smell?' she asked, coming over to sniff. 'It's very nice.'

Melanie put down the vacuum cleaner to walk over and have a sniff as well.

'Hmm. Very erotic,' was her murmured comment, bringing a sharp look from Jade. The woman had sounded wistful, yet sensual. It wasn't the first time Jade had thought their housekeeper had a strong sexual streak in her.

'What's it called?' Ava asked.

'Desire.'

Melanie lifted her dark eyebrows and turned away to plug in the vacuum cleaner. 'Sorry to put an end to our chat, but I must get on with this. You do look lovely, Jade. I hope your day is a big success.'

'How can it help but be?' Ava said, smiling. 'Jade doesn't have to win the race, only sash the winner and look pretty for the photos. Isn't that right, dear? Now let's go downstairs and show your father how beautiful you look.'

'Do we have to?' Jade groaned.

'You can't,' Melanie said from behind them. 'He's gone out.'

Jade breathed a sigh of relief.

'Darn,' Ava grumbled. 'Where's he gone?'

'To golf.'

'Golf?' He can hardly walk upstairs, let alone around a golf course.'

'He bought one of those driving carts.'

'Truly. Nobody tells me anything around here.'

'He did mention it last night, Auntie,' Jade recalled, 'but you were watching a movie.'

'Oh…yes, well, people shouldn't tell me things when I'm watching a movie. You know what I'm like.'

Jade laughed and linked arms with her aunt. 'We certainly do, darls, especially when the movie's a romance.'

'Don't call me that,' the older woman complained. 'I hate it. Frankly, it's high time you stopped using that term altogether. It sounds cheap.'

'Cheap?' Jade was astonished.

'Yes, cheap!'

'Then it won't pass my lips again,' she promised faithfully. 'My days of cheap are over.'

'And about time too!' her aunt announced firmly as they went downstairs.

They were just stepping on to the rug at the bottom of the stairs when the buzzer near the front door announced a visitor wanting entry at the gates. Instant butterflies crowded Jade's stomach as she hurried over to flick the switch on the security intercom.

'Is that you, Kyle?'

'It is.'

'Sorry about the gates. I'll open them for you.'

'Thank you.'

So chillingly polite, she thought, and shivered. Suddenly, the day ahead took on a bleak reality. She should never have listened to Lenore, should never have allowed her hopes to be raised.

Closing her eyes, she just stood there. Her breathing came deep and even as she tried desperately to compose herself, to hide her misery behind a cool calm façade.

'Are you all right, dear?'

Jade swung round, her eyes flying open to see her aunt's concerned face.

'Yes, of course. I was just daydreaming.'

'You like Mr Armstrong, don't you?'

Jade stiffened. 'I admire him. Yes.'

'I see,' the other woman said slowly. 'Well, have a nice time, dear, and we'll see you when we see you.'

The front doorbell rang and Jade went to open the door. Her insides tightened as her eyes swept over the man she loved.

How handsome he looked. That black suit did things for

his colouring that no other colour did. And his body di(
things for the suit in return that not many men's would.

'You're a little early,' she said stiffly.

The corner of his mouth lifted in a small, sardonic smile
'Maybe I was anxious to see this vision of loveliness.'

Jade froze. Was he mocking her? Or could Lenore have
been spot on? 'You…you really like what I'm wearing?'

He seemed surprised by her obvious lack of confidence
'Don't you?'

'I just didn't think this was me.'

'Well, if it isn't you,' he said drily, 'then, whoever it is
don't bother to change. What you're wearing is perfect.'

Jade could feel the heat gathering in her cheeks. 'I have
to get my purse. Do you want to come in?'

'No. I'll wait here.'

Jade hurried upstairs to her room where she snatched up
the pearlised clutch purse she'd also bought the other night
then took one last glance in her dressing-table mirror.

'He likes how I look,' she whispered happily. 'He really
does.'

Eyes bright with relief and excitement, she came downstairs, trying not to hurry too much. Lenore had insisted
she be pleasant, but not too anxious to please. Sweet, bu
not cloying.

Once on the front patio with the front door closed behind
them, Kyle took her elbow and gallantly escorted her dowr
the steps, opening the door for her and seeing her properly
seated and belted before striding round to the driver's side
Jade tried hard not to let her gaze follow his every move
but to no avail. She couldn't seem to get enough of him
today, even if it was only with her eyes.

'Yes?' he asked after belting himself in and noticing tha
she was still staring at him.

'Oh… I—er—nothing.' God, but she was hopeless! Le
nore would be grimacing, if she could see her now.

Kyle started the car and they were away. Jade focused
straight ahead, determined not to move her head an inch

his way until they arrived at the racecourse. The silence
between them lengthened, the atmosphere becoming terribly tense.

'Jade...' he began at last while they were stopped at a
red light.

'Yes?' She kept her eyes on the road ahead.

He sighed irritably. 'This is more damned difficult than
I thought it would be.'

'Well, it needn't be,' she suddenly snapped, mortified
that she'd started hoping stupid hopes. What a fool she was!
'I realise you're only taking me to the races today because
you have to. I'm not under any illusions that this is a date
or anything. You told me to get all glammed up so I did.
There's no reason for you to feel you have to treat me any
differently than you do at the office these days. You've
made it perfectly clear you don't want any relationship with
me other than a working one, even if I still do, so I...I...'

Jade refused to burst into tears at this juncture but she
just couldn't go on. She'd already said far too much. So
she simply stopped talking and stared through the passenger
window. But it was an unseeing stare. When the car drew
to a halt again, she presumed it was because of another red
light.

'Jade. Turn round and face me.'

Angry blue eyes whipped round at his demanding tone
to find he'd pulled over into a side-street and parked. 'What
do you want now?' she snapped again. 'Haven't you done
enough yet, Kyle? Must you keep on crucifying me?'

Jade was taken aback by the truly pained look that
crossed his face.

'God, is that how bad it's been? I'm truly sorry, my
darling. Truly, truly sorry.'

Jade gaped at him. My *darling*? What was going on
here? What cruel game was he playing at now?

Suddenly, he unsnapped his seatbelt, leant over and
kissed her startled mouth, softly, sweetly. 'I didn't mean to
make you suffer,' he murmured, lifting his head, then smil-

ing a faintly sardonic smile. 'Well, I might have...a little...at first. But afterwards, I knew it was the only way I
could be sure, the only way I could make you see the truth.'

'What truth?' she asked, utterly confused now.

'That you really loved me. That it wasn't just sex.'

'Of course I really loved you, you stupid man!' she burst
forth. 'I knew that! Why didn't you? My God, are you
saying you loved me all along? If you are saying that, Kyle
Armstrong, then you'd better get out of this car and start
running because I...'

He kissed her again, kissed her and told her he loved her
over and over till she was crying with joy and relief and
so many mixed emotions, not the least of which was total
bewilderment.

'I still don't see why you couldn't tell me you loved me
before,' she cried.

'The way you told me, perhaps? Think, Jade. What *did*
you tell me? That you didn't know what you felt for me
except that the sex was great, that you were never going to
marry or have children, and that once you learnt my job I
was expendable.'

'Oh!' An embarrassed heat crowded her face. 'But I...I
didn't realise at that stage how much I loved you!'

'Exactly. You didn't realise because I was confusing you
with sex and generally being a precipitate fool. I pulled
back, Jade, hoping a break would force you to see the truth.
I thought you might be in love with me but I couldn't be
sure. I'm sorry if it hurt but I've been hurting too.'

Jade stared at him. 'But I...I might have ended up hating
you instead.'

'You didn't, though, did you?' he smiled.

'When...when did you fall in love with me?'

'I think the process began that first night at dinner. Do
you remember when I started coughing?'

'Yes...yes, I do.'

'You'd just smiled over at me. Such a sad smile, my
darling. It tore at my heart and made me want to take care

of you, to comfort you. It came to me then that you were
the woman I was going to marry.'

'*Marry*!' she squawked. 'I thought you only lusted after
me that first night.'

'That too. I fought both impulses, I can assure you. Told
myself that I couldn't possibly bed my boss's outrageous
daughter, let alone want to marry her. But my subconscious
obviously didn't agree because before I knew it I was contriving to have you work with me, pretending it was for
your own good when in fact all I wanted was any excuse
to have you around me. God, how I wanted you!'

He laughed softly. 'I did quite well to last till the Friday,
don't you think? The straw that broke the camel's back was
thinking you might actually go out and go to bed with some
other man. I couldn't have that when I knew it was *me* you
wanted. I decided then and there to be your next lover, no
matter what. But then I found out you were nothing like
you pretended to be. Nothing at all! You were sweet and
innocent and adorable and I fell for you like a ton of hot
bricks.'

'But you very definitely said that night you didn't love
me,' Jade recalled, frowning. 'You said you never fell in
love.'

'I never have. I've always been a cold, controlled bastard: I've never known love, you see. My parents died when
I was just a baby and I was put into a boarding-school when
I was a tot. It took a very special person to make me fall
in love, Jade, and *still* I didn't recognise the emotion. I
knew I liked you and admired you and desired you, but it
wasn't till you teased me that day in the office about having
no control that I finally saw the truth. You see, I've never
not been in control with a woman before.'

Now Jade did frown. 'But why did you back away? I
still don't understand...'

'Don't forget what you'd just said to me that day, about
never wanting to get married or have children. Not to mention that crack about my being your toy-boy right at the

same moment I realised I loved you. You were denying me what I wanted most in the world. *You*, as my wife and the mother of my children. I lashed out in frustration and I'm terribly sorry. I regretted everything immediately I stormed out, but my pride wouldn't let me come back. I was off my head, thinking your only interest in me was carnal.'

'Oh, Kyle…'

'It wasn't till I'd calmed down that I realised you might love me underneath that flighty façade you hide behind, and which I already knew was a lie. I also decided to gamble that your decision about marriage and children was a backlash against your parents' miserable marriage, not to mention your mother's appalling treatment of you. I began to have faith that you really loved me, but I had to convince *you* of that, so I put your love to the test these past few weeks and you came through, darling Jade. *We* came through. We love each other, really love each other. It's not just lust. It's true love. Marry me, darling. Marry me and I'll make you happy, I promise…'

By this time tears were misting Jade's eyes. She reached out and picked up his hands, squeezing them to her heart. 'Oh, yes, Kyle. Yes…'

'And babies?'

'As many as you like.'

The joy on his face moved her so much that more tears followed.

'You don't know how happy you've made me,' he choked out, taking out his pocket handkerchief and wiping her streaming cheeks.

'I've ruined my make-up,' she laughed. 'Do we still have to go to the races?'

'The races! My God, I forgot.' He glanced at his watch. 'We have to go, Jade. I can't let people down like that. Damn, I wanted to… Oh, well, I guess that can wait until tonight…

'I have to confess I'm a little afraid of horses,' Jade nervously told the PR person from the racing authority as the

winner of the Whitmore Opal Stakes was brought back to
be weighed. Jade eyed the sweating animal with growing
temerity as the jockey slid off and they waited round till
weight was declared right, after which Kyle made a small
speech on behalf of Whitmore Opals and presented the
owner with a trophy and an opal ring.

Jade watched, fascinated and admiring, Kyle's absolute
composure and confidence. If it had been her up there she
would have been umming and aahing everywhere. There
again, a man like Kyle only came along once in a million
years, she believed. And he was going to be her husband.
She sighed with happiness.

'Time to sash the winner now, Miss Whitmore,' the PR
man whispered in her ear.

Jade took a deep breath and stepped forward.

'Thank God the poor thing was too tired to do anything
but nod,' she said afterwards to Kyle, curling a happy arm
through his. 'Can we go home now?'

He smiled down at her. 'My home or yours?'

'Ours.'

'Ours?'

'You did ask me to move in with you, didn't you?' she
said. 'How about tonight?'

'I do like the way you make decisions, Ms Whitmore.'

They were just turning away when someone tapped Kyle
on the shoulder.

'Kyle? Is that you?'

Both of them whirled round. A striking blonde in bright
pink was standing there, giving Kyle a peeved look.

'So it *is* you!' she said, throwing a curious glance Jade's
way before returning her gorgeous green eyes to Kyle's
stony face. 'Well, what have you got to say for yourself,
Mr Gainsford? I've been waiting weeks for you to call as
you said you would,' she tripped off, not sounding overly
upset. 'Still, I'm not one to hold a grudge. Call me when
you get back to Tassie. I'll be waiting. Ta-ta!'

She walked off, waving coyly, the crowd soon swallowing her up.

Jade wished the ground would open and swallow her up as well. She was an intelligent girl and it didn't take long to put two and two together. What a pity four was such a nauseating number. A nauseating, despairing number. With a tormented groan, she lifted distressed eyes to the man standing stiffly beside her.

'Well, Mr Gainsford,' she said shakily, 'or whoever you are—want to tell me what that was all about? Make it good, because there are laws in this state against false representation.'

His expression did not reflect the expression she might have expected on an exposed con-man. He'd become Mr Cool again. Or was it Mr Arrogant?

'For God's sake, Jade,' he ground out. 'You're jumping to all the wrong conclusions. Hell...' His hands raked through his black curls, giving him a less cool image. 'Why did that stupid bitch have to show up today, of all days? And here, of all places!'

'I dare say you slept with her, and conned her too.'

'If anyone was doing the conning on that occasion, it was the lady,' he countered harshly. 'She turned out to be a gold-digger.'

'Well, she struck out with you, didn't she? What happened? Did you use your rich mate's name with her, and she thought it was you with the millions? Yes, of course that's what you did. How silly of me. *You're* the gold-digger this time, though, aren't you? Do tell me, Kyle. Is it me you're after, or the company?'

'Just you.'

She gasped her shock that he could admit such a thing. 'But I'm not that rich!'

'I know that. But *I* am. And my name *is* Gainsford. I'm probably one of the richest men in Australia.'

Jade's head jerked back. '*What*?'

'You don't have to take my word for it. Check me out

if you like. But before you put your pretty foot further into your pretty mouth, let me give you the simple facts, the same ones I would have told you before the races, if I'd had time. Hell, I shouldn't have put it off, but I guess I wanted to live the fantasy a little longer.'

Jade blinked, her brain still blank with shock.

Kyle sighed. 'This will probably sound pretty farfetched but it's the truth. I assumed a false name and false work record to get an ordinary job and live an ordinary life, because I wanted to find a woman who would love me for who I am, not what I owned.'

Jade blinked some more.

'God!' He pulled her to him, his grip unyielding, black eyes blazing with a dark passion. 'Do you hear what I'm saying? I wanted to get married and have a family, and I wanted my wife to really truly love me. Me, the man, not me, Mr Moneybags. Well, I found her. And I love her like mad, and I'm not going to let her go. Not ever. Believe me when I say that, even if you don't believe anything else.'

Jade was still having trouble taking it all in, though there was no doubting Kyle's sincerity. But what an amazing, incredible story! Perhaps she should have been angry with him for such a deception, but instead she was deeply moved. Kyle's upbringing sounded as awful as her own. And just as lacking in love. No wonder they'd been drawn to each other.

'There's no mysterious Mr Gainsford, then?' she asked. 'You're him?'

'I am.'

'Then that night on the houseboat… You were talking about yourself?'

He nodded and she remembered all that he had said about not liking the man he'd been once, but liking him more now.

'Why did you choose Armstrong?' she asked, still a little dazed.

'It's my secretary's surname.'

'Your…your secretary?'

'My secretary's a man, before you jump to any more false conclusions,' he added drily. 'It was he who rang me at the office that day, not a woman.'

'Oh…' She frowned up at him as a thought struck. 'If you're so rich, why doesn't your name ring a bell?'

'My parents were American.'

'I thought you were Tasmanian?'

'I am. When I was born my parents received a kidnap threat which they took seriously. They emigrated to Tasmania, where they bought a secluded country property, thinking they'd be safe. But that was in 1967, the year of Tasmania's worst bushfire. They perished in it, but somehow I survived, heir at six months old to billions of dollars. I grew up being given everything but love, Jade. And over the years, I tried everything but love. Then one day I saw the emptiness of my life and knew what I had to do. I came looking for love. And I found it.'

Jade felt like crying, till she thought of something. 'Does my father know all this?'

'Not a word of it.'

'Goodness. He's going to be furious with you for deceiving him.'

'Let's not tell him just yet. I like working at Whitmore's, Jade. I'd like to see if together we can really rescue the place and make it a success.'

'Oh, yes, I'd like that. But he's still going to be furious when we eventually tell him.'

'Not if you present him with a son-in-law and a grandchild.'

'A grandchild?'

'I want a family, Jade, and I want it soon.'

'I…I still want a career at Whitmore's, Kyle.'

'Of course you do. Of course! I would never ask you to give up your life's dream. I'll help all I can. And I think I can afford a nanny or two, don't you?' he added, smiling.

Jade thought of the pills she'd thrown away after that

awful incident at the office and her heart squeezed tight. 'We could start trying tonight, if you like.'

He seemed startled. 'You mean that, Jade? You've still got this year to go at uni.'

'True... Well, perhaps we should only practise for a month or two, before we try to hit a home run.'

Kyle laughed and hugged her. 'I do so love you.'

'You'd better,' she warned. 'And soon. I've been going mad, missing you.'

'*You've* been going mad! Tell you what, I'll race you to the car.'

'Don't be ridiculous, Kyle,' she reproached. 'Have some decorum.'

While he was looking suitably chastened, she slipped off her shoes and made a dash for it, whooping as she went.

Kyle swore and took off after her. He should have known white lace hadn't made her into a lady. But then, he didn't want a lady, did he? He wanted his Jade.

He began to run faster.

CHAPTER FIFTEEN

AVOCA beach was fairly deserted, partly because it was Monday, but mostly because the weather had turned nasty overnight. A southerly change had blown in a couple of minutes after midnight, bringing with it freezing winds from the Antarctic. Gemma knew the exact moment the change had struck, because she'd been wide awake in her bed. Wide awake and alone. Again.

Tucking her hands under her arms, she put her head down and kept walking along the sand, hoping the sharp breeze would brush away the cobwebs from her mind so that it could focus on reality rather than romantic fantasy. Had she expected too much from her marriage? Had she painted Nathan in her mind as some sort of god, and not a human being with human failings?

She stopped, and stared out to sea, her hair whipping across her face, salt-spray stinging her eyes. The water was very choppy, the waves building as the tide came in. A walk around the rocks was out of the question. Only a madman would do that. Or a potential suicide.

Gemma shuddered, then frowned. Fancy thinking such a thing! Things weren't as bad as that! Every newly married couple had adjustments to make, especially once the honeymoon was over.

But the honeymoon *shouldn't* be over yet, an inner voice niggled. You've only been married two and half weeks. Just because Nathan's doing a little writing...

A *little*? that insidious voice scorned. That was the understatement of the year!

She'd woken in the early hours of yesterday morning feeling cold, only to find Nathan's side of the bed empty. Slipping a robe over her naked body, she'd gone in search of her husband, trying the kitchen first. But it too was empty. Maybe he was in the bathroom. She was walking back to the bedroom when she'd noticed the light under the den door at the end of the hallway.

Relieved, she'd hurried down and gone in, startled to find a fully dressed Nathan sitting at his computer, tapping away like a man possessed. Despite her abrupt entry, he'd kept typing away for at least a minute before looking up and snapping, 'What?'

'I...I was wondering where you were?'

'Well, now you know. I'm in here and, as you can see, I'm working.'

Gemma was so stunned by his brusque manner that she just stood there, speechless.

'Go back to bed,' he ordered, his eyes already back on the screen, his fingers flying over the keys. 'And close the door on your way out.'

She'd retreated, telling herself over and over that it was absurd to feel so hurt. He hadn't meant anything personally. He'd been preoccupied, that was all. She'd known he was a writer when she married him. Kirsty had often spoken of his obsessiveness when creating, so she'd even been warned about it.

Determined not to let things flare out of all proportion, she'd made herself a hot drink and gone back to bed, feeling confident that Nathan would join her later. Now they were married, he didn't seem able to stay away from her for long, wanting to make love morning, noon and night. Yes, no doubt he'd join her long before breakfast.

But he hadn't joined her. Gemma had woken shortly before nine, still alone. And worse was yet to come. Nathan had stayed in that damned room all Sunday, scowling at her the one time she'd dared enter to bring him a tray of food.

'I can't stop to eat now,' she'd been told, his tone irritable and exasperated. 'Oh, just leave it. I'll have something shortly. Why don't you go for a walk? Or a swim? I *have* to finish this scene, Gemma. I shouldn't be much longer.'

By Sunday evening, Gemma's mood had swung from distress to depression. Was this what marriage to Nathan was going to be like from now on, long lonely hours stretching into even longer lonelier days and nights? How would she fill her time? Nathan didn't want her to work or have children for a couple of years, saying a couple had to get to know each other before they introduced a baby into their lives.

Getting to know each other...

Gemma had mulled over that thought all Sunday evening. She didn't really know Nathan any better today than she had on their wedding-day. How could that be when they'd spent every minute of every day together up till now?

The truth was they'd done little else except eat, sleep and make love. Physically, they'd become attuned as Nathan had said they would, and yes, he only had to look at her a certain way to spark her own increasingly demanding desires. But was such sexual intimacy *real* intimacy? She wanted to know Nathan's mind, as well as his body, and vice versa.

Gemma had finally fallen asleep on the Sunday night, feeling unhappy and disturbed. When she'd woken the following morning, still alone, a surge of anger had seized her and before she could think better of it she'd flounced down to that infernal room and walked right in.

Nathan had been sprawled on the sofa, sound asleep.

Her anger evaporating, she had sighed and shaken her head, for he looked rather sweet and vulnerable, lying there like that, his hair dishevelled and a five o'clock shadow on his chin. He'd also looked cold, his knees drawn up in a foetal position, his arms wrapped around himself. Smiling softly, she had collected a blanket from the spare bedroom and spread it over him, bending to smooth that wayward lock of hair from his forehead. He'd moaned softly and turned over. So had her heart. Dear lord, but she loved him so much. What a fool she was to get herself all worked up over his writing for a day or two! As for their getting to know one another... They had their whole lives to do that.

She had been tiptoeing out when she spied the messy printer read-out all over on the floor. Now wasn't that just like a man? Shaking her head, she'd gone over and tidied up the pages, and had been about to put them on the corner of the desk next to the computer when the title of the play jumped out at her.

In Darkness He Stirs.

Intrigued, she had been about to start reading further when the pages were snatched out of her hands and thrown into a nearby chair. 'Nobody reads what I write unless I ask them to,' Nathan snarled, glaring at her with cold fury.

She simply stared up at him, eyes wide, a trembling deep inside. Her father had looked at her like that. Often.

Suddenly, Nathan groaned, and grabbed her to him, embracing her fiercely. 'Don't look at me like that,' he said huskily. 'God, I'm sorry. I didn't mean it. Always remember that, Gemma. When I'm writing, I'm not myself.'

He held her away from him then, his eyes dark and haunted. 'Tell me you understand, Gemma. Tell me you don't mind. It would kill me if you minded, because I *have* to write. I simply have to.'

'It's all right, Nathan,' she lied. 'I...I don't mind.'

'I've been neglecting you, I know,' he growled, cupping her chin with a less than tender hand. 'I don't mean to. I'll make it up to you. I won't be much longer, darling. After I've finished this next act we'll be together again.' He kissed her, quite passionately, then sent her away, unfulfilled and aching for him.

That had been six hours ago. In the end, unable to stand the house any longer, Gemma had walked down to the shops and bought herself an ice-cream, then gone down to the beach, hoping to make some sense of the storm gathering inside her.

A gust of wind hit and she shivered. I'll have to go back, she thought wretchedly. Back to that horrible house.

Gemma didn't go back straight away, however. As she passed the old picture theatre, she noticed a session was about to start so she went in. At the back of her mind she knew she was only delaying a possible confrontation between herself and Nathan, plus their first marital argument. But she was only human, and the thought of conflict upset her.

So she sat for the next couple of hours and watched one of those mindlessly violent action movies where the hero looked like an overmuscled freak and couldn't act to save himself. She counted forty-four corpses and left the theatre, feeling like one herself.

Taking a deep breath, she set off up the hill and was labouring up their steep driveway when Nathan burst out on to the front veranda, looking like the hounds of hell were after him. 'Gemma! Where on earth have you been? I've been looking everywhere for you!' He came racing down the steps, grabbing her shoulders and looking her over as though expecting to find bullet holes in her. 'I've been worried sick. I searched everywhere and couldn't find you. I was just about to call the police.'

Oddly enough, his frantic concern irritated her. 'Really?' She pushed past him and marched up the steps and into the front living-room. 'I was at a movie, if you must know,' she threw back over her shoulder, sensing him behind her.

When he grabbed her and spun her round she was about to lash out some more when he yanked her hard against him, holding her head against his loudly thudding heart. 'You don't understand. I thought you might have gone round the rocks. I thought…hell, I thought so many things. If anything ever happened to you, I'd die, Gemma.'

'You weren't too worried about me while you were writing,' Gemma said in a voice she could hardly believe had come from her. It sounded cynical and bitter. But, having started, she didn't seem able to stop. 'You might as well know right from the start, Nathan. I have no intention of living the rest of my life like this.'

Nathan released her abruptly, and stepped back, staring down at her. 'You're leaving me,' he stated, looking appalled, yet sounding oddly resigned.

His face and words stunned her. Yet, in a weird way, they totally defused her anger. Was this what happened to a person after they'd gone through a divorce? Gemma shook her head in disbelief that he would even *think* such a thing.

'Of *course* I'm not leaving you! I was talking about my going to work, Nathan. You might not realise this but I was very disappointed about that, especially after mastering my basic Japanese. I might not be a genius but I do have a mind and I do get bored, especially when you leave me alone as long as you have these past two days. I understand you need to write. It's part of who you are. But I can't just sit around all day doing nothing.'

Nathan's smile was a mixture of relief and joy as he swept her back into his arms. 'Of course you can't, darling. Of course. I've been very selfish. It's only logical that you'd want to work, a smart girl like you. Look, I'll buy us a unit near town. We'll live down there during the week and up here at the weekends.'

'That sounds wonderful,' Gemma murmured, a little dazed at how quickly Nathan had resolved what could have become a big problem between them.

'It *will* be wonderful,' he reassured, 'because I have a wonderful wife and if I ever forget that again I hope she'll keep reminding me.'

Gemma smiled softly and reached up to rub Nathan's bristly chin. 'You need a shave.'

'And a bath. Care to join me?'

Her eyes rounded, yet she shouldn't have been surprised. Already Nathan had brought her round to a lot of activities she might once have found shocking. 'You're a wicked man,' she teased, though a little breathlessly.

His eyes narrowed on to her mouth. 'You could be right,' he muttered, and bent to kiss her. 'Did you miss me?' he rasped against her lips.

'Yes.'

'Do you want me?'

'Yes.'

'Tell me you love me?'

'I love you.'

He groaned, and, sweeping her up into his arms, carried her down towards the bathroom.

PASSION & THE PAST

CHAPTER ONE

ROYCE TOOK ONE LOOK at the huge black opal on display in the shop window, and wanted it.

He'd always been like that. Swift and sure about deciding what he wanted, and obsessive about gratifying those wants. As a ten-year-old boy he'd wanted to be go-cart champion of south-east England. By fourteen, he was. Nineteen saw him coveting the world championship in formula-one motor racing.

This time, however, it had taken him thirteen years to achieve his ambition. Thirteen long, hard, dangerous years. He'd subsequently gone on to win the championship in back-to-back years, then stunned the motor-racing world by announcing his retirement. But what had been the point of going on? The challenge had been met, the wanting satisfied. Time to move on and find a new goal.

That had been eighteen months ago, during which time he'd been travelling the world, seeing all those places he'd never really seen from behind the wheel of a racing car. He'd also developed a penchant for collecting antiques and art and artefacts. Already, he'd sent home crateloads of treasures to help fill the sixty rooms of the eighteenth-century Yorkshire mansion he'd purchased two years ago, and to which he would soon return.

Now that he was no longer risking his neck every week by hurtling round a track at two hundred miles an hour, friends thought he might contemplate marriage and a family. But marriage had ever been, and never would be, on Royce's 'most wanted' list.

His gaze returned to the opal in the window, while his mind drifted off on a tangent. He started wondering what Australian women would be like. Not that he'd had time to meet any yet.

He'd only landed in Sydney the previous afternoon, the hire car bringing him straight from Mascot Airport to the Regency Hotel where he'd flaked out till late this morning. He'd just been for an after-brunch stroll, and had been wandering past the shops in the foyer of the hotel on his way back to his suite when the opal in the window had caught his eye.

His eyes refocused on the sign sitting on top of the security glass box that housed the large chunk of gemstone. It said:

The Heart of Fire. A rare and precious pinfire black opal of 1260 carats, to be auctioned as an uncut collector's piece at the Whitmore Opals Annual Ball to be held in the Regency Hotel ballroom on Friday night, July 21st. Tickets for the ball may be purchased within or at the Whitmore Opals store on the Rocks. The belle of the ball will be presented with a magnificent solid opal pendant valued at twenty thousand dollars.

An auction, Royce mused. On the twenty-first of July. That was over a month away, well after he'd have moved on to Melbourne. Still, from his experience, an item being auctioned did not preclude an interested party making a bid beforehand. He would simply make an offer that the head of Whitmore Opals could not refuse.

Royce was wondering who the head of Whitmore Opals was and how much money it would take to get what he wanted when his attention was captured by a woman standing at one of the counters inside the shop—a black-haired, black-eyed woman with skin like porcelain and a face that belonged to an Italian master's painting. She was talking to one of the salesgirls, showing her something in a plastic bag.

Royce was entranced by her lovely but rather serious face. Her eyes, especially, reflected an inner sadness. A remoteness. He was thinking he'd never seen such an odd combination of beauty and bleakness, when suddenly she smiled, a smile so vibrant and stunningly sensual that he was powerless to stop the automatic response of his male body. Royce's wanting the opal immediately took second place behind a more immediate and primitive want.

With a surge of adrenaline setting his blood racing, he watched her covertly through the window, his mind searching for some way to meet her, his narrowed eyes roving over her now with a more intense awareness of her physical beauty. Never had he seen a face so perfect, a neck so elegant, a mouth so lush. He felt irritated that what she was wearing hid her body completely. Why would a woman so beautiful dress herself in such awful clothes? That drab green trench-coat was awful. The black dress underneath looked almost as bad as her chunky black shoes.

The only black Royce liked to see on a woman was in the underwear department, and then only in passing. If she were *his* woman, he'd dress her in a deep red, or emerald-green, or peacock-blue. And he'd adorn those gorgeous slender ankles of hers with the highest strappiest sexiest shoes he could find.

Hell, she was leaving!

Not one to be slow off the mark, Royce leapt into action, contriving to bump into the woman as she exited the shop.

'I am so sorry,' he apologised, gripping her elbow to steady her. 'Are you all right?'

'Perfectly, thank you,' she said crisply.

Up close she was even more exquisite, he thought, his desire for her increasing with each second. God, if only they were back in the caveman days...he'd knock her on the head and drag her back to his lair where he wouldn't let her see the light of day for weeks!

'I should have been watching where I was going,' he said, relieved to find that her hands were ringless. He always steered well clear of married women. 'Could I offer you a cup of coffee, perhaps, by way of apology?'

Those incredible black eyes of hers blinked wide as they lifted to his face, fear immediately shooting into their inky depths.

Royce was shocked. What had she seen in his face to make her react like this? He thought he was being all smooth charm; that his carnal intentions were well hidden behind a suitably suave façade.

'No, thank you,' she whispered shakily. 'I…I have to go.' And before he could blink, she bolted across the foyer and out through the glass doors, diving into one of the taxis waiting there. She was gone before Royce could gather his wits enough even to note the number and make of the cab.

'Damn,' he muttered, hating to lose, even in something as transitory as a passing fancy.

A passing fancy?

That didn't do justice to the passion that had possessed him on looking into that dark, tempestuous gaze. What he wouldn't give to see them fling wide with ecstasy, not fear!

An idea leapt into his belatedly clearing brain, and, whirling, he strode into Whitmore Opals.

GEMMA WAS standing there, thinking about Melanie's unexpected visit, when someone coughed. Startled, she looked up to find a man on the other side of the counter, a tough-looking man with intense blue eyes and a five o'clock shadow on his chin.

'Excuse me, miss,' he said in a Michael Caine accent. 'That lady you were just talking to. The lady with the black hair. I'm sure I know her. Was she English, by any chance?'

'Melanie? Oh, no, she's Australian. At least, I think she is…' Gemma frowned, realising she knew nothing much about Melanie except that she'd been the housekeeper at

Belleview for a couple of years, and had an unhappy past, her husband and baby having been killed in a car accident some years ago.

'You mean you know the lady *personally?*' the English tourist was asking.

She smiled at him. 'Yes, I do. She works for my father-in-law.'

'Your father-in-law,' he repeated, giving her an incisive look. 'But you look far too young to be married.'

'Well, married she is,' announced another male voice.

'Nathan!' Gemma exclaimed, delight quickly changing to consternation when she saw how her handsome husband was scowling at the Englishman. Surely he didn't think the man had been flirting with her!

'This is my—er—husband,' she said, feeling flustered with Nathan's display of jealousy. It wasn't the first time he'd made things awkward when he thought a man was paying attention to her. At first, she'd found his possessiveness flattering, but not so much any more.

'Nathan Whitmore,' Nathan said coldly, and held out his hand.

The Englishman shook it. 'How do you do? Royce Grantham.'

'I thought I recognised you,' Nathan remarked, not sounding overly happy about this man's identity. 'So what is the one and only Royce Grantham doing in our small corner of the world?'

Gemma stared hard at the man but was none the wiser. The name and face meant nothing to her. Which wasn't surprising. She'd only begun to appreciate her ignorance of the world at large since she'd started work in this store two months ago. The Regency Hotel was a mecca for celebrities passing through Sydney. They often browsed through Whitmore Opals, the rest of the staff teasing her over how she always failed to recognise them.

'I'm holidaying,' Mr Grantham said. 'I've just arrived in your beautiful city and have been admiring the sights.'

'So I noticed.'

Gemma cringed at her husband's dry tone.

Their visitor, however, was undeterred. 'I saw that magnificent opal in the window and thought I'd come in and ask about it.'

Gemma's eyes flew to the man's. That was a lie. Or, at least, a twisting of the truth. He'd come in primarily to ask about Melanie.

'I'm afraid I won't still be here for the auction on the twenty-first,' he went on. 'I take it, Mr Whitmore, that you are the owner of Whitmore Opals?'

'No, I am not.'

When Nathan wasn't forthcoming with further information, Gemma stepped in. 'Whitmore Opals belongs to my husband's father,' she volunteered, her stomach tight with agitation. Why did Nathan have to act like this? She hated it. Thank the lord Mr Grantham didn't seem offended. He looked very tough indeed.

'The father-in-law you mentioned?' he asked, one eyebrow lifting.

'Yes, that's right. Mr Byron Whitmore.'

'And where would I be able to contact him?'

Gemma picked up and handed over one of their business cards which had the head office address and telephone number listed as well as the two city stores. 'The head office is not far from here,' she told him, hoping the smile mitigated her husband's rudeness. 'Byron should be there till five at least. If he's not in, you could ask to speak to his daughter, Jade, or to a Mr Kyle Armstrong. He's head of marketing.'

The Englishman smiled at her. 'Thank you for all your help, Mrs Whitmore. You've been most kind. Mr Whitmore,' he nodded curtly, and strode from the shop.

Now that Mr Grantham was gone Gemma couldn't look at Nathan. She knew if she did she wouldn't be able to keep the exasperation out of her eyes.

'I thought I'd drop in and take you out for a surprise

lunch,' he said, then added drily, 'It looks as though I arrived just in time.'

Now her eyes snapped up. 'And what does that mean?'

Nathan flashed her a frustrated look. 'Just get your coat, Gemma. I don't want to argue with you in front of people.'

Gemma glanced around the store and noticed that a couple of customers were throwing curious glances their way. The rest of the staff were diplomatically ignoring them. Feeling disconcerted, Gemma hurried into the back room where she dragged her coat down from the coat-stand and picked up her handbag.

'I'm going to lunch now,' she said as she walked past the other two salesgirls. 'I should be back by two.'

They murmured their assent and soon Nathan was guiding Gemma from the hotel entrance and out into the city street.

'There was no need for you to be so rude to that man, Nathan,' she blurted out at last.

'There was every need,' he bit out, his fingers digging into her arm through the coat. 'I suppose you're going to tell me you don't know who Royce Grantham is.'

'No, I don't. All I know about the gentleman is that he's English.'

'He's no gentleman. Not even remotely.'

'You know him, do you?'

'I've read about him.'

'What is he, then? A movie star or something?'

Nathan's laughter was harsh. '*Or something* just about describes him, I would think. He won the Formula One world championship two years on the trot, and has a reputation for being the most cut-throat ruthless driver that ever drew breath.'

'So? What has that got to do with me, or what happened just now?'

'He also has a reputation for being just as ruthless with women. The man's a predator of the worst kind, and I won't have him hanging around *my wife.*'

Oh, how Gemma was beginning to hate the way Nathan said that! *His* wife. She had a name, didn't she? She was a person, not a possession.

'You've got it all wrong, Nathan,' she sighed. 'He wasn't the slightest bit interested in me. If you must know, he came in to ask about Melanie.'

'Melanie ?'

'Yes. She'd just been in to show me what she'd bought for Jade and Kyle for an engagement present, and to make sure we hadn't forgotten about the dinner Byron is having for them tonight. Mr Grantham had apparently glimpsed her through the window and thought he knew her.'

'Good God, Gemma, don't you know that's the oldest trick in the book? It's you he wanted to meet. As if a man would look twice at Melanie when he had someone as breathtakingly lovely as you in his sight. Lord!'

Nathan ground to a halt and turned Gemma to face him, his expression reflecting frustration and concern. 'When are you going to realise what this world is really like, darling? It's rotten through and through, and most of the people in it.'

Gemma groaned. 'I hate it when you talk like this, Nathan. I've always believed that most people were good and I want to keep holding on to that belief. Please don't try to change me.'

His face softened as love filled his gaze. Now Gemma melted. When he looked at her like that she forgave him anything, even his persistent jealousy and world-weary cynicism. 'As if I would ever want to change you, my darling,' he whispered, cupping her face and kissing her gently on the lips. When his mouth lifted, then returned for a fiercer kiss, she drew back.

'Nathan, we're in the street!'

'So?'

'Do you like embarrassing me?'

'Maybe I like checking that you can still *be* embarrassed,' he said darkly. 'Come on, let's go and have some lunch and you can tell me what Melanie was doing in the city anyway. Never known that woman to set foot outside of Belleview except to visit her brother every Sunday!'

MELANIE PAID OFF the taxi and dashed inside, relieved to be safely home at Belleview.

That awful man, she thought breathlessly. Trying to pick me up like that. Did he think she didn't know what he wanted, or that she hadn't met the likes of him before?

But that wasn't the worst of it. The worst was the way he'd made *her* feel for one mad moment. As though she actually wanted to go with him!

Melanie had been struggling to keep that appalling realisation at bay all the way home in the taxi. And she'd managed fairly well by concentrating on feelings like outrage and indignation. But now that she was alone, she could no longer find the will to deny the truth.

Yes, she'd found him instantly attractive. Yes, she'd been flattered by his obvious pass. Yes, she'd been momentarily tempted to have coffee with him. And maybe more...

Her moan of bewilderment and dismay came from deep within her soul.

She'd been so *sure* no man could ever make her feel like that again, so sure that that part of her life was dead, as her husband and baby were dead. After what happened with Joel, she wanted to have nothing more to do with men and, quite frankly, there hadn't been one incident in the past few years to shake her belief that she would live the rest of her life in a sexless void.

Till today...

A memory of the man's ruggedly handsome face and hard, sexy blue eyes flashed into her mind and she shuddered. Maybe it was a one-off thing, came the clutched-at hope, an aberration never to be repeated. If it was, then she was safe. After all, she would never see him again. Sydney had four million people in it and, given her tendency to leave Belleview only rarely, the odds of running into that individual again were not worth worrying about. Besides, he had sounded English. No doubt he was a tourist, just passing through.

Her logical thoughts having soothed her near panic, Melanie levered herself away from the front door to make her way shakily across the wide marble foyer. But as she passed the huge Italian gilt mirror that hung on the wall, her reflection halted her, a gasp of shock flying from her lips.

Was that her, that flushed impassioned-looking creature with pink cheeks and eyes like glittering black coals?

A cry of torment flew from her lips and she dropped her handbag on the marble console beneath the mirror, leaning on both with white-knuckled intensity.

'Melanie! Are you all right?'

Gathering herself with great difficulty, Melanie sought for the impassive face she usually found comfort behind, but it took its time in coming. Only by the greatest effort of will did she turn a composed face to the plump woman sweeping down the marble staircase.

'It's that time of the month, I'm afraid,' she lied valiantly. 'I'll be fine in an hour or two.'

'You shouldn't have gone out shopping,' Ava said kindly. 'I could have bought whatever it was you had to buy. Oops...'

Melanie froze when Ava's foot slipped on the bottom step and she almost went flying. Luckily, she was able to grab the corner of the balustrade to right herself and Melanie heaved a ragged sigh of relief. Thirtyish and overweight, Ava Whitmore was the most accident-prone person she had ever known. Hardly a day went by without her either falling over, or crashing into someone, or breaking something.

Melanie felt sorry for her employer's younger and only sister. What sort of life did she have, spending all her days painting watercolour landscapes that she never finished, then filling her evenings watching endless movies on television and video? Ava had never had a real job or a real boyfriend in her life. Apparently, Byron had routed a few males of the gold-digging variety in her earlier days, leaving the woman with little self-esteem and a tendency to cocoon herself from real life.

Yet she was a warm, motherly woman with a lot to offer the right man. Not bad-looking either, with lovely blue eyes and a pretty mouth. All she needed to look presentable was to lose a few pounds and get that awful ginger hair dyed back to its original brown.

Melanie found it ironic that she would want for Ava what bitter experience told her was a hazardous path to happiness. Wasn't Ava's self-imposed seclusion a safer option to her going forth into the world and putting her future into the hands of a member of the opposite sex? Melanie was not nearly as vulnerable a type as Ava, yet the man *she'd* trusted and loved had ultimately destroyed her life, along with her capacity either to trust or to love a man ever again.

She'd thought Joel had also destroyed her capacity to respond in *any* way to a man again. But it seemed she'd been wrong about that, she realised with a shudder of self-disgust.

'I think you should come with me to the kitchen,' Ava suggested, taking her elbow with uncharacteristic firmness, 'where you can sit down while I make you a cup of tea.'

Melanie gave in gracefully and was soon seated at the breakfast bar while Ava busied herself making the tea, during which activity she first spilt the sugar, then dropped a mug which, luckily, didn't break.

'I must have the dropsy today,' she said breathlessly.

Finally, the tea was safely made and Ava hoisted herself up on to a stool to devour her own, along with several chocolate biscuits. Melanie wished she wouldn't eat so many sweet things but didn't say anything.

'What do you think of Jade and Kyle Armstrong becoming engaged so quickly?' she said instead. 'Not to mention her moving in with him.'

Ava shrugged. 'Young people don't know how to wait for things these days. Still…I would never begrudge Jade any happiness. She's had a hard time of it lately, what with her mother dying in that boating accident and all.'

'That's true,' was Melanie's non-committal remark.

Privately, she thought Jade was better off without her mother, who'd been an atrocious neurotic who'd thankfully spent more time in sanatoriums than home with her husband and daughter at Belleview. She'd been in one such place when Melanie had originally accepted the position as Byron's housekeeper. She might not have come to Belleview at all if Mrs Whitmore had been in residence at the time, for it had infuriated Melanie to watch a mother being so emotionally abusive of her daughter. Didn't she know how lucky she was to *have* a child? Luckily, Jade was a girl of some spirit. A more timid person would have withered under Irene Whitmore's constant criticism and sarcasm.

As for Jade's father…Byron Whitmore was a patriarch of the old-fashioned type, overbearing, bossy and chauvinistic. Clearly, he'd found his daughter's rebellious teenage years a bewildering experience, failing to understand what lay behind her outrageous escapades. From what Melanie herself had witnessed, Irene had been very clever and sly in her parental tyranny and Byron never saw first-hand what his daughter had to put up with. It was no wonder the girl had sought love outside the home. She'd received little enough within its walls.

Jade deserved a break in Melanie's opinion, and the break had come along in the guise of Kyle Armstrong. The new marketing manager for Whitmore Opals was just what that girl needed, a strong hand and a loving heart. Best of all, he seemed to have cured the girl of her one-time infatuation for Nathan, who was not the man for any young girl.

Which brought Melanie to thinking about Nathan's recent marriage to Gemma.

She frowned. From the moment Nathan had brought Gemma home to Belleview a few months ago, it had been obvious the girl was smitten with him. And why not? Nathan was incredibly handsome in the golden-boy style of a young Robert Redford. At only twenty and country-naïve, Gemma was no match for a thirty-five-year-old sophisticate hell-bent on sampling her glorious innocence.

What Melanie—and quite a few others—had not expected was that Nathan would marry the girl. His ex-wife had been as stunned by the union as everyone else, because Nathan had vowed never to remarry, his divorce only having come through two years ago. His daughter Kirsty had been very upset, because she'd hoped that her parents would ultimately reconcile. A foolish hope, given that the pair had never been in love. Or so Ava had told Melanie when Lenore and Nathan had called their marriage quits some time back.

'I'd give Kyle's and Jade's marriage a far better chance of success than Nathan and Gemma's,' Ava suddenly said, as though her mind had been going along the same track as Melanie's.

'I have to agree with you on the age-difference alone,' Melanie commented. 'Fifteen years as opposed to what? Six or seven? How old is Kyle, exactly?'

'Twenty-eight, I think.'

'Still,' Melanie mused, 'Gemma seemed happy enough when I saw her in town today.'

'It's only been a few weeks. Wait till the honeymoon wears off and Nathan shows his true colours.'

Ava's tartness surprised Melanie. Was it possible she had once been infatuated with Nathan herself? Though herself immune to his brand of sex appeal, Melanie had seen it in action plenty of times. Yet as a person he remained an enigma to her. What lay behind the cool glamorous mask he wore? What kind of man was he really?

'Tell me about Nathan, Ava,' she asked carefully, sipping her tea in a casual fashion. 'He was only sixteen when Byron adopted him, wasn't he?'

'He'd turned seventeen by then,' the other woman corrected, an acid tone in her voice. 'Seventeen, going on thirty. Understandable, considering the kind of life he was living.'

'What kind of life was that?'

'The kind a lot of street kids fall into up at the Cross, I suppose. Living off his wits. *And* his body.'

Melanie sat bolt upright. 'Are you saying Nathan prostituted himself?'

Ava shrugged. 'Not exactly. But I overheard Byron telling Irene about finding him living with a woman of forty! If that's not a form of prostitution I don't know what is!'

'But he was only a boy then, Ava. If that was what was going on, surely the woman was the one to blame, not Nathan! Besides, I can't see Byron bringing anyone basically bad into his own home.'

'My brother can be very blind sometimes. All he would have seen was a boy in need, a soul in danger of being lost, and he would have been compelled to save him. To give him credit, Nathan has done Byron proud in most respects. He worked hard to learn the opal business and his plays have taken the world by storm. Though God knows why. I think they're over the top.'

'I've never seen one. What's over the top about them?'

'The way the characters behave. They're so emotional in a frightening, out-of-control way. The stories are cruel and violent as well. His plays don't entertain you. They disturb you. I only went to one and one was enough, thank you.'

'Yet Nathan is a very controlled person himself,' Melanie murmured thoughtfully.

'Yes. Odd, isn't it?'

'Maybe…'

Ava sighed. 'He's a puzzle all right, I'll give you that. Still, he's always been a good father to Kirsty and at least he did marry Gemma. Though I wonder if he only did that because of Byron.'

'Why because of Byron?'

'You know what a stickler Byron is for doing the right thing, and Nathan does like to keep in Byron's good books. Byron thinks the sun shines out of him. Of course, there have been certain incidents with certain females in the past that Byron never saw and which I for one would never enlighten him on. But who knows? Maybe I'm wrong. Maybe Nathan's changed. Maybe he genuinely loves Gemma. We can only hope, I suppose. But, as they say, leopards don't change their spots.'

A pensive silence developed, broken when the telephone on the kitchen wall rang.

'I'll get it,' Melanie said immediately, fearful that any hurried movement of Ava's might result in another accident.

'Belleview,' she answered.

'Byron here, Melanie. There'll be another person for dinner tonight. A gentleman. I hope that will be all right.'

'Yes, of course.'

'Sorry to give you such late notice. Must go. I have some important business to finish up and I don't want to be late home.'

The line went dead and Melanie rolled her eyes.

'What is it?' Ava asked. 'Is there anything wrong?'

'No. Just Byron adding another head to the dinner party tonight.'

'Oh? Who?'

'I don't know. A gentleman. Look, if I don't get a move on there won't be any dinner party tonight. At least, not one with food.'

'Can I help?'

'Oh—er—no, I don't think so, but thanks for offering. Rita will be here later to set the table and help serve. You go and make yourself pretty. Who knows? The gentleman Byron's bringing home might be an eligible bachelor.'

'Even if he is, he won't look at the likes of me,' Ava said bleakly.

'Don't sell yourself short, Ava. You've got a lot to offer a man.'

'Only my money.'

'That's not true. You're a very attractive woman.'

'I'm too fat. Most men only want slim and sensational.'

'More fool them.'

Ava was startled by the bitter tone in Melanie's voice. She had never heard the other woman sound so vehement. Come to think of it, Melanie wasn't her usual self today. She seemed…agitated. And it had nothing to do with the time of the month. Something had happened during her shopping trip, something that had upset her.

Ava wished she could ask her about it but Melanie might think she was prying. Byron's housekeeper was a very private person who kept her own counsel and clearly liked it that way. Ava sighed and slipped from the stool, her heavy landing reminding her of her weight.

No man is ever going to look at me, she thought wearily. Why I bothered to go and buy that new outfit I have no idea. Still, I might as well go and try to make a silk purse out of a sow's ear. I've got nothing else to do.

CHAPTER TWO

By six-thirty that evening Melanie was grateful she'd chosen a menu which was deceptively easy to prepare, because, where Ava had had dropsy earlier, *she* had now developed a severe case of distraction.

The reason did not elude her. It was crystal-clear. Irritatingly so. She could not get the incident with that man out of her mind.

'Damn him,' she muttered, banging the cutlery drawer shut.

'I hope you're not talking about me.'

Melanie swung round as her employer strode into the kitchen from the direction of the garages.

'You're early home for a Friday,' she said, sidestepping Byron's comment.

'I wanted to be showered and changed by the time Royce arrived. I told him seven, which means if he's on time I'll have him to myself for a while. The others aren't due till seven-thirty.' He was taking off his tie as he hurried through the room. 'Make sure both ice-buckets in the drawing-room are full, will you, Melanie?'

Byron was gone before she could do more than draw breath. Ever since his shattered leg had finally mended, he'd been a whirlwind of energy, his mind going as fast as his body. Though fifty next birthday, he was by no means middle-aged, either in looks or manner. An exceptionally handsome man, with thick wavy black hair, elegantly grey at the temples, he propelled his impressively proportioned body around with a dynamism that a man twenty years his junior would envy.

A thought suddenly crossed Melanie's mind.

I wonder what Byron does for sex these days?

Instant irritation sent her winged black brows drawing together. There she was again, thinking thoughts that wouldn't normally occur to her these days! It was all that damned man's fault. Him and his sleazy looks and filthy desires.

Filthy?

Now Melanie brought herself up short. She'd never been one of those women who'd thought sex dirty or filthy. She'd always enjoyed making love, even those first nervous attempts with her high-school sweetheart.

A smile of wry remembrance pulled at her generous mouth. What a hopeless pair they had been! His name had been Grant, and he'd been rather sweet and shy, even at eighteen. They'd been going together for a couple of years before he'd drummed up the courage to ask her to go all the way. His lovemaking had been very basic and fumbling, and, while Melanie could not say she'd ever seen stars, she had loved the feel of his hands on her body, loved the warmth and intimacy of it all.

Grant had lasted all during her year at secretarial college, right up till she secured a job as a secretary-receptionist for Eagles Advertising Agency, an American company with a highly successful branch in Sydney. There, she'd caught the eye of an up-and-coming advertising executive named Joel Lloyd. From the moment Joel Lloyd decided Melanie Foster was the woman for him, poor Grant didn't stand a chance.

A bitter taste invaded Melanie's mouth as she thought of the difference between her two lovers. Two years it had taken Grant to work up the courage to consummate their relationship. Joel had seduced her in the company store-room two weeks after they'd been introduced. And she'd very definitely seen stars!

But that had been typical of Joel. He was one of those men who took risks, who dared while other men dithered. He'd been a ruthless man, there was no doubt about that. What a shame she hadn't realised right from the start just how ruthless he was, then maybe her baby would still be alive...

Melanie shuddered before giving herself a mental shake. I'm not going to think about the past any more. If I do, I'll go mad. I'm going to concentrate on the here and now of my life, which is that all of a sudden a man has sparked an unexpected and unwanted sexual response in me. With a bit of luck, that spark will snuff out again, quite quickly. I'm certainly going to work on it, because sex can make a woman vulnerable to a man, and I am never going to be vulnerable to a man again. Never ever!

Melanie set about the final preparations for the evening meal, annoyed to find that her train of thought had made her uncomfortably aware of her woman's body beneath her simple black skirt and white blouse. Her breasts felt tight against her bra, and when she walked she was conscious of her stockings brushing together at the tops of her thighs. God, but it was proving hard to concentrate on doing even the simplest task.

What a pity that tonight of all nights Rita couldn't come to lend a hand. Rita's teenage son had come down with the chicken pox and with her husband not due home from work till late she felt she had to stay home. Melanie could have rung round the assortment of casual helpers she had on her books, but that would have taken as long as just doing it all herself. Normally, she could have handled a dinner party for seven standing on her head, but tonight she was not her usual efficient self.

Now what was it Byron had asked her to do? Oh, yes, the ice-buckets in the drawing-room. Melanie hurried to collect the buckets and was filling them with ice-cubes from the freezer when the front doorbell rang. The clock on the wall said five to seven, which meant Byron's special guest was early—a most uncommon occurrence these days. Muttering, Melanie sped back to the drawing-room, replaced the buckets in the drinks cabinet and dashed to answer the door, smoothing any stray hairs back behind her ears as she went.

Feeling quite harried, she couldn't even drum up a polite smile as she opened the door.

Even if she had, it would have frozen on her face.

'You!' she exclaimed, black eyes rounding. 'What... what are you doing here?' she cried, quickly followed by an outraged, 'How dare you follow me?'

Too late it occurred to Melanie that the unwanted personage on the front doorstep was wearing a dinner suit. This afternoon, he'd been dressed in faded blue jeans and a brown leather jacket. Would a would-be pursuer put on formal dress simply to chase after a female prey? And would he have waited till evening to knock at her door? Not very likely.

Reality returned with crashing embarrassment.

'You're Byron's extra guest,' she realised aloud, groaning silently. This was fate at its most wicked! 'Royce Something-or-other,' she added in a raw whisper.

To her mortification, he laughed. 'That's me all right. Royce Something-or-other.'

Her temper rose at his obvious amusement, and she had to fight for composure. 'Byron didn't tell me your full name,' she said agitatedly.

'He didn't tell me yours, either. Melanie what?'

Those sharp blue eyes locked on to hers and in that moment it came to her in a swamping wave of shock that she'd been right the first time. He *had* followed her. Somehow. This was no fickle finger of fate. This was man at his most dangerous and predatory. She didn't know how he'd found out where she lived or how he'd wangled an invitation to dinner tonight, but she knew, without a shadow of doubt, that he had. He was another Joel, this Royce Something-

or-other. She recognised the type as forcefully as her sub-conscious had recognised it earlier in the day.

Unfortunately, she still seemed to find this type insidi-ously attractive.

Her breath caught in her throat as her eyes swept over him once more. The dinner suit lent an urbane elegance to his hard lean body. His thatch of thick straight brown hair had been tamed with some gel and swept back from his high forehead. The five o'clock shadow he'd been sporting earlier in the day was gone, replaced by an aftershave that was fresh and tangy. But despite his superb grooming there was still something uncivilised about him which made her heart leap and her senses spring to attention.

It was his eyes, she realised, that gave him away. For their expressive blue depths were the windows to his soul. And his soul was the soul of a dark and dangerous man, a man who didn't know how to lose. Oh, yes, she recognised the type, only too well.

But forewarned was forearmed and be damned if she would let him know her susceptibility to such men.

'My name is Melanie Lloyd,' she said coolly. 'I am the housekeeper here at Belleview. I am thirty-two years old and a widow. I do not date. *Ever*. Do I make myself clear, Mr Royce Something-or-other?'

'Perfectly. For the record, my name is Royce Grantham. I am thirty-six. Single. And I do date. A lot. On top of that I think you are the most exquisitely beautiful woman I have ever seen.'

Her mocking smile would have put off most men, as would the acid tone of her words. 'How very original of you, Mr Grantham. Do come in. Byron is looking forward to your no doubt entertaining company. But might I give you a word of warning? He's not a man who likes flattery so try not to indulge your obvious tendency for flamboyant exaggeration.'

'You know Byron well, do you?' his guest drawled as he followed the wave of her hand inside.

For a second Melanie's nostrils flared, her eyes flashing with fury at the implication behind his words. But she refused to give this horrid creature the satisfaction of an angry retort. Gathering herself, she dredged up one of her frostiest faces and turned its chill upon him full blast. 'I've been Mr Whitmore's housekeeper for two years, during which time I have come to appreciate the genuine gentleman he is. Now if you will come this way, Mr Grantham, I'll settle you in the drawing-room and find out what is keeping your host.'

Melanie was sure she didn't breathe till she left the drawing-room. Her head was whirling and she had to stop on the first step of the staircase to pull herself together. Their visitor had not said another personal word to her, but she had felt the magnetic pull of his eyes, even as she left the room.

Why he should be as interested in her as he so obviously was, amazed her. She'd long passed the days when her looks had stopped men in their tracks. Oh, yes, there had been a time, in the early years of her marriage to Joel, when that had happened. Joel had been a man of great sophistication and taste, and known exactly how to make her over from the pretty teenager he had married into a very striking woman. He'd dressed her in vivid colours, and in simple but daring styles which more often than not required a minimum of underwear. And of course her long black hair had always been worn loose then.

But Melanie was under no illusion about her appearance these days. She mostly wore black and in unbecoming styles. She used no make-up and her hair was always pulled back in a severe knot or roll. If that wasn't enough to deter a man, her aloof manner usually polished off any burgeoning interest.

Yet something—some perverse appeal—had made this man fancy her enough to pursue her. And he didn't mean to give up. If Melanie knew anything about this type of male, it was the stubbornness of his ego. He would be merciless in the chase. And bold.

It was the boldness that bothered her the most.

Because boldness had once excited her. Very much.

'Did I hear the doorbell ring just now?'

Melanie glanced up to see Byron hurrying down the stairs towards her. Also dressed in black dinner suit, he was much more traditionally handsome than the man seated in the brocade armchair in the drawing-room. Why didn't Byron excite her? Why didn't *his* sexy blue eyes send her blood racing?

'Melanie?' Byron stopped to touch her on the shoulder, concern on his face. 'Are you all right, my dear?'

She stiffened under his touch, for it left her cold, as his eyes left her cold.

Her covering smile was born of panic, for she couldn't bear for Byron to get a hint of what was troubling her. 'Sorry. Just wool-gathering. Yes, that was the doorbell. I put your Mr Grantham in the drawing-room. He said he'd wait for you to join him before he had a drink.'

'Good.' Byron reached up to give his black bowtie a last straightening. 'So what did you think of the famous Royce Grantham, eh, Melanie?'

'Famous?' she repeated blankly.

'You mean you don't know who he is?' Byron seemed amused. 'Isn't that just like a woman? I'll bet Ava doesn't recognise him, either. Royce Grantham happens to have won the Formula One world championship not once, but twice! He retired at the height of his career a couple of years back.'

'What's he doing here?' Melanie asked, her throat dry.

'He's passing through Sydney on a world tour and staying at the Regency. Apparently he's become quite a collector during his travels, and when he saw our Heart of Fire opal in the hotel shop he came to see me, thinking he could persuade me to sell it to him before the auction. He's got Buckley's, I'm afraid. But he insisted on a further chance to persuade me so I invited him along tonight. Who knows? Maybe we'll be able to get him to buy some of our other opals instead. He's damned rich enough to afford a swag.'

Byron moved on, leaving Melanie to stare after him with a sinking feeling in her stomach. A world champion racing driver... She should have guessed he'd be something like that. A risk-taker of the first order. A thrill-seeker extraordinaire. A raving lunatic!

When her heart began to beat even faster, she groaned anew. Turning, she fled back to her kitchen, determined to hide there till circumstances forced her to leave.

The first circumstance was the front doorbell ringing at twenty to eight. Muttering to herself, she hurried to answer it, meeting a nervous-looking Ava in the foyer. Melanie was taken aback to see the other woman wearing a surprisingly elegant royal-blue silk trouser suit whose simple long-line jacket and loose-legged trousers hid her plumpness very well.

'My, don't you look nice!' she complimented warmly. 'That's new, isn't it?'

Ava flushed with pleasure. 'You really like it? I bought it at a boutique Lenore told me about which specialises in making big women look better. I'm thinking I might go back and splurge on some more outfits.'

'Why don't you? That one looks great.'

The doorbell rang again.

'Do you think that's Byron's gentleman guest?' Ava whispered, looking a little more confident now.

Melanie's insides contracted at this reminder of Royce Grantham. 'No, he arrived half an hour ago.'

'He did? Goodness, he was early. What's he like? Don't tell me he's an old fogy!'

'Hardly. He's one of those crazy Formula One racing drivers,' Melanie bit out. 'Byron says he was once world champion.'

Ava's eyes lit up. 'You mean he's Italian?'

Quite clearly, Italian men figured largely in Ava's romantic fantasies. 'Sorry. British. A Mr Royce Grantham. I must answer the door, Ava,' she excused herself. 'Why don't you go along to the drawing-room? Byron and Mr Grantham are having pre-dinner drinks in there.'

'I think I'll wait and go along with whoever is arriving.'

Melanie opened the door to find both couples standing there, waiting. Nathan and Gemma. Kyle and Jade.

What a striking foursome they were, she thought: Nathan, coolly resplendent in a white dinner-jacket; Gemma, lush in wine-coloured velvet; Kyle, wickedly handsome in black and Jade, dazzling in a red wool dress that showed every curve of her spectacular figure.

Melanie began to appreciate how Ava must feel sometimes, having to compete with her glamorous family, though at least tonight Byron's sister could hold her own. She really did look very attractive in that blue. Melanie's compliment seemed to have done wonders for her confidence as well, for she came sashaying forwards without putting a foot wrong and proceeded to shower everyone with warm kisses, adding hearty congratulations to the newly engaged Kyle and Jade.

Melanie extended her own best wishes as she hung up various overcoats, and, when she got the chance, drew Jade over to the console in the hall where she had placed the present she had bought them earlier that evening.

'I saw this and couldn't resist,' she explained on handing the prettily wrapped package to a startled Jade.

'Oh, how kind of you! Wasn't it kind of Melanie, darling, to buy us a gift?' she directed at Kyle, who joined them, smiling.

'Very kind,' he agreed.

Melanie was pleased that both of them seemed to genuinely like her present—an antique photograph frame made in real silver, with a scrolly edge that was both intricate and romantic-looking.

'I thought you could put one of your wedding photographs in it,' she suggested. 'When is the big day to be? Have you set a date yet?'

Jade flashed her fiancé a surprisingly coy look. 'Soon, I think,' she murmured.

'Very soon,' Kyle insisted.

Jade laughed, her eyes still on the man she loved. 'Perhaps we'll elope, like Nathan and Gemma here.'

'I think Byron might appreciate the privilege of giving his only daughter away, don't you?' Kyle advised gently.

'Speaking of Byron,' Ava piped up, 'you'll never guess who he has in the drawing-room.' She glanced around the group, looking and sounding like a little girl, dying to tell a secret.

'You're quite right, Ava,' Nathan said drily. 'We couldn't guess, so just tell us. But if you say Celeste Campbell then I for one won't believe you.'

'Neither will I,' Jade laughed.

Now if there was one thing Melanie would have liked to find out about her employer it was what lay behind the feud between him and Celeste Campbell. But she doubted she ever would. Byron's hatred of his half-sister-in-law and main business rival was only exceeded by his reluctance ever to discuss her. She was verboten in this household!

'Don't be ridiculous, you two,' Ava said reproachfully. 'Hell will freeze over before Byron invites Celeste Campbell to Belleview. No, it's Royce Grantham. You know... the champion British racing car driver!'

'*Really?*' Jade exclaimed, the only one of the foursome to look pleased by the news. Kyle was frowning, and Nathan exchanged a glance with Gemma that bespoke more than a passing irritation at the news of an additional guest. Privately, Melanie agreed that Byron shouldn't have imposed a virtual stranger—no matter who or what he was—on what was essentially a family occasion. But Byron was not large on sensitivity. Unfortunately.

Oblivious of the sudden atmosphere, Jade breezed forward and slipped an arm through Ava's elbow. 'I've read about him. He's supposed to be a one with the ladies, if I recall. You'd better watch yourself, Auntie. You're looking rather scrumptious tonight in that blue suit. Have you been on a diet?'

'Not really.'

'Well, you're looking fab, so I'm going to stay close and ward off Mr Grantham's passes. Or do you want him to make passes? Yes, of course you do. How silly of me!' She was off and propelling Ava down to the drawing-room before any of the others could stop her. Nathan urged Gemma after them, Kyle dragging the chain, his frown deep and dark.

Melanie could only assume that Kyle had met Royce at Whitmore Opals head office today, and either didn't like him, or didn't like his trying to persuade Byron to sell the Heart of Fire before the ball. Why else would he be perturbed by the Englishman's presence? It wasn't as though Jade was upset by her father's inviting an extra guest, even if Nathan was.

Whatever, it seemed Melanie wasn't the only person who didn't want Royce Grantham's presence here this evening. Still, not wanting him here wasn't going to change anything. He was here. Neither could she do what she would dearly love to do, which was vanish herself for the next few hours. She had to serve dinner, from the hors-d'oeuvres to the last cup of coffee. All she could do to cope was hide her agitation behind a coolly controlled façade.

Everyone else would probably think she was in one of her remote moods. But tonight, it would all be acting. Melanie felt far from remote when she thought about being in the same room as Royce Grantham. And far from coolly controlled.

CHAPTER THREE

GEMMA COULDN'T believe it!

Nathan could, of course.

Even as they'd been driving through the gates of Belleview a few minutes before, he'd made another pointed remark about her naïveté over men. She'd scorned his opinion that Royce Grantham would show up to bother her
again, and what happened? Her supposed admirer turned
up here as a dinner guest tonight.

Coincidence was impossible. That infernal man had deliberately wangled an invitation from Byron so that he
could see Melanie again. But since Nathan hadn't believed
her assertion the first time that it was Byron's housekeeper
the Englishman was interested in, then he wasn't going to
the second time either.

Even if Royce Grantham *had* taken a fancy to her,
Gemma would still have been upset with Nathan's attitude.
It took two to tango, didn't it? Where was his faith in her
love, his trust? Did he honestly believe she would go off
with some stranger? She loved Nathan to death and no
other man interested her. Yet her husband was looking dag-
gers at her as they traipsed after Jade and Ava. Anyone
would think, by the expression in his eyes, that she had
planned this all herself!

'Ah, there you are,' Byron boomed as they entered the
drawing-room. 'Come and meet Royce. I'm sure the men
will recognise him, if not the ladies.'

Gemma, for one, almost didn't. *Again.* What had the man

done to himself since lunchtime? Where had the rough and tough image disappeared to?

In its place was a suave, elegant, almost handsome creature who looked like he'd stepped out of one of those fashion magazines. His black dinner suit fitted like a glove, its satin lapels as sleek and shiny as his hair. Amazing!

She stiffened as those sharp blue eyes of his started running over their group, seemingly searching for something—or someone.

Melanie, Gemma hoped, and held her breath. She couldn't help sighing with relief when his gaze slid right over her without stopping, a fact which Nathan couldn't have failed to notice.

'Clever bastard,' Nathan muttered in her ear. 'He doesn't want to look obvious.'

Gemma could have screamed. Only by clenching her teeth hard in her jaw did she stop her frustration from finding voice. Better not to say anything, she decided. Arguing with irrational people was a waste of time.

A disturbing thought jumped into her mind as she stood there, seething silently. This was exactly the tack she'd been forced to use with her father in the weeks leading up to his death. For some reason, after she left school, he'd become extra paranoid and possessive about her, refusing to let her leave Lightning Ridge to find work, and often losing his temper if she was five minutes late home. At first she'd stood up to him, but when he retaliated with violence she'd begun to handle his irrational outbursts with silence. And while this was physically safer, she'd hated the triumph in his eyes when he thought she'd been cowed into submission.

Gemma slid a frowning glance up a her husband. Surely her relationship with Nathan wasn't going to develop the same minefields as her relationship with her father? She didn't want to have to tippy-toe around his moods for fear of potential outbursts, didn't want to feel she couldn't *talk* to him, couldn't discuss things in a sane, logical fashion.

Once again, she was struck by how little they did actually talk. This lack of communication had raised its ugly head on their honeymoon at Avoca, but she hadn't noticed it so much since they'd returned to Sydney to live and she'd started working. Maybe she'd been too busy. True, Nathan did make an effort to stop his writing as soon as she came home of an evening, but more often than not they went out—first to dinner and then to the theatre or a movie. It was hard to have meaningful chit-chat in a restaurant, or in a crowded theatre. Then, when they finally returned to the flat, Nathan would take her to bed and make beautiful love to her, after which he would promptly fall asleep.

Still, most women would have thought Gemma had it made. She lived in a glamorous unit overlooking Elizabeth Bay, had a glamorous job working in a ritzy opal store, wore glamorous clothes which cost more than most people earned in a year, and had a glamorous husband who was mad about her. In a way, she felt impatient with herself. What more did she want?

The answer was crystal-clear. To have a truly close relationship with her husband, where they knew and understood each other deeply, intimately, where their love was expressed in other ways besides sexually, where she was his friend and confidante, not just his lover.

Gemma dragged herself back to the present to hear Nathan explaining to Byron that they had already met Mr Grantham earlier that day.

'Really? Where?'

'At the Regency shop.'

'Ah, yes, of course. Royce said he'd been there, looking at the Heart of Fire. But what were you doing there, Nathan? I thought you were well into a new play.'

Nathan shrugged. 'I've had to put it aside for a while. It's not working out.'

'In that case you should consider my other offer.'

'What other offer?' Gemma joined in, frowning. Why hadn't he told *her* his writing wasn't going well?

'I'm having trouble finding the right director for the play of Nathan's that I'm producing. I've asked Nathan to consider doing it himself. He'd be perfect. Still, we'll talk about that later. Jade, come over here. Kyle, where are you? Why are you lurking back there near the door? Come and join Jade so that we can finish these introductions and then break open the champagne to toast your engagement.'

Kyle came forward, a wry smile on his face. 'Mr Grantham and I are also previously acquainted,' he said, slipping an arm around Jade's waist and kissing her on the cheek. 'There's nothing for it, darling. We'll have to tell everyone the truth before your father's guest lets the cat out of the bag.'

'The truth?' Ava said, blue eyes blinking wide with curiosity. 'What truth?'

Kyle cleared his throat. 'My last name is not Armstrong, but Gainsford. I've been going under an alias since coming to live here in Sydney.'

Byron was truly taken aback, an angry flush slanting across his high cheekbones. 'Why the devil would you do that? God, you're not some kind of con-man, are you?'

Royce's dry chuckle sent everyone's eyes his way. 'I wouldn't worry about your future son-in-law, Byron, if I were you. The reason Kyle and I know each other is because he was one of my financial backers during my last years on the track. I suspect he could buy you and me both out and still have the odd billion or two left over.'

This news brought an assortment of gasps and stares, plus a mischievous giggle from Jade. 'See the trouble you've got yourself into?' she told her fiancé. 'I told you we should have told everyone before, but no, you said you were enjoying your anonymity too much. Next time you'll listen to me, won't you? Ah, here's Melanie with some much needed refreshments. I think we need something to pop into all the goldfish mouths around the room. Melanie, did you hear Kyle's little confession? Ah, yes, I can see by the look on your face that you did. Well, go on, darling,' she went on, jabbing Kyle in the ribs. 'Trot out the reason behind your deception. Truly, everyone, it's better than Zorro. I haven't heard it nearly often enough yet. It's so wonderfully romantic. And then, when you're finished, we'll drop our other bombshell, shall we?'

Kyle groaned. 'I can see there'll be no stopping you.'

'There never has been any stopping my daughter,' Byron said drily.

'You're right about that, Byron,' Kyle agreed, giving Jade a look of such love and approval and understanding that Gemma's heart turned over. If only Nathan would look at *her* like that. Passion was all very well, but sometimes it wasn't enough.

'If you don't tell us the story soon, Kyle,' Ava spluttered, 'I'm going to explode!'

'I'm rather curious myself,' Mr Grantham said, amusement glittering in those expressive blue eyes of his.

Kyle sighed. 'This will probably sound hopelessly sentimental and melodramatic, but here goes. The fact is…I've always found my inherited fortune a huge barrier when it came to relationships. It brought me plenty of attention from the opposite sex, but experience gradually taught me that it was very difficult for a man as rich as myself to find a woman to truly love him. I was reaching the age where I wanted to marry and have a family, so I decided to move interstate and assume a false identity where I could look for a wife as an ordinary chap with an ordinary job. I knew Jade was the girl for me the first day I saw her, and luckily she felt the same.'

'I always thought there was something fishy about you,' Nathan said with an ironic chuckle.

'Well, I didn't!' Byron muttered crossly.

'I'm sorry I had to deceive you, Byron,' Kyle went on. 'But I've tried to do a good job at Whitmore's and I'd like to continue as head of marketing. To be honest I'm enjoying the challenge. There's no need for my secret to go any further than this room for a while yet, is there? Jade and I plan to have a very private garden wedding with only her immediate family present so there shouldn't be any problem with publicity.'

'But what about your family, Kyle?' Gemma asked. 'Don't you want to invite them to your wedding?'

'I don't have any family here in Australia. My parents were killed in a bush fire when I was only a tot. I am...' he smiled down at his fiancée '...the classic poor little rich boy who's been lucky enough to find a woman who loves him for himself.'

'And who's going to have his baby,' Jade murmured before throwing her father a slightly worried look.

She needn't have worried. Byron's initial shock soon gave way to a wide beam of delight. 'A baby! My first grandchild! How wonderful!' He came forward to hug his daughter and shake Kyle's hand. 'The wedding will be soon, I hope.'

'As soon as it can be arranged.'

'Well, this does call for champagne. Lucky we put a *couple* of bottles on ice, eh, Royce? We have two reasons to celebrate now. What a night this has turned out to be!'

Amen to that, Melanie thought ruefully as she moved around the room, serving a silver tray of hors-d'oeuvres while Byron and Royce handed out glasses of champagne. She lingered with Nathan and Gemma, exchanging pleasantries, then chatting to Jade till she saw that Royce had moved away to take a glass of champagne to Ava. Melanie filled in a little more time telling Byron about Rita's inability to help tonight, but finally had no option but to approach the enemy. By this time, he was standing in front of the fire, leaning a casual elbow on the mantelpiece while he sipped champagne and listened attentively to a highly animated Ava.

'I really shouldn't,' Ava murmured when presented with the tray.

'I don't see why not,' her companion said, managing to bestow a charming smile upon her while his eyes were all for Melanie. Her black gaze bored back into his, conveying an icy contempt for what he was doing, bewitching poor Ava while secretly lusting after the household help.

Did he think such tactics would make her jealous? He had a lot to learn about Melanie Lloyd if he thought he could manipulate her. Oh, he could set her heart beating with those sexy eyes and that hard virile body of his but never would she let him know it. She'd rather die than give a man—especially a carbon copy of Joel—the slightest power over her again.

'Will you stay and have a glass of champagne with us, Melanie?' Ava asked innocently.

'Can't, I'm afraid, Ava. Rita couldn't make it tonight so I'm all alone in the kitchen.'

'I'm pretty good in a kitchen,' Royce drawled. 'Want a hand?'

'Thank you for the kind offer,' she said with false sweetness, 'but I'm sure Byron wouldn't appreciate a dinner guest spending the evening in his kitchen.'

Her smile was pure acid before she turned away, having decided to leave the food behind as self-serve and escape this corrupter's presence post-haste. But when she bent over to lower the tray on to the nearby coffee-table, her straight black skirt rode up slightly at the backs of her legs, as well as pulled tight across her hips and buttocks. Despite her back being to Royce, the hairs on the nape of her neck suddenly stood up on end and she just knew he was watching her intently, not only watching her but undressing her with his eyes.

Appalled at the persistent sexual nature of her thoughts— not to mention the undeniable heat coursing through her veins—she swiftly straightened, wiping sweaty palms down the sides of her skirt. 'When do you want me to serve dinner, Byron?' she asked, amazed to hear that her voice sounded steady.

'Not for another half-hour, Melanie,' her employer informed her. 'The food won't spoil, will it?'

'Not at all.' The smoked salmon entrée was already on its serving plates under cling-film and would keep indefinitely. The Thai pork main course was an easy stir-fry with all the ingredients pre-prepared, and the coconut caramel pudding was sitting in the refrigerator, only needing to be popped in the microwave for a couple of minutes.

Melanie had found through experience that dinner parties went more smoothly if as much of the menu as possible could be prepared or cooked beforehand. That way, delays posed no real problem. It also eliminated the possibility of last-minute cooking disasters.

Of course no amount of 'being prepared' could have prepared her for the perturbing influence of Mr Royce Grantham.

'Before I go, Byron,' she said, still marvelling at the coolness she was superficially exhibiting, 'I took the liberty of choosing the table wines for you. I hope you don't mind, but the whites did have to be chilled. The reds, of course, can easily be changed, if they don't meet with your approval.'

'Melanie, my dear, your ability to choose wines to complement your excellent cooking is only exceeded by your unflappability under fire. I was telling Royce earlier what a treasure you are. He seemed to think that my inviting him home to dinner at the last minute might cause a stir, but I assured him you were rarely rattled by anything.'

'And I told Byron,' Royce said from beside her shoulder, 'that if he didn't watch it, I might steal you away from him. I am in need of a housekeeper of your calibre for my home back in England.'

'My God, did you hear that, everyone?' Byron laughed. 'He's trying to seduce Melanie away from us. You've got Buckley's, Royce. Melanie's practically one of the family. Besides, she knows I'd be lost without her. Ava, my dear, your glass is nearly empty. Come over here and I'll top it up.'

'I'll double your salary,' Royce offered quietly before Melanie could escape his insidious presence.

She glanced up over her shoulder at him, only to have those wicked blue eyes clamp on to hers with a resolve that was frightening.

'I'll give you anything you want,' he stated boldly, 'if you come with me.'

'What I want, Mr Grantham,' she returned shakily, 'is for you to leave me alone.'

'Liar.'

Melanie turned fully to stare at him. 'How dare you?' she whispered fiercely under her breath.

'Are you Byron's mistress? Is that it?'

Now her eyes and nostrils flared wide, and a small smile pulled at his hard mouth. 'Don't bother to answer. I can see that you aren't. Just as well. I wouldn't have liked that. No, I wouldn't have liked that at all.'

His voice was low and hushed, so that the others could not overhear. But for all its softness, it was no less commanding, and quite terrifyingly hypnotic. 'Sorry to be this crass—it's not normally my style—but I have so little time. I've always found that if you want something badly enough, then sometimes the only way to get it is to go after it, boots and all. I want you, Melanie Lloyd. It's as simple as that. I find you breathtakingly beautiful and incredibly intriguing and so damned sexy I'll have to have ten cold showers when I get back to my hotel room tonight. Unless, of course, you're there with me...'

Melanie caught her breath. My God, did he honestly expect her to do such an outrageous thing? Had other silly females come running when he clicked his fingers at them?

Yes, she realised with a chilling acceptance of this man's success rate with women.

Fortunately, she had previous experience with a similar man which spelt out for her the danger inherent in surrendering one's will to an individual whose only concern was self.

Melanie summoned up what she considered her most withering look.

'I take it that's a no?' he drawled.

Without lowering herself even to give him an answer, she whirled away and strode rapidly from the drawing-room, hoping that her haste was construed by the others as need to hurry back to the kitchen and not the fleeing of a panic-stricken woman.

For underneath her very real fury at Royce for his arrogant presumption lay a startling susceptibility to his compliments.

It wasn't often that a woman was told she was breathtakingly beautiful and incredibly intriguing. Nor that she was so sexy that her pursuer would do anything to have her. Such talk could turn the head of any woman, let alone one as intrinsically lonely and possibly as frustrated as Melanie.

She had to constantly remind herself over the next half-hour of the type of man she was dealing with here. He was a daredevil who would employ any audacious tactics to get what he wanted. And that included flattery and outright lies. Next, he'd be telling her he *loved* her!

Still, it was damned hard not to imagine what spending the night in Royce Grantham's bed would be like.

It was all Joel's fault, she decided savagely as she raged around the kitchen. He had taught her how exciting sex could be with a man like him: how addictive even. She'd thought she'd been cured of such needs by his treachery, but it seemed she hadn't. Obviously, she was still a woman in its most basic sense, still a female animal, compelled by mother nature to mate with the male of her species.

I am not an animal, she argued as she set about removing the film on the entrées and arranging them on a tray. I am a human being. I do not have to give in to my baser instincts. I have will-power and pride to protect me from that marauding male in the drawing-room.

Ah, yes, pride. I've always been big on pride. Maybe too much so.

But not this time. This time pride will serve me well. Do I want to be reduced to nothing more than another sexual scalp on Royce Grantham's belt, another notch on his gun, another trophy for his memoirs?

'Over my dead body,' she muttered angrily.

Melanie glanced at the clock and felt her stomach tighten. Time to summon the guests to the dining-room and start serving the meal. Time to test her pride.

She did surprisingly well, she thought afterwards, though grateful that there was no soup on the menu. She probably would have slopped it everywhere, especially that first time their eyes met and he had the gall to smile at her.

Ten o'clock found her removing the plates from the main course and checking that everyone wanted dessert, and whether they wanted cream or not.

'Only a small helping for me, please, Melanie,' Ava said, smiling coyly. 'And no cream.'

'I thought you said you weren't dieting, Auntie,' Jade piped up.

Ava blushed. 'I'm not.'

'She certainly doesn't need to,' Royce put in suavely. 'I like a woman with a bit of meat on her.'

This comment was accompanied by a direct glance at Melanie's well-rounded bust. When an embarrassing heat zoomed into her cheeks she wanted to curl up and die. Gemma, for one, was looking at her curiously, as was Nathan. They know what's going on, she realised, and blushed all the more.

'Same here, Royce,' Byron was saying, totally ignorant of the by-play between his housekeeper and his guest. 'Once a woman reaches a certain age she looks better with her bones well covered.'

'I think that depends on the woman,' Jade said. 'Celeste Campbell must be pushing forty and she's reed-thin. I saw a photo of her in a women's magazine the other day, hosting some harbour party on her yacht. She was dressed in a bikini and looked sensational. I'd like to look half as good when I'm her age.'

'She probably does a lot of exercise,' Ava said with a sigh.

'Yes,' Byron snapped. 'All in her bedroom! For pity's sake, Jade, what is your fascination for that atrocious woman? You're always bringing her up.'

'Well, she is my aunt, you know,' Jade defended. 'Not to mention Whitmore Opals' main competition.'

'Maybe not for much longer.' Byron's smile was vengefully smug. 'I hear their sales are suffering since those reports appeared on television about their bribing Japanese tour companies to bypass all other duty-free stores in favour of theirs. I was wondering if you had something to do with those stories, Kyle. Not that I'm objecting, mind.'

'I may have dropped the right word in the right ear a while back,' he admitted coolly. 'I happen to own a part-share in the first television station to run that particular exposé.'

Byron laughed. 'I can see you're an invaluable man to have on our side. But surely, you're not going to continue being Whitmore's marketing manager indefinitely, are you?'

'No, I'm grooming Jade to take over next year. I really will have to get back to overseeing my own interests by then.'

'But surely Jade's too young and inexperienced!' her father argued. 'And she's going to have a baby. Her place is in the home, not in business!'

'Jade's place is where she's happiest,' Kyle defended firmly. 'Most women can combine a family and career these days if that's what they want. As for her being young and inexperienced...she's actually better qualified than I am. Most of the new ideas Whitmore's have been successfully putting into practice over the past few weeks have been hers. I have great faith in her and I suggest you should too.'

'Enough of that, darling,' Jade intervened, laughing. 'I appreciate your support but I can fight my own battles. Pops, shut up and drink up. Melanie, I'll have a double helping of dessert, since I'm eating for two!'

Melanie suddenly realised she was still standing there, agonising over her earlier embarrassment, instead of getting the dessert. She'd even forgotten who wanted cream and who didn't. All she could remember was that Ava only wanted a small helping. Flustered, she fled the room, deciding to put the cream in a jug so that people could serve themselves.

She waited as long as she could before putting the dessert plates on a tray and making her way back to the dining-room. The conversation around the table had moved on to the opal Royce supposedly wanted to buy, with both Jade and Kyle strongly vetoing any sale before the ball.

Melanie put the tray on the sideboard, placed the jug of cream in the centre of the table, then started placing a serving in front of each person, the smallest going to Ava, the largest to Jade.

'You'll have to stay on in Sydney for the auction if you want the Heart of Fire that badly,' Byron was saying to Royce as she gave her employer his slice of pudding. 'What's another fortnight to secure something so unique and precious? You won't get another opportunity, you know. Thanks, Melanie.'

Once again, Royce managed to catch her eye as he spoke. 'I couldn't agree more. Yes, I think I will stay till the ball, after which I'm going to take my unique and precious find straight back to England. I've a mind to see it adorn my home there. I have just the spot—in the master bedroom.'

Melanie reefed her eyes away. Was he really talking about the opal? Or herself? Despite all her earlier resolves, she found her mind filled with images of herself in that master bedroom. Herself and Royce.

Help me, pride, she prayed. Help me…

'But what if someone bids higher?' Gemma asked.

'I doubt they will. I've always been prepared to spend as much money as is necessary to get something I really want.'

Now Melanie's black eyes flashed his way again from where she was standing behind Byron's shoulder. So that was his strategy, was it? If all else fails, bring out the cheque-book. My God, did he honestly think he could *buy* her?

'You really want our pride and joy that much, eh?' Byron said.

'I certainly do.'

'Then we'll see you at the ball?'

'Most assuredly. I'll pop down to the shop and pick up tickets tomorrow morning. You'll be there, will you, Mrs Whitmore?' he directed at Gemma.

'Yes, of course,' she smiled, thinking to herself that he really was quite charming. And obviously very taken with Melanie. Why, he couldn't take his eyes off her every time she came into the room.

'No, I'm afraid you won't be, darling,' Nathan said, astonishing her. She sat there stunned for a second, while he spoke directly to Royce. 'Gemma and I will be spending the day with my daughter. My ex-wife has an—er—appointment she can't get out of.'

'But…but…' Gemma finally started stammering.

He took her hand and patted it. 'I forgot to tell you about it, darling. But not to worry. I'll telephone the store manager personally and smooth things over for you. They can call in one of the casuals. Really, there's no big problem, is there Byron?'

'Of course not. You're only working there as a little hobby, after all, Gemma.'

CHAPTER FOUR

GEMMA'S ANNOYANCE with Nathan was momentarily exceeded by outrage at Byron for speaking so patronisingly about her job.

Why, her sales figures were better than any of the other girls'! And she spoke Japanese much more fluently than anyone in the store, because she'd worked very hard at mastering the difficult language. Neither did she shy away from using it as some of the others did. In fact, she'd been so successful with Japanese tourists that they often asked especially for her.

'I don't think of my job as a hobby, Byron,' she said, trying not to sound as hurt as she felt.

'I should say not!' Jade jumped to her defence. 'What an old chauvinist you are, Pops. Take no notice of him, Gemma. I don't.'

'So I've noticed,' her father retorted drily. 'I'm glad Kyle's taken over your reins, daughter, dear. It'll be good to let someone else worry about you in future.'

'Why should I worry about Jade?' Kyle shrugged. 'She's a grown woman with a mind of her own and more nous than most men I know. As for taking over her reins...my God, if I started telling Jade what to do or how to behave, she'd have me for breakfast.'

'You'd better believe it,' she said with a determined-sounding laugh. 'You're going to marry a liberated lady here and don't ever forget it!'

'Better you than me, Kyle,' her father pronounced.

'There again, to each his own. I have to admit that I prefer the old-fashioned kind of wife.'

'Amen to that,' Nathan muttered under his breath.

Gemma closed her eyes momentarily against the gatherings of a headache. Jade had just put her finger on the root cause of her unhappiness, and Nathan had just verified it. He didn't want the sort of partnership Kyle and Jade had, where they shared everything on an equal footing— careers included. He wanted a wife of the old brigade, one who always deferred to her husband's opinion, one whose needs and ambitions were not considered or taken seriously, one whose only job was to keep her hubby happy—especially in the bedroom.

No doubt, at the appropriate time and when it suited him, Nathan would make her pregnant, after which she would be expected to give up her 'hobby' and retire to become an old-fashioned mother.

Gemma found it incredible that the thought of having Nathan's baby no longer gave her the pleasure it once would have. Dear heaven, hadn't she told Ma just before leaving Lightning Ridge that her dearest dream was to marry a nice man and have loads of babies? And hadn't she written to her old friend after marrying Nathan and told Ma she couldn't wait to have that big family she'd always wanted? Now here she was, shrinking from even having *one* baby.

But how could she look forward to a pregnancy, if it meant she would have to leave a job she enjoyed, only to be imprisoned at home with no one to talk to and nothing to do? Nathan would probably also veto her doing any of the housework and cooking, just as he'd started vetoing other things he thought weren't good for her, such as seeing Royce again.

The bottom line was he was treating her like a child, making decisions for her, not trusting her judgement, acting like an autocratic father rather than the caring, loving husband she'd mistakenly thought he would be.

'Coffee, Gemma?'

Gemma opened her eyes and smiled a wan smile over her shoulder at Melanie. 'Yes, please.'

Melanie's returning smile as she placed the cup of coffee on the table had a sisterly understanding behind it that made Gemma feel better, and oddly stronger. In the absence of Ma, Gemma considered calling Melanie some time in the near future and asking her for advice on how best to tackle her problem. After all, she'd been married once. Maybe Melanie could advise if a new bride should fight openly for what she wanted right from the start, or try to achieve change in more subtle manipulative ways.

Take the problem she was faced with tomorrow. Gemma wanted to go to work. She suspected that Nathan's excuse about their having to take out Kirsty was probably a lie. Even if it was true, she knew darned well that the last person Kirsty wanted to spend the day with was herself. The girl still hadn't really forgiven her for marrying her father, and thereby smashing her dream of her father getting back with her mother. Not once since their marriage had Kirsty visited them, or wanted Gemma with her father when he took her out. Even on her recent birthday, she'd bluntly told Nathan that Gemma wasn't welcome at her party.

Gemma believed if she didn't go to work tomorrow she would end up spending the day in the unit alone, just because Nathan had some weird idea in his brain that Royce Grantham was interested in her. What was wrong with her husband? Hadn't he seen for himself the various looks the Englishman had given Melanie all evening? He'd hardly given *her* a glance, or directed more than polite conversation her way.

Gemma suspected that this was one problem that couldn't be solved with subtle methods. She would have to stand up for her rights and make Nathan understand how she felt about his treating her like some silly girl with no mind of her own.

Yet the thought of an argument later than night was an upsetting and daunting one. Things had already been strained between them since their confrontation over Royce earlier in the day. Maybe she should just give in to Nathan's wishes this once. Gemma supposed it wasn't every day that a champion racing car driver would cross her path. It was probably his reputation with women that was bothering Nathan.

This thought started her thinking about what such a man would want from Melanie. Was he only looking for a holiday fling, some woman to show him a good time while he was here in Sydney? Or was the attraction deeper than that? Maybe he was on the lookout for a wife, now that he'd retired from his dangerous sport. Though, somehow, Gemma doubted it. Royce Grantham didn't look the marrying kind. Which only left an affair.

But Melanie was not the sort of woman to indulge in casual sex, of that Gemma felt certain. Frankly, in the months Gemma had known her, she'd shown no interest in men whatsoever. At first, Gemma had believed this had been due to her husband and baby being killed in that accident, but as she'd got to know her better Gemma wondered if her marriage had been a happy one. Sometimes Melanie showed an icy contempt for the male sex that the tragedy alone could not explain.

Before tonight, Gemma would have thought any man's chances of attracting Melanie were less than zero, but there was no doubting Royce Grantham had made an impression on the normally indifferent housekeeper. A couple of times Gemma had caught them exchanging highly charged looks, and once Melanie had actually blushed. This in itself was so unlike the other woman that Gemma had to revise her thinking on what Melanie might and might not do. Gemma herself knew how vulnerable a female could be when a man had set his sights on her seduction.

When she sighed, Nathan turned to her. 'You haven't

drunk your coffee, darling. Is there anything wrong with it?'

'What? Oh…no…no, I was just daydreaming.'

'About what?'

'Nothing really. I'm tired, I guess.'

'Then perhaps we should go home. Byron, Gemma's a bit on the weary side. Would you mind if we left as soon as we've finished our coffee?'

'But it's only eleven,' he complained. 'And I was going to talk to you about the play.'

'There's no need. I've already made up my mind about that. I'll do it.'

'You *will*? Even with Lenore in the leading role?' Clearly, Byron was astonished. So was Gemma. She simply stared at her husband, totally speechless.

'I don't see why that should present a problem,' he drawled dismissively. 'Our divorce was quite amicable, no matter what others believe. To be honest, now that Lenore and I are no longer living together, we're better friends than ever.'

Gemma's whole insides contracted as a past incident suddenly jumped into her mind. It had happened the very first day Nathan had brought her here to Belleview to be his daughter's minder, at a time when she had already fallen under his spell, and when he'd subsequently claimed he was already smitten with her. Yet that night she'd stumbled across him kissing Lenore in the billiard-room, their embrace so passionate that neither of them had seen her standing in the doorway. She'd always meant to ask Nathan about that kiss, but had never seemed able to drum up the courage. Then, when he'd asked her to marry him, scorning any feelings for his ex-wife, she'd driven any worry about that kiss—or his still being in love with Lenore—to the back of her mind.

Now the worries resurfaced. She didn't want him directing Lenore in that play, didn't want him spending that much time with her. The woman was exquisitely beautiful, her elegance and sophistication always making Gemma feel a little gauche by comparison. No doubt she knew exactly how to please a man sexually, whereas Gemma still had moments of shyness and inhibition in that department.

Gemma's stomach churned when she thought of Lenore happily having pleasured Nathan in all sorts of erotic ways during their marriage. Feelings of inadequacy and jealousy burnt within her, and she resolved that she would be more daring in the bedroom in future, and not pull back from some of Nathan's more adventurous suggestions like some prudish virgin. Usually he laughed gently at her embarrassed reactions, then simply moved on to some other more acceptable activity or position. But how soon before his outer patience waned and he began to find her boring?

With these new concerns revolving round in her mind, Gemma decided not to make an issue of going to work tomorrow. Best take the line of least resistance this time. She didn't want Nathan angry with her when he started directing Lenore in that play...

But all her good intentions went out the window when, a few minutes into their silent drive home, Nathan said crossly, 'I don't like it when you sulk.'

Indignation and a sudden flaring of temper sent her eyes snapping his way. 'I'm not sulking. But even if I were, then you shouldn't be too surprised. I would just be acting the way you've been treating me all night. Like a child!'

'Don't be ridiculous, Gemma. I've done no such thing.'

'What do you call it then when you tell me I'm not going to work tomorrow, simply because you think Royce Grantham might make a line for me? Blind Freddie could see that the woman Royce has set his sights on is Melanie, not me. Good grief, Nathan, didn't you see the way he looked at her tonight?'

'I saw. But I know Melanie. She won't come across, which means Mr Grantham will be left with a severe case of frustration which he will seek to ease with the next available female. Namely you!'

Gemma threw her hands in the air. 'I don't believe this. Anyone would think I didn't have any say in who I chose to go to bed with. Why would I want Royce Grantham when it's *you* I want, *you* I love? Or don't you believe I truly love you, Nathan?'

There was an electric silence till they pulled up at a red light, where Nathan slowly turned his head her way. His face was irritatingly unreadable, those grey eyes of his both cool and steady. 'All I'm trying to do is protect my wife from the sort of man most women have few defences against, let alone a young inexperienced girl like you. This is not a question of love, Gemma, but a question of lust. Believe it or not, a woman can love one man and still be made to feel lust for another.'

'I don't believe that.'

'Of course you don't, but there again, you're only twenty years old. Your opinion might change in a few years. To give you an example, however, my erstwhile ex-wife loved another man during our entire marriage. But she thoroughly enjoyed going to bed with me, I can assure you.'

Gemma gasped her shock. 'I don't believe you.'

His mouth twisted into a sardonic smile. 'Which part don't you believe?'

Gemma's thoughts whirled. She could hardly refute that Lenore enjoyed Nathan making love to her. She'd seen the evidence before her own eyes. As for Lenore's being in love with someone else... If Nathan said that was so she supposed it was. It would certainly explain the divorce, and his bitterness. Despite what he'd said tonight at dinner, he hadn't been happy about the divorce. Was that because he *was* still in love with Lenore? Maybe, when he spoke of being able to love one person and lust after another, he was talking about himself.

A grim bleakness swept into Gemma's heart. Maybe Nathan had married her simply because he lusted after her.

Maybe he'd never loved her. Now that she thought about it, he'd never actually said he did. He'd said he wanted her and adored her but he never used the word 'love'.

'Do you love me, Nathan?' she asked shakily.

Now, his steely composure broke. 'What kind of stupid question is that? Of course I do. Good God, why do you think I married you?'

'I'm not sure,' she said, bewildered and unhappy. 'Why don't you tell me?'

'I married you because I love you, dammit! Surely you're not going to be one of those women who want to be told that every day, are you?'

Gemma shook her head. Why did admitting that he loved her make him angry? Or was it her forcing him to *talk* that made him angry?

'No,' she sighed, still not at all sure that he did. It brought her mind back to the woman at the core of her doubts. 'Who is Lenore in love with?'

'I'm not at liberty to say.'

'Why not?'

'The man's married and still living with his wife and family.'

Gemma gasped. 'And Lenore's sleeping with him?'

'You don't think she's living the life of a nun, do you? Who do you think she's spending tomorrow with?'

'My God…'

'Does that shock you?' His laughter was harsh and dry. 'Good. Maybe now your rose-coloured glasses about people might begin to smear a little.'

Gemma fell silent, her mind fighting to separate reality from Nathan's cruel cynicism. He wasn't above trying to paint Lenore as morally and sexually loose, simply to persuade her to his point of view that most people were like that—or *could* be like that, given the right circumstances.

Gemma's natural aversion to such cynicism had her trying to put aside her natural jealousy of Lenore and see her as she really was. Past memories provided a picture, not of a Jezebel, but a strong-minded woman of good character and strength. Lenore was a decent woman, Gemma decided, not a scarlet one.

'Are you suggesting Lenore slept with this man while she was married to you?' she asked, disbelief in her voice.

'How should I know? Maybe she did and maybe she didn't. She *says* she didn't. But as I've already said, Lenore wasn't unhappy in my bed, which proves my point that love and lust can coexist in the same person.'

'Maybe with Lenore but not with me,' she stated firmly. 'And not with a lot of other people, I'll warrant.'

'You say that because you're young, and inexperienced.'

'I thought you *liked* the fact that I was young and in-experienced,' she argued, her frustration acute.

'I do,' he insisted.

'Maybe you'd rather I was more like Lenore?' she flung at him, stung by a mental image of Lenore doing those things she still felt inhibited about.

'Good God, no! Why ever would you say such a thing?'

'Perhaps because I saw you kissing Lenore one night and *both* of you were certainly enjoying it, not just your ex-wife!'

Thank God they were stationary, the way Nathan's head whipped round. 'What in God's name are you talking about?'

She told him, watching as his frown smoothed into a sardonic smile. 'Oh, yes, I remember.' He laughed then. 'I suppose you won't believe me when I say that wasn't Lenore I was kissing that night. It was a certain young woman in a sexy pink sundress who'd aroused me to a fever pitch of desire. Lenore said something that touched a nerve and before I knew it I was taking my frustration out on her. Being the mature, sensible woman that she is, she went along with it for a diplomatic minute or two before kicking me delicately in the shins and thereby bringing me to my senses.'

His self-mocking tone did not entirely soothe Gemma's doubts. 'So you're not still in love with her?'

'Heaven forbid! But your wording suggests I once was. I never loved Lenore, nor she me. She flirted with me one night in an attempt to get back at her beloved who would have none of her, and I took her up on the unspoken invitation. We went to bed and she got pregnant with Kirsty. She refused to have an abortion and I refused to spawn a bastard, so we got married and tried to make the best of it.'

The light turned green and the Mercedes purred forwards. Nathan's smile was relaxed now as he looked over at her. 'Have you been harbouring these silly doubts all the time?'

She nodded, indeed feeling silly. But none of this entirely eliminated the fact that Nathan clearly had no faith or trust in a woman's love, hers included. No doubt Lenore's behaviour was responsible for this. It seemed incredible to Gemma that a woman could love one man and enjoy sleeping with another. Though she had to concede that if that man was Nathan there were extenuating circumstances. Not only was he incredibly handsome with a beautiful body, but he was a superb lover, very knowledgeable about a woman body's and how to give it pleasure. He seemed genuinely to adore female flesh. The feel of it, and the taste. He did things to her with his hands and mouth that made her quiver all over just thinking about them.

She jumped when his hand came over and covered her knee.

'Wait till I get you home and I'll show you just how much I love you,' he rasped.

Gemma tried not to tense. Was this his only way of showing her he loved her?

For the rest of the drive home, Gemma couldn't help mulling over what he'd said about lust and love. Could people always differentiate between the two? Might someone think they were genuinely in love when in fact they were in the grip of lust? If so, what happened when their lust began to wane, when suddenly there was nothing left to base a relationship—or marriage—on?

Gemma arrived back at their unit, tense and afraid. The last thing she wanted now was for her husband to make love to her.

CHAPTER FIVE

MELANIE WAS STACKING the dishwasher when Royce walked into the kitchen, a brandy balloon in one hand and a cigar in the other. Melanie didn't say a word, eyeing him coldly as he walked over and slid up on to one of the breakfast bar stools. He eyed her back with an insouciant smile, giving the amber liquid a couple of swirls before lifting it to his lips.

'Good cognac, this,' he said, putting the drink down to take a deep drag on the cigar.

'I don't allow smoking in my kitchen,' she said frostily, and slid a small souvenir ashtray on to the counter in front of him.

'No trouble.' Stubbing the end of the cigar into the picture of the Opera House, he left its smouldering remains there and returned to a leisurely sipping of the cognac.

Melanie folded her arms and glared at him. 'If you're going to offer me a job as your housekeeper again, then forget it. There isn't enough money in the world to induce me to work for you.'

'Not to worry. I've given up on that idea.'

'But you haven't given up on *me*, have you? If you had, you wouldn't be here now.' Her hands unfolded to rest on her hips, her aggressive stance allowing her simmering fury better expression. 'What excuse did you give Byron for a trip to the kitchen? Or is this a detour from the powder-room?'

'Carrying cognac and a cigar? Hardly. No, I told him the truth.'

'You told him you wanted to chat up the cook?'

'*Chat up* the cook?' His expression was one of mock innocence. 'Now why would I want to chat up a woman who's made it perfectly clear she's not interested in me? Or am I mistaken…?' His eyes narrowed upon her face and its undeniably high colour. 'Perhaps you always play this game with men who are as passionately attracted to you as I am. Perhaps it adds something to your eventual capitulation to give them a hard time first.'

'You're mad!' she gasped.

'Yes,' he agreed smoothly. 'About you. And I don't think you're as indifferent as you pretend to be. Your body language is a dead giveaway, Melanie, as is the intensity of your so-called outrage. I think you just might want me as much as I want you.'

Melanie achieved composure with a supreme effort of will. Her gaping mouth snapped shut, her lips pursing in a parody of primness. She consoled herself with the fact that Royce couldn't possibly see into her mind, into the awful fantasy that was video-playing there in full CinemaScope.

'What a ghastly man you are!' she snapped, angrier with herself than with him. 'And you couldn't be more wrong. I detest men like you. *Detest* them, I tell you!'

'"The lady doth protest too much methinks,"' he drawled, and drained the brandy.

Much to Melanie's consternation, he put down the now empty balloon, slid off the stool and began making his way around to where she was virtually imprisoned in the galley-style kitchen, her only escape quickly blocked by Royce's approaching body.

She shrank back into the far corner, eyes wide, heart beating wildly in her chest. 'If you touch me, I'll scream!'

He stopped an arm's length away from her, his almost handsome face tipping to one side as he surveyed her own stricken features with curiosity and dark puzzlement. 'I think, perhaps, you mean it.'

'I *do*!'

For several tormenting seconds he just stood there, watching her, narrowed eyes raking over the rise and fall of her breasts before lifting once again to her flushed face.

'No,' he denied at last with a confidence that totally threw her. 'You don't.'

If he'd grabbed her roughly, she might still have screamed. But he didn't. He drew her trembling body to his quite slowly, tipping her chin up even more slowly, holding her wide black eyes with his hard blue eyes for ages before his mouth descended.

Melanie hated herself for standing there and allowing him to kiss her. She especially hated that it was *her* lips which parted first. Immediately, Royce deepened the kiss, shattering any illusion Melanie might have been holding that she could resist this man. Her bones went to water beneath the onslaught of his mouth and tongue and soon she was clinging to him, clinging and moaning softly.

'Oh, God, Melanie,' Royce groaned, breaking the kiss to press impassioned lips to her throat. 'Come back to the hotel with me tonight. I've already asked Byron if you could have tomorrow off. I said I was going to ask you to show me around Sydney but he seemed to think you wouldn't agree.' His mouth covered her ear, making her shiver uncontrollably when his tonguetip traced the shell-like opening then dipped inside. 'He doesn't know the real you, does he?'

The real you...

Royce's words cut through the haze of her arousal like a knife, stabbing deep into her heart.

The real you...

She wrenched back out of his arms and might have slapped him across the face if she'd been quicker. But he easily grabbed her wrists, holding them in front of her heaving chest while he shook his head in wry reproach. 'Don't, Melanie. It's not necessary. I *like* the real you.'

'You don't know what you're talking about,' she cried,

humiliation sparking a defiant anger. 'You don't know the real me. You'll never know the real me!'

'Then I'll settle for the Melanie I just kissed, and who kissed me back with such passion. That's the Melanie I want to know.'

'Oh, I don't doubt it,' she scorned, yanking her hands out of his grasp. 'The trouble is, I don't want you to know *any* Melanie. I don't like you, Royce Grantham.'

His laughter was dry. 'Then you have a funny way of showing it.'

'Has it occurred to you that you might have struck me at a weak moment?' she flung at him, determined to dent his ego a little while finding an escape for herself. 'Maybe I'm simply in need of a man. *Any* man. You know what widows are like,' she jeered. 'They can get quite desperate.'

'And is that what you are, Melanie?' he taunted softly. 'Desperate?'

'Not so desperate that I would go to bed with the likes of you!'

His eyes darkened, his face hardening. 'I'm getting tired of this game, Melanie. You're going to spend the weekend with me and that's that!'

'I most certainly am not!'

She could see the muscles clenched hard in his jaw. 'Don't be so bloody stupid.'

'And don't you be so bloody arrogant!'

'Melanie, for pity's sake…'

She laughed, a hard, bitter sound. 'Don't you talk to me of pity, Royce Grantham. That word isn't in your vocabulary. Now go away. I have no intention of going back to your hotel with you tonight or of showing you around Sydney this weekend.'

He slanted her a long, thoughtful look. 'Is that your final word on the matter?'

'It is.'

'I could kiss you again, you know, and show you up for the hypocrite you are.'

Fear zoomed into her eyes, bringing irritation and confusion to Royce's face.

'I don't understand you, Melanie Lloyd. If you weren't attracted to me, I could accept being rejected. If you were involved with another man, I might even back off in gracious defeat. But there is no other man, is there? I wonder what it is that frightens you so much about me...'

'You don't frighten me,' she defended, but lamely.

'Oh, yes, I do. I terrify the life out of you. And I aim to find out why. I'll accept your right to say no tonight, but this isn't the end of us. Not by a long shot. I'll be calling you tomorrow, and the next day, and the next. And sooner or later you'll either tell me the truth or you'll give in and go out with me.'

Whirling on his heels, he strode back around the long counter and stalked from the room. Melanie was left to stare blankly after him, her panic receding once he disappeared from view, quickly replaced by outrage. The hide of the man, the utter gall! He needed to be taught lessons in humility *and* rejection. And by God, she was going to teach them to him.

Oh, really? came a darkly mocking voice from deep inside. Easy to say but not so easy to do. What happens if he kisses you again? Can you honestly say that he couldn't make you want him as you were wanting him a little while ago? What if he'd pushed that encounter a little further, touched your breasts for instance?

Melanie shuddered as just thinking about Royce touching her like that had her nipples hardening inside her bra. God, but he probably could have had her here tonight, in the kitchen, if he'd been daring enough.

She groaned her dismay. Had he known that? Had he sensed her vulnerability to daring men? Was that why he'd kissed her even after she'd warned him not to?

She sincerely hoped not. What hope did she have of warding him off if he realised her response to that kiss had resulted from his being bold, if he knew she found his ruthless resolve to pursue her both exciting and arousing? Her only salvation was making him believe she'd been simply suffering from a momentary frustration tonight. She *was* a widow, after all. A widow who didn't date. Ever.

The noise of footsteps had Melanie's eyes jerking round in the direction of the open doorway. But it was only Byron, undoing his cufflinks as he walked in.

'Well, that's it,' he pronounced. Everyone's gone home. Kyle offered Royce a lift back to town and he went. I dare say I have you to thank for his early exit.'

'Me?'

Byron chuckled. 'He seemed most put out after his little visit to the kitchen. I did warn Royce that you wouldn't go out with him, but he simply wouldn't listen. Our Melanie never goes out with men, I said. You're wasting your time.'

Melanie stiffened. For some reason, Byron's amusement rankled. 'How do you know that?' she challenged.

Byron looked up from his cufflinks. 'Know what?'

'That I don't go out with men.'

Byron looked startled before a frown settled on his handsome features. 'What are you trying to tell me, Melanie? That you *do?* I'm afraid I don't believe that. You've made your feelings quite clear about men, my dear. And I understand. Truly.'

You understand *nothing,* Byron, she thought bitterly. You *know* nothing.

'Did Royce do or say something to upset you?' Byron asked abruptly.

'No, of course not,' she sighed.

His glance was thoughtful. 'Maybe you should have gone out with him. Maybe it's time…'

Her chin shot up. 'Time for what, Byron?'

'Time you started living again,' he said. 'You've changed lately, my dear. Haven't you noticed? You're taking more of an interest in things around you instead of just going about your work like some robot. When I told Royce you'd become like one of the family, then you have, of late.'

Melanie was taken aback by Byron's observation till she realised it was true. The change had probably started with Nathan bringing both Kirsty and Gemma home to Belleview to live some weeks back. It had been impossible to maintain a remote distance from two such engaging young people. Suddenly, the household had been full of laughter and fun. Melanie's coldly bitter heart had started to thaw, there was no doubt about that. She'd begun to care about people again. Why, when Nathan and Gemma had eloped, she'd really worried about that girl. That was why she'd gone to town today to visit Gemma and to reassure herself that the girl was happy.

She frowned when the thought came that Gemma hadn't seemed too happy tonight at dinner...

Melanie jumped when Byron suddenly touched her on the shoulder. 'Go to bed, my dear. You look tired. Don't worry about breakfast for me in the morning. I'll be up early going to golf. I'll get myself something at the clubhouse. Thanks again for that splendid meal tonight. You do spoil us, you know. Lord knows what we'll do if you ever decide to leave us.' With a warm smile, he turned and left the room.

Melanie sighed and turned away to finish clearing up the kitchen. Yes, she mused as she worked, she had changed. Her emotions, once dead, had stirred to life. Byron was right. Time to live again. In a fashion...

She would never be the same person she'd been before Joel. That was impossible. The one emotion she could never recapture was the ability to love and trust a man. Which meant marriage was out. As for having another baby... She could never face motherhood again, either. Even looking at a baby sometimes brought so much pain that she avoided women with prams.

So, if she was going to live again, what was she going to do differently in future?

Melanie hated the way her mind automatically flew to Royce Grantham. But it very definitely did. And it stayed on him. Stayed and stayed and stayed.

'Damn the man!' she muttered, and, with the last dirty plate cleared away, she marched down to her bedroom which was opposite the laundry.

She undressed quickly and angrily, throwing her skirt and blouse across her chair and stuffing her stockings and underwear into the small cane linen basket in the corner. But as she went to snatch the nightie out from under the pillow she caught a glimpse of her naked body in the cheval-glass in the corner. Her breath caught, her heart thudding as she stared at herself.

As though compelled, she turned and walked over to survey her nude body, her hands lifting to cover herself in an oddly defensive gesture, as though by doing so she wouldn't see the evidence of her own arousal. Slowly, shakily, her hands slid down from her hard-tipped breasts to her tensely held stomach, and finally, finally, she accepted the strong possibility of her having an affair with Royce. He'd been so right. She wanted him probably more than he wanted her, wanted him so much it was an ache deep inside her body.

A shudder ripped through her with this acceptance, a wave of heat following in its path. Reaching up, she took the pins from her hair and let it tumble in blue-black waves around her shoulders. She imagined what it would feel like to stand like this in front of Royce, to watch those sexy blue eyes of his take her in, watch them glitter with desire.

The intensity of her response to such thinking shook her. God, but she had no hope of resisting him, no hope at all!

And why *should* you resist him? suggested a wicked voice she didn't recognise as her own. Why shouldn't you have what men like Royce have been having for years? An exciting sex life without any strings attached, without consequences, without commitment? Let's face it, there's no chance of you falling in love with a man like him. You've been down that path before and have no intention of going down it again. All you have to do is protect yourself...

Melanie stared at herself in the mirror, appalled yet intrigued. Being appalled won in the end and she spun away, dragging out her nightie and pulling it down over her head. She dived into bed and buried her face in the pillow, doing a good imitation of pretending to go to sleep.

But that insidious idea wouldn't let go. It kept coming back, as ruthless as the man who'd inspired it. Desire invaded her mind, but so did a strange strength of will, a new sense of herself as a living breathing female. Apparently, the shell she'd cocooned her sexuality within for years had been smashed with a vengeance today, and a new woman was emerging, a tougher, harder, but highly sensual creature who would have what she wanted without putting herself at risk of the sort of pain she'd endured in the past. It was love that brought pain, she decided, not passion. She would have one without succumbing to the other. She would have Royce, but on *her* terms, not his.

Coming to such a scandalous decision rocked Melanie. Was this the woman who had allowed Joel to control every aspect of their life together, who had always had difficulty making decisions of any magnitude? The one time she *had* made a big decision had resulted in tragedy. Maybe this would have a similar outcome...

Don't be ridiculous, the new Melanie argued. Would you rather become a wimpy victim, waiting anxiously for Royce to call, worrying over when he was going to seduce you, seemingly against your will? Where's the pride in that, let alone the self-respect? You're a grown woman, with normal healthy needs and desires. Who better to satisfy those needs and desires temporarily but a man like Royce who is just passing through?

Do it, that wicked voice tempted. But do it your way!

Before she could think better of it, Melanie jumped out of bed and hurried out into the corridor and along to the kitchen where she wrenched open the cupboard that housed the telephone directories. On finding the number of the Regency Hotel, she jotted it down on the notepad she kept near the phone, ripped off the page, shoved the directory back, slammed the cupboard door and returned to her room with its own private line.

Her hands were shaking as she dialled but she was determined not to back out. The receptionist at the hotel put her straight through to Royce's room, despite the hour—it was after one. Her nerve only began to fail when no one answered for ages. At last, the receiver was disconnected and Royce snapped hello.

'Royce?' she said, nerves making her voice curt.

'Yes,' he grunted. 'Who is this?'

'It's Melanie.'

The line fell silent.

Melanie gulped, then plunged on. 'I've decided to make a counter-suggestion for tomorrow, if you're still interested.'

Again, all she got was dead silence.

'Well, are you?' she snapped.

'I'm getting over my shock, if you don't mind.'

Her laugh was harsh. 'What shock? You were pretty confident of success with me, weren't you? I've decided to simply pre-empt your next move and go straight to the heart of the matter.'

'Which is?'

'Our going to bed together.'

She had to smile over his sharply indrawn breath.

'What's the problem, Royce? Did I read you wrong? Are you saying all you wanted me for was as a tour guide after all?'

'For God's sake, Melanie, stop talking like this. It isn't you at all!'

Again she laughed. 'As I told you before, Royce, you don't know the real me.'

'Are you saying this is the real you?'

'Could be. It's certainly the only one you're going to get. Take it or leave it.'

He startled her with another elongated silence.

'I'll take it,' he said at last, his words brusque.

'I thought you might. Do you have a pen and paper handy?'

'I think so…' She heard the sound of a drawer opening and shutting. 'What am I supposed to be writing down?'

'An address where you can pick me up tomorrow night.'

'Why not at Belleview?'

'Oh, no, I can't have that. What would Byron think?'

'Who gives a stuff what Byron thinks?'

'I do. Can you get a car? I have an aversion to taxis, especially on a Saturday night. They drive like lunatics.'

'I can hire one, I suppose.'

'Good. Here's the address…' He repeated it back to her after he'd written it down. 'If you get a map you should be able to find it easily enough. After all, you've got all day.'

'What time do you want me to pick you up?'

'Eight. On the dot. Oh, and Royce…'

'Yes?'

'Don't come in. Blow the horn and I'll come out.'

She hung up, her heart pounding in her chest, her face flushed and her hands shaking. Yet when she'd spoken, she'd sounded so cool, so controlled. Had she developed a split personality? Was that it? The old Melanie and the new. If so, it was the old Melanie that resurfaced once she realised what she had done.

Oh, God, she groaned inwardly. God…

Her head dropped into her hands but there was no going back, no changing her mind. The new Melanie would not have allowed that. She'd set both Melanies on a course that had no turning. It went straight to hell!

CHAPTER SIX

'GEMMA!' Melanie exclaimed on opening the front door shortly before eleven on the Saturday morning. 'What are you doing here?'

'I came to see you.'

'*Me?*'

'Yes. Can we go somewhere private to talk? Who's home? Ava, I suppose. What about Byron?'

'Byron's at golf and Ava, surprisingly, has gone out. I think she's shopping and having her hair done.'

'So we're alone?'

'Yes, if you don't count the gardener out the back.'

Gemma sighed and stepped inside. 'That's a relief. I won't have to smile sweetly and pretend everything's fine.'

Gemma avoided Melanie's sharp look, turning away to take off her brown suede jacket and hang it up in the coat closet. One part of her wished she hadn't come—it was hard to admit to anyone at Belleview that her marriage to Nathan was already in trouble—but common sense told her she needed advice, preferably from an intelligent, level-headed woman of experience. Who better than Melanie?

Turning back, Melanie was still looking at her with a concerned expression on her face.

'You haven't left Nathan, have you?'

Gemma closed her eyes for a second. How odd that Melanie's question didn't produce the shock that it would have a few weeks back. When Nathan had assumed, after their first little spat on their honeymoon, that she was leaving him, she'd been appalled. For *her* marriage was for life, not till divorce us do part. Now, she had to admit that leaving Nathan had crossed her mind. Especially this morning...

'Gemma?' Melanie repeated, sounding really worried now.

Sighing, she opened her eyes. 'No. I haven't left Nathan. Not yet, anyway.'

'That sounds ominous. Look, let's go sit together somewhere and you can tell me what's troubling you. Where shall we go?'

'How about the family-room? I always liked that room when I stayed here. It's not quite as intimidating as the rest of the house. No antiques or treasures to worry about knocking into.'

Melanie smiled a typical Melanie smile, Gemma thought. Very dry. She looked extra drab today too, her face devoid of all colour, her hair even more savagely scraped back than ever.

As she followed Melanie into the family-room, Gemma conceded that Royce Grantham wasn't going to succeed with her. Nathan had been right about that. Pity. It might have solved one of her own problems.

Sighing heavily, Gemma settled into one of the squashy brown leather armchairs facing the huge television set, a long low coffee-table in front of her.

'Shall I get coffee?' Melanie offered. 'I was just about to have a cup myself.'

'That would be nice. Thanks.'

'I'll also bring some of Ava's store of chocolate biscuits. She says she's not going to eat any more and you look as if you could do with some energy food.'

'I didn't sleep much last night.'

Gemma was taken aback by the odd expression that flashed across Melanie's normally expressionless black eyes. It was almost as if the other woman had been *amused* by something she'd said. Did she perhaps think Nathan had kept her awake all night making wonderfully satisfying love to her?

Gemma groaned silently. Maybe if that had been the case, she wouldn't be sitting here this morning. Oh, he'd wanted to make love, as usual, but the tension of the evening had taken its toll and for the first time she hadn't been able to respond to Nathan's kisses and caresses. Nathan had become quite frustrated by her lack of response. His love-making had finally turned rough, as though he thought he could make her feel something if he kissed her more savagely, touched her more forcefully.

But his semi-violent attentions set off memories from the past that Gemma thought she'd forgotten. Suddenly, Nathan's mouth had become *his* mouth, Nathan's hands, *his* hands. She'd frozen beneath him, as she had once frozen beneath that vile brute. But where *he'd* been unable to do more than touch, Nathan was not similarly impotent.

When her husband drove his impassioned body deep inside Gemma, and set up a relentless rhythm, she was shocked out of her catatonic state. Guilt consumed her as she realised this was the man she loved, not some pig assaulting her. Just to lie there under him, frozen and unresponsive, was a dreadful thing to do.

So Gemma set about doing the one thing she thought she'd never have to do. Fake her pleasure. And she'd done it very well, so well that Nathan had groaned in triumph, his own climax seemingly more intense than ever before.

'You're still mine,' he'd muttered into her hair, possessive hands keeping her joined to him for a long, long time. When finally he'd fallen asleep, she'd eased her aching body away from under his and lain there, staring at the ceiling for hours. She'd felt empty and cold and unbearably depressed. She hadn't succumbed to sleep till shortly before dawn.

Nathan had woken her around nine with a breakfast tray and the message that he'd already rung her work to say she wouldn't be in. He'd kissed her, then stunned her by ordering her to stay home and not to answer the telephone or the door. When she'd gone to argue, he'd cut her dead, saying if she loved him she would do this for him. He would have taken her with him, he'd said but Kirsty still didn't want her to come. Interpreting her angry silence as co-operation, he'd congratulated her on showing good sense at last, reassured her he would be back in plenty of time to take her out tonight, kissed her again, then left.

For at least half an hour she'd lain there, not knowing what to do or where to turn, till she'd thought of Melanie. Immediately, she'd thrown back the duvet and leapt out of bed, showered and dressed, then driven out to Belleview. Now, here she was, sitting in the family-room, waiting for Melanie to return, feeling very uptight.

Leaning back in the softly padded chair, she took several steadying breaths, managing to feel a bit more relaxed by the time Melanie returned with the coffee and biscuits on a tray.

'I have to admit you've surprised me coming here this way,' Melanie said as she poured the coffee. 'When I dropped in to see you at work yesterday, you seemed so happy. What happened after I left you to change the *status quo?*'

Gemma shook her head. 'Well you might ask.'

'I *am* asking,' Melanie said, and handed her a cup of coffee.

'Royce Grantham happened, that's what,' Gemma said ruefully, and started sipping the coffee.

After a few silent seconds, she looked over to see Melanie was staring at her with a startled look on her face.

'Don't get the wrong idea,' Gemma rushed on. 'He didn't make a line for me or anything. I'm not blind, Melanie. I saw last night he was very taken with you. You're the reason he came into the shop in the first place. He…he must have seen you and fancied you. He came in and asked about you, said he thought he knew you.'

'That old chestnut.' A sardonic smile pulled at her

mouth. 'One would have thought he'd have had more imagination. Still, it worked, I suppose. He found out where I
was.'

Gemma couldn't quite make out Melanie's attitude. Was
she glad Royce was interested enough in her to pursue her?
Or angry? She sounded half amused, half bitter.

'What exactly did you tell him about me?' Melanie
asked.

'Nothing much, really. Just that you worked for Byron.
He started talking about the opal in the window after that.
You know…the Heart of Fire. And then Nathan walked in
and all hell broke loose.'

Melanie was taken aback. 'In what way?'

'Nathan recognised him. Naturally, I hadn't. I don't have
a wide knowledge of world celebrities, especially sports-
men. Frankly, I'd never heard of Royce Grantham, let alone
recognised him.'

'That's nothing to be ashamed of. Neither had I.'

'Yes, but I never recognise *anyone*. Anyway, Nathan assumed he was trying to chat me up. He refused to believe
me when I said he was interested in you. He went on and
on about him being a dangerous man when it came to
women and said he was sure to show up to pester me again.
I told him he was crazy and we…well…we had a bit of an
argument about it. You can imagine what he thought when
we arrived last night and ''guess who'' was already here.
I nearly died.'

'You weren't the only one who was surprised,' Melanie
admitted with understated sarcasm.

Gemma frowned. 'Don't you like him, Melanie? I
thought…'

'He's a rogue and a scoundrel,' she snapped. 'I wouldn't
trust him as far as I could throw him.'

Gemma's heart sank. 'That's what Nathan said. I…I
thought he was rather nice.'

'*Nice?* He's a snake!'

'I suppose you think I'm naïve too.'

'I think you're very young.'

'Young and stupid,' Gemma muttered, miserable now. She'd thought Melanie would be on her side. Clearly, she'd been wrong.

'I didn't say that, Gemma. You're far from stupid.'

'Well, Nathan thinks I'm stupid. He treats me like a child most of the time. He wouldn't let me go to work today simply because he thought Royce might drop in. He also ordered me not to answer the telephone or the door.'

'Oh, dear... He's trying to protect you, I suppose. Men like Royce Grantham can be very persistent, not to mention unscrupulous. Your being married wouldn't deter him, Gemma. Not even remotely. Still, I don't think you're in any immediate danger.'

'I wish you'd convince Nathan of that. The man's paranoid! Doesn't he realise that Tom Cruise could walk into my life and I wouldn't look at him twice? I love my husband, Melanie. Why doesn't he trust that love?'

'I don't know, Gemma. Nathan's a complex man. None of us knows him very well. I think things happened in his childhood and adolescence that affected him very deeply. Maybe if you asked him about his mother, and his upbringing...'

Gemma's laugh was caustic. 'I've tried that, believe me. He won't talk about the past, not even *mine!* Soon after we met, he told me he wanted to know all about my life up till now, but every time I start telling him about Lightning Ridge and my life with my father he finds some way of changing the subject.'

'To what? How?'

Gemma blushed. 'Mostly he starts making love to me. I...I like making love, but not as a substitute for every other kind of intimacy. I was watching Kyle and Jade with each other last night. Their camaraderie. Their sense of sharing. Their friendship. I felt so jealous. That's what *I* want, Melanie. That's what I *need.* I can't spend my whole life being nothing but a...a...'

'Possession?'

Gemma blinked.

'Well, that's all you feel like, isn't it?' Melanie went on with brutal frankness. 'Nathan's pretty little possession. His private toy. His very own creation.'

Gemma's eyes rounded. 'Yes! Yes, that's exactly what I feel like.'

'God help me for suggesting this,' Melanie muttered, 'but would a baby help, do you think?'

Gemma shook her head. 'Nathan says it's too soon.'

'What do *you* say?'

'I...I think it's too soon too.'

Melanie was clearly taken aback. 'You've surprised me. I would have thought motherhood was very important to you.'

'It is. It's just that... I'm not sure...'

'Of what?'

Gemma looked at Melanie, her eyes pained. 'I'm not sure Nathan really loves me.'

Melanie nodded, slowly, ruefully. 'I see.'

'I think he *thinks* he loves me,' she rushed on.

'But you think it's just lust.'

'I'm not sure...'

A silence fell between them for a short while.

'And what about you, Gemma? Are you sure what it is *you* feel for Nathan?'

Gemma's big brown eyes rounded. 'What...what do you mean? I love him.'

'Do you really? As I said, you're very young and he's a very handsome, virile man. Women can feel lust too, you know. Sometimes with dire results. Sometimes it propels them to marry men they should never have married. It blinds them to reality. And sometimes, sometimes it makes them do really dangerous things...'

Her voice had lowered to a husky whisper, her eyes glazing with a faraway, almost haunted look. But then suddenly, she snapped out of it, and that cold mask was solidly back in place.

'Only time will tell, I suppose,' she said firmly. 'Lust, you see, has a tendency to run its course. One day, if your feelings are only sexual, then the scales will fall from your eyes and you'll see the real man, not the mirage, and vice versa. So I think you're very wise not to have a baby, Gemma, till you are sure, both about *your* feelings, *and* Nathan's. Meanwhile, you must not let Nathan treat you in any manner which doesn't feel right to you, and that includes sexually. He has no *right* to your body, Gemma, just because he married you. If you don't want to make love, then say so.'

Gemma flushed, thinking about the night before. 'But what about…when *he* wants to, and you…well…you don't really mind but you can't seem to…enjoy it?'

'That's a difficult one. Most men feel like sex more than their wives, and if the wife's not tired or sick or anything, then mostly—if she wants the marriage to be a happy one—she gives him what he wants.'

'But does she have to pretend she likes it as well?'

'You mean fake orgasm?'

Gemma cringed a little. How awful that sounded. Luckily Melanie swept on without her having to say anything further.

'I dare say there aren't too many wives—or women—who haven't faked it at some time or other. But I think, if the relationship is good between husband and wife, she shouldn't have to. Her husband should understand that she's not a machine, and he should be damned grateful that she's giving him satisfaction while not getting any herself. Unfortunately, sometimes a man's ego gets in the way. He takes it as a personal insult if he can't satisfy his wife every time. He might even think that she's stopped loving him, which is crazy.'

'That's one of the reasons I pretended last night,' Gemma admitted unhappily.

Melanie stared at her, clearly astonished.

'I...I was upset,' Gemma elaborated with an embarrassed shrug. 'And tired. Nathan wanted to make love and I just couldn't feel anything. He started getting a little rough and he...he frightened me, so I...I...pretended.'

'Bastard,' Melanie hissed, black eyes blazing with fury. 'That was tantamount to rape, Gemma. Can't you see that?'

Gemma was startled by Melanie's fierce words. She instinctively shrank from thinking what Nathan had done was even *close* to rape. 'No, it wasn't,' she denied hotly. 'He...he's my husband!'

'God in heaven, does that give him the right to take you by force?'

'No, of course not, but he wouldn't have been expecting me not to like it, and I think he was upset too,' she argued, worried now that she was asking advice from the wrong person. She'd never realised before how much Melanie hated men. She wasn't even *trying* to see Nathan's point of view.

'You shouldn't have to pretend,' Melanie muttered. 'You shouldn't have to squash your own feelings in favour of his all the time. You're right to envy Jade and Kyle. The ideal relationship *is* a partnership in every way. A woman has to have her own individual identity besides being a wife, otherwise, in the end, the husband loses all respect for her. He thinks he can do as he pleases. He thinks he's all powerful. Give a man that sense of power and God knows what terrible things might happen.'

Gemma stared at Melanie, at the passion in her voice—and the hidden anguish. Dear heaven, what had happened in that marriage of hers?

Melanie must have seen the way Gemma was looking at her, for suddenly she seemed to forcibly gather herself, adopting one of those cool calm faces she was famous for. 'Sorry. I was getting carried away. There's no blueprint for marital happiness, Gemma. It's pretty much a play-it-by-ear arrangement. What works for one couple might not work for another. But there's always a period of adjustment before a man and woman really understand each other. Of course it would help if you and Nathan talked things out more. Now drink up that coffee and get a couple of those biscuits into yourself.'

Gemma did just that, endeavouring to see things in a more logical, less emotional way. She'd been making mountains out of molehills, she decided. So Nathan was a bit over-possessive and over-protective. So what? That showed how much he loved her, didn't it? She would go home and cook him a lovely dinner, saying she'd prefer to stay home tonight and just be with him—alone. She'd chill his favourite wine and put on some of his favourite music, or maybe the television. Then, while they were stretched out on the sofa, she might take a bit more of the initiative in lovemaking. She might even…

A delicate shudder rippled through Gemma. No, not that. She couldn't do that just yet.

'You should come and visit more often,' Melanie suggested as they walked together to the front door. 'The house is so empty now. I know Byron gets lonely sometimes. And so does Ava.'

'And you, Melanie? Don't you get lonely?'

'Occasionally.'

'Would you go out with Mr Grantham, if he asked you?'

'On a date, you mean?'

'Yes.'

'Never in a million years.'

'Why not?' she asked while she retrieved her suede jacket and slid into it.

'Because I don't like him.'

'I could have sworn you did. Last night you…you…'

Melanie actually blushed as she had blushed during the dinner party. Now Gemma was *certain* the other woman had found the Englishman attractive.

'He has undeniable sex appeal,' Melanie conceded stiffly, pulling open the front door to let in some watery winter sun. 'But far too much ego. I don't like egocentric men.'

'I wasn't suggesting you *marry* the man, Melanie,' Gemma said with mild exasperation.

Their eyes locked for a second before Melanie answered, 'I'll keep that in mind.'

'So you will go out with him if he asks you?'

'Oh, go on with you.' Melanie practically pushed her out on to the front patio. 'Go home and don't do anything your mother would be ashamed of. Oh! Speaking of your mother, has that private investigator come up with anything?'

'Not a darned thing. It's so hard to get anything out of people at Lightning Ridge. They're naturally suspicious and secretive. As far as the public records are concerned, neither my father nor my mother officially exist. Dad never even filed a tax return. The only place he could be officially found was in the Department of Transport files—his driver's licence and registration of his old truck. But even then he used false documents for ID. I told Nathan not to bother spending any more money for now.'

'What a shame.'

'Nathan says it's all for the best, of course. He says some people's pasts are best left there.'

'Really? Well, I suppose I might be forced to agree with him on that score,' Melanie said drily.

'I don't. It's a horribly empty feeling not knowing who your mother was, or her real name, or what she was like. I haven't given up hope yet. One day soon, I'll go back to Lightning Ridge and see what I can find out myself. I might do better than a stranger.'

'That's true.'

'I'd better go. Thanks for everything, Melanie. I feel much better having talked to you.'

'I'm not sure I helped much.'

'Oh, you have. Bye for now.' Waving, she tripped down the steps and climbed into her new white sedan, a recent present from Nathan. Recalling this—and all the other presents he kept giving her—brought a soft smile to her lips. Nathan loved her. How could she ever have doubted that? Gemma drove home, determined never to doubt her husband's love again.

CHAPTER SEVEN

WHEN MELANIE HAD ASKED Royce to pick her up at her brother's house at eight, she assumed she would have the place to herself. Ron took Frieda down to the local Workers' Club every Saturday night without fail, leaving the house around six-thirty and never returning till after ten. They only had the one child, a son, Wayne, who was nineteen and very good-looking.

According to Frieda he spent every weekend at his girlfriend's house, much to the girlfriend's mother's annoyance. But when Melanie drove up shortly before seven, planning to leave a note for Ron and Frieda which said she had to go to a school reunion near by and did they mind if she stayed the night, she was confronted by her nephew, very much at home, tinkering with one of his infernal motorbikes on the front porch.

'Damn,' she muttered under her breath.

Wayne looked up as she pushed open the squeaky front gate. 'Oh, hi, there, Aunt Mel,' he said. 'What are you doing here? You do know the oldies are down the club, don't you?'

'Yes, Wayne, but I needed to get a dress I left here. I...I'm going out.' Actually, Melanie kept all her old clothes here, the ones she'd worn as Mrs Joel Lloyd. She'd lived here with Ron and Frieda for some time after her breakdown, in the bedroom she'd grown up in. This was the Foster family home, Ron having inherited it after their parents passed away in quick succession several years back.

Melanie had been dismayed at being left nothing in the

will except her mother's personal effects, but her father had been the last to go and he'd held old-fashioned views about men and women. Melanie, who was nearly twenty years younger than her brother—she'd been a change-of-life baby—had always been treated as an inferior being, her father believing women had no real worth except as wives and mothers.

She sometimes wondered if she had subconsciously absorbed this none too subtle brainwashing, for she'd given up work after her marriage, despite being terribly bored at home till she learnt to fill her days up with classes that turned her into a social hostess and housewife the envy of every woman and man in the advertising set around Sydney. It had been these skills that had qualified her for the role of housekeeper at Belleview, a job which she did with ease and total efficiency.

Thinking about her marriage to Joel brought a bitter taste to Melanie's mouth and she dragged her mind back to the present, where Wayne was following her inside, clearly having found a welcome distraction for his own boredom.

'You're really going out, Aunt Mel?' he was saying as he traipsed after her right into her bedroom, draping his none too clean self all over the floral-quilted bed. 'The oldies *will* be pleased. Where are you going?'

'For goodness' sake, get off that bedspread, you grub!' she exploded, avoiding a direct answer. 'Your mother will kill you if you get grease on it!' Frieda was a very particular woman who fussed a lot over the house.

Wayne grudgingly hauled himself off the bed and sprawled on to the chair in the corner. 'Don't start getting like Mum, Aunt Mel,' he grumbled, which brought Melanie up short.

Melanie liked her sister-in-law, who'd been very kind to her after the accident, but she did have some irritating ways. Melanie's brother was his father's son and had typically married a woman who was a professional housewife and who wouldn't dream of having an opinion that didn't match her husband's.

Melanie was aware she'd been much the same with Joel. It was only in hindsight that she realised what a mistake it was for a woman to bury her own personality and identity like that, how it only led to an eventual breaking point. Even Frieda had had a small crisis about a year ago, stunning Ron when she left him for a few days, saying she would only come back if he started taking her out at least once a week. Hence their Saturday nights at the club.

Melanie's mind flashed to Gemma and her visit that morning. Hopefully, the girl had enough common sense and spirit to buck Nathan's attempts to rein her into being that sort of meek and mild submissive wife.

'Mum never lets up,' Wayne continued to grumble. 'It's always "Wayne, don't touch that," or "Wayne, don't sit there!"'

Melanie smiled at her nephew, seeing both points of view. 'Come now, Wayne, you do get pretty messy working with those bikes of yours. Maybe if you could remember to clean up a little before coming into the house.'

'Yeah, maybe.' His sullen face suddenly broke into a cheeky grin. 'I guess you'd be just as bad if I came into that big fancy house you look after with grease all over me.'

'You'd better believe it.' Still, Melanie understood now why he spent every weekend at his girlfriend's house. To avoid the nagging.

'Why aren't you at your girlfriend's tonight?' she asked, turning to open the wardrobe and start searching through the dresses. In a way, it was good to have Wayne here. It stopped her nerves from taking over.

'We're having a break,' he said.

'Oh? Is that your idea or her idea?'

'Hers,' he sighed.

'Why do you think she wants a break?'

'Dunno, really. She says it's because I take her for granted.'

'And do you?'

'I guess so.'

Melanie found the red dress she was looking for and turned to face her nephew. 'Have you been sleeping with her?'

Wayne went bright red. 'Gee, Aunt Mel…'

'*Have* you?'

'Well…sure! Everyone does these days. You…you won't tell Mum and Dad, will you?'

'Wayne, do you honestly think they don't know? Don't take the oldies for fools. I hope you've been using protection,' she warned, her stomach turning over as she thought of what she had bought on the way over here. And what was lying in the bottom drawer of the dressing-table in this very room.

'Course,' he muttered. 'I'm not stupid, you know.'

'It's stupid to do something just because everyone's doing it. Making love should be special, Wayne, with someone you really love and care about. It should…' She broke off, guilt and shame consuming her. Who am I to lecture anyone on matters of sex, tonight of all nights?

'Wayne, I really must get ready,' she said brusquely. 'My date is going to be here at eight and it's already gone seven.'

'OK.' He levered his six-foot frame out of the chair. 'Am I allowed to ask where you're going?'

'To dinner. In the city,' she added curtly. 'Now out!'

'OK, OK, don't get your dander up. Gee, Aunt Mel, a date, eh?' His eyes swept over her as if wondering what man would want to take out his drab, thirty-two-year-old Aunt Mel. Shrugging, he left the room, shutting the door behind him.

By five to eight, Melanie had been reduced to a quivering mess. She's already poked herself in the eye with her mascara wand and smudged her nail polish—twice! But at last, she was ready.

Standing back, she surveyed her reflection in the mirror, hardly recognising the woman who stared back at her. She'd been so used to seeing herself as Wayne saw her, drab and dreary. What on earth had Royce seen in her yesterday to make him want her? He could have his pick of women.

The woman in the mirror, however, would turn any man's head. This was the woman Joel had created, and displayed. Vibrant and vivacious and yes…sensual.

The red woollen dress with its low scooped neckline and long tight sleeves hugged her womanly curves down to her voluptuous hips, where it flared out into a softly gored skirt falling to mid-calf. Delicate black sandals with ankle-straps had replaced her normal chunky black shoes, silken sheer stockings in barely black caressing her shapely legs instead of her usual thick beige ones.

Red suited her colouring, bringing a warm glow to her fair skin and highlighting her blue-black hair which was no longer up, but falling in its naturally lush waves to her shoulders from a side-parting, sweeping slightly over her left eye. Her black eyes were strikingly made up with plenty of black eyeliner and mascara, her generous mouth filled in with a scarlet gloss that matched her dress—as did her nail polish. She'd put blusher on her cheeks, despite not needing any. Her colour was high tonight, as her pulse-rate was high, riding on fear more than desire, nerves rather than courage.

Where is that new Melanie when I need her most? she asked her reflection.

Wayne simultaneously knocked and burst into her room. 'Aunt Mel, a black…' He broke off mid-sentence to stare at his aunt who'd swung round at his sudden entrance, the red skirt flaring before settling into more sedate folds around her legs. Wayne's stunned gaze swept up from those legs to her face. 'My God,' he whispered on a low, shocked note. 'I…I…'

Melanie's smile was wry. 'You were saying, Wayne?'

Her nephew walked forward to survey her further, shaking his head. 'Aunt Mel, you're…you're *gorgeous!*'

She had to laugh. 'Your words are complimentary, nephew, dear, but your expression isn't.'

Wayne didn't have the grace to look embarrassed. 'Well, you're usually so…so…' Now he was really at a loss for words.

'Plain?' Melanie suggested.

'No, not actually plain…' His face screwed up into a puzzled frown.

'Never mind, Wayne, what was it you wanted to tell me?'

His face cleared and brightened. 'Oh, yes, I think your date's arrived. In a black Ferrari, no less.'

'A what? Never mind, I heard.' Could one hire a Ferrari? She supposed so. But if he'd arrived, why hadn't he blown the horn?

Her answer to that came when the front doorbell rang.

'I'll get it, Aunt Mel,' Wayne immediately offered, and was gone before she could stop him.

'Damn, damn and double damn,' Melanie muttered. Wayne was sure to recognise Royce. Her nephew was a racing car nut! Things were going from bad to worse.

Melanie breathed in then let out a ragged sigh. She should have known she wasn't cut out for this kind of thing. Her stomach was in instant knots. Her heart was racing, and her palms were clammy.

Wayne soon reappeared in the doorway, looking stunned. 'Aunt Mel! You…you do realise who it is you're going out with tonight, don't you?'

Melanie sighed again. 'Yes, Wayne, I do. It's Royce Grantham.'

'But it's…*the* Royce Grantham. You know?'

'Yes, that's right. *The* Royce Grantham, the Formula One driver.'

'God.' He stared at her with awe in his gaze. 'Fancy that. Royce Grantham, taking out *my* aunt. Wait till I tell my mates. Wait till I tell Mum and Dad. They'll be wrapped!'

Melanie opened her mouth to implore Wayne not to tell anyone then shut it again. Suddenly, the new Melanie swept back in, bringing her a lifted chin and renewed defiance. They might as well know that change was on the way. After all, Royce might be the first man she'd gone out with in four years, but he wasn't going to be the last. Once Royce had gone back to England there would be more dates with more men. Even the old Melanie couldn't bear to look at the rest of her life with no outings and no male company. The new Melanie wasn't going to do without sex, either.

Still, no point in Wayne giving Ron and Frieda false hopes.

'It's only a date, Wayne,' she reminded him drily. 'I met Royce last night at Belleview and he's a stranger to Sydney. I said I'd show him the sights of the city on a Saturday night. Now, where have you put him?'

'He wouldn't come in. He's waiting on the front porch.'

'Did you introduce yourself?'

'I sure did. There's no flies on me!'

'And what do you think of him?' she asked as she put a few things into the black beaded evening bag she'd selected earlier.

'What do I think of him?' Wayne looked perplexed. 'What's to think, Aunt Mel? He's Royce Grantham, for Pete's sake!'

Melanie suddenly understood what Kyle had been talking about last night when he said rich men had a real problem finding a woman to love them for themselves. The rich and *famous,* she decided, had double trouble. People were blinded, not only by their money, but by their aura of success. Maybe that was why Royce had never married, because he lived in an artificial environment where people were automatically impressed without even knowing him. That could be a very corrupting way to live.

'Ready, Aunt Mel?' Wayne asked agitatedly. 'He's waiting, you know.'

'Well, let him wait!' she snapped, annoyed with herself for starting to think of Royce as a real person with real problems to contend with. She only wanted to think of him as a male body.

Such thinking was back on track once she sighted him standing there under the light of the front porch. He looked lethally attractive in a grey woollen suit, with a sexy black T-shirt where another man would have put a stuffy shirt and tie. Suddenly, her stomach curled over and, while some deeply embedded instinct kept warning her to run as far away from this man as she could, her body had ideas of its own.

Wayne was hot on her heels as she walked down the corridor, so Melanie stopped for a second and hissed over her shoulder for him to get lost.

'Aunt Mel,' he groaned. 'Don't be a spoil-sport.'

'Wayne, I mean it,' she said darkly.

'Yeah...right...OK. Have a good time. Don't do anything I wouldn't do,' he muttered as he loped off, back in the direction of the kitchen.

I won't, Wayne, Melanie thought with black humour, and, taking a steadying breath, continued the long walk to the front door, aware that Royce was staring at her as much as she was staring at him.

'I thought I told you not to come in,' she said straight away, her voice a little strangled with nerves. Did he like the way she looked or not? Why was he frowning at her as though he was a psychiatrist and she was his trickiest patient?

'Mr Hyde, I presume?' he mocked, ignoring her complaint and letting those sexy blue eyes of his sweep over her once more.

'Mr Hyde?' she repeated thickly, aware of little but the

lump in her throat and the mad thudding of her heart against her ribs.

'As in Jekyll and Hyde.'

The analogy shocked her for a second till she accepted it had some essence of truth in it. She was distracted and disappointed, however, by his not directly complimenting her appearance. 'Are you saying you don't like how I look?'

'Do you think I'm crazy? You're absolutely stunning. Shall we go?'

He took her elbow and guided her quickly down the front steps and out to the pavement where a black sports car was indeed parked behind her small grey sedan.

'Wayne tells me this is a Ferrari,' she remarked as Royce opened the passenger door and stepped back to wave her inside.

'If it isn't,' he said drily while she folded herself into the low-slung seat, 'then I know a certain car rental agency that's going to get sued.'

He slammed the door shut and strode around to slip in behind the large steering-wheel. Melanie couldn't quite make out his mood. Was he angry with her? If so, why? He was getting what he wanted, wasn't he?

'I think you, of all people,' she said, agitation making her voice sharp, 'would know a Ferrari when you saw one.'

'True. I drove for them once. They say all Formula One drivers should drive for Ferrari at least once, so that they're damned glad to get back to driving for someone else!'

'If they're so difficult to drive for, then why do it at all?'

'For the money. What else? So where are we off to, sweet Melanie? Dinner and dancing? A movie, perhaps? A romantic stroll under the moonlight? You forgot to tell me while you were delivering your orders last night exactly what was expected of me after I'd honked.'

His hypocritic sarcasm sparked a surge of anger, which she just managed to keep under control by clenching her teeth hard in her jaw.

'But you didn't honk, did you?' she bit out.

'No. Funny, that. I have a natural aversion to following orders.'

'Then why ask me for more? Oh, just drive straight to your hotel, Royce. I'm not in the mood for games.'

'Really? From what I can see,' he said, eyes raking over her hair and face, 'your whole damned life is one big game. Talk about Dr Jekyll and Mr Hyde.'

'Just drive, damn you!' she spat, glaring at him.

He glared right back for a long moment, before reefing his eyes away and firing the engine. 'Put your seatbelt on,' he ordered curtly. 'You're going to need it.'

That was the understatement of the year.

The Ferrari screeched round in a savage U-turn and careered down to the corner where without hesitation it swept out on to busy Parramatta Road. There was no doubting Royce's skill as they darted in and out of the trucks and cars, changing lanes, overtaking, braking and accelerating with heart-stoppingly small margins for error. After five minutes of sheer terror, Melanie's nerve broke.

'If you don't slow down,' she cried out, 'I'll grab that wheel and to hell with the consequences.'

Royce said nothing, making her gasp again in fright as he wrenched the wheel left, just missing a car, then lurched round a corner on squealing tyres before screeching over to the kerb and braking to a shuddering halt.

'You stupid bastard!' she flung over at him, her face still flaming with surges of fear-filled adrenalin. 'How dare you drive like that around city streets? How dare you risk my life and others in such a pathetic display of schoolboy arrogance! What did you think you were proving by hurtling around in this elongated tin can like you were driving in a Grand Prix? That it made you into more of a man?'

Melanie had little time to register the dangerous glitter in those hard blue eyes. Neither did she have any chance to extricate herself from her low-slung prison before Royce swiftly unsnapped his seatbelt, swivelled and loomed over

her. There was the fleeting impression of a whooshing
sound, of the scent of expensive after-shave, of a darkened
face overhead, and then all there was were his hands capturing her face, his mouth prising hers open, his tongue,
driving deep.

Melanie moaned beneath the onslaught, her already
heated blood quickly changing from anger to arousal. And
with the change came a passion even she had not envisaged. It took possession of her body with a vengeance,
making it throb as the still running engine beneath her feet
was throbbing.

Hard wild kisses followed with even harder, wilder
kisses. Soon, Melanie's lips felt raw and swollen. When
Royce ran his wet tongue over them, she trembled. When
he sucked each lip in turn into his mouth, she groaned at
the bittersweet sensations.

'You drive me wild,' he muttered huskily. 'Do you know
that? Touch me, Melanie. Touch me…'

Her hands parted his jacket and ran over the black
T-shirt, his chest muscles well-defined beneath the thin material. She could feel his chest wall rising and falling rapidly, feel his sharp inward breath whenever her fingers
found a male nipple. His response to her touch excited her
unbearably and her impassioned fingers travelled downwards till he gasped, then groaned, then grabbed her hands.

'No,' he growled. 'Not here. And not like that.'

She stared up at him, eyes glazed, no cohesive thought
in her head. Her eyes blazed with a blind passion, wanting
nothing but to have this man make love to her. Her yearn-
ings burnt within her hot black gaze, telling him she was
his in whatever way he wanted her. For a second he stared
at her, as though disbelieving of this wicked new Melanie.
Disbelieving, yet fascinated.

'Hell,' he muttered under his breath, then, shaking his
head, sagged back into his seat. Another sideways glance
betrayed a continuing bewilderment. 'Who are you, Mela-

nie Lloyd? *What* are you? No, don't answer. I don't think I want to know.'

Firing the engine, he negotiated a much safer U-turn and headed once again in the direction of the city.

Melanie sank back into her seat, her eyes closing as the confusing reality of what had just happened settled into some order in her mind. Unbelievably, it seemed Royce was able to arouse her much more quickly and intensely than Joel. She also seemed to want him even more than she had ever wanted Joel.

Now that didn't seem right. She'd loved Joel. This...this was just a sexual thing. Superficial and shallow, with no depth of feeling or caring. Yet it had sent her spiralling out of control, made her ready to do anything to please him. That wasn't right. It just wasn't right.

Melanie frowned, trying to make sense of it.

Maybe it's because I'm older, she decided. She'd read that women reached their sexual prime much later than men. And she had to be extra frustrated, not having been with a man in years. Yes, that had to be it. For what else could it be?

A shocking thought had her slanting a panicky glance over at Royce, at his ruggedly handsome face and his long strong hands, gripping the wheel with white-knuckled intensity. As if sensing her eyes upon him, his head jerked around, but she quickly looked away, afraid of what *he* might see, afraid of what *she* might feel.

It can't be, she told herself shakily. I don't believe it. I won't believe it! It's just sex. Nothing more. I can't cope with anything more!

Gradually, she calmed, common sense telling her that she was merely trying to justify what she was doing. That was all. This was her first venture into a strictly sexual affair, her first foray into lust. Next time, she decided with a twisting of her heart, it would be easier.

CHAPTER EIGHT

THE REGENCY HOTEL was one of the newest in Sydney, nestled in a side-street down towards the Quay, where all the rooms could have a view of the harbour. The atmosphere and décor was rich and plush, with lots of wood-panelled walls and velvet curtains and gold fittings, reminiscent of some of the older, ritzier London hotels.

Royce's suite—Melanie told herself she should have guessed he'd have a suite—was on the tenth floor, and comprised an elegant sitting- and dining-room in peach and green, which led discreetly to a master bedroom in the same colours, off which came a sumptuous bathroom which went for broke in cream marble with gold taps. Fresh flowers sat in the corners of the triple vanity and the shower alone would have housed six people.

Melanie had tried to settle her nerves on arrival with a visit to the bathroom, where she replenished her lipstick and combed her hair, all the while desperately battling to find a suitable façade to get her through the coming ordeal. But, much as she tried to summon up the new Melanie, she continued to elude her. Instead, all she could find was a brittle sarcasm to shore up her imminent disintegration.

'You like to live well, Royce, don't you?' she said drily on exiting the bathroom after trying out the toilet and matching bidet. Nerves always did have an unfortunate effect on her bladder.

He was standing in the bedroom doorway, watching her with a thoughtful expression on his face. 'I've earned it,' he said.

'You're lucky you've lived to spend it,' she flung at him, 'the way you drive.'

He laughed and turned to disappear back into the sitting-room. 'Come out here and have a drink with me?' he called out. 'I think we both need it.'

'I don't usually drink,' she said on joining him, sitting down on one of the low green linen sofas and placing her purse on the coffee-table. 'But I think you're right,' she went on ruefully. 'I certainly could do with one.'

He shot her a puzzled look, then shrugged and turned to open the cabinet that housed the mini-bar and bar fridge. 'What shall we have? Scotch?'

'Whatever,' came her taut reply.

She didn't watch as he poured the drinks, feigning an interest in the view afforded by the floor to ceiling windows on her right. She'd never seen the Opera House framed by peach velvet curtains before, but she supposed it looked as spectacular as ever with its incredible roof of interlocking sails. From this height and at night, surrounded by darkly lapping waters, it really stood out. As did the Quay area, lit for the tourists all year round. But in truth, Sydney harbour and the postcard beauty of its surroundings couldn't distract her from her growing agitation.

Melanie's relief when Royce handed her a glass then settled himself on the sofa opposite showed itself in a deep sigh. The coffee-table between them provided an adequate barrier to his touching her in any way, even her foot. Why the idea of his touching her filled her with such alarm all of a sudden she couldn't fathom. One would have thought that would have been what she wanted. After all, once he started making love to her she would probably forget everything else, as she had in the car.

Which reminded her. She had to discuss certain matters with him.

Shifting nervously on the sofa, she recrossed her legs and stared at the view some more. The sensible words she should have been saying just wouldn't come.

'You haven't done this type of thing before, have you?' Royce said abruptly, but with an odd note of surprise in his voice.

It brought her eyes round with a jerk. 'Why do you say it like that?' A frown drew her dark brows together. 'Did...did you think I had?'

His laugh was sardonic. 'After last night's phone call? What do you think I thought?'

'Oh...' An embarrassed heat flooded her face at the realisation that she must have sounded like the toughest old tart in the world. Lifting the glass to her lips, she took a deep swallow before spluttering and grimacing down at the amber liquid.

'You didn't want it straight?' he asked. 'Here, give it back to me and I'll add some soda. Or would you prefer ginger ale?'

'No...' She shook her head. 'No, it's all right.'

'Are you hungry? Would you like me to order some supper from Room Service?'

She stared at him. 'Why...why are you being so nice to me?' she croaked.

He seemed startled by her question. 'What did you expect? That I would rip off your clothes the moment I shut the door and ravish you on the floor?'

Her eyes dropped. 'I...I don't know. Maybe it would have been better if you had.' Her voice sounded bitter yet all she was feeling was a black emptiness. 'It's what you brought me here for, after all.' She gulped some more whisky then placed the glass on the coffee-table with a shaking hand, unknowing that the eyes she lifted held a haunted look that would have moved the hardest of hearts.

'No, Melanie,' Royce denied in a low, measured voice. 'Maybe that's all *you* came here for, but that's not the way I do things with women I really like. I'll order us some supper. Do you like seafood?' He stood up and she had to crink her neck to look up at him.

'I...yes, yes, I do.'

'Good.' His smile was far too sweet and she quickly dropped her eyes again, hiding her fluster by picking up the glass again and sipping the rest of her drink. But while her ears automatically listened to him moving over to the phone on the desk in the corner behind her, where he proceeded to order a platter of seafood, crusty rolls, champagne and fresh strawberries, her mind was whirling.

She was liking him too much, she realised. Far too much. This was not what she wanted, for it made her feel emotional and vulnerable. This wasn't supposed to be a warm romantic encounter, simply a sexual one.

'Can I get you another drink?' he asked on returning. 'Or will you wait for the champagne?'

'I'll wait,' she said tautly.

'Then so will I.'

As he settled back down on his sofa, she said abruptly, 'I want you to use protection. If you don't have any I've brought some with me.'

His silent stare unnerved her.

'I…I *am* protected against pregnancy,' she went on agitatedly, 'but there are so many other risks these days, risks not covered by…by…'

'I will use protection, Melanie,' he agreed, 'though I am not one of those risks.'

'I only have your word for that, though, don't I?' she snapped.

'You do.' His tone was quite cold. 'I presume my word holds little value for you?'

'I have learnt not to trust the word of men like you,' she returned just as coldly.

'You know, Melanie, that's the second time you've used that phrase in connection with me. What kind of man is a man like me? Are you referring to the fact that I'm a so-called swinging bachelor, or something even less savoury?'

'Let's just say I'm not convinced of your honour or sincerity where women are concerned. You tried to pick me up that first day, Royce, without even knowing me. I suspect you might have brought me straight up here, if I'd let you.'

There was no escaping the guilt that flashed across his face. 'Probably,' he confessed. 'But it's not my usual style. Yours was an unusual case, Melanie Lloyd.'

'I don't see how,' she remarked with contempt in her voice.

'I'm not sure I do either, but it's true. Still, I can see I have little chance of convincing you that I've never felt anything as powerful as what I felt on seeing you yesterday.'

'It's called lust, Royce. L-U-S-T,' she spelled out sharply. 'Though frankly, I'm not sure how I could have inspired *anything* yesterday. I looked like a dog.'

His laughter broke the angry tension that was developing between them. 'You could never look like a dog, Melanie. Unless you're talking about a sleek pedigreed variety. You have lines that no clothes could hide, and a face only a master could do justice to.'

Melanie didn't want to feel pleasure at his extravagant compliments, but she was doomed to failure. Her cheeks pinked and she hastily looked down into her lap lest he see her vulnerability. It was to be thanked that she was sitting down for she suspected her knees had just gone to water.

'Why don't you come over here and join me?' Royce murmured. 'You're too far away.'

'You're the one who sat over there,' she countered, her eyes snapping up in rebellion against her moment of weakness. 'Why don't you come over here?'

His grin showed her the ease with which she'd just trapped herself. 'I thought you'd never ask.'

God, but he was a quick mover, over beside her and drawing her into his arms before she could say Jack Robinson.

'No, I...' was all she got out before his lips closed over hers and the room around them receded.

Somehow her arms ended up around him under his jacket

and she was pulling him closer and closer, the urge to remove all air between their bodies as compulsive as the urge to have his tongue drive deeper and deeper into her mouth.

The sound of a knock on the door had them gasping apart, Melanie's black eyes wildly dilated as she stared into Royce's equally stunned face. Both his hands lifted to rake his now dishevelled brown hair back from his forehead, a wry smile curving his rather cruel mouth as he surveyed her swollen lips.

'Have I got lipstick all over me?' he asked.

'Yes…'

He nodded. 'In that case, *you* answer the door while I pay a visit to the bathroom. Or aren't you liberated enough to reverse roles?' he mocked lightly.

A giggle escaped her lips before she could stop it. But his words about reversed roles had sent an image into her mind, a very sexy image of her on top.

'Melanie Lloyd,' he said teasingly, 'that was a very naughty giggle. I'll want to know what brought it on when I get back.'

Kissing her on the cheek, he was gone, leaving her to do as he asked and answer the door.

'Good evening, madam,' the waiter greeted her, then wheeled in their supper on a trolley-style serving table. When he went to remove the covers on the food, she told him just to leave it. When he started formally setting the dining-table, she told him to leave that as well. Frowning, then shrugging, he wished her a pleasant evening, gave a small bow and left, closing the door quietly behind him.

Royce rejoined her without his jacket, and what she'd thought was a black T-shirt actually had long sleeves. Most men looked sexy in black, she conceded. Royce, however, looked dangerous as well. She found it impossible to stop her eyes from coveting his broad-shouldered, lean torso as he walked towards her.

'Mmm,' he said, his arms snaking around her waist to draw her hard against him. 'You can look at me like that

any time you like. Now kiss me, wench, and make it good.
I've already forgotten what you taste like.'

She kissed him. And then *he* kissed *her,* and soon it was
clear that any eating was going to be postponed. Royce
found the zip at the back of the dress, swearing when his
efforts to rid her of her clothing were hampered by the
tightness of the long sleeves. Several savage tugs later, the
dress pooled at her feet while he attacked her bra, only to
swear again.

'It's a front-opening clasp,' she told him shakily, her
bones having melted to mush. He whirled her in his arms
and she sank back into him while he fumbled and fiddled,
still swearing.

'I always have trouble with black lace bras,' he growled.
'They do things to me.'

Finally, the bra fell apart under his fingers and Melanie
groaned aloud. But oh, the feel of his hands on her bare
breasts.

'Royce...'

'Shut up, Melanie, I'm enjoying myself.'

She whimpered her own pleasure as he teased her nipples
into hard pebbles of the most exquisite sensitivity. At last,
he turned her round and swept her up into his arms, laying
her down on the nearest sofa then kneeling down beside it
and bending to delight her breasts further with his mouth.
He seemed to know just when she wanted him to lick her
softly, when to suck a little more firmly, when to nip and
bite till she was beside herself. Then and only then did his
hands move to peel her tights and black lace briefs down
her legs, though once again he found an impediment to his
progress in the guise of the ankle-straps of her sandals.
Some more swearing followed—quite colourful, really—
and she laughed.

'You won't be laughing soon,' he warned darkly.

And she wasn't.

The shoes and undergarments finally discarded, he
started working his way back up her legs, kissing her, lick-

ing her, caressing her, past her calves, her knees, her thighs. When he pushed one of her legs off the sofa, then raised the knee of the other, she was beyond protest. A soft moan was all she could manage as his fingers and tongue started to work in unison.

Melanie's hands lifted to fall across her eyes which were squeezing tight in an effort to stop her body from doing what Royce seemed intent on making it do. Her heart was beating faster and faster and everything inside her was twisting tighter and tighter. She wanted to cry out for him to stop but suddenly her pleasure burst like a mini-explosion and her back arched, her mouth gasping wide for air. The spasms seemed to last forever and by the time her heavy arms finally slumped away from her eyes, one falling limply over the edge of the sofa, she was feeling totally drained.

'She liked that, methinks,' Royce chuckled softly and her eyes fluttered open to find him still kneeling beside her but rapidly stripping. His black sweater was reefed over his head to reveal a lean-muscled chest with a triangle of dark curls in the centre. She smiled in languorous amusement when he sat down on the floor and wriggled out of his trousers and underwear, amazing herself when she reached out without hesitation to stroke his beautiful erection.

'God, Melanie,' he protested at last. 'Don't keep doing that. I'm a man, not a machine. Besides, I have to go and get something.'

'Open my bag,' she ordered huskily. 'Behind you, on the coffee-table.'

He twisted round and did, his eyes flinging wide. 'Good God, how many did you buy?'

She blushed prettily. 'They…they were cheaper by the dozen.'

'Thank heaven for small mercies. For a minute there I thought you were expecting me to use the lot! Now there's a thought.' He grinned over his shoulder at her as he ripped one of the packets open. 'Maybe I could look upon this as a new challenge. Damn, do you think I could have some help here?' he asked, turning back to her without the slightest embarrassment. 'I'm all fingers and thumbs thinking of my new challenge.' And he pressed the condom into her hand.

She gave a low, husky laugh. 'Well, we can't have that, can we?' But once she started to do what he'd asked, her throat went dry and her own fingers started shaking. Even so, they kept caressing him long after the task was completed. And he let her, urging her to use her mouth as well, to pleasure him as he had pleasured her. Stunned a little at first, she did what he wanted, surprised when she found a pleasure in it that she never had when Joel had coerced her into such intimacies.

Maybe it was because of the way Royce was touching her while she did it. Stroking her hair so tenderly, all the while telling her that what she was doing felt fantastic, that she was incredibly sexy and ravishingly beautiful and that he adored her.

'Enough,' he murmured at last, and tenderly lifted her into a sitting position in front of him, stroking her thighs apart and bending forward to kiss her on the mouth while his fingers caressed her open for him. Melanie was all heat and liquid by the time he eased himself into her, but still, her eyes flung wide at the feel of his flesh fusing with hers.

'Royce,' she moaned softly.

'Hush. Don't talk. Put your arms around my neck.'

She did so, gasping when he cupped her buttocks and lifted her forward so that his penetration was even deeper.

'Now kiss me,' he urged thickly.

She kissed him. And it was while her own tongue was sliding in and out of his mouth that he began an almost parallel rhythm with his own lower body, quickly taking her to a place where nothing else existed but his flesh inside hers, and the slow-building tension gripping every internal muscle she owned. Soon, her hips began to pump in response to his movements, her mouth was gasping away from his, and she was giving voice to her need in hot, wild words. Her nails dug into his neck and she felt herself reaching for release once more.

It came like a volcano, bursting upwards through her, making her cry out in shock at the stunning nature of her pleasure. For it was not just sexual. It was a complete experience, both physical and emotional, especially when she heard Royce's answering cries of satisfaction. God, but she'd never felt anything like it. Not ever. Their bodies pulsating as one, meeting each other's needs, sharing in each other's pleasure.

She clung to him, raining kisses on his neck and shoulders, telling him that he was the best lover in the whole wide world. In reply, he held her just as fiercely, rocking her slowly back and forth as the tempest calmed, allowing her to savour every last sensation, seemingly not wanting it to end any more than she did. She groaned when he finally laid her limp body back on the sofa and deserted her for a while, her eyes and limbs growing heavy as all the energy drained from her satiated flesh. She was lying there, half asleep, and feeling deliciously languid, when a still naked Royce loomed over her, dry amusement on his face.

'Oh, no,' he laughed. 'This will never do.'

Scooping her up, he carried her through the bedroom and into the shower with him, making her squeal and struggle in his arms under the sudden blast of cold water.

'Wake up, witch,' he growled as he held her ruthlessly beneath the spray. 'I haven't had enough of you yet.'

At long last, the water turned warm and he lowered her spluttering self to her feet, effectively stopping any further protest with another of his highly distracting kisses.

'Hungry now?' he asked thickly after a minute or two.

'For food? Or other things?'

'Both.'

'You're insatiable,' she laughed when his hands started working on her breasts again.

'Just trying to keep the engine running. And well oiled,' he added hoarsely, one hand having found its way down between her legs. 'No trouble there, I see.'

She blushed. 'You're terrible.'

'And you're gorgeous.' Groaning, he pulled her to him for another round of kisses while water cascaded down over them.

'I think we should return to the living-room,' he muttered at last.

'The seafood calls, does it?'

'No. That's where your bag is.'

It was a crazy, incredibly sexy evening, with their making love at regular intervals and in the most adventurous ways, laughing in between, getting drunk on champagne and generally acting like honeymooners. Royce did his level best to meet his new challenge but fell short by three or four. As for Melanie, she adored the way he could spin her into a daze of desire and delight that had no thought of tomorrow or the past or anything. She'd never felt so totally sensual as she did beneath his lips and hands, never so complete as when he drove his body deep inside hers.

They finally made the mistake of making love in the bed, its comfort seducing them to sleep afterwards. The last thing Melanie remembered was telling Royce she had to go home, that it was terribly late, but then she drifted off...

At some time during the night, she roused sufficiently for her sleepy arm to steal round his naked waist and pull him close back into her. She snuggled around him, spoon-fashion, loving the feel of his hard male body. So strong, yet warm and sweet and cuddly. Her lips pressed to his back, his shoulder, his arm. I wish I could do this every night, she thought dreamily. I wish...

Melanie snapped awake, eyes wide. Dear God, what was she doing? No...what had she *done*? There was to have been no feeling, no emotion, no silly *wishing*. Royce was just a body to be used for a while, then discarded afterwards, without afterthought, without pain.

Oh, God, what a fool she was! She'd felt the warning signs, but she hadn't heeded them. She should have known she wouldn't be able to give her body so totally and not be in danger of giving her heart.

Yet the man lying beside her had no use for foolish women's hearts. Oh, he wanted their bodies, as often and in as many varied ways as he could have them. But it was strictly sex on his part. Never anything more. She should have followed his example.

Well, there was only one solution. She had to break with him now, while her feelings still fell short of love. Yes, she would never see him again. Never ever. She would have to be strong, have to resist temptation, have to say no if he asked her out again.

He might not ask you out again anyway, came the added bitter thought. They'd done just about everything last night, everything a man and a woman could do. Whatever sexual challenge she had represented to him had been well and truly met. Whatever fantasy he'd wanted her to fulfil, she had. Besides, one-night stands were called that because they lasted one night. End of story.

Feeling totally wretched, Melanie crept out of the bed and gathered up her clothes, taking them into the bathroom where she dressed quickly and quietly. The sight of towels spread on the floor from one of their encounters jolted her for a moment, but she steadfastly refused to accept shame or guilt. She'd clearly needed sex, needed Royce—the man. What she didn't need, however, was to start needing Royce—the person.

It was just on four when she let herself out of the room. By four-thirty the taxi was dropping her off at home where, thankfully, no one woke up. Not that she didn't creep around like a mouse. She soon tumbled her weary body into bed, where she fell into an exhausted sleep.

CHAPTER NINE

'IT'S ABOUT TIME you got up,' Frieda said accusingly when a yawning, dressing-gown-clad Melanie walked into the kitchen shortly before noon on the Sunday. 'Royce said not to disturb you, that you'd got in rather late, but truly, Melanie, it's very rude to invite a man over for the day then not be out of bed when he arrives. It's also rude not to tell your own family that you've decided to start dating again. You know how pleased we would have been. I can't understand why you kept it a secret.'

Melanie's hand fluttered up to her throat. 'Royce is *here? Now?*'

'Well, of course he is! Why look so surprised?' Frieda's face showed irritation. A thin, wiry woman, with sharp features and impatient blue eyes, she moved quickly and spoke quickly, with an easily exasperated manner. 'You told him eleven, didn't you? And it's way past eleven. I wish you'd thought to leave me a note since he'll be here for lunch. As it is, I had to move the roast dinner from tonight to lunchtime. It'll be ready around one-thirty. I hope he likes lamb,' she muttered, and started slicing beans into a saucepan in the sink.

'Where...where is he?' Melanie asked, sitting down at the kitchen table before she fell down.

'Helping Wayne with his bike in the back yard. Seems he knows something about engines.' Frieda glanced up, her expression dry. 'There again, he would, wouldn't he, him being a world champion racing car driver and all?'

'You…you know about that too, do you?' came Melanie's weak comment.

'Hard not to. Wayne was raving on about him to his father and me over breakfast this morning. Not to mention how you looked last night. Done up to the nines, it seems. So what is going on between you and this man, Melanie? Where did you meet? Are you serious about each other? I still can't understand why you didn't tell us, your own flesh and blood!'

'Goodness, Frieda,' Melanie gasped. 'Don't get so carried away. Didn't Wayne tell you I was simply doing my boss a good turn, showing one of his clients around Sydney while he was here? You do realise Royce is only in Sydney on holiday. And I didn't invite him here for the day. We were supposed to be going out, sightseeing.'

I'll kill him, she was thinking as she desperately tried to extricate herself from this horrible mess.

'That's not the impression he gave me, Melanie,' Frieda countered archly. 'He told me he was fed up with doing the tourist scene and that he was looking forward to spending a day relaxing with a nice normal Australian family with no pretensions. He said you'd told him what a good cook I was and that he couldn't wait to sample an old-fashioned home-cooked meal. He said he had had it up to here…' Melanie blinked as Frieda whipped the bean-slicer up to eye-level '…with hotel food.'

'He did, did he?' Well, that's not the impression *she'd* got when he devoured the seafood platter last night, Melanie thought sourly. But it was a clever manipulative lie, trotted out by a rogue intent on having his wicked way with her. *Again.* No doubt he'd woken this morning to find her gone, and—not ready yet to give up such a delicious morsel—he'd set out to secure seconds for himself by fair means or foul.

Melanie sat there, fuming. She should never have let Royce pick her up here. She should have taken a taxi to his hotel and met him there. Now, he'd backed her into a corner from which it would prove difficult to escape.

Difficult, but not impossible. She would simply have to go along with this charade till she could get him away from here. And then she would let him have it, right between the eyes. No man backed Melanie Lloyd into corners these days, certainly not a scoundrel like Royce Grantham!

'Melanie, surely you're not going to just sit there in that ghastly old pink dressing-gown,' her sister-in-law berated sternly. 'Royce could come in at any moment and see you like that with no lipstick on and your hair a mess. Go and make yourself presentable immediately!'

Melanie stayed exactly where she was, though she did scoop her hair back from her face, sighing as she did so. 'You haven't been listening to me, Frieda. There is nothing serious between Mr Grantham and myself. Not even remotely! Neither have I put myself on the marriage market again. I've simply decided to date occasionally and, when Royce asked me to show him around the city, I decided why not. Frankly I've been wanting to start going out again for a while, but I don't meet many eligible men at Belleview. Most of Byron's friends are married for starters.'

'Well, he's not any more.'

'Who? Royce? I didn't know he'd ever been married at all!'

'No, not him,' came Frieda's frustrated-sounding reply. 'I was talking about Byron Whitmore.'

Melanie couldn't help showing amazement. 'What are you suggesting, Frieda? That I should actually make a line for Byron?'

Frieda shrugged. 'He's a very handsome man. And very eligible. I think he likes you, too. Remember when we talked you into answering his advertisement for a house-keeper and you said you didn't stand a chance because you had no real experience?'

'Yes. But I don't see...'

'For pity's sake,' Frieda huffed. 'Why do you think he

hired you above all the other applicants? Because he liked the *look* of you. Maybe because he was *attracted* to you.'

'Oh, don't be ridiculous, Frieda!' Melanie laughed. 'He hired me because he *wasn't* attracted to me, that's why. That wife of his had an eagle eye when it came to her husband and other women, I can assure you. No, Frieda, you're wrong. Byron hired me for the opposite reason, because he knew I'd be the last woman on earth to make a line for him. Besides,' she added drily, 'he's not my type.'

'Not like your racing car driver, eh?' Frieda suggested with a smirk. 'He's your type, isn't he? Physical, yet clever. Don't look so surprised. I know the sort of man who would attract you, Melanie. A man like Joel. Yes, I saw the similarity straight away, but where Joel had a hard, almost ruthless streak in him, Royce is more of a cheeky, naughty boy.'

Melanie stared at her sister-in-law, never having realised she was so intuitive. But she was right, of course. Royce didn't seem to be as ruthless as Joel had proven to be. And he could charm the birds out of the trees when he put his mind to it. But that didn't mean he wasn't a dangerous man to start feeling things for other than the most superficial. He was still a very selfish, conscienceless individual, as evidenced by his coming here today without an invitation. Did he honestly think she would be *pleased* to see him, that she would welcome this intrusion into her private and personal life with open arms? The man was in for a shock if he did.

Unfortunately she wouldn't be able to show her displeasure while the others were around. His ticking-off would have to wait.

'Is Ron out with Royce and Wayne?' she asked, frowning.

'Melanie, where *are* your brains this morning? You know he coaches the under-twelves' soccer team, and that they play a match every Sunday during the winter months. He won't be back till four at the earliest. I'll have to put his dinner on a plate and reheat it. Look, if you're determined not to get dressed yet, why don't you get yourself a cup of coffee?' she went on. 'It might wake up that sleepy head of yours. Still, you must have had a good time last night, if you got home so late.'

'What? Oh, yes...yes, it was very nice.'

'Royce is nice too. I have to admit I was pleasantly surprised by him. You rather expect the rich and famous to be stuck up, but he's very down-to-earth. What a pity he's going back to England so soon. End of July, he said.'

'It's not a pity at all,' Melanie said sharply. 'You know I have no intention of marrying again. Don't start trying to matchmake me. You'll only be wasting your time. And don't go telling Royce what happened to Joel and David. He knows I'm a widow and that's all he's going to know. I'm not in the business of pity.'

Frieda put down the bean slicer, her face softening with just that emotion. Pity. 'You can't go on grieving forever, love. I thought...after last night...well, I hoped...'

'Well, you hoped wrong,' Melanie said, looping a stray lock of her hair back behind her ear and gnawing at her bottom lip.

The back wire-screen door opened at that vulnerable moment and in walked Royce, wearing a spiffy grey tracksuit and trendy black running shoes. Despite having dark rings under his eyes and sporting a five o'clock shadow, he looked far too attractive to her eyes. A hot awareness of her nudity under the dressing-gown had her clutching the lapels tightly over her chest and battling an irritatingly embarrassed feeling. Silly, really, in the circumstances. There wasn't an inch of her he hadn't already seen. *And* from very close quarters!

Wayne blundered in after Royce, looking chirpier than he had the night before. 'Hi, Aunt Mel. Royce here fixed my bike. That's worth one of Dad's beers, don't you think?'

'Indubitably,' Melanie said, throwing Royce a dry look.

He returned it with arrogant confidence, coming over to pull out a chair next to hers. Melanie resisted the temptation to flee to her bedroom, decided it just might do him good to see her in her ancient pink dressing-gown and bare feet. Till she remembered he'd found her madly attractive *before* she'd done herself up last night, when she'd been dreary Mrs Lloyd—housekeeper. Lord knew why.

'Hi, Mel,' he said, adopting Wayne's casual abbreviation of her name. 'How's the bod this morning? Stiff and sore, I'll bet.'

Melanie stared at him.

'From all that dancing,' he added, a wicked gleam in his eye.

'I used to love dancing,' Frieda said wistfully from behind her bean slicing. 'But Ron doesn't take me any more. I'm hard pushed to get him to take me to the club for a meal and a game on the pokies. He says you get beyond dancing.'

'Well, his sister's not beyond it,' Royce said. 'No, siree. Never been with a better mover in all my life.'

Melanie glared at him but he merely winked at her.

'Get that into you,' Wayne said, plonking a can of beer down in front of Royce, who popped the can and drank deeply.

'Ah,' he sighed afterwards. 'Never thought I'd like cold beer but it sure hits the spot after a bit of physical work.'

'Dad'll be pleased the bike's going at last. He wasn't too happy with me buying it and all, was he, Mum?'

'You can say that again. So tell us, Royce, what are you going to do when you get back to England? Wayne tells us you've retired from Formula One racing.'

'I have, indeed. Other than refurbishing a house I bought a while back, I've no definite plans. I might take up playing polo. I've always wanted to do that.'

'And what about your family?' Frieda persisted, much to Melanie's annoyance. 'Any brothers and sisters?'

'Nope. I was an only child. After my mother had me,

she declared having babies her least favourite pastime, with being poor a close second. She left us that same year. I haven't seen her since, but I heard she was married to some rich aristocrat in London. Actually I never missed her at all, but Dad was pretty cut up about it for the rest of his life. Poor sod. Still, he's dead now...'

Though these words were delivered in a very casual fashion, Melanie could not help but hear the bitterness in Royce. Possibly this was the reason he'd never married, a thought Frieda must have had as well.

'And you never married yourself, Royce?' she asked. 'Melanie wasn't too sure if you ever had or not.'

'Really?' He slanted her a dry look. 'I thought you knew I was a confirmed bachelor.'

She shrugged. 'One can't always believe what one reads in the magazines and newspapers.'

'I'm so glad you think like that. Now I won't have to work so hard to convince you that all you've read about me isn't true.'

Her returning look was sardonic. 'I see no reason for you to convince me of anything.'

'Oh, dear,' Frieda piped up into the sudden, tense silence. 'I've just remembered, we've nearly run out of milk. Wayne, could you run me down to the shops? Melanie, you wouldn't mind if we used your car, would you?'

'I could take you,' Royce offered.

'Oh, no, you're a visitor. You stay and talk with Melanie. Even if she *isn't* dressed.' This last remark was delivered with a look which implied she was blowing her chances with this man, presenting herself in such a dishevelled state and being generally awkward.

Melanie handed over her car keys with some reluctance, not because she was afraid Wayne would wrap it round a pole, but because she didn't want to be alone with Royce. The banging of the back door, followed by the sound of her car being started up, signalled for her to extricate herself from the kitchen post-haste. She stood up, scraping back the chair as she resashed the old robe tight around her naked flesh.

'I'd love to stay and chat,' she said sarcastically. 'But I really must go and dress.'

'Not on my account,' he drawled, tipping up the can to finish his beer. 'I prefer you with as few clothes on as possible.'

Melanie counted to ten, all the while glaring at him. 'I'd ask why you're here, if I didn't already know.'

His hard blue gaze swept up her body to her flushed face. 'So why *am* I here? I'd really like to know what you're thinking. It could be interesting, being privy to that schizophrenic mind of yours. In fact, it might satisfy a little of my curiosity about what makes you tick, Melanie Lloyd.'

Her black eyes spat angry fire at him even as she laughed. But her anger and fire hid a dangerous excitement and arousal. Melanie's earlier resolve to go along with his charade for a while was swamped by an urgent need to get him out of this house and away from her. *Now!*

'Then you'll have to satisfy your curiosity without any help from me,' she flung at him. 'And you'll have to satisfy your *other* needs in future without any help from me as well. I'd have thought you'd have got the message when you woke to find me gone. I don't like post-mortems to my one-night stands, or encores. So if you'll just toddle off back to your cave I'll find some excuse for your absence when Frieda and Wayne return.'

'No,' he said. Simply. Casually.

Everything inside Melanie began to disintegrate—her confidence plus her desire to resist what he so obviously wanted. Those sexy blue eyes told her everything as they locked with hers.

'I...I don't want you here, Royce,' she said, trying to sound very firm but failing abysmally. 'I didn't invite you. I want you gone. I...I don't want to see you again. Ever.'

'What an incorrigible liar you are, Melanie. First of all, you don't have one-night stands. Secondly, you don't want

me gone at all, and you sure as hell want to see me again.'
He got to his feet and walked slowly round to where she
was standing at the end of the kitchen table. The steely
resolve in his gaze both excited and frightened her. When
his hands shot out to pull her hard against him, she pan-
icked.

'No!' she cried, struggling in his arms so that his mouth
could not find its target. 'Let me go!' She began to hit him
everywhere, flailing arms connecting with his arms, his
chest, his shoulders, his head.

She twisted and he pushed till her struggles were half
defeated by the backs of her thighs digging into the edge
of the kitchen table. His hard elbows pressed her arms
down uselessly by her sides while strong hands captured
the sides of her head, holding it still for his marauding
mouth.

She could have bitten him, if she'd really wanted to.
Could have still kicked him in the shins or brought her knee
up into his groin. But Royce had been right, of course. She
didn't want him gone at all. At least…her body didn't.

God, but she hated the way it sagged submissively beneath his, a moan escaping her mouth as her lips fell helplessly apart.

He needed no further invitation, using his considerable
kissing skill to bend her further to his will, to bend her
back on to the table and peel open her dressing-gown. She
knew what she was allowing was shocking and decadent,
but she couldn't seem to resist with his mouth all over her
like that.

Till she dazedly remembered something…

'No, you can't,' she croaked, battling to lift her head a
little.

But then his lips found the ultimate target and her head
clunked back on to the table, her protest dying. Oh, God,
he was good at that. So very, very good.

At least that was safe enough, she told herself weakly

And with a soft moan, gave herself up to the heady delight: his lips and tongue were evoking.

Only it wasn't safe. For at a point when her head wa: whirling, and her body was shattering into a million pieces things changed swiftly and smoothly to the real thing. By the time her befuddled brain could react to the difference Royce was already pumping his seed deep into her body into her unprotected, possibly fertile body.

'Oh, no,' she sobbed, struggling to sit up. 'No...'

Tears of despair and horror welled up in her eyes, flood-ing over. She scrambled back on to the table, sending for-tunately empty beer cans flying, kicking him away from her, hating him. 'Go away. Get out. Get *out!*'

He stared at her, clearly stunned. 'Melanie, for God': sake! What's wrong? Why are you acting like this? You wanted it. You know you wanted it!'

He was hurriedly fixing his clothes when there was the sound of a car pulling into the driveway, the sound of doors opening and closing. Melanie's horror soared, stricken eyes flying to the back door.

Before she could do anything, Royce acted, sweeping her off the table and carrying her quickly down the hallway eyes darting from side to side till he found the bathroom. He placed her down on unsteady feet, wrapping and sashing the robe tightly around her.

'I'll tell them you're showering,' he said, and went to leave. But then he glanced back at her standing there, cry-ing, and groaned.

'Don't cry,' he said raggedly, and swept her back into a fierce embrace. 'There's no reason to cry, dammit! What is it? Are you worried because I didn't use anything? I told you before that I was no risk to your health and since you're on the Pill there's no harm done.'

Oh, God, he thought she was on the Pill. But she wasn't She'd used a diaphragm last night, and it had been removed this morning when she'd woken up.

'You don't understand,' she sobbed against his chest.

'No. No, I don't understand. I don't understand you at all, Melanie.' He held her away from him with firm, steadying hands. 'And I'm not going to go away till I do.'

Her blurred eyes flew wide but he was gone, striding back down the hall, his strong male voice floating back for her to hear. 'That didn't take you long, Frieda. Here, can I help you with that? Melanie's popped into the shower. She won't be long. So tell me, is there anything else I can do? Some veg to peel, perhaps?'

Frieda's laughter was coy. 'What kind of a hostess would I be, making the visitors do the vegetables? No, you go out on to the back porch and have another beer with Wayne. I'll send Melanie out to join you when she's looking more presentable.'

Melanie shut the bathroom door and clasped anguished hands to her head. What was she going to do?

Maybe you'll be lucky, the voice of desperate hope suggested. Maybe you won't get pregnant. There's no need to panic yet. No need to do anything. Pull yourself together, girl. The last thing you want is Royce getting a whiff of what might have occurred just now. Men like him had a very possessive streak about things they thought they owned. Children they fathered came under that category. After that ball next month, he'll be safely on his way back to England. By then you should be sure one way or the other and, if the worst comes to the worst, you will have to take the appropriate steps.

A shudder ran through her right down to her toes. For she suspected she might not be able to do that, take an innocent child's life as Joel had taken an innocent child's life. But what was the alternative?

Snapping on the shower, she threw aside her dressing-gown and stepped under the icy shards of cold water. It beat down upon her body, stinging and harsh. I'm being punished, she thought. Punished.

But for what? What have I ever done that was so wicked? Have I deceived anyone, betrayed anyone, destroyed anyone? I was the victim in my marriage, not the villain. But I'm not going to be a victim again in any relationship, however fleeting it may be. Not now. Not ever!

By the time she stepped out of the shower, the new Melanie was back in control.

CHAPTER TEN

BY THE TIME Melanie emerged, dressed in washed-out jeans and a dark purple mohair jumper, her black hair caught back with a black velvet ribbon, her only makeup some burgundy lipstick, she was fully composed. Frieda waved her out of the kitchen, having always been possessive about her cooking, so Melanie had no option but to wander out on·to the back porch where Wayne and Royce were stretched out in the watery winter sun, drinking another beer.

'You'll be over the driving limit if you don't watch it,' she warned drily, dragging up a deckchair and settling herself next to Royce, while doing her best to ignore his smouldering gaze. God, did he have to look at her that way, as if he was remembering what she looked like without any clothes on?

'It's light beer, Aunt Mel,' Wayne informed her. 'Only two per cent. He can have quite a few and still be fit to drive.'

Melanie laughed. 'I doubt Royce is ever fit to drive on normal roads. You should have seen him last night. We went careering up Parramatta Road like we were in the Indianapolis 500.'

'She's exaggerating,' Royce refuted. 'Your aunt's a bit of a nervous Nellie in a car.'

'Well, that's only to be expected, I suppose,' Wayne muttered, giving his aunt a sympathetic look. 'What with the car accident and all.'

'You were in a car accident, Melanie?' Royce asked, turning a disarmingly concerned face towards her.

'No, I—'

'Not Aunt Mel,' Wayne interrupted before she could shut him up, though she snapped forward on her chair and shot him a warning glare.

'Sorry, Aunt Mel,' he mumbled. 'I...I forgot you don't like to talk about it. Maybe I'd better make myself scarce.'

'Maybe you should,' she bit out, before relenting. 'Don't be silly, Wayne. There's no reason Royce shouldn't know. My husband was killed in a car accident. That's what he was going to say,' she finished firmly, hoping Wayne got the message that David was not to be mentioned.

'I see,' Royce said, eyeing her closely. 'I'm sorry. And I'm sorry for the way I drove last night. I didn't realise...'

'How could you?' she said nonchalantly, and leant back, her cool façade not betraying her twisted insides.

'I guess I couldn't, since you didn't see fit to tell me,' he said with reproach in his voice. 'How long ago did this happen?'

'Four years.'

'Four years...and were you married long?'

'Eight years,' she admitted curtly.

'That's a long time to be married without any children,' he remarked.

'Yes, it is, isn't it?' she returned airily.

Wayne started coughing at this point and stood up, saying he was going to see if he could help his mother.

'A discreet retreat,' Royce murmured once the wire door banged shut. 'I like that boy.'

'He's hardly a boy,' she snapped. 'He's man enough to be sleeping with his girlfriend without truly caring for her, like most macho males. Luckily, she had enough common sense to give him the heave-ho.'

'Would you like me to give him some words of worldly advice?' Royce countered caustically. 'I could suggest he

start sending the girl red roses and telling her he loves her
every other day. Women go for that.'

'You've tried it, have you?' she asked tartly.

'No, but I've seen it work for other men.'

'You don't need such niceties, though, do you? You do
extremely well on the *"veni, vidi, vici"* style of operations.
"I came, I saw, I conquered." It must be great to be so
goddamned irresistible!'

'Irresistible, am I? How flattering. I didn't realise. So tell
me, darling Melanie,' he whispered, leaning close so that
she could feel his warm breath on her cheek, 'have I conquered you?'

She was infuriated by the way her heart flipped over at
his cynical endearment, not to mention his closeness. Her
unwanted reactions sparked a bitter anger that found solace
in fighting words.

'You've got to be joking, lover,' she spat at him. 'What
happened last night was all *my* idea, not yours. I needed a
man at long last, and I decided you would do better than
most for reasons which should be obvious. You danced to
my tune, Mr King-of-the-Road, not the other way around!'

His hand shot out to grab her chin, twisting it cruelly
with steely fingers. 'And the episode just now on the
kitchen table?' he derided. 'Who was dancing to whose
tune then? I had you in the palm of my hand, lover. Literally. And I could have you again, any time I want.' He
released her chin with a flick of his hands, his mouth curling.

'You wanna bet?' Her glittering black eyes locked with
his, challenging him, despising him. 'Why don't you kiss
me, Royce?' she hissed. 'Go on, I dare you to. Kiss me
and feel my coldness. Kiss me, and feel my contempt. Kiss
me, and feel my hatred for men like you!'

His head jerked back, blue eyes wide as he stared at her
in horror and what might have been hurt, if he'd been capable of really being hurt. Merely a bruised ego, Melanie
decided bitterly. Men like Royce didn't feel real pain.

'I see you're finally getting the message, Royce,' she resumed in the cool, remote voice she'd been comfortable with for years, but which had deserted her since meeting Royce. Thankfully, it was now back to save her. 'It's over. *We're* over. I do hope you will respect my wishes and not try to contact me again after today. If you do, I might have to complain to Byron that you're sexually harassing me. I doubt he would look kindly on that. Byron is rather a stickler when it comes to moral issues.'

Royce's stunned face gradually took on a stony mask, his eyes hardening to blue chips of ice. 'In that case, he wouldn't look kindly on his housekeeper whoring around with a man she'd just met!'

Melanie paled, and for a second Royce actually looked stricken with a type of remorse. But then Wayne called through the screen door that dinner was ready, and any expression of apology melted away.

'Let's cool this for your family,' he muttered. 'There's no need to upset them, is there? This is just between us, after all.'

Melanie found dinner an awful strain. Royce carried off the charade of superficial politeness the better of the two. Over coffee, he actually pulled photos out of his wallet, showing the others snaps of the sixty-room mansion that awaited him back home. It was, indeed, magnificent. Almost a castle, set in huge grounds rather like a park.

'It's so big!' Frieda exclaimed. 'I wouldn't like to have to keep it clean, I can tell you.'

'Looks good to me,' her son joked. 'I could be as messy as I liked and no one would find out for six months. It'd take that long to get round all the rooms.'

Royce chuckled. 'It would if only one person had to do all the work. But I have an army of cleaners and gardeners who are getting everything into shape. I'm going to open it to the public during the summer months, then in the winter I'm going to hire out the grand dining-room and the ballroom for functions and parties. Hopefully, that will pay for the tax and upkeep, which is astronomical. It sent the lord who used to own it stony broke.'

'I suppose you bought it from this poor bankrupt aristocrat for a song,' Melanie said, unable to hide the hostility in her voice. Frieda shot her an amazed look which she steadfastly ignored.

'I did get it for a song,' Royce admitted drily. 'But the poor bankrupt aristocrat had actually passed on to that great polo field in the sky, and since he'd neither married, nor had any living relatives, the place was put up for auction by the charity he'd left it to. Yours truly made the winning bid.'

'Who are you going to leave it to when you go, Royce?' Wayne asked innocently. 'You're not married either, and don't have any children. Or do you?' he added with a cheeky wink.

'Wayne!' his mother reprimanded.

Melanie found her hand automatically resting on her stomach, butterflies crowding in as she thought of the possible consequences to what had happened in the kitchen earlier. What would she do if she were pregnant? If she did decide to keep the baby, she would have to quit her job and come back to live with Ron and Frieda. She had no money except for her meagre savings from her salary over the past two years, Joel having left her nothing from their marriage. Their fancy furnished house had been rented, and his small insurance payout had only just covered the cost of the funerals and her medical expenses afterwards. Even the car he'd driven had been leased. They had owned nothing of any value except two wardrobes full of very expensive clothes.

She was reefed back to the present by Royce's droll answer.

'As far as I know, I have no offspring,' he was saying. 'And believe me, Wayne, if a man in my position fathers a child, he doesn't get away with it these days. The lady in question would have me in court quicker than you could blink, with DNA tests and God knows what else to prove her case. So I can safely say I have not added to the population problem of this world. Now to answer your original question, I dare say I too will end up leaving my fortune to charity. Cancer research perhaps.'

'My mother died of cancer,' Frieda said sadly. 'It's a dreadful disease.'

'Yes, it is.'

'Must we talk about such wretched topics?' Melanie said, leaping up to start clearing the table. It was nearing three and she wanted to steer Royce out of here before her brother came home at four. She had just about had enough of worrying over what would be said next.

Royce must have been of a similar mind because he stood up also, and offered to help with the washing-up.

'No need for that,' Frieda smiled. 'Ron bought me a dishwasher for Christmas last year. Maybe you and Melanie might like to go for a drive?'

'What a good idea. What do you say, Mel? You were going to show me Darling Harbour today, remember?'

Her eyes met his, warning him that her agreeing was a white lie simply to get them out of the house. 'Yes, all right. But we'll have to drive both our cars into the city. It's too far for me to drive back here and then back to Belleview.'

'Fair enough. You can lead and I'll follow. That way you can't accuse me of driving recklessly.'

Melanie made no comment on that, merely said she had to collect some things from her room. Packing her housekeeping clothes in a plastic bag, she emerged looking collected, though her insides would continue to churn till she was safely away from Royce and back in Belleview.

'Ron's going to be annoyed that he missed you, Royce,' Frieda said as she walked with them out through the front gate and into the street. 'Maybe you'll be able to come back for dinner again some time soon.'

'I'm not sure I'll have another opportunity,' Royce returned. 'I'm flying to Melbourne in the morning.'

'But I thought you were staying in Sydney till late July!' Frieda protested, echoing Melanie's surprise.

'You must have misunderstood me,' he explained smoothly. 'I *will* be back in Sydney for a day or two around then to go to an auction, but meanwhile I'll be travelling around the rest of Australia.'

'What a shame! So this is goodbye, then?' She held out her hand.

He took it, giving her a warm smile. 'I'm afraid so, but it's been a grand day. I'll remember it always.'

Against all common sense Melanie felt tears pricking at her eyes. So this really was goodbye...

Gathering herself, she cleared her throat, thanked Frieda once more for the meal and strode over to her small, second-hand sedan. Royce slipped in behind the wheel of the Ferrari, the engine rumbling to life immediately. Melanie belted up and started her engine, signalling carefully before she negotiated a slow U-turn and crawled down to the corner. A glance in the rear-view mirror showed the black sports car close to her bumper-bar, a wry expression on Royce's face.

Undeterred, she crawled out on to Parramatta Road where she proceeded sedately along in the slow lane. Royce was content to follow for a short distance till suddenly he zapped out from behind and drew alongside, gesturing for her to pull over in the next side-street. When she shook her head vigorously, he merely cut her off and forced her to turn or have a small collision.

She was shaking by the time she pulled up. But with what? Nerves? Anger? Fear? She was still sitting there, quivering, when Royce jumped out of his car, slammed the door and stalked back with thunder on his face. Reefing open her door, he stood glaring down at her, hands on hips.

'Why couldn't you just damned well turn when I asked

you? Or did you expect me to crawl after you at ten miles an hour all the way into the city?'

'I don't expect anything of you, Royce Grantham,' she bit out, a clenched jaw the only way she could stop her teeth from chattering.

'Fine! Because I'll like nothing better than to live down to your low expectations. I won't say it's been a pleasure knowing you, my dear. It's been sheer torture! With a bit of luck I'll find some nice normal lady in Melbourne who'll be so uncomplicated she might even prove boring. But I'm sure I can cope with some boredom after you. Hell, yes!'

He laughed and straightened, looking down at her coldly now. 'I won't kiss you goodbye. You might have painted your lips in some deadly poison like all black widows. One word of warning, though, before I go. Don't get into the habit of insulting your lovers after you've finished with them. You never know who or what they might be. I'd hate to wake up one morning and read about the beautiful house-keeper of Belleview found murdered in her bed!'

Whirling, he strode back to the Ferrari, climbing in without a backward glance. Gunning the engine, he scorched round in a sweeping curve and was gone, leaving nothing behind but the smell of tyres burning.

Unless one counted the shattered woman sitting, sobbing, in the front seat of the plain grey car. Or the child of his she was possibly carrying.

GEMMA ARRIVED AT WORK on the Monday morning, feeling better than she had in ages. She'd made up with Nathan on the Saturday night as planned, they'd enjoyed a wonderful meal at home that she had cooked, and, best of all, she'd had no need to pretend a thing later in bed. It had been marvellous, even if she remained as conservative in her lovemaking as ever. The icing on the cake had been that Nathan hadn't fallen straight to sleep afterwards, but held her in his arms, and actually talked to her about his writing.

Not much, mind. But a little, telling her that the play he'd been working on was not going according to plan—something to do with his characters not being able to find the right emotion—and that he was actually looking forward to directing the play Byron was producing, which was called *The Woman in Black*.

When she asked him what it was about, he declined to tell her, saying that he would prefer she knew nothing about it till she saw it on opening night. Which would be when? she asked. Months away, he told her. They hadn't even held auditions yet for the roles. But Lenore didn't have to audition, she slipped in. Why was that?

Gemma had been pleased by her husband's answer. It had nothing to do with him. Apparently, Byron had promised her the role some time back and refused to go back on his word. Nathan was not thrilled, but what could he do? He conceded Lenore probably would have been one of the favourites for the role, even if she had auditioned, because she was the right age and physical type for the part, and was one of Sydney's most experienced and professional stage actresses. Still, he would not tolerate any rumours of nepotism where she was concerned. If Lenore didn't come up to scratch she'd be out on her ear like a rocket. He had Byron's agreement on that.

Gemma had been soothed by Nathan's dismissive and dispassionate manner when talking about his ex-wife. He seemed to consider her presence in the play a mild irritation, but certainly not worth getting het up over. Gemma could hardly keep thinking he still harboured deep feelings for her, in the circumstances.

Oh, yes, Saturday had been a success all round, especially when it came to improving their communication. Gemma decided it had been worth the sacrifice to her pride not to make a fuss about Nathan's cavalier and chauvinistic behaviour that morning. Her patience had been rewarded by a happy evening, crowned by an even happier Sunday.

Kirsty, at long last, had telephoned her, and they had the

loveliest long chat. Apparently Nathan had torn strips off his daughter the day before, castigating her for her immature and selfish attitude towards Gemma. After he'd left, she'd chatted with her mother and had finally seen the error of her ways. She'd been all apology and sweet forgiveness, so much so that Gemma had been touched beyond belief. She hadn't realised till then that Kirsty's withdrawal of her friendship had been like a huge shadow over her marriage to Nathan. Now, that shadow had lifted and she felt so happy that she couldn't stop smiling as she dusted the counter and waited for her first customer of the day.

Unfortunately, that first customer wiped the smile from her face.

'Mr Grantham!'

'Royce, please.'

Her eyes darted nervously towards the door, afraid all of a sudden that Nathan would come in and catch them together again. Crazy, since she knew he'd gone straight to Byron's office where they were going to discuss more arrangements for their production of *The Woman in Black*. Still, Whitmore's head office wasn't all that far away and it wouldn't take Nathan long to walk along here if he chose to for some reason.

'I...I can't talk to you,' she whispered agitatedly.

'Why not, for heaven's sake? Oh, I see. You're worried about your bully-boy of a husband seeing us together.'

'He is not a bully-boy,' she defended hotly. 'How dare you call him that? Why, he's...he's...'

'*Can* it, sweetie. I'm not in the mood this morning. I wouldn't have come in here at all except I was on my way to the airport and spied you in here and I just couldn't leave without having my curiosity satisfied about one thing. Was Melanie happy in her marriage or not? Or don't you know the answer?'

'I...I don't have any first-hand knowledge,' Gemma stammered, flustered by the whole scenario. 'I...I didn't know Melanie back then, before her husband and baby were killed, that is.'

'*What* did you say?'

'I said I didn't know her back then.'

'No, no, not that. The bit about her baby being killed. She had a *baby?* And it was killed in the same accident that her husband died in?'

'Yes, that's right. I was told it happened in front of her very eyes, down the street from her home. Apparently, she was devastated for ages and still hasn't really got over it. At least...' She had been going to add that she thought Melanie might have been on the road to recovery with her obvious attraction for *him*. But since he was leaving Sydney, there was no point in telling him that, was there?

'Good God,' he muttered.

It was then that Gemma noticed how terrible he was looking. Bleary-eyed and unshaven, like he'd been out drinking all night.

'Poor bitch,' he added, shocking Gemma.

'You shouldn't talk about Melanie like that. It's... it's...disrespectful.'

'It's the bloody truth. Hell, I wish I'd known this sooner.'

'Why? Do you think you could have persuaded her to go out with you if you'd known more about her?'

Gemma was taken aback by the odd gaze he set upon her. Was he laughing behind those harsh, glittering blue eyes—or crying? Why did she suddenly feel so terribly sad looking into them?

'Royce,' she said gently, reaching out to touch him on the arm, 'if this means anything to you, I think she liked you, despite everything.'

'I doubt that, sweet child. I doubt that very much. Still, it's a nice thought to leave on. A very nice thought...'

'You won't be back for the ball, then?'

A haunted look joined the weary sadness. 'I'm not sure. Maybe, if I want to punish myself a little more. Will she go, do you think?'

'Melanie? No, I don't think so. She never goes out anywhere, except to her brother's for dinner every Sunday. She's a very sad, lonely lady. For...for what it's worth, I don't think she was happily married.'

'What makes you say that?' he asked sharply.

Gemma shrugged. 'It's only a hunch, really. Sometimes, when Melanie talks about marriage and men, there's a certain bitterness in her voice that can't be explained by the accident. She doesn't talk about the past, but it's always there, I think, colouring everything she does and feels.'

'I can appreciate that,' he said ruefully. 'The past can have a way of poisoning the present. It's like a festering sore that needs to be cut out before it contaminates everything. Still, that's easier said than done, isn't it?' he finished drily. 'I suppose you'll be at the ball with your bodyguard hovering by your side?'

Gemma blushed at this description of Nathan. 'I...yes, I suppose.'

'Then I'll do you a favour and ignore you.'

He swung round then, and walked over to stare at the opal in the window. 'How much do you think it will take to secure this rock?'

'A million. Maybe a lot more if you've a serious rival for its possession.'

'That's a lot of money for something you can only look at...'

Whirling suddenly, he strode from the store without saying goodbye, without looking back. Gemma was left staring after him, an overwhelming feeling of depression descending to blot out her earlier happiness. What a shame nothing had come of his interest in Melanie. It was quite clear he'd been very taken with her. In Gemma's opinion, Melanie was a fool to turn her back on life, and such a nice man. No matter what Nathan said, no one would ever convince her that Royce Grantham wasn't a decent type, that his intentions hadn't been honourable. One only had to see the look in his eyes to see he was a very disappointed man.

Finally, she gave herself a mental shake and turned away to get on with her cleaning, but, try as she might, she couldn't recapture the same optimism about the day or the future that she'd woken with. Something Royce had said kept coming back to bother her as well, something about the past being like a festering sore, spoiling things in the present. Once again, she started wishing Nathan could confide in her about *his* past, as well as let her explore her own more fully. The idea she'd once had about going back to Lightning Ridge to see what she could find out for herself resurfaced.

And while it continued to tease her all day, she knew she would not mention it to Nathan that night, which underlined the continuing delicate nature of her relationship with her husband. Last Saturday night hadn't changed the *status quo* much after all, and this thought made her miserable. Suddenly, the future seemed intolerably grim, and she wanted to sit down and cry.

The arrival of a group of Japanese tourists put paid to that idea. Gemma sighed, dredged up a smile and walked over to them.

CHAPTER ELEVEN

'I'M SO EXCITED!' Ava said, and put down her paintbrush. 'Only one more day to the ball. Do you really like my dress, Melanie?'

Melanie glanced round from her dusting and smiled at Ava. 'You've already asked me that a dozen times since I came into the room. Yes, I like your dress. It's lovely and you'll look lovely in it. Blue is definitely your colour.'

'It is, isn't it?' Ava jumped up, almost knocking the easel over. She grabbed it just in time, heaving a sigh of relief and throwing Melanie a sheepish look. 'I might have lost a few pounds lately but I still haven't lost my clumsiness.'

'Maybe not entirely,' Melanie agreed, 'but you've definitely improved. Do you realise you haven't broken anything in ages? And we all knock into things occasionally, you know.'

'I suppose so,' Ava smiled, then walked over to admire her dress once more.

What a sweet nature that woman has, Melanie was thinking as she watched her. She was so grateful to Byron for offering to take her to the ball, when in truth her big brother probably didn't have anyone else to take, and he'd be too proud to arrive at the Whitmore-sponsored Opal Ball unaccompanied.

Melanie sighed wearily at the cynicism of her thoughts. Maybe she was doing Byron a disservice. He had changed somewhat since the accident that had claimed his wife, actually developing a slightly more caring and considerate nature.

Still, he *was* a chauvinist, and a typical man. Men, she'd found, rarely appreciated a woman's way of looking at things. Men lacked sensitivity. They were also incredibly selfish and self-absorbed.

Such thinking sent her mind flying to Royce, and her heart twisted with a rueful anguish. She wouldn't mind betting he hadn't given her more than a passing thought since his departure from Sydney.

There again, why should he? Her behaviour had been as appalling as his had been. The weeks since his leaving had given her plenty of time to look back and try to understand how she had come across to him, how he would have perceived her as a woman.

And she didn't like the answers she'd come up with. Dear lord, he'd had every excuse to treat her as he had treated her. And to leave her in the manner he had. She'd deserved no better.

But she had suffered for her misdeeds and reckless foolishness. She was still suffering.

Her eyes dropped to her wristwatch. It was almost eleven. She'd promised to ring the doctor this morning and give him her final decision. She was booked into a small private clinic for the following Sunday evening, and while she knew a termination was the most logical and practical solution to her problem—she tried to keep thinking about the baby growing within her as a *problem* and not a little person—there were moments of weakness and confusion when she just didn't know what to do.

Her doctor had counselled that he didn't think she was emotionally strong enough to have a baby alone after what had happened, that she would probably become an overprotective, exceedingly fearful mother who might eventually have another breakdown. The decision was up to her, of course, but it was clear what he was advising.

But he was a *man*, she worried anew. And an unmarried, childless one at that. What did he know of being a mother? Melanie had known plenty of women over the years who'd been less than thrilled to find themselves pregnant, but who, by the time the baby came, were besotted with their infant. Mother nature worked miracles with mothers, sometimes.

But maybe not with you, Melanie. What of the dreams just seeing a baby can evoke in you? No, not dreams. Nightmares!

Maybe the doctor was right. You can't take the risk. It wasn't fair to the child to have a permanently frightened mother.

The buzzing on the portable intercom in Melanie's pocket startled her, perhaps because it didn't buzz all that often. If people were expected at Belleview—visitors or tradesman or the casual staff—then the gates were left open for them to simply drive in.

Drawing it from her pocket, she flicked the switch and spoke into the miniature microphone. 'Yes?'

'A delivery of flowers for a Mrs Melanie Lloyd.'

Ava swung round to stare at her. 'Flowers, Melanie? For you? Goodness, I wonder who they're from?'

Melanie's stomach did a somersault as the answer to Ava's question popped into her mind. Royce. It *had* to be Royce.

He'd said he was coming back for the ball. She'd thought he might change his mind and simply go straight back to England. But he hadn't. He'd come back to get his opal. And perhaps to say farewell to her in the only way he knew how.

A searing heat raced up her body and into her face, making a mockery of her recent decision never to sleep with any man ever again. The bitter realisation came that of course she had meant *other* men, not Royce. Nevertheless, it upset Melanie to think that, after all that had happened, she was still so susceptible to him. One would almost think that...

No, no, you fool, don't start thinking any such thing. What you feel is nothing more than it ever was. A strong physical attraction. A chemistry. A passion. Don't try to justify yourself any more by calling it love. You're a lot of things but never a hypocrite.

'I'll open the gates for you,' she told the waiting delivery man in cool, crisp tones. 'Go round to the side-entrance near the garages.'

Melanie pressed the control that automatically opened the gates and hurried from the room, Ava bustling after her. 'Melanie?' she panted, breathing heavily in order to keep up. 'Who are the flowers from, do you know?'

Melanie saw no point in not telling the truth, especially with an avid Ava breathing down her neck. 'Yes, I think so. Royce Grantham.'

'But…but…'

'I'll explain later, Ava,' she said briskly. 'Right now I have to get to the side-door.' She increased her stride.

By the time Melanie reached the bottom of the marble staircase Ava had been left far behind. Despite her apparent composure upstairs, her pulse was racing madly by the time she reached the side-door. The sight of the delivery man holding a huge box with at least three dozen long-stemmed red roses resting under its transparent lid stopped her heart-beat for a second, before it lurched back into its pounding rhythm.

'Mrs Lloyd?' the delivery man checked, a slight frown on his face as he took in her drab appearance.

'Yes.'

He shrugged. 'Then these are definitely for you. You know, I usually only deliver this many roses to the maternity sections of hospitals. You have one very keen admirer here.'

Melanie took the roses, closed the door and leant against it, her fingers fumbling as she took the attached card out of its envelope. It simply said—'I've missed you, Royce'.

Missed me, have you? she thought angrily. You lying bastard! I know what you've missed. And I know what these roses represent. A ruthlessly cynical gesture, echoing your scathing remark that women fall for flower-giving and false avowals of love.

Tears pricked at her eyes as she realised how much she would give for him genuinely to have missed her, genuinely to have sent her these flowers out of true affection.

Oh, God…maybe I do love him.

No, you don't, argued back a darkly bitter voice. You're just thinking that because you've conceived his child, because you're trying to find an excuse to keep it. Grow up, Melanie. This is the real world and this is real life! So you have to make a tough decision here. Don't go all sentimental and wishy-washy on me. Do what has to be done!

Squaring her shoulders, she marched back along the corridor and into the kitchen where she would have dumped the roses in the garbage with the respect they deserved except that a breathlessly curious Ava was waiting for her there, ready to pounce.

'Oh, my goodness, I've never seen so many red roses! Oh, how beautiful they are. But horribly expensive. And were they from Royce Grantham?'

'Yes,' Melanie admitted curtly, which brought a sharp glance from Ava.

'You don't sound all that pleased, Melanie. Most women would be over the moon.'

'Naturally. That's what he's bargaining on.'

Now Ava was frowning. 'I don't understand. Actually, I don't understand any of this. I didn't know you even *knew* Royce Grantham in a personal way. Have you been seeing him since he came to dinner here that night?'

Melanie prayed for patience, and an inventive mind. 'Not the way you mean. I did go out with him once back then. But only once. He left Sydney several weeks ago and I haven't seen him since. I think he's come back for the ball and the auction of the Heart of Fire, and probably wants me to go with him. Celebrities don't like showing up in public without a partner. Don't make too much of the flowers, Ava,' she went on drily. 'Royce is a very wealthy man.

He likes to impress ladies with grand gestures, that's all. It means little.'

'Are you sure? I mean, he must like you a lot, Melanie, to send so *many* roses. Goodness, I'm quite shocked, do you know that? I didn't realise you went out with men at all. I thought…well, I thought…'

'You thought correctly, Ava. I don't go out with men as a rule. This was a one-off thing. He was a stranger in Sydney and simply wanted someone to show him around one weekend. I did it as a favour,' she lied valiantly. 'As far as I know he flies out for England the day after the ball, so don't start making more of this than there is. It's a friendship of convenience at best, certainly not a romance.'

'Oh, what a pity! He was such an interesting and clever man. Just the sort who would have suited you, Melanie.'

Melanie laughed. 'You are an incorrigible romantic, Ava.'

'Perhaps, But what's wrong with that? This world could do with more romance, I say.'

'Yes, I'm sure it could,' Melanie agreed ruefully.

'You…you should think about getting married again, Melanie,' Ava continued gently. 'I know what happened to you was tragic but life does go on and you're a beautiful woman, no matter how hard you try to hide it. You shouldn't waste the rest of your life looking after Byron and me in this mausoleum. You should be looking after your own home, with a husband of your own, and children. Oh, yes, you should have more children. Do you think your poor little boy would want you to grieve for him forever? You'd make a wonderful mother. You…oh, no, what have I done? Oh, Melanie, I'm so sorry. I shouldn't have said anything. I…I…oh, please don't cry, Melanie. I'll go away. Yes, I'll go away right now and I'll shut my stupid mouth and I won't say another word on the matter ever again!'

'No, don't go!' Melanie cried, her whole being awash with floods of emotion. 'I…I'm not angry with you. It's just that…oh, just hold me, Ava. I really need someone to just hold me.'

Ava could do nothing to stop tears of heartfelt sympathy and remorse from rushing into her own eyes. Dear lord, she had never seen such misery, such emotional torture as was reflected at that moment in Melanie's eyes. And *she* had caused it, stupid fool that she was.

Clasping the weeping woman close to her not inconsiderable bosom, she hugged her and soothed her with halting and probably ineffectual words. 'I'm so…sorry. It's none of my business…what you do. And who am I to talk? Miss Coward herself…staying at home all the time…hiding from life…pigging out on junk food…pretending…fantasising…'

Soon, it was Ava crying the harder of the two and Melanie doing the soothing. 'No, you were right to give me a talking-to,' she reassured, reaching for a handful of tissues from the box on the counter behind them and sharing them out. 'But you're wrong about yourself. You're still relatively young, Ava, with most of your life left ahead of you. Do something with it before it is too late.'

Ava sniffled, dabbing at her eyes with the tissues. 'You really think I could?'

'Yes, I do. Get out of this house more often. Get a job of some sort, or volunteer for some charity work. Join a club. Anything! Only don't bury yourself in your room all the time. You can't make your dreams come true if you never give them a chance…'

'That's what Jade's always telling me. She gave me her mother's jewellery, did you know? Told me to sell it and use the money to go to proper art school, or go on a world cruise.'

'What a clever girl she is. Proper art school. Now why didn't I think of that?'

Ava sighed. 'Perhaps because I don't have any real talent in that department.'

'Ava! How can you say that? You *know* you have talent.'

'Byron doesn't think so,' she muttered.

'Well, pooh to Byron!'

Ava looked shocked. 'Pooh to Byron?'

'Yes, pooh!'

Ava started to giggle. 'I like that. Pooh to Byron.' Her giggles became real laughter. 'Pooh to Byron! I'll remember that the next time Byron tells me I'm stupid or I can't do something.'

'That's the spirit!'

'And you're going to look around for a nice man to marry,' Ava insisted in return.

Melanie smiled a wry smile. 'I can't promise miracles, but I'll certainly make some changes and decisions. And I'll stop running away from life too.'

'What a pity Mr Grantham is going back to England. He might have been your new Mr Right.'

Melanie's heart contracted. 'I think not, Ava. He's not the marrying kind.'

'No, I suppose not. Well, we're a right pair, aren't we? Blubbering on each other's shoulders and generally being silly-billies.'

'We all need a good cry occasionally.'

'I'm sure you're right, but I think I'd better go upstairs and wash my face. Some people can cry and still look gorgeous with big luminescent eyes but others we shall not name go all blotchy and puffy.'

Melanie laughed. 'Oh, go on with you.'

'I am going. In fact, I'm gone!' She waved airily over her shoulder as she hurried from the kitchen.

Melanie turned to look at the roses again. Ava was a dear but she just didn't understand. One couldn't always do what one might want to do down deep in one's heart. Sometimes, one had to be sensible...

Her hand was actually reaching up for the telephone to call her doctor when it rang. For a second, Melanie stared at it, intuition telling her, as it had with the flowers, who it was on the other end of the line. Feeling like a hunted animal, she suddenly wanted to run and hide, but what would be the good of that with a man like Royce? If she refused to talk to him on the telephone, he'd simply show up on her doorstep. Best to see what he wanted this time. As if she didn't already know.

Steeling herself, she lifted the receiver out of its cradle on the wall and placed it to her ear and mouth.

'Belleview,' she said crisply, 'Melanie Lloyd speaking.'

Royce's wry chuckle came down the line. 'Oh, yes, indubitably that is Melanie Lloyd. Who else could make me feel like a chastened schoolboy so quickly?'

'Royce,' she said in a flat, resigned tone.

'You remembered me? Or is it that my roses have arrived?'

Melanie swallowed the lump gathering in her throat. Why, after all these weeks, could the mere sound of his voice do this to her? Her heart hardened at her own stupidity.

'Yes, your roses have arrived,' she admitted in clipped tones. 'Am I to expect an imminent avowal of undying love as well? Or are you bargaining on our little separation having whetted my widow's appetite further for male company?'

His weary sigh made her feel guilty, her guilt alternately making her feel even angrier. 'What do you want, Royce?' she snapped. 'We said our goodbyes when you were last in town. Maybe I didn't make mine clear enough. Goodbye. I don't want to see you again.'

'Don't hang up on me!' he blurted out. 'Please, Melanie, don't hang up on me,' he repeated in a voice that stunned her. It was almost pleading, and highly emotional. It was not what she would ever have expected from Royce Grantham.

She didn't hang up.

'I'm sorry,' he said simply. 'For everything.'

It threw her. 'You...you behaved no worse than I did,' she found herself saying.

'I don't think so. I was the instigator of everything. I pursued you mercilessly, took advantage of you, exploited your vulnerability. Maybe I didn't realise quite why you were so vulnerable, but I was deliberately blind to your feelings, simply because I wanted you so much myself. I was selfish and arrogant and I'm deeply, deeply sorry if I hurt you.'

He sounded so sincere, as though she really meant something to him and he really cared. Melanie's heart leapt and, against all common sense, a vain hope sprang into life.

'Come to the ball with me tomorrow night,' he invited softly. 'I have tickets for two.'

She automatically cringed away from the Whitmores' seeing her at the ball with Royce.

'Melanie?'

She bit her lip and dithered.

'Don't you have anything to wear, is that it?'

'No, I have plenty of ballgowns I could wear over at my brother's place. My marriage was a very social one,' she finished with acid remembrance.

'I don't want you wearing any of those,' he said brusquely. 'I'll buy you something new and have it sent over.'

'Don't be silly, Royce. I might not like it and it probably won't fit.'

'If you like it and it fits, promise me you'll wear it.'

'You're being silly.'

'I'm being a man. *Promise* me.'

'All right, I promise. But only if I like it and only if it fits.'

'Fair enough. I'll have it to you by noon tomorrow. Is that in enough time?'

'Yes.'

'And I'll pick you up at your brother's place at eight again.'

'I...I don't recall agreeing to go with you to the ball in the first place. I think I've just been conned.'

'Would I con you?'

Yes, you would, she accepted bitterly.

Especially if the end result was to have her in his bed once more. God, Melanie, one phone call after all this time, for no other reason than he happened to be in town again, and you're hoping stupid hopes and agreeing to see him again. If he'd missed you so much and cared about you so deeply, where has he been for five weeks? He doesn't want anything different from what he did the last time. He's simply come up with a different approach this time to succeed and he just has.

'Are you still flying home to England the day after the ball?' she asked.

His hesitation to answer was very telling.

'That depends,' he said at last.

'On what?'

'I'll tell you tomorrow night at the ball.'

Melanie sighed. This is your chance to tell him that there isn't going to be a tomorrow night. So why aren't you saying something?

She did. 'All right.'

'Melanie…'

'Yes?'

'Thank you.'

'For what?'

'For saying yes. You won't regret it.'

But I already do, she sighed wearily as she hung up. Nothing had changed. Royce still didn't want marriage or forever. He wasn't in love with her. And he *had* just conned her.

So why had she agreed to see him one last time?

Perhaps because she knew that was what it was. One last time. One last night to remember, forever. A proper farewell for the father of her child.

Melanie sighed again, knowing at last what she was going to do. Picking up the telephone again, she checked the number of her gynaecologist and dialled. The receptionist answered and in due course she was put through to Dr Hyland.

'Melanie Lloyd here, Dr Hyland. Thank you for all your advice, but I...I've decided to keep my baby.'

CHAPTER TWELVE

'ARE YOU SURE this neckline isn't too low, Nathan?' Gemma asked, coming out of their bathroom with a frown on her face.

Nathan had commissioned the gown to be specially made for her, having found the style in a period costume book of Regency England. He'd said it was just the thing for her to wear to the ball, and Gemma had complied because her own sense of fashion was still a little unformed and she did like to dress to please her husband. Made of cream chiffon and lace, the high-waisted flowing style had looked all demure innocence in the book, but the wide square neckline had turned out to be more revealing than she'd realised, especially with her new underwear.

'I...I thought it was all right when I last tried it on, but that corset thing you bought me pushes my breasts right up and together, and with my hair up, I...I feel almost naked.' She placed a modest hand over her cleavage and smiled nervously at him. Frankly, the neckline wasn't all *that* low, but Nathan's previous displays of jealous possessiveness had made her careful over doing anything to encourage any untoward attention from other males. 'If you like, I could change.'

Nathan, who was looking impossibly handsome in a black formal dinner suit with white ruffled dress shirt and black bowtie, stared at her for several seconds before walking slowly around the foot of their king-sized bed, his eyes never leaving her. Picking up the covering hand, he lifted it to his mouth and kissed it. 'Don't be silly. You look

delicious. Every man there tonight will be envious of me.
The neckline is a little bare, but I've a special something
for you to wear tonight that might help solve the problem.'

'Nathan, you haven't bought me more jewellery, have
you?'

His head lifted, a frown settling into his beautiful grey
eyes. 'You object to my giving you jewellery?'

'No, of course not, but you've given me so many presents since we've been married. Not a week goes by without
you coming home with something.'

'Most women would be delighted,' he said stiffly.

'And so am I. Truly. But what are you going to do when
Christmas comes? Or my birthday? They won't seem special if you give me things every other day.'

A wry smile pulled at his sensuous mouth. 'What a treasure you are, my darling. Not only sweetly innocent and
delightfully modest, but totally without greed. Maybe that's
why I like giving you things, because you don't ask for or
expect anything.' Still smiling, he bent to kiss her lightly
on the lips. 'You are a pearl beyond price. Which reminds
me. Come over here...'

He drew her over to her dressing-table which was so full
of his previous presents—other jewellery in a magnificent
jewel box; bottles of perfume; cosmetics; delicate porcelain
figurines; even a silver-handled brush and mirror set—that
she wondered how he had found room for this new dark
blue velvet jewel case.

'Open it,' he ordered.

She obeyed, her heart turning over at the sight of the
triple pearl and gold necklace and matching drop earrings.
If they were real pearls—and of course they were—they
would have cost a small fortune. Gemma tried to feel
happy, but her gasp and smile of pleasure felt false.

Over the past few weeks, the pattern of their marriage
had changed. And so had Nathan.

He no longer burst forth from his study when she came
home from work, eager to spend the entire evening with

her, mostly because he himself was rarely home when she got in. He was still out holding auditions for his play—which was proving difficult to cast—or discussing sets with the set designer, or costumes with the costume designer, or whatever else a director did.

Invariably, when he came home he was tired and pre-occupied, not wanting to go out so much. Not wanting to make love so much either. In fact he hadn't touched her this past week, which was beginning to bother Gemma a little. Her niggling concern that he would one day grow bored with her in that department was never far from her mind.

But one thing remained the same. She still felt like a highly prized possession, not a real wife, unless one thought of a wife as a totally submissive little thing who only opened her mouth to say, 'yes, sir, no, sir, three bags full, sir'. Nathan still made all their decisions without consulting her. Where they went, what they did, whom they invited over. The one time she'd been asked out by some of the girls at work for a girls-only night out, he'd made such a fuss—ranting and raving about the dangers of women being out at night without men to protect them—that she hadn't gone in the end.

'I thought pearls were just the thing for this dress,' Nathan was saying as he did up the clasp on the necklace, which had proven to be a choker and no real cover for her cleavage at all. 'Now that you're keeping out of the sun, your skin has lightened to a gorgeous honey colour.'

He trailed his fingers over her skin, then bent to press moist lips to the area of bare shoulder between the necklace and the beginning of the softly draped sleeves. Gemma shivered, but not, as she usually did, from pleasure. There was something odd about Nathan tonight, something dark and pensive that she didn't like. He seemed distracted, yet watchful. Every time he looked at her she had the feeling he was trying to see something. But what?

She suppressed an urge to sigh. Would she never get to

know what he was thinking? Never find out what brought about the strange changes of mood that sometimes afflicted him? They'd be going along quite happily together when suddenly—was it something she did or said?—he'd become silent and almost morose, often giving her the blackest, most suspicious look. .When that happened, she was at a loss what to do, as she was at a loss tonight.

She glanced in the mirror at Nathan standing behind her shoulder, and he was once again staring at her with that peculiarly intense expression in his eyes. Without stopping to think, she spoke her frustration aloud. 'Why do you keep on looking at me that way tonight, Nathan? You've been doing it ever since you came home.'

Immediately, his face was wiped of all expression and she could have screamed. As always when she dared to question him, he slotted that smooth mask into place, hiding everything from her. 'And what way is that, darling? You must know that I've always had trouble keeping my eyes off you. Especially in a dress like that.'

Their eyes met in the mirror, Gemma's angry with him for sidestepping her question. 'You were looking at me oddly long before I put this dress on, Nathan, and you know it. Why can't you just give me a straight answer for once? Every time I ask you a question you try to distract me with sweet talk so that you don't have to answer me.'

'What rubbish! I do no such thing. You women always imagine things. So I've been looking at you tonight. So what? You're my wife, aren't you? If you want me to be bluntly honest, Gemma, I've been wanting to make love to you from the moment I walked in the door, but you were busy getting ready for the ball, so I did the right thing and left you alone. I'm sorry if my eyes couldn't be similarly gallant,' he ground out, and, spinning away, strode angrily from the room.

Gemma stared after him, knowing in her heart that he was lying. She knew exactly the way he looked at her when he desired her, and that was not how he'd been looking at her tonight. The fact that he felt he had to lie over such a thing brought a rush of suspicions.

Was it that he couldn't bring himself to tell her that she was beginning to bore him? Had he perhaps met with Lenore today, and spending time with his beautiful and sophisticated ex-wife had made him see what a fool he'd been to marry a naïve child by comparison?

Gemma grabbed on to this last sickening suspicion, and ran with it. Maybe Nathan had not only seen Lenore today but lots of other days. Maybe the reason he hadn't been making love to *her* lately was because he didn't need to. Maybe he...

Gemma brought herself up with a jolt. This was all sheer speculation, the imaginings of a young and insecure bride. Still...it would put her mind at rest if Nathan would tell her where he'd been today, whom he'd been with. Surely she had a right to know that. Steeling herself, Gemma went in search of her husband.

She found him in his study, sitting at his desk and reading what looked like a report. Clearly, her sudden appearance in the doorway surprised him, for he jumped slightly in his chair.

'Good God, Gemma, you startled me. What do you want? Are you ready to go?'

'What are you reading?' she asked, more to see if she could get a straight answer for once instead of real curiosity.

'Nothing important. Just a quarterly report from one of my investment consultants.' He folded the sheets of paper, replaced them in a large brown paper envelope which he slipped into the top desk drawer. 'They're trying to get me to put some of my money back into the stock market.' His gaze raked over her. 'I see you haven't put your earrings in yet so you can't be ready. Surely you haven't come along here to keep on about my looking at you, have you?'

Gemma swallowed. 'No,' she lied. 'But I...I want you

to tell me something, Nathan, and please…just tell me the truth.'

His grey eyes cooled at this implication that he might not always tell her the truth. 'What is it?'

'I want to know where you went today. What you did. Whom you saw.'

'What is this, Gemma? What have I done to deserve the third degree?'

Panic at his continuing evasion stretched her nerves to breaking point. 'Once again you're going to side-step my questions, aren't you? Why can't you just tell me your movements, like any normal husband? What have you got to hide, for pity's sake?'

'Hide, Gemma? I'm not trying to hide a thing.' He got slowly to his feet, buttoning up his dinner-jacket as he made his way around the large desk. 'Look, I know I've been a bit distracted lately. This directing business is proving to be more time-consuming and involving than I realised.'

His handsome face melted into a disarming smile as he came up to her, curling gentle hands over her shoulders. 'As for telling you what I did today…I didn't realise you'd find it interesting. But if you must know we held more auditions for the part of the man opposite Lenore, and I'm glad to report we've at last found someone who might be able to carry off the demanding role.'

'*We*, Nathan?' Gemma pounced. 'Are you saying Lenore is always with you during these auditions?'

His smile faded, his eyes carrying total exasperation. 'Don't tell me you're still worried about Lenore. Good God, of *course* Lenore is present at the auditions! She does the reading with them. I have to see how they look and sound together. They have to spark off each other. Dammit, Gemma, if anyone has reason to be jealous in this marriage it's me! You've always got other men lusting after you.'

'That's not true!' she protested, her face flushing with frustration and fury.

'You don't see what happens behind your back, my dear,' he responded with dry sarcasm.

'If it does, then it's certainly not my fault,' she snapped. '*I* don't encourage them.'

'I know. That's why I do my best to protect you.'

'Then why let me wear this dress tonight?' she flung at him. 'Aren't you taking a risk, letting me show off my lust-inspiring body? Not that it seems to be inspiring much lust in *you* lately!'

When she went to whirl away he grabbed her, spinning her back hard against him, his fingers biting cruelly into her upper arm. 'You little cat, don't flex your claws with me or you might find yourself suddenly out of your depth.'

He grabbed both her arms and dragged her upwards till their eyes were level. And their mouths. 'I've a good mind to rip that bloody dress off you right here and now and give you a taste of *real* lust. Then you wouldn't be so ready to be so damned nice to some of the men who flirt with you. You might also appreciate what it is I've been trying to protect you from!'

Gemma's eyes had rounded, her mouth falling open in utter shock. This was a Nathan she had never seen before. And he terrified the life out of her.

Did he see the terror in her eyes? Was that why he suddenly set her back down and released her arms, stepping back with a small shudder.

'I'm sorry if I frightened you,' he muttered. 'Not that you didn't deserve a shaking-up, Gemma. You're still incredibly naïve. But I shouldn't have lost my temper and threatened you like that. It won't happen again. Go and put your earrings on,' he ordered brusquely. 'We have to leave for the ball, or we'll be late.'

Nathan watched her stumble from the room, his face tight as a drum. Once she was gone he consciously relaxed his clenched fists and turned to go over to his desk where he pulled open the top drawer and stared down at the brown envelope.

The investigation into Gemma's past had cost him a small fortune, but the man Zachary had recommended had come through with the truth at last, complete with documentation. Unfortunately, the truth was so appalling that he had made the difficult decision to keep Gemma's past a secret, especially from her.

Difficult decision?

His mouth pulled back into a darkly rueful smile. It hadn't been all that difficult, had it, Nathan?

Shutting the drawer, he locked and removed the key, slipping it in his pocket. Smoothing the grimace of self-disgust from his face, he walked from the room.

'OH, MELANIE, you look lovely!' Frieda exclaimed. 'That dress fits you like a glove.'

'It does, doesn't it?' she said, still surprised. One would have thought it had been made for her, not bought off the peg.

She twisted to examine the dress in the mirror from all angles. The colour was deep purple, the material satin, the style sleek and sophisticated with a tightly fitted elongated bodice that swished out into a long flowing skirt. It had long tight sleeves and a low off-the-shoulder neckline that showed off her pale creamy skin to perfection, not to mention her bust.

Included in the dress box that had been delivered to Belleview by express courier at eleven that morning had been a black satin evening bag, black satin pumps—which also fitted perfectly—and a black satin ribbon choker to wear around her neck, a gold heart centring it.

Melanie had loved everything on sight but she was still amazed at the supcrb fit. 'I'd love to know how Royce...' Suddenly, the penny dropped and she whirled round. 'It was you, wasn't it?' she accused her sister-in-law. 'You gave Royce some of my clothes. And a pair of my shoes!'

Frieda didn't look at all shamefaced. 'Well, of course I did! The man's mad about you, Melanie. And I think you're mad about him. I'd have done anything he asked me to if it meant getting you two happily together again.'

Melanie shook her head in exasperation. 'You're almost as bad as Ava. Don't you know the sort of man Royce is? He's an adventurer where women are concerned. A regular Don Juan. He's been travelling around the world, no doubt bedding some woman in every city he visited. I was simply his Sydney woman.'

Frieda was taken aback by Melanie's startling admission. 'You *were?* You mean, you and he…'

Melanie said nothing.

'I suppose I shouldn't be surprised,' Frieda muttered. 'You're so beautiful…'

'And he's a highly skilled seducer of beautiful women,' Melanie inserted drily. 'So please, Frieda, let's have no more of talk of Royce being mad about me. Royce is not mad about me, except in as far as I can give him what he wants till he sets forth for home.'

Frieda flushed a bright pink, her face shocked. 'And you're still going to go to this ball with him?'

Melanie patted her hand gently. 'Don't worry about me, Frieda. I know what I'm doing.' In a fashion, she added silently and with a pang of real doubt. Presenting herself in public at this ball as Royce Grantham's partner might damage her in the eyes of her employer. Byron Whitmore would correctly conclude that Melanie had become Royce's lover during his stay in Sydney, and she had a feeling he wouldn't like that.

'But are you going to let him?' Frieda asked with round-eyed wonder. 'I mean…you know…' Her pink face became bright red.

'I…I'm not sure,' Melanie hedged, not wanting to shock Frieda too much. For she had thought of nothing else all day but being in Royce's arms again.

'Well, if you do,' Frieda whispered, 'don't forget to be careful. You don't want to be getting pregnant, do you?'

Melanie didn't know how she kept a straight face. 'I'll

be very careful,' she returned, her lips twitching with the
irony of it all.

'I think it's just as well Ron's having his Friday night
drink with his mates,' his wife said, 'so that we don't have
to explain any of this to him.'

'I couldn't agree more,' Melanie said, turning to give her
hair a final brush and spray, then applying a liberal amount
of Arpège perfume. 'Where's Wayne, by the way?'

'Over at the girlfriend's place.'

'Oh? Took him back, then, did she?'

'Yes, today. But you've got no idea what that boy did.
Spent a fortune on sending her flowers. Long-stemmed red
roses, would you believe? But it did the trick. She was on
the telephone immediately, cooing like a dove. Silly twit
of a girl! Still, I shouldn't complain. I'm fed up with having
that boy underfoot all the time. You've no idea how noisy
and messy he is. Betty's mother's welcome to him! Oh,
my, there's the doorbell. That'll be Royce. After what
you've just told me I hope I can keep a civil tongue in my
head. And let's hope he's come in something different from
that sports car he was driving last time. Your lovely dress
will crush if you have to squash yourself into one of those.'

He'd come in a white stretch limousine with grey velvet
interior. And Frieda not only kept a civil tongue in her
head, she fairly gushed all over Royce, who switched on
the charm full-blast from the moment she opened the door.
But he did look splendid in a black dinner-jacket with satin
lapels and cummerbund which complimented Melanie's
gown to perfection.

Melanie felt her stomach flip over at first sight of him,
but it was his reaction to *her* that rattled her. Why did he
stare so? Why look at her as though he'd never seen her
before, or didn't know she could scrub up so well?

They didn't dilly-dally, and before long Melanie was settled in the spacious interior of the chauffeur-driven limousine and they were on their way towards the city.

'A glass of champagne for the lady?' Royce asked suavely, indicating the built-in bar.

'Why not?' She shrugged, and watched him fill the delicate flutes without spilling a drop. He handed her one glass and raised his in a toast. 'To the most beautiful woman in the world.'

'We're toasting Elizabeth Taylor?' she said drily.

'Please. I'm British. Though I was thinking of a certain dark-eyed, dark-haired beauty. Her name, however, is definitely not Elizabeth.' He clicked her glass and drank, his eyes never leaving hers.

Melanie had to admire his style. If she hadn't had some experience of Casanovas and con-men, she might have really been taken in by Royce. Still, that didn't stop the pain she felt when he worked his superficial charms upon her to such good effect.

In danger of succumbing to a sudden depression, Melanie lifted the glass to her lips and drank deeply. She'd promised herself not to become maudlin tonight. She'd accepted what he was and wanted their last night together to be a happy, carefree one. She took another swallow of the champagne.

'I know about the baby,' Royce said so unexpectedly that if there had been more champagne in her glass Melanie would have spilt it all over her dress. As it was, her hand shook terribly as she took the glass from her lips to stare at him in stark horror.

Seeing the glass tipping dangerously to one side, Royce swept it from her hands and put it back in the safety rack, along with his own. Melanie's trembling hands came to rest on her stomach, perhaps in an automatic and instinctively defensive gesture.

'You…you couldn't,' she rasped. 'I…I didn't…t…tell…'

'Yes, I know, but I asked Gemma.'

'Gemma?' she repeated blankly.

He frowned. 'Yes, Gemma. Mrs Whitmore. The one who works in the opal store at the Regency. I dropped in there on my way to the airport on the Monday morning after we parted, driven to find out something about your marriage. She told me that it wasn't just your husband who was killed in that car accident, but a baby as well.'

Melanie shuddered with a type of perverse relief when she realised what baby Royce had meant. Then she shuddered again.

'I can't tell you how sad I felt for you,' he said softly. 'And how guilty. As I said on the telephone yesterday, I knew there had to be things in your past that made you act the way you were acting, but I didn't want to know in the beginning. I wanted you in my bed and I was prepared to turn a blind eye to your pain to achieve that end.'

Still in shock, Melanie just nodded, unable to say a word.

He picked up her closest hand and started gently stroking her fingers. 'I haven't been able to get you out of my mind, Melanie. I've tried. Dear God, I've tried, but I couldn't. I had to come back, had to find out if what I was feeling was more than I've ever felt before. And now I know. I think I love you, Melanie. I think I've loved you all along.'

Melanie's heart squeezed so tight that she thought it had to break. The roses had been bad enough, but did he have to follow them up with this? God, didn't he know it wasn't necessary? She'd already decided to go to bed with him again. A cold fury descended to rescue her from imminent disintegration, encircling her heart within an icy shell, holding it together, holding *herself* together.

'Is this what you told Wayne to tell his girlfriend?' she mocked. 'Don't look so puzzled, Royce. You did tell Wayne about the red roses strategy when you picked up my clothes from Frieda yesterday, didn't you?'

He was frowning at her. 'Surely you aren't angry with me for borrowing some of your clothes, Melanie, or for giving the poor boy a little advice? He looked so down-in-the-mouth. I couldn't let a fellow male suffer so I gave him a few clues. Did they work, do you know?'

'Oh, they worked. There again…they always work, don't they? I'm here, aren't I?'

'Melanie, for pity's sake, you don't think…' He groaned. 'God, what a bloody fool I am! I thought…I just wanted to… God-damn it, woman, I simply wanted to show you that you were different from any of my previous women. I never send flowers. Never!'

'You've never had to before,' she reminded him caustically.

He stared at her. 'What did that bastard of a husband do to you to make you like this? Don't deny it. I know he made you miserable. Gemma told me that…'

Her brittle laughter cut him off. 'Gemma? What would Gemma know of my marriage? Nothing! And that's exactly what *you're* going to know. My past is mine alone, and I don't appreciate people poking and probing into it, *or* talking about me behind my back. Accept victory gracefully, Royce. You've got what you wanted. I'm going to the ball with you. Though frankly, I only agreed to come tonight because you were going home to England tomorrow and I felt badly about how we separated the last time. I like you. I really like you. You can be a sweet charming man, and you're an incredible lover. But don't insult my intelligence by talking of love. You don't love me. You don't even *know* me.'

'I'd damned well *like* to know you, but you won't give me the chance!'

'No, I won't.'

'Why?'

Why? She stared at him, steadfastly ignoring the confusion in her heart that he was talking like this, and grasping instead the certainty in her mind. Royce was another Joel. She'd sensed that the very first day they'd met, and she still sensed it. He'd come back to Sydney, not because he loved her, but to buy that damned opal. Royce did not really love her. No way. And she was never going to become involved with another man who didn't really love her.

'*Because,*' she said firmly.

'That's no answer.'

'It's the only one you're going to get.'

He shook his head, sighing in weary exasperation. 'I don't understand you. I don't think you understand yourself. Still, who am I to reason why?' he went on bitterly. 'My job is to pour champagne, be charming and an incredible lover, then get the hell out of your life in the morning. Simple. I've been doing that with women for years. I can do it on remote control. Would you like a little pre-ball sampler to show you what a good time you're in for tonight?' Abruptly, he pulled her into his arms.

'Royce, don't!' she cried, placing both hands on the hard wall of his chest and pushing at him quite ineffectually.

'Don't?' he scorned, his eyes contemptuous as he stared down at her trembling mouth. 'You mean *do,* don't you, Melanie? I seem to recall that your protests meant very little in the past.'

'Bastard!' she cried, tears springing into her eyes.

He stared at her for a long moment, then groaned and cradled her head against him, stroking her hair and speaking to her in softly soothing words. 'Let's not punish each other like this. It's cruel. And it's futile.' His sigh was ragged. 'You have every right to your privacy, if that's what you want. And every right to live your life as you see fit. I won't keep on making things difficult for you, sweetheart. I promise. We'll just enjoy tonight for what it is, right?'

'Right,' she whispered back weakly, then shivered.

He pulled back, a wickedly sardonic smile curving his mouth to one side. 'Then let's drink up,' he said, and reached for the champagne. 'We have a lot of memories to pack into one short night!'

CHAPTER THIRTEEN

THE BALLROOM at the Regency was a magnificent recreation of some of the European ballrooms of the past, with mirror-panelled walls, elaborate gilt-edged frescos on the high domed ceilings and chandeliers so ornate and large that they must have been hoisted into place with cranes.

Melanie peered over the shoulders of the group of people standing in front of them, trying to distract her churning stomach by admiring the surroundings. She'd no idea each couple was going to be formally presented as they arrived and she felt sick with nerves.

'Stop looking so worried,' Royce whispered. 'There's not a woman here to touch you. You'll be the belle of the ball.'

Melanie blinked over at him. Did he honestly think it was her appearance she was worrying over? It was her being here at *all* that was bothering her. She should have confessed to Ava and Byron she was coming.

Suddenly, there was nothing between herself and the roll of red carpet running right up the middle of the ballroom, along which each couple walked after being presented. Her eyes darted around the huge room, past the magnificently decorated banquet tables that lined the walls, down to where groups of people were gathered near the stage and the orchestra.

The first person Melanie saw was Byron, his wavy blue-black hair gleaming high above the two females flanking him. Jade was on his left, looking sensational as usual in a long scarlet strapless sheath. Ava stood on his right, very elegant in her cleverly draped cornflower-blue gown. Even her hair looked good, now that she'd had the frizzed ends cut off and the rest permed into a soft cap of golden-brown curls.

As Melanie watched them chatting away to each other, Kyle joined the threesome, bringing with him a couple of glasses of champagne. Gemma and Nathan were nowhere in sight.

The man whose job it was to present everyone stepped forward, dressed like a footman from the Regency period, with a powdered wig, red coat, white breeches and highly polished black boots. Royce handed him the gilt-edged tickets, whereupon the 'footman', after giving Melanie a highly appreciative look, assumed a suitably formal expression and announced in a loud, very Shakespearian voice, 'Presenting Mr Royce Grantham...and Mrs Melanie Lloyd!'

Heads twisted, mostly to stare first at Royce—he was the celebrity, after all—then at his companion. One selected group, however, stared straight at Melanie.

'Good God,' Byron gasped. 'That can't be *our* Melanie Lloyd.'

Ava was totally speechless, an affliction that Jade rarely suffered from.

'It most assuredly is,' she confirmed, smiling ruefully at the sight of their normally drab housekeeper making her way slowly down the red carpet, looking like a film star on her way to collecting an Oscar. A very *sexy* film star...

'Mmm,' was Kyle's only comment, but it brought a jealous glare from his fiancée.

'Down, boy,' she hissed, and he chuckled.

'I don't believe it,' Byron was muttering. 'What is she doing here with Royce? I thought she'd turned him down that night after dinner.'

Ava finally found her voice. 'Oh, no, she went out with him. She told me. And he sent her flowers yesterday.

Masses and masses of long-stemmed red roses. I was there when they arrived.'

Byron turned on his sister. 'You *know* about this… liaison, and you didn't tell me?' he asked, sounding both amazed and annoyed.

'It…it's not a l…liaison, Byron,' Ava stammered. 'Melanie says it's a…a friendship of convenience.'

'Good God, woman, open your silly eyes! No woman dresses like that for a simple bloody friendship!'

'Why so upset, Pops?' Jade queried archly. 'You wouldn't be jealous, would you?'

'Jealous? Why would I be jealous? Don't be ridiculous, Jade. I just don't like to see a nice woman like Melanie being taken advantage of by a man like Royce.'

'That's a fairly harsh judgement, Byron,' Kyle intervened smoothly. 'Your housekeeper is what? Thirty?'

'Thirty-two.'

'And a widow of some years?'

'Yes.'

'Then I doubt any man could take advantage of her, especially a man of Royce Grantham's obvious reputation. Mrs Lloyd strikes me as a lady who knows her own mind and wouldn't easily be fooled. I think she deserves more credit for common sense than you're giving her. If she's having an affair with Royce Grantham then it's because she wants to. She's a grown woman, Byron. And a very beautiful one. Did you think she was going to spend the rest of her life in total celibacy?'

'You don't know the whole story where Melanie is concerned,' Byron grumbled.

Now Jade was frowning. 'That's true, Kyle. She…oh, dear, they're coming over. Be nice, Pops. There's nothing to be gained by making things awkward, is there?'

'I guess not,' he muttered, and somehow found a charming smile for the new arrivals. After all, he couldn't really afford to alienate the main bidder for that infernal opal, could he? But it was to be hoped Royce would take both it and himself back to England tomorrow and leave Melanie alone. She deserved better, the poor woman.

Poor woman? Good God, she looked anything but poor tonight. She looked glamorous and gorgeous, and so bloody sensual he couldn't take his eyes off her. A definite prickling in his loins brought him up with a jolt. Damn, but he would have to find himself a woman. And soon!

'Melanie,' he said warmly, extending his hands to take both of hers. 'What a dark horse you are, sneaking out to this ball like Cinderella! But what a glorious gown. And how stunning you look in it, my dear.' Dropping her hands, he turned to shake Royce's hand and deliver some more polite patter, even if he was still somewhat rattled inside.

Melanie smiled a stiff smile and looked nervously round the group. Ava was staring openly. Jade was frowning slightly. And Kyle was smiling, thank God.

'You do look stunning, Mrs Lloyd,' he said.

'Do call me Melanie.'

'Very well. You must save a dance for me later, Melanie. That is…if my gaoler here will give me the key for a while.'

Jade bestowed a very possessive look his way, linking her arm with his and clasping it tightly against her side. 'I never thought I'd have to protect my man from *your* clutches, Melanie.'

Melanie laughed. It was all rather funny, in a way. Byron had done his best to cover his shock but it had been there in his eyes. There'd been something else in his eyes as well which bothered her a little. The last thing she wanted was for *Byron* to start lusting after her.

'You look very beautiful, Melanie,' Ava said enviously.

'And so do you, Ava. Doesn't Ava look lovely tonight, everyone?'

Everyone said she did.

A sudden awkward silence descended on the group, and into that silence came an astonishing announcement.

'Presenting Mr Damian Campbell and Ms Celeste Campbell!'

A sound like rushing water rippled round the room as most people either gasped or murmured something. The ones who weren't staring with their mouths open, that was.

Melanie was as shocked as everyone else, her eyes flying to Byron to see what his reaction would be. But where she had expected him to be blustering with fury and outrage, he was actually ashen-faced. And ominously silent. He stood there, staring at the woman, as were most people in the room by now, even the ones who had no idea who she was.

There was no doubt Celeste Campbell was worth staring at.

Rising forty, she looked at least ten years younger, her striking face unwrinkled, her sultry mouth painted and pouting, her long tawny blonde hair tumbling in glorious disarray around her shoulders and halfway down her back. But it was her body that riveted all the men's eyes, her tall athletic body, honed to perfection and outrageously displayed tonight in a dress that was both spectacular and shocking at the same time.

Champagne in colour, it might have been sewn on, so tightly was it fitted, following the curves of its female wearer right down to her trim ankles and dainty feet, which were sexily shod in gold sandals. The style was basically strapless, with a sheer layer of champagne chiffon that reached high round her neck and down her arms to her wrists. This alone would have been quite modest—despite the tightness—if it hadn't been for the selected gold beading on the body of the gown.

From a distance the beading stood out, the rest of the skin-coloured material taking on the appearance of bare flesh. It looked as if she was wearing a very skimpy costume, something like an exotic dancer would wear. A small area of beads covered each nipple area, one large bead rested over her navel, while more intense beading formed a provocative V at the juncture of her thighs.

When she turned side-on—the sides did not have beads—one gained a fleeting impression of nakedness right up to her armpits. The back of the dress—easily seen in the mirror panels on the wall as she walked up the carpet—was sheer chiffon to where the beading began on her buttocks. A slit right up to her bottom might have been there for movement. But Melanie doubted it. The legs on display were as sensational as the rest of her body.

Melanie found it impossible to take her eyes off the dress, and the woman in it. Byron, she fancied, was similarly hypnotised since he hadn't moved an inch since sighting her.

'One has to admire her gall,' Jade said at last.

'I was admiring more than her gall,' Kyle added drily. 'That is *some* dress.'

'It's disgusting,' Byron snapped, reefing his eyes away at last. 'That woman's disgusting.'

'What's she doing here?' Ava whispered, still gaping.

'To spite me, no doubt,' Byron snarled. 'What else?'

'Who's that she's with?' Ava went on avidly. 'He's years younger than Celeste. I suppose he's her newest toy-boy lover.'

'For pity's sake, Ava,' Byron snapped. 'Weren't you listening just now? That's her snake of a brother, Damian. Don't stare at him!'

Melanie had not noticed the brother. She'd been too busy staring at Celeste Campbell. Her eyes went back to where Ms Campbell and her male companion had stopped to speak to a couple they obviously knew, and her breath caught. Dear God, but that was the most beautiful man she had ever seen.

Beautiful. But yes…Byron was right. There was something about him, something…slimy.

Was it the way his jet-black hair was slicked straight back from his forehead? Or the way his deeply set dark eyes were moving almost slyly around the room while he dragged on a cigarette?

Impossible to narrow it down to one thing. It was an overall impression.

His heavy-lidded gaze landed on her and she stiffened. He didn't smile. He simply stared. A chill invaded Melanie and she wrenched her eyes away with a shudder of revulsion.

'Something wrong, Melanie?' Royce whispered.

'No...no, I'm fine.' But she wasn't at all sure that she was. Could evil be projected across a room like airwaves? Or was she becoming fanciful? Maybe Byron's contemptuous description of the man had coloured her thoughts.

'Let me get you a drink,' Royce suggested. 'I can see one of those red-coated waiters coming our way. What would you like?'

'Oh—er—champagne would be nice.'

'Champagne coming up. Anyone else for a drink? Ava, your glass is nearly empty.'

Conversation revolved around what everyone was going to drink next. They all agreed on another champagne for this round.

'Oh, look,' Ava exclaimed after her first sip. 'It's Nathan and Gemma at last. Oh, doesn't Gemma look enchantingly pretty in that sweet dress?'

Now Melanie had never felt Gemma looked enchantingly pretty in anything. Her body was too lush and earthy, her face too exotic with its almond-shaped brown eyes, high cheekbones and generous mouth to be labelled 'pretty'. Still, that air of youthful innocence she unconsciously carried was still there—despite her marriage to Nathan—and that dress might have been virginally sweet on another less voluptuous female, so she could understand how Ava could be misled into such a description. Ava's own ingenuousness where sex was concerned lent a naïveté to her opinions that would not have been echoed by any of the men looking at Gemma at that precise moment.

A sudden thought struck Melanie and, very, very carefully, she snuck a glance over at Damian Campbell. Oh, my God, she thought, her stomach contracting. Just look at the way he's staring at her. No, not staring, *eating* her up with his eyes. Suddenly, Melanie felt afraid for Gemma, which was crazy really. Nathan was an extremely possessive husband, and not one to allow men like Damian Campbell anywhere near his lovely young wife. Just look at how he'd reacted to Royce going into the shop and asking her a few simple questions.

Still…

Her gaze returned to Gemma as Nathan guided her down the red carpet. She doesn't look happy, Melanie thought. And neither does Nathan. He dredged up one of his smooth smiles as he approached, though it stiffened once he saw Royce, then faded entirely to a look of shock once he recognised Melanie.

'Don't say it, Nathan,' Jade warned laughingly. 'We all have and Melanie's sick of it, aren't you?'

'That depends on what he says,' she smiled. 'Hello, Nathan…Gemma. What a lovely dress.'

There followed quite a bit of discussion over Gemma's dress, till Ava suddenly grabbed her brother's arm. 'Good God, Byron,' she hissed, 'Celeste's coming over. Oh, my goodness. Oh, heavens…'

'Pull yourself together, woman,' he growled, though the blood had drained from his face again, Melanie noted. What *was* it between these two?

'Good evening, everyone,' Celeste drawled as the group parted like the Red Sea for her arrival. Up close, she was even more beautiful, with the most unusually captivating eyes. Almost oriental in shape, they were a sherry-yellow in the middle, rimmed in a dark brown, and lashed thickly with long curly brown lashes. They were quite magnetic in their exotic feline beauty. Melanie could not stop staring at them.

When she did finally look away it was to find the others

still staring at the woman with some interesting expressions on their faces. Byron, now that he'd had a moment to gather himself, was clearly furious. Ava was goggle-eyed. Jade was wryly admiring, while Kyle and Royce were simply wry, as though they recognised the type and were content just to look.

Gemma was the only one whose attention was not on Celeste Campbell, which was because she was frowning up at Nathan who, quite frankly, seemed the most uncomfortable of everyone. He was glaring at the woman with an expression bordering on explosive. Every muscle in his stiffly held body shouted an inner tension that was killing him.

'Byron, darling,' Celeste began silkily, not giving the rest of the group a single glance, let alone a word of greeting. Her eyes were all for Byron, only for Byron. 'It's so long since I've seen you. *Too* long. Not that I haven't got a bone to pick with you. What naughty person at Whitmore's has been spreading nasty rumours about Campbells' duty-free stores? Not you personally, I hope, though a little birdy told me it was. Truly, Byron, I didn't think you would stoop to such low tactics. Not a man of *your* honour.'

Did he wince at this last, barely hidden barb? Melanie couldn't be sure. He certainly seemed to stiffen slightly. Whatever his reaction, to give Byron credit, once he'd gathered himself, he was superb. 'You know what they say, Celeste,' he drawled. 'If you can't beat them, join them.'

'How divinely original! Are you saying you sincerely believe that I *do* give bribes and kickbacks as a normal business practice?' she delivered in a sweetly poisonous voice. 'Because if you do, and you say it out loud and in company, I might just have to take you to court for slander.'

'Do that,' he agreed without batting an eyelash.

'But before you do, Ms Campbell,' Kyle joined in in his usual cool fashion, 'I suggest you have a little chat with your sales and marketing manager.'

'Damian?' She flicked an eye over her shoulder to where

her brother was still talking to the couple on the corner. 'Now why should I do that?' she asked nonchalantly, though anyone could see that Kyle had struck a raw nerve.

'Just a suggestion,' Kyle drawled.

His drily triumphant tone wiped the smile from her face. 'And who are *you?*' she asked curtly.

'He's Whitmore's brilliant new marketing manager,' Jade jumped in. 'Not to mention my fiancé.'

Those cat's eyes narrowed upon this young upstart in the red evening gown, then widened. '*Jade?* God, surely you're not little *Jade!*'

Jade drew herself up tall. 'I certainly am. But I'm not so little any more, Aunt Celeste.'

'Goodness, no,' Celeste returned drily. 'You certainly aren't. And haven't you done well for yourself?' she added huskily, appreciative eyes travelling over Kyle.

'What in hell are you doing here, Celeste?' Nathan suddenly snapped, jerking everyone's eyes his way. Nathan was usually so cool and composed. This wasn't like him at all.

Celeste turned to face him, her expression withering in its contempt. 'Well, well, well, if it isn't Byron's bad-boy-makes-good protégé . Yet this doesn't appear to be the wife I last saw you with…' She flicked a knowing look over Gemma. 'Exchanged her for a younger model, have you? How very predictable of you. But to answer your oh, so polite question, Nathan, this ball was open to anyone who purchased tickets, which I did. But I don't mind you knowing my main reason for coming here. I've come to get something back that belongs to me.'

'There's nothing here that belongs to you, Celeste,' Nathan flung at her, a cold fury in his eyes.

'Oh, really?' Celeste scorned. 'Then take a look at that opal up there on the stage in that display cabinet. The one with the security guards flanking it. At least *half* of that belongs to me. Or, more accurately, to the Campbell family. David Whitmore robbed my father of his share nearly forty years ago. Frankly, I'm intrigued to find out how it comes still to be in the possession of the Whitmores when it was reportedly stolen over twenty years before.' She swung back to face Byron, her eyebrows arching. 'Byron? I think I deserve an explanation.'

'What you deserve, Celeste,' he said darkly, 'is not fit for the ears of the ladies present. I'll have you know that my father offered that opal to your father in 1945, gratis. But your father refused to take it.'

'That's a lie,' she countered icily. 'My father said your father cheated him while he was away, fighting for his country. And I believe him. No one hates that long and that well for *nothing!*'

Their eyes clashed, and everyone watching them knew that Celeste was no longer talking about their fathers but themselves. Celeste hated Byron, and it wasn't for nothing. Neither was it because of that opal.

'The Whitmores owe the Campbells nothing,' Byron bit out. 'You want the Heart of Fire back, Celeste? Then you bid for it! I'll find it rather ironic to fund some of the changes we're making at Whitmore's with Campbell money.'

Her cool voice was not matched by the fire still burning in those yellow eyes. 'My, my, I can see that Irene's passing hasn't sweetened your temper at all. And there I was, thinking you'd be a different man now that you were free of my appalling half-sister. My apologies, Jade, for speaking about your mother in such a fashion but you, better than anyone, must have known what a monster she was. Pity her husband didn't as well,' she finished savagely, and, turning on her heels, she departed as swiftly and angrily as her dress would allow.

Gemma stared after the woman, stunned. She'd heard a lot about Celeste Campbell, but the reality had far exceeded her expectations. The woman was outrageous in every way. And yet…one had to admire her style, her spirit and her overwhelming self-assurance. There wouldn't be too many men who'd tell her what to do, or what to wear, or how to act. No, sirree!

'I'll buy that damned opal myself,' Nathan muttered, 'rather than let her have it. God, what an appalling woman she is!'

Byron threw him a surprised look. 'And since when did Ms Campbell deserve *your* derision? I always thought you rather admired her.'

'Admire that slut? You'd have to be joking. She's perversely amusing from a distance but I don't want to spend time breathing the same air she does. That goes for that lecherous brother of hers too. If he looks at Gemma one more time, I'll thump the bastard.'

'Nathan, he *hasn't* been looking at me at all,' Gemma sighed wearily.

'I think,' Kyle interrupted diplomatically, 'that the ushers are trying to direct people to their seats so that the banquet can be served. Shall we, darling?' he asked his fiancée, and steered her away.

Melanie was relieved that she and Royce were not seated right next to the Whitmores' group. Much as the interchange between them and Celeste Campbell had been fascinating in a way, she could do without that sort of tension tonight.

She almost enjoyed the meal, possibly drinking too much wine, but the alcohol dulled the pain lurking deep in her heart, making her light-headed and slightly silly. She laughed at all of Royce's jokes, accepted his flirtatious comments and outrageous compliments without making a single sarcastic retort and generally played the role of agreeable female companion to perfection.

'I like you when you're happy,' Royce whispered into her ear while she was spooning a brandied strawberry into her mouth.

'And I wike you aw the time,' she said, the strawberry in her mouth making it impossible to say 'l'. It sounded so funny, she started to giggle.

He leant over and kissed her, prising open her lips and taking the half-eaten strawberry right out of her mouth into his. Her head jerked back to stare at him as he proceeded to eat it, stunned, yet aroused by the startling intimacy of it all.

'You're looking at me like that again, woman,' he said in a low voice. 'Don't do it, or I'll have to take you up to my room right here and now. In fact, that's a splendid idea.' He scraped back his chair and stood up, his sexy blue eyes hard upon her. 'Coming?'

She gaped up at him, then snapped her mouth shut and stood up as well. 'Yes.'

The triumph in his eyes brought a shiver of sexual excitement. He took her hand and began to drag her with unceremonious haste along behind the tables and chairs.

'What…what if they auction the opal while we're gone?' she whispered shakily once they were outside the ballroom doors.

'Don't worry about the opal,' he replied thickly. 'I have that matter well covered. Let's go.'

GEMMA SAT SILENTLY by Nathan's side, playing with her dessert, moving the cream aside and searching for the smallest strawberry. Seeing herself in this dress tonight had made her wonder if she should try to lose some weight. Lenore was so slim…

Suppressing a sigh, Gemma looked up and locked eyes with a man seated a fair way down the table on the opposite side. He winked saucily at her before she realised whom he was sitting next to. The infamous Celeste Campbell.

So this was the man who was supposed to have been ogling her obscenely earlier in the night, this incredibly handsome man with sparkling dark eyes and an open boyish grin. Yet Nathan had made him sound like Satan himself, probably because of his sister, who was, indeed, dressed in as scandalous a fashion as she was reputed to live her life. And there *she'd* been, worrying over a small amount of cleavage. Imagine how Nathan would have reacted if she'd come out in Celeste Campbell's dress.

And imagine how he would react if he noticed her looking down at the dreaded Damian Campbell!

Gemma dropped her eyes back to the strawberries and shifted them around some more. Truly, she had no appetite tonight. In fact, she felt generally wretched. What *was* she going to do about her marriage?

Nothing, she supposed. This was real life and real life was difficult at best. Hadn't she learnt that when she was a little girl? Why did she think falling in love would make it easier?

'You're not eating your dessert,' Nathan commented.

'No.' She stopped pretending and put down her spoon. 'I'm not hungry.'

'Or talkative. You haven't said a word to me since you sat down.'

'That should suit you, then,' she snapped. 'You don't like talking to me.'

'Certainly not in your present mood,' he grated out and turned away to speak to Byron on his left about the man they'd contracted today for the play.

Gemma made no attempt to listen. She hated that play and wanted to know nothing about it. And she hated Nathan tonight.

Feeling mutinous, she glanced down the table again in the direction of Damian Campbell, startled to find he was already looking at her. She felt an odd little flutter in her stomach when his smiling eyes narrowed to an intense gaze. And while there was something slightly disturbing about the way he was looking at her, it was also oddly compelling and she found it difficult to pull her eyes away. In fact, she couldn't, and soon she didn't even want to—

'Gemma!' Nathan snapped from beside her, and she jumped.

'W...what?'

'Ava was talking to you.'

'Oh...sorry...I...I...was daydreaming,' she said, feeling flustered and oddly guilty. What had happened just then? She couldn't quite understand it.

'Yes, Ava?' she asked distractedly, focusing at last on Byron's sister.

'I was wondering if you'd come shopping with me some time. Now that Nathan's so busy with the play you must have some spare time.'

'Oh, yes,' she said wearily. 'I have plenty of spare time.'

Had she said that loudly? Or did it fall into a momentary hush at the table? Whatever, her words seemed to echo around her ears, and when she slid a surreptitious glance down the table Damian Campbell's dark eyes were still intent upon her. A slow smile pulled on his attractive mouth and, before she could stop herself, Gemma was smiling back.

CHAPTER FOURTEEN

'GOOD EVENING, Mrs Whitmore.'

Gemma whirled as she let go of the ladies'-room door to stare down the corridor to a dimly lit corner in the distance. The red glow of a cigarette butt gleamed momentarily, just before Damian Campbell stepped out of the shadow into the light.

'Oh!' she exclaimed. 'It's you!'

He dropped the cigarette and crushed it underfoot. 'Come down here. I must speak to you privately for a moment. It's important.'

Gemma glanced nervously around, half expecting Nathan to materialise at any moment. 'I...I can't,' she whispered weakly.

'Why not? Won't the boss approve?'

'The boss? You mean Byron?'

'No, I mean your husband.'

'Nathan's not my boss!' she protested.

'Isn't he?' he said softly. 'I've never seen a wife so under the thumb. Or so nervy. Or so lonely.'

'I...I'm not any of those things. How dare you say such things to me?'

'I would dare to say a lot of things to you.'

She stared at him. 'What...what do you want?'

His laughter was low. 'Now that's a question. If I said a dance, would you dance with me?'

'I *can't!*'

'How about a quiet talk about anything you'd like to talk about?'

'No, I...I...'

'You can't,' he mocked. 'Better come down here, Mrs Whitmore,' he went on drily, 'before someone sees you already talking to me. Come on. I won't bite...'

Almost against her will, she found herself walking towards him, his darkly compelling gaze luring her on.

When she stopped short he reached out and drew her into an alcove, pressing her against the door-frame of a recessed door.

'What...what are you doing?' she protested breathlessly.

'Making sure your husband doesn't see us together, since that's what you're so afraid of.' He let her go to lean on the other side. 'Does he mistreat you?'

'No!' she cried, shocked.

'Oh, yes, I think he does. Maybe not with physical violence but in many subtle ways. You see, I know a lot about Nathan Whitmore. He's a twisted introvert, your husband. Not fit material as the life partner of a young vibrant woman like yourself. He'll stifle you, smother you, destroy you.'

'You're wrong!'

'Am I? We'll see.'

'Why are you saying these things to me?' she sobbed. 'They're wicked. And cruel.'

'Sometimes you have to be cruel to be kind. Look, I'm sorry if I've hurt you by speaking out, Mrs Whitmore. But I couldn't see you leave tonight without knowing that somewhere in this big bad city you have a friend. If you ever need one.'

'But I...I don't! I mean—'

'You will,' he interrupted firmly. 'How old are you, Gemma?'

'How...how did you know my name?'

'I know a lot of things about you.'

'But how?'

'This place is full of Whitmore employees. You've no idea how they like to gossip about their employer, and their employer's family. So, Gemma, how old are you? That's the one thing no one seemed sure of.'

'T...twenty.'

'Tch tch. And Nathan's what? Thirty-five, or -six?'

'What has Nathan's age got to do with anything?'

'It has everything to do with everything. You don't think he married you for your intellectual company, do you?'

Gemma stared at him.

'To be brutally frank, my dear, Nathan Whitmore does not love you. And one day soon you'll realise that. When you do, you'll need a friend, someone who can appreciate the beautiful, bright young woman that you are. The whole woman, not just the body.'

Her eyes had opened wider and wider with his coldly delivered yet oddly passionate words, her heart beating faster and faster.

'Yes, open your eyes to the truth, Gemma,' he went on relentlessly. 'Nathan Whitmore only wants you for one thing, and soon he won't even want you for that. I know his type. Believe me.'

'I don't believe you!' she cried. 'You're wrong. I won't listen to any more you've got to say. I won't!'

And she ran, back along the corridor, back into the ballroom where the milling throng of dancers covered her flight and her fluster. She slowed her steps, trying to cool her face so that by the time she rejoined Nathan at the table she would be fully composed. But she wasn't entirely, and he noticed, his glance one of dark suspicion.

'You were a long time in the powder-room. And you look flushed.'

'I...I'm finding it terribly hot in here. Do you think we could go home?' She stayed standing, hovering, hoping.

'It's really not that hot in here, Gemma. In fact, it's a little on the cool side.'

'Well, *I'm* hot!' she argued, knowing she sounded like a petulant child, but unable to stop herself. She had to get out of here. Had to! 'I want to go home, Nathan. If you won't take me, I'll take a taxi.'

He stared up at her, eyes narrowing. 'The auction's about to start. Do you think you could wait till it's over?'

'No.'

'Don't be ridiculous, Gemma. It won't take long.'

'Nathan, I don't ask you to do much for me but I'm asking you this. Please take me home.'

'I can't go home before the auction, Gemma. I'm going to bid.'

Her eyes flung wide. 'But *why?* Don't tell me it's just to stop Celeste Campbell getting the Heart of Fire! Who cares if she buys it? Why should it matter?'

'Would you keep your voice down?' he demanded impatiently.

'No, I won't! I'll speak as loudly as I damned well like. This is a free country.'

His frustrated sigh made her feel guilty. She was behaving *very* badly now, but something—was it fear that what Damian Campbell had said to her was true?—was driving her on. Maybe she was testing Nathan's love, trying to make him prove that his feelings for her went far beyond the physical.

'I was going to buy it for *you,* Gemma.'

Another present, she groaned silently, but with growing distress. I'm not a *real* wife. I'm little better than a mistress, to be soothed with gifts and side-tracked with smooth lies. Damian was right. Nathan does only want me for sex, and he doesn't even want me for that any more. Oh, God...

'Sit down, Gemma.'

She stared down at her husband, stared deep into his eyes and saw nothing but a reflection of her own misery and uncertainty in those implacable grey pools. Suddenly, all the other warnings people had given her about Nathan rushed back with a vengeance.

Gemma's head was beginning to whirl. Out of the corner of her eye she saw Damian Campbell return to his seat and,

once again, she felt the need to get away from both him
and Nathan. She needed time to think. She needed to
breathe some clean fresh air.

'No, Nathan,' she said shakily but with a surprising
amount of resolve. 'I am not sitting down. I am going
home. You stay and bid for the opal, by all means. But if
you're successful, don't bother giving it to me. I don't want
it! I haven't wanted it since I found out my father stole it.'

'For God's sake, stop being so melodramatic,' Nathan
ground out in a low, but clearly furious voice. 'That opal
is your birthright and I want you to have it. Now, will you
please sit down and stop making a scene in public?'

'Have you listened to a word I said, Nathan? I doubt it.
I don't want to sit down. I don't want that rotten opal. I
want to go home. *Now!*'

'Go, then,' he bit out. 'Don't let me stop you. All little
girls should be home in bed by now, anyway.'

'Yes, they should,' she hissed back. 'But they shouldn't
be sharing their beds with men old enough to be their fathers!'

Gemma's last glimpse of Nathan's face haunted her as
she swept from the ballroom. God, but she'd hurt him.
She'd really hurt him.

Go back, her heart whispered as she hurried on, out
through the foyer of the hotel and towards the bank of taxis
waiting just outside the main doors. Go back. Apologise.
Kiss and make up.

But she didn't go back. She swept on, out of the hotel
and into a taxi.

'WE'RE JUST IN TIME!' Royce said as they slipped back into
the ballroom. 'The auction's starting. Let's stay and watch
from back here.'

'But won't they have difficulty seeing you bid?'

'I'm not going to bid. I have an agent up front bidding
for me. I've given him a ceiling.'

'What if Celeste Campbell goes higher?'

'Then she can have it.'

'But I thought… I thought…'

His gaze held a steely resolve. 'I came back to Sydney to secure only one treasure, Melanie, and she's standing right next to me. I love you, and I want to marry you. I don't care about the past, either yours or mine. I won't take no for an answer so you might as well just say yes.'

Melanie froze. How ironic that his final sentence contained the very same words Joel had used when he proposed to her. And right after he'd just made delicious love to her. Oh, with hindsight, it couldn't compare with what she'd just shared with Royce, but she hadn't known that back then. At the time, she'd thought Joel was an incredible lover. She'd been blinded by the sex and the charisma of the man, by his boldness and never-say-die determination. So she'd just said yes and in the end her blind faith in his love had cost her baby son his life.

How could she just say yes again, on so brief an acquaintance, even if she did yearn to do so? Maybe if it had just been herself then perhaps, yes, she would take the risk. But there was another child's life at stake. She or he deserved better than potentially divorced parents…

'I…I thought you were a confirmed bachelor,' she said.

'I was. Till I met you.'

'Royce, I…'

'Hear me out before you say no.'

She closed her eyes against the weakness already invading her.

'I love you,' he rasped into her ear. 'I know you don't believe me but it's true. I never meant to fall in love, never meant to take the risk of going through the hell my father went through. But all that went by the board the moment I set eyes on you, Melanie Lloyd. You love me too. I *know* you do.'

She opened her eyes and turned their luminescence upon him. 'Hush up, Royce,' she said softly. 'The bidding's starting.'

'Stuff the bidding! Come back upstairs with me.'

'No,' she said firmly, knowing that was where she was the weakest, in his arms. 'I want to see this. We...we can talk afterwards.'

'Oh, all right,' he grumbled. 'Might as well watch my own money being spent.'

Melanie was grateful to the auction for its distracting qualities. Bidding was spirited till the figure reached the million-dollar mark, then things slowed right down. When it finally passed one and a half million, Royce sighed.

'Well, that's me out. I'm no fool. The thing's not worth that much.'

'I wonder who's left in?' Melanie said, trying to see.

Royce craned his neck. 'Byron's bidding. And my God, so is Nathan! What's the matter with those two, bidding against each other? That's insane! No, there's someone else bidding as well. Not that Campbell woman, though. She's sitting perfectly still. Nathan's just dropped out. Byron hasn't. The man's lost his head! Hell, some idiot's bid two million.'

The auctioneer looked at Byron for a counter-bid but no, he was shaking his head. Melanie felt relieved, a sentiment echoed by Royce.

'Thank God Byron came to his senses in time. Whoever just bid that two million will be getting themselves a damned expensive trinket!'

'Two million once,' the auctioneer intoned pompously. 'Two million twice... Sold, for two million, to the gentleman over there.'

A balding gentleman rose, then turned to smile at Celeste Campbell, who got slowly to her feet, her expression triumphant.

'Oh-oh,' Melanie groaned.

Celeste mounted the stage to quite a few murmurs, mostly because of what the slit in the back of her dress was showing. When she reached the microphone she just stood there for a few moments, waiting like a golden god-

dess while her subjects gradually fell silent. Which the
did.

'You are looking at one very happy lady,' she said in he
slightly husky and very sexy voice. 'You may not know thi:
but the Heart of Fire was once owned jointly by the Whit
mores and the Campbells, but through…circumstances…
became the sole property of the Whitmores. You may als
not know that many many years ago, it mysteriously dis
appeared—presumed stolen. I, for one, was astonished t
learn of its equally mysterious reappearance. But Mr Byro:
Whitmore seems content to leave that a mystery. Unless, o
course, we can persuade him to come up here and enlighte:
us…'

Heads turned to Byron. Even from that distance, Melani
could see his face was like granite, his folded arms an
wide-legged stance showing a controlled anger. Murmur
changed to clapping, and soon Byron was being urged o
to the stage. He went with obvious reluctance and annoy
ance.

Celeste's pointy chin lifted as he approached, but for on
who had invited this confrontation she was suddenly look
ing far from comfortable. Of course, Melanie could not se
the expression in Byron's eyes as he mounted the steps
since his back was to everyone else. Still, she knew hov
formidable and intimidating Byron could be when his blooe
was up. And she could well imagine he was close to losin;
his temper.

Yet when he turned to face the curious crowd, his hand
some face was lit by a charismatic smile, his quite beautifu
blue eyes glittering with what most people would hav
taken for indulgence or dry amusement. But a more intui
tive onlooker might have seen a hint of malevolent intent
of an underlying hardness that bespoke hatred and fury.

'My dear Celeste,' he said smoothly into the micro
phone as she took an almost nervous step sidewards, 'I hav
long wanted to put to rest the ancient and quite erroneou
rumours that a feud exists between our two families. Al

there is, folks, is a healthy competition between two similar businesses. Contrary to popular opinion, I am delighted that a Campbell has purchased our marvellous opal.'

'Really, Byron?' Celeste scoffed with a small smile, seemingly having recovered her composure. 'Which is why you were the underbidder, I suppose? Because you sincerely wanted me to have the Heart of Fire?'

Some muted gasps rippled through the room.

Byron's smile sent a shiver down Melanie's spine. She'd never seen him look so dangerously wicked.

'My dear lady,' he drawled, 'perhaps I was merely bluffing you into paying more. As for your other query…I wish I could relate a wildly romantic tale for everyone to hear about the opal's reappearance, but I'm afraid I cannot oblige. The tale is a very simple one. An old miner died recently and the opal was found in his possession, recognised, then returned to its rightful owner. The only mystery is how an opal stolen from my home here in Sydney turned up over twenty years later in the hands of an old derelict at Lightning Ridge. What do *you* think, Celeste? Could you supply a solution to this mystery?'

Celeste's frozen face was broken by a brittle laugh. 'What do I think? I think that's your story, Byron, and you're obviously going to stick to it.'

More laughter erupted from the ballroom. Byron grinned knowingly and said, 'True.'

Celeste looked furious and was about to say something else when a man in a black dinner suit and a black balaclava pulled over his head suddenly strode on to the stage. Everyone gasped when he put a pistol to Celeste's head, snaked an arm around her waist and dragged her to one side, well out of reach.

'It's all right, folks,' the masked man said with coldly controlled menace. 'I won't shoot Ms Campbell here if you all stay nice and quiet and don't move.'

There was a stunned silence when another balaclavaed criminal suddenly appeared on the stage, waving a lethal-looking rifle at the security guards while he disarmed them, then proceeded to put the Heart of Fire into a canvas sack along with the opal pendant sitting on a side-table that was to be presented to the belle of the ball later in the evening.

Melanie was as stunned as everyone else.

Byron, she noted, had gone a pasty shade of grey.

When someone pushed her own startled body away from the wall and jabbed something in the small of her back, it took a few seconds before she realised she had just been taken captive as well.

Royce was contemplating slipping through the back doors on his right to raise the alarm when a low voice whispered in his ear. 'Don't even think about it, mate. There's a gun pointed straight at your girlfriend here and if you move she's dead.'

He looked over and saw Melanie's wide frightened eyes and wanted to kill the bastard standing behind her. But how could he without endangering her life? He'd never felt so powerless. Or more sure that he loved this woman. God, if anything happened to her, he wouldn't want to live any more!

'Keep calm, everyone,' the head of the trio called out from the stage in his coolly arrogant voice. 'We're leaving now, but we're taking along a couple of hostages to make sure none of you does anything stupid till we're well clear. Come on, sweetheart,' he said to Celeste. 'We're *definitely* taking you. And my friend has chosen another delectable little honey from down the back, in case all you distant folks are thinking of doing something foolish.'

Heads swivelled to see a pale-faced Melanie being pushed towards the back doors by her captor. Royce groaned his frustration. What should he do? What *could* he do? If he made a move, Melanie might be killed. Yet he'd heard experts advise never to let a criminal take a person away from the scene of the original crime. Experience spelled out that the danger to their personal safety increased with that move. But dammit, the gun was rammed right in her back!

The other two gunmen were by now making their way down the steps of the stage, Celeste Campbell in front of them. An equally frustrated-looking Byron stared after them, clearly appalled at what was happening.

When Celeste hesitated at the foot of the steps her kidnapper pushed her roughly ahead of them so that she stumbled to her knees. Gasps of horror punctuated the hushed room when he viciously yanked her upright by the hair.

It was then that the most astonishing thing happened. Celeste Campbell spun round with a cry of raw rage, her body lifting from the ground, her left leg sweeping round in an arc so quick and so expert that all the onlookers could do was gasp. Her assailant was rendered unconscious with one karate kick to the head, and within seconds the second man fell to a similar blow.

Unfortunately, the third man, the man with the gun at Melanie's back, was some distance from everyone and had pulled Melanie round in front of him for protection. Royce saw the man's panicky agitation at what was happening, heard him cock the gun. There was a loud crack, and a red flower bloomed in Melanie's upper chest. Her arms flung wide as she lurched forward, as did her eyes and her mouth. She twisted to stare blankly at Royce as she crashed to the ground, and he cried out his anguish. In a wild fury, he wrenched the gun away from her assailant and smashed his fist into the masked face. Smashed it again and again till he crumpled.

But it was all too late. Too late.

'Melanie,' he moaned, sinking to the floor and scooping her limp body up in his arms. Tears flooded his eyes at her deathly stillness. 'Oh, my love...my love...'

ROYCE SAT ALONE in the waiting-room, anguished and ill. It was four in the morning and he'd been back from the police station for over an hour, waiting for word of Melanie.

'She's in Theatre,' the night sister told him when he arrived. 'The surgeon will speak to you as soon as he's finished, Mr Lloyd.'

Royce had not bothered to correct the nurse's misconception of his identity. What did it matter who she thought he was?

Jumping up, he began to pace. Maybe he should ring Frieda and Melanie's brother. No, better to wait. Why wake them up and worry them when they couldn't even see her? Maybe, in a short while, he'd have good news. Then, he'd ring them.

He swung round at the sound of the door opening. But it wasn't a doctor entering. It was Byron, looking every one of his forty-nine years.

'God,' Byron sighed. 'What a night. The police have finally let Celeste go home. Not that she hasn't stood up to the ordeal quite well. That's one tough woman, I can tell you. And an amazing one. Who would have believed she was a martial arts expert?'

'Pity she chose that moment to demonstrate her skill,' Royce bit out. 'Because of her, Melanie could be dying.'

'That's a bit harsh, Royce. Celeste simply reacted to the treatment that bastard was handing out. She didn't stop to think. And Melanie's not going to die. The sister on the desk has just told me the operation went well. The doctor will be in to see you shortly.'

Royce's shoulders sagged with relief. 'Thank God.'

'You look as if you could do with a cup of coffee,' Byron said, and made his way over to the automatic drinks machine.

'No, thanks. I couldn't drink a thing.'

'No? Well, I think I'll have one.'

It was while Byron was getting himself a hot drink that a harried-looking, green-robed individual strode in. He looked appallingly young to be a surgeon, Royce thought. Or was it that he felt appallingly old?

'Mr Lloyd?' he asked, glancing from one man to the other.

Royce stepped forward, still not in the mood to explain anything. Better they keep thinking he was Melanie's husband. That way, he'd find out everything he wanted to know. 'That's me,' he said, hoping his firm tone would keep Byron's mouth shut.

'Your wife's doing quite well, Mr Lloyd,' the doctor told Royce. 'The bullet punctured her left lung and ripped through quite a bit of bone and tissue, but fortunately it missed her heart and the major blood vessels. She's resting quite comfortably and you should be able to see her shortly.'

'Then she's completely out of danger?' he asked, still shaken by the storm of emotion inside him. 'I mean... Everything's going to be all right? Absolutely everything?'

'If it's the baby you're worried about, Mr Lloyd, then let me put your mind at rest. Everything's fine in that department too.'

Royce swayed on his feet, grasping at the doctor's arms. 'Baby? Melanie's having a *baby?*'

'Good God, man, didn't you know? She's talked of nothing else, even under the anaesthetic. We had to save her baby. That was all that mattered.'

'Oh, God...' Royce spun away, his head dropping into his hands.

The doctor placed a hand on his shoulder. 'I'm sorry. I didn't realise she hadn't told you yet. Perhaps you'd better not let on that you know till she tells you. We certainly don't want her upset just now, do we?'

Royce's nod was grim, his heart in turmoil. A baby... Dear God... And she wasn't going to tell him...

'I'll send a nurse in when you can see her,' the doctor said, and made a discreet departure, leaving Royce with his churning thoughts. He didn't understand how it could have happened. Or when?

And then he realised. On that Sunday…in the kitchen. She'd been very upset afterwards… He'd thought she was on the Pill, when clearly she hadn't been. She'd used some other method the night before, a method which was no longer protecting her that morning.

'I ought to throw this coffee in your face, you bastard,' Byron ground out.

Royce's head jerked up and around, distressed eyes slowly hardening when he saw Byron's fury. 'Don't jump to conclusions, Byron. This is not what you think.'

'You mean it's *not* some worldly womanising bastard taking advantage of a lonely woman? And what would have happened if *this* hadn't happened tonight? You'd have been winging your way back to England tomorrow without a damned care in the world, while poor Melanie's life will have been destroyed once again!'

'That's not true! I told Melanie I loved her tonight and I asked her to marry me. I am *not* going to go back to England tomorrow. I cancelled my flight the moment she agreed to come to this ball with me, the moment she gave me the chance to prove to her how much I love her and want her.'

'My God, you actually almost sound sincere!'

'I *am* sincere, dammit. And if there's anything you know about Melanie that you think I should know then tell me, man. *Help* me! She's having my baby, for pity's sake.'

Byron's frown was troubled, then pensive. 'Melanie's a very tragic lady,' he said slowly, 'with a very tragic past.'

'I've gathered that, but she won't tell me anything. She loves me, Byron, I'm sure of it, but she refuses to trust me.'

'That's understandable. I think she would have trouble trusting *any* man, let alone someone of your reputation. But that's beside the point. You can't change your past any more than Melanie can change hers. In the circumstances, however, I think you have a right to know what you're up against.'

He dragged in a deep breath then launched forth. 'When Melanie answered the advertisement I put in the paper for a housekeeper over two years ago, she actually told me very little about herself except that her husband and baby son had been killed in a car accident two years previously, and that she hadn't had a job since. Most of my knowledge of her past comes from a private telephone conversation I had with her brother, Ron. Have you met him?'

Royce shook his head in the negative. 'I have met his wife, Frieda, and his son, Wayne, but Ron's been out every time I've been to the house.'

'Pity. Ron might have filled you in on things. He's no gossip but he does care about his sister. He only told me the sordid details because I'd hired her for a live-in position.'

'Good God, I knew that bastard of a husband had done something bad to her,' Royce muttered.

'That bastard,' Byron continued, 'went by the name of Joel Lloyd. He was an ambitious and reasonably successful advertising executive, handsome as the devil and a good ten years older than Melanie. They met when she joined his company as a receptionist at the tender age of nineteen. Apparently he swept her off her feet, married her within months, made her stop work, then proceeded to turn her into the perfect executive wife. She took lessons in everything, from grooming to interior decorating to cooking to floral arrangements. Ron hated him, said he was all show and no substance, though he admitted he had style and charm and more hide than a herd of elephants.

'The marriage seemed happy enough, however, till Melanie started wanting a baby. Joel kept putting her off. Years went by, so one day Melanie just went ahead and got pregnant, and, surprisingly, once presented with the baby her husband was tickled pink. Adored the child apparently. They called him Peter. But then things started going wrong in his career, and dear Joel became a cocaine addict. No one's sure which came first. It came out at the inquest that he'd also been having affairs since shortly after his honeymoon, though he'd hidden them well. Melanie had found out not long before his death about the coke but not the women. Worried about him one day, she came to the office and caught him in some store-room having sex with the mail girl.'

'Hell.'

'The story goes she didn't say a word, simply went home and started packing. Joel came barging home after her, screaming all sorts of verbal abuse and warning her not to take the child. When she picked the baby up and went to leave, he snatched the child out of her arms, shouting at her that if he couldn't have the child then neither could she. He threw the baby into the front seat of his car, and drove off at breakneck speed. Melanie was running after him down the street when the car veered off the road and straight into a telegraph pole. It exploded into flames on impact and she had to watch while her husband and baby were incinerated right in front of her eyes. Apparently, she had a severe emotional breakdown afterwards.'

'My God, no wonder. And no wonder she lost faith in men. I...I wish I'd known some of this earlier...'

'Would it have changed anything, I wonder?' Byron said with a sigh. 'Knowing things about a woman doesn't seem to change how you feel about them, or how you act with them. Lust has a way of making bastards of the best of men.'

'What I feel for Melanie is not just lust,' Royce denied heatedly. 'I love the woman more than life itself.'

'Perhaps you do, Royce. Perhaps you do. And Melanie must love you to have your child. I would have sworn she would never have a child again. Who knows? Maybe she *is* ready to live again. With you.'

'God, I hope so.'

'But if you ever hurt her,' Byron warned darkly, 'you'll have me to answer to.'

An efficient-looking nurse bustled in. 'Mr Lloyd?' he directed straight at Royce, who nodded. 'Doctor says you can see your wife now. Come with me, please.'

'I'll go home, Royce. Ava will be worried sick. Ring me if there are any changes and don't forget to contact Melanie's family.'

'I won't.'

Royce's heart turned over when he saw her. She was so pale and still, a tube running from her arm to one of those plastic fluid bags. 'Is...is she awake?' he whispered.

Before the nurse could answer, Melanie's eyelids fluttered, then lifted, revealing those beautiful black eyes of hers. But how haunted they looked with those deep black rings under them.

'I'm awake,' she croaked.

'Just a few minutes,' the nurse warned, and left the room.

Royce pulled up a chair on the side without the tube and picked up her hand. How cold it felt, and how frail. 'You're going to be all right,' he said, trying to rub some warmth into the hand.

Her weak smile moved him. 'And you're going to miss your plane.'

'The next plane I catch for England,' he told her gently, 'will be with you by my side, as my wife.'

She closed her eyes for a few seconds then opened them again. They were wet.

A huge lump filled Royce's throat and he just couldn't speak.

'I...I think I have something to tell you,' she said at last. 'I...hope you won't be angry with me.'

Royce swallowed and forced himself to speak. 'I could never be angry with you. Melanie...darling...you don't have to say a word. I know about the baby. The doctor let it slip, and I'm so happy I could burst.'

'But you...you don't understand... You don't know...'

'I know about everything and I understand everything. All I can say is that I *do* love you, darling. Really truly love you. When I thought you might die I wanted to die myself. You're all I will ever want. You and our child, and perhaps some more children. Would you like that?'

She nodded, tears spilling over to run down her cheeks. Royce battled to keep his own eyes from flooding.

'Making my family happy is going to be my next goal,' he promised. 'And it will be the best ever goal in the world because it will never end. Say you'll marry me, darling. I'll die if you don't.'

Her smile widened a little. 'Well, we can't have that, can we?'

His heart turned over. Oh, my beautiful Melanie. My beautiful brave Melanie. How could anyone have hurt you like that? I'll make it up to you, my darling, all the days of my life. He lifted her hand to his lips and kissed it.

'I love you,' he said in a strangled tone.

Melanie closed her eyes, her heart swelling with an emotion she thought she would never feel again. Not just love, but faith. This man truly loved her. She knew it. She *felt* it. It was real.

It had taken a near tragedy to make her see the truth clearly. With the danger had come a certain clarity of mind. She'd known, in those few seconds before she lost consciousness back in that ballroom, when she'd thought she was going to die, that if she had a second chance, if God was good enough to give her that, she would grasp it with both hands.

Her eyes opened and she smiled up at Royce, a dazzling smile that came from the heart. 'And I love you, darling,' she said. '"Till death us do part".'

CHAPTER FIFTEEN

'WHAT'S THE NEWS?' Gemma asked anxiously when Nathan put down the phone. 'It sounded hopeful from here.'

'She's going to be all right.'

Gemma dropped down into the sofa, all the air rushing
from her body. Suddenly, she started to cry.

'Gemma…darling…' Nathan sat down beside her and
pulled her into his arms. Gemma went because she didn't
have the strength to fight him any more. She'd wanted to
fight him by the time he got home from the ball, the hours
of anxious waiting obliterating any wish to make up. She'd
paced the apartment, wondering where on earth he was and
why he didn't come home. It was to be thanked Lenore
hadn't been at the ball or she would have started imagining
all sorts of things.

Then, shortly after three, the key had turned in the lock
and she had stiffened, ready for the fray. But then she had
seen his face and known that something dreadful had happened, something that made their squabbles seem insignificant.

The whole horrific tale had tumbled from his still
shocked mouth and she'd listened to it all in appalled silence. They'd all been kept at the ball for ages by the police, after which he'd driven Ava home to Belleview for
Byron because he had to go with Celeste down to the police
station, being one of the main witnesses to the robbery and
the aftermath. Nathan had returned to the police station
where he'd waited till Byron was free to go, thinking Byron
might need a lift home, but he wanted to go back to the

hospital. By this time, Nathan had been thinking he'd better be getting home himself, Byron promising to ring as soon as he knew anything.

'I could do with a drink,' Nathan said with a ragged sigh after Gemma's weeping had subsided. 'I think you could do with one too.' He rose and went over to the well-appointed bar in the corner and poured them both a brandy, returning to give Gemma hers before slumping down in an armchair opposite with his. She sipped obediently, while wondering why he hadn't sat back down next to her.

'Byron says Melanie's expecting Royce Grantham's baby,' he said at last.

Gemma's teeth rattled against the glass before it dropped down to her lap. Her eyes were wide upon her husband's.

'He *says* he's going to marry her,' he added sceptically. 'He *says* he loves her.'

'Maybe he does,' she returned with more venom than she'd intended. 'Some men do fall in love, you know.'

Their eyes met and Gemma would have given the world to know what lay behind that cool grey gaze.

'I realise that. But rarely men like Royce Grantham. And never men like Damian Campbell,' he finished coldly.

'Why on earth not?' she defended, despite a guilty heat entering her cheeks. 'They're human beings too, aren't they? They're as capable of falling in love as…as you and me.'

'I suppose Royce could be,' he said, idly twirling the brandy balloon in his fingers. 'But not that bastard Campbell.'

'He speaks highly of you as well,' she snapped before she could bite her tongue.

Those silvery grey eyes darkened to slate. 'So the truth is out at last,' he drawled. 'He did speak to you, didn't he? When you were so long away at the Ladies' and you came back to the table, all hot and bothered. What did he say, Gemma? What clever line did he spin you?'

'Why should I answer your questions when you refuse to answer mine? Or when you *lie?*'

'When have I lied to you?'

'Earlier this evening when you said you wanted to make love to me. That was a lie.'

His steely gaze dropped to the rapid rise and fall of her breasts and her breath caught. Now he *was* looking at her with desire. She'd never be mistaken about *that* look. Worse, her body leapt in instant response. God, but he had her well trained, didn't he? Like a dog. One tug on the leash and she was panting to do his commands.

She watched with a dry mouth while he drained the glass and placed it down on a side-table, standing up and stretching out one of his hands. 'Come to bed,' he invited darkly. 'And I'll show you just how much I was lying.'

'No,' was her defiant reply, though inside she was quivering with an excited expectation.

'Don't play the coquette with me, Gemma,' he snapped, and, grabbing one of her hands, reefed her to her feet. Infuriated, she threw the rest of her brandy in his face, thrilling to his look of shock, then quavering to his answering fury.

'You little bitch,' he hissed. 'You'll be sorry you did that.' Knocking the glass out of her hand, he gripped the back of her head and kissed her savagely, forcing her lips open and thrusting his tongue inside her gasping mouth. Amazingly, and for the first time, Gemma experienced a hot stab of arousal at this display of male aggression.

Her moan was one of raw desire. But perhaps it sounded like something else, for suddenly, Nathan jerked his head upwards, his face twisting with self-disgust. And bitter remorse. His eyes fastened on her still parted, still panting lips, then lifted to where her eyes began searching his with a stunned bewilderment.

For she had wanted him to ravish her just now. Ravish…not make love. Wanted him to be rough. To take, and not ask. To demand, and not draw back.

Her groan showed true torment, and she spun away, lest he see the truth in her eyes. Instinct warned her that Nathan would hate her to have wanted something like that. He would rather she be boring in bed than depraved. And it was depraved, wasn't it, to want your husband virtually to rape you?

His hands curled over her shoulders and drew her back against him.

'I…I'm sorry,' he murmured thickly. 'Forgive me.'

She could feel his hot breath on her neck, and her body ached to whirl in his arms, to pull his mouth back down on hers, to propel him back into that mad whirlpool of passion. But she didn't. She stayed frozen in his arms, every muscle straining to keep herself in check. She flinched when his fingertips momentarily bit into her flesh, then shuddered when he released her.

'Go to bed,' he said in a hollow voice. 'It's been a long day and you must be tired.'

She went, thoroughly ashamed, not only of herself, but of all the doubts she'd been harbouring about Nathan's love. If he'd married her for lust alone, he wouldn't have stopped just now. Damian Campbell was wrong. Nathan loved her. Really loved her. God, what a fool she'd been tonight. What a silly little fool!

A long time later Nathan walked into the bedroom to stare down at his sleeping bride. His darkly brooding gaze gradually turned to one of black resolve, and he turned, walking with quiet footsteps over to Gemma's dressing-table. Taking the three packets of pills from the top drawer, he took them out to the kitchen and ground each one down the garbage disposal.

She wanted a baby? Well, he would give her one. He would give her anything she wanted to keep her in his bed. Anything!

Where love comes alive™

From first love to forever, these love stories are
for today's woman with traditional values.

A highly passionate, emotionally powerful
and always provocative read.

V *Silhouette®*

SPECIAL EDITION™

Emotional, compelling stories that capture the
intensity of living, loving and creating a family in
today's world.

V *Silhouette®*

ΙΝΤΙΜΑΤΕ ΜΟΜΕΝΤS™

A roller-coaster read that delivers romantic thrills
in a world of suspense, adventure and more.

SINTMAG